Suzanne Wright lives in England with her husband and two children. When she's not spending time with her family, she's writing, reading or doing her version of housework—sweeping the house with a look.

She's worked in a pharmaceutical company, at a Disney Store, at a primary school as a voluntary teaching assistant, at the RSCPA and has a First Class Honours degree in Psychology and Identity Studies.

As to her interests, she enjoys reading, writing, reading, writing (sort of eat, sleep, write, repeat), spending time with her family, movie nights with her sisters and playing with her two Bengal kittens.

To connect with Suzanne online:

Website: www.suzannewright.co.uk
Facebook:
www.facebook.com/suzannewrightfanpage
Twitter: @suz_wright
Blog: www.suzannewrightsblog.blogspot.co.uk

By Suzanne Wright

The Dark in You
Burn
Blaze

SUZANNE WRIGHT
BLAZE

piatkus

PIATKUS

First published in Great Britain in 2016 by Piatkus

3 5 7 9 10 8 6 4

A CIP catalogue record for this book
is available from the British Library.

ISBN: 978-0-349-41317-4

Typeset in Goudy by M Rules
Printed and bound in Great Britain by
Clays Ltd, Elcograf S.p.A.

Papers used by Piatkus are from well-managed forests
and other responsible sources.

MIX
Paper from
responsible sources
FSC® C104740

Piatkus
An imprint of
Little, Brown Book Group
Carmelite House
50 Victoria Embankment
London EC4Y 0DZ

An Hachette UK Company
www.hachette.co.uk

www.piatkus.co.uk

To all those who agree with me that archdemons should be real.
Sure, they'd be powerful enough to destroy the world, but we
can't let a little thing like that get in the way, right?

Acknowledgments

Firstly, I have to thank my family for somehow managing to live with someone who spends so much time in her own head—playing with fictional people, no less. Even I know that's just weird. Although it does beat being alone.

Big thanks to my hyper imagination . . . you worked yourself hard during this book and I appreciate that.

Of course I have to sincerely thank my assistant, Melissa, who not only supports me and works her ass off, but also saves me from my unsociable self during book signing events.

I wish to also thank everyone at Piatkus, especially Tara Loder, who is exactly what every writer wants in an editor.

Last but not whatsoever least, thanks to all my readers. Each and every one of you is *the shit*—pure fact. If you wish to contact me, you can reach me by email at suzanne_e_wright@live.co.uk or via social media.

BLAZE

CHAPTER ONE

———◆———

"Stop right there, bitch!"

Snapping her gaze from her cell phone to the pistol now aimed at her head, Harper Wallis froze. Well, shit. She couldn't deny that she had some karma to burn off. She was no angel. Being a demon, she was quite the opposite, in fact. But having a gun pointed at her by a human with a shaky hand and dilated pupils that said he was drugged up to his eyeballs . . . well, it just felt like the universe was being a little unfair, that's all.

"Put the phone on the ground!"

She *so* didn't have time for this. She'd taken a quick break from work so she could head to the ATM—

"Put the phone on the ground!"

"Do I really have to?" The floor of the alley was covered in grime, cigarette butts, glass fragments, and dirty rain puddles. Then there were those dubious-looking stains . . .

"Don't make me repeat myself."

With an inward sigh, Harper slowly did as he asked.

Note to self: Stop taking shortcuts through alleys. It wasn't exactly a scenic route with the dumpsters, trash bags, moldy walls, and the scent of rotting food . . . although the graffiti was pretty cool. The artist definitely had potential.

"Hands up and keep them up!"

She raised her hands, all the while staring into blue eyes that flickered with nervousness. Sparky here wasn't as confident as he was trying to appear. But he had every reason to feel at least a little confident. They were alone except for the rats, she was small where he was burly, and he had a weapon while she was unarmed—or, at least, that was what he thought. Not that the stiletto knife tucked into her boot was going to do her much good against a gun.

Really, she should know better. This area of North Las Vegas was high in crime . . . which, incidentally, was why her family fit right in. The Wallis demons were pretty notorious for doing exactly what all imps did: mostly lying, stealing, tricking, cheating, and, of course, breaking and entering. Although Harper was a sphinx like her mother, she'd been raised by her paternal family and was an imp by nature.

"Now throw me your purse!"

"You told me to keep my hands up," she pointed out.

"Well, now I'm telling you to give me your damn purse."

Okay, that was going to be a problem. It had been a gift, and she wasn't going to hand it over to anyone.

"*Now*, bitch!"

How rude. Not that he was wrong. She was a bitch and she took pride in it. "I'm afraid I can't do that."

His brows drew together. "What?"

"See, someone very important to me bought me this. I tell him not to keep buying me shit, but he doesn't listen. He likes to spoil me, even though it makes me uncomfortable—"

A burger wrapper crumpled under his foot as he took an aggressive step forward, lips flattening. "Throw. Me. The. Purse."

Her inner demon snarled, eager for Harper to either slit his throat or do something equally entertaining. Like shifters, demons had a dualism to the soul. Shifters shared their soul with an animal. Demons, however, shared theirs with a dark entity—an entity that was without conscience, possessed a strong sense of entitlement, and lacked both empathy and the ability to emotionally connect. "Come on, give a girl a break."

"Oh, I'll give you something," he said, a lewd gleam in his eyes.

Like *hell* he would. A dark yet protective power unfurled from within her and rushed to her fingertips, making them prickle. Her demon urged her to release it on the human, but there were other ways of dealing with him.

"You don't want the purse," she said in the compelling tone that all sphinxes were gifted with, enabling them to confuse people. Satisfied when his eyes glazed over, she continued. "You don't want to hurt me. You want to drop the gun." She wished she could compel him to never do it again or to confess his crimes to the police, but her compulsions wouldn't hold that long.

A car honked in the distance, making him jump, and the glaze fell from his eyes. "Give me the purse!"

"This is getting tedious." She flinched at a loud bang. *Motherfucker.* The human had shot at the ground in front of her feet. She wasn't sure if he'd purposely missed; she had no interest in finding out. Before that shaky hand could shoot again, she acted. Faster than he could ever hope to be, she whipped out her knife, kicked the gun out of his hand, slammed him into the wall, and put her blade to his throat.

Breaths quick and shallow, he stared at her through wide eyes. Well, he'd be a lot more scared if she'd granted her demon's request and infused hellfire into the knife. It would be pretty funny to watch his face go slack, but that would expose herself as inhuman and ... and was it just her or had the temperature dropped seriously quickly? It was also darkening fast. She looked up. A dark, heavy, ominous-looking cloud had formed.

Harper's eyes snapped back to the human as a large, sweaty hand crushed her wrist and sharply yanked it, making her drop her blade.

His free hand wrapped tight around her throat as he spun them, slamming her into the wall. The breath whooshed out of her lungs. Fisting her hair, he rammed the back of her skull against the wall, and there was the sickening sound of bone hitting brick. Spots danced in front of her eyes and a ringing sound filled her ears.

"Bitch!" He bit down hard into her cheek as he roughly tore open her fly.

Motherfucking bastard. She slapped her palm to his forehead, and the power prickling her fingertips shoved its way inside him.

With an agonized sob, he dropped to his knees and slapped his hands against his head.

A little on the dizzy side, she rapidly blinked. The bite mark on her cheek was throbbing like a bitch. Watching him whimper pathetically at her feet, she gently probed the lump that was quickly forming on the back of her head. Fucking ouch.

Giving up any pretense of being human, Harper crouched in front of him. "Do you know why one simple hit to your body took you down? Because my touch can cause soul-deep pain. I can't really empathize, because I've never felt it myself. I'm told that the pain burns each nerve ending, cuts through each organ, slices through each bone and then lances through the very soul, making it feel like it's shattering. Does it?" She was genuinely curious.

Eying her with a newfound terror, he clumsily scrabbled away from her.

Understandable, really.

His gaze fell to the gun, but it was too far away and he was in too much pain to get up.

"You might as well lose the dream of shooting me," she told him, grabbing her cell phone off the floor and tucking it into her purse. "Now, what should I do with you?"

A cold wind blew through the air, flapping her T-shirt and causing her loose hair to whip at her face. Looking up, she saw that the murky cloud was bigger and darker. The air felt ... charged, somehow. Wary, she slowly stood upright.

Ping. Ping. Ping.

Something hard and sharp bounced off her hand onto the concrete. Wincing, she frowned down at the small white ball. *Hail.* "Well, shit."

In a matter of moments, a torrent of icy pellets was raining down on them, stinging the skin of her face and hands. She shrugged off her jacket and held it over her head. But, like the rest of her clothes, the material couldn't protect her from the hard sting of the hailstones.

The deluge was *deafening*. Each pellet pounded into the ground, hammered into the garbage cans, and splashed out of the rain puddles. The pellets weren't big, but the force of them was bad. They were no doubt chipping windows and denting cars all around.

Seriously, where the fuck had this storm come from? One minute the weather was mild, the next there was a hailstorm and she was *freezing*. If it was anything like the other recent strange storms, it would end as abruptly as it had begun.

She could hear raised voices coming from the end of the alley; watched as people scrambled to escape the torrent. She would have followed their lead and run for shelter, but there was good ole Sparky to consider. She was going to have to do something with the little bastard, who was now crawling toward the gun, proving yet again that he was indeed a bastard.

She kicked it far out of his reach, and it slid into a slushy puddle.

With a groan of defeat, he rolled onto his side and curled up into a fetal position, shielding his face with his thick arms. Like her, he was wet and his teeth were chattering. Maybe she should have felt bad for him but, well, she just didn't. He'd freaking *attacked* her.

A very familiar mind slid against hers. *Harper, where are you?*

Even telepathically, her mate's voice was like an erotic stroke to her senses. Hell, everything about Knox Thorne stroked her senses. But seriously, his smoky, velvety rumble was pure liquid sin.

Caught in a hailstorm, she told him. He was no doubt warm and dry in a conference room somewhere in Chicago.

I know you're stuck in the storm. I want to know where exactly you are.

She frowned, wondering how he could possibly know. Now that the deluge had abruptly begun to slow, she scooped up her blade with cold fingers and returned it to the sheath inside her boot.

Tell me where you are; I'll come for you.

Hearing another groan, she looked down at Sparky. He was shivering even worse than before. And Harper ... yeah, she still wasn't feeling bad for him. *It's sweet that you'd offer to pyroport all the way from Chicago, but it's not necessary.* Right now, she wouldn't mind having that ability herself – traveling by fire would at least warm her up.

I'm at your studio, I've been waiting for you.

Well, then it would seem that he'd cut his business trip short. But why? Uneasy, she asked, *Is something wrong?*

Harper, where are you?

She narrowed her eyes. *You avoided my question.*

You avoided mine.

Well, yeah. *The storm is actually easing off.* The rumble of pellets had slowed to light individual pings. *You don't have to come for me.*

Harper, he growled.

Okay, but you have to promise not to lose your shit. But considering she had bite marks on her cheek, a goose-egg on her head, and the buttons of her fly had been ripped off, there was little chance of that. She wasn't averse to seeing the sick-ass motherfucker on the ground die a painful death, but it was never a good thing for Knox Thorne to lose control.

Only a handful of people—including Harper—knew what breed of demon he was. Still, he was both feared and respected within the demon world since he was rumored to be the most powerful in existence; a demon that could call on the flames of hell. It was a rumor that very few knew to be true. And since nothing was impervious to the flames of hell, he could, literally, destroy the freaking world.

A vibe of anxiety touched her mind. *Harper, where the fuck are you?*

Sighing in resignation, she lowered her soaking wet jacket. *The alley between the ATM and the deli.* An alley that was now dotted with icy pellets. Well, at least it smelled better; ozone and water beat pigeon shit and grime any day of the week.

Fire roared to life a few feet away, causing Sparky to cry out in terror. The fire hissed and spat until the flames quickly calmed. And there was Knox. Piercing, deep-set ebony eyes locked on her, and the intense potency of his natural sex appeal swept over her, causing her body to hum. Well over six feet of danger, power, solid muscle, and a raw sexual magnetism, Knox Thorne was both a mouthwatering and intimidating sight.

As always, he looked like something out of GQ with his black tailored suit, sexily confident stance, and his short, dark stylishly cut hair. He exuded an aura of self-assurance that said he could handle any situation with total ease. At that moment, he was also radiating a fury that thickened the air. Crap.

"I'm fine," she assured him.

"Nothing about this situation is fine," said Knox, stalking toward her. He sounded completely calm. Composed. Casual. But she knew he was none of those things.

"What I mean is that I'm okay." Albeit wet and cold.

"You're soaked, shivering, and bleeding." He lightly breezed his warm thumb over the skin beneath the throbbing marks on her cheek, and his fury became almost tangible. "The human's mental shields are weak. I can see what he did to you, I can see what he planned." Knox turned to the human, who was now shaking like a shitting dog. "You've mugged and raped many women, haven't you? Young girls, too. You should have been put down long before now."

Menace stamped into every line of Knox's face, he grabbed the human by the throat and lifted him off the floor. The air chilled even further as his eyes bled to black— his inner demon was now in control. The entity had claimed her as its mate, though it didn't "care" for her; it lacked the emotional capacity to do so. However, it had formed a very firm attachment to Harper. It was as possessive and protective as Knox. It viewed her as something it owned; something it had collected and intended to keep.

Glaring at the human through cold eyes, the demon spoke in

a flat, disembodied voice that would give anyone the chills. "You hurt what belongs to me. No one does that and lives."

Hellfire rushed from its hand to completely engulf the human's body; it happened so fast that the guy didn't have a chance to cry out. Fire crackled and popped as his skin blistered, melted, and peeled away. Her nose wrinkled at that the God-awful stench of burning flesh. The alley smelled bad once again.

As the body slumped in its grip, the demon dropped him and watched with clinical detachment while it vaporized right in front of them. Good ole hellfire sure was a bitch.

Obsidian eyes cut to Harper, still cold as ever. The demon prowled towards her, and she had to force herself not to tense. She knew that she wasn't in danger, but the entity still unnerved the ever-loving shit out of her. It did a slow blink. "You should have called for me, little sphinx."

That made her and her inner demon bristle. "I handled the situation."

One brow slid up. "Pride can be a weakness." The demon tapped her lip. "Take better care of what's mine." It then retreated, and Knox's dark eyes once again held hers. And it was clear to see that he wasn't happy. Evidently, he agreed with his demon.

She sighed. "I was dealing with the guy just fine on my own. If I'd thought I needed your help, I would have called for you."

Knox slowly splayed his hand around her throat and circled her pulse with his thumb. "Really?" His tone called her a liar.

"Yes. I'm stubborn, not stupid."

"Then you'll have no problem making me a promise here and now."

She didn't like the sound of that. "Oh yeah?"

"Promise me that if you ever need my help, you'll call for me."

"I told you I will. I meant it."

"Then this will be an easy promise for you to make."

Damn, she'd walked right into that one. "Fine, I promise."

"Good girl." He kissed her, boldly licking into her mouth. The kiss was as aggressive as it was possessive; she could taste his anger, his concern, and his determination to keep her safe. He ended the kiss with a sharp, punishing bite to her lower lip. He wasn't quite calm yet.

A car horn honked, and Knox said, "Time to go. We need to get you warm." He guided her to the end of the alley where a sleek, top-of-the-line Bentley waited. Well, that was the kind of thing you could afford when you were a billionaire who owned a chain of hotels, casinos, restaurants, security firms, and bars.

Like all demons, Knox hid in plain sight, blending in easily with humans. Their kind often sought jobs that granted them power, control, challenges, and respect. Many were entrepreneurs, stock brokers, CEOs, politicians, bankers, surgeons, lawyers, police officers, and celebrities. Harper wasn't so big on power, but she did enjoy the challenges of co-owning a tattoo studio.

Knox was as influential in the demon world as he was in the human world. He was a powerful Prime of a fairly large lair that spanned most of Nevada and a good portion of California. In addition, he owned a subterranean version of the Las Vegas strip known as the Underground. It was a busy place, given that demons were impulsive, forever restless, suffered from instant gratification issues, and had a bad habit of trying to deal with their oppressive boredom using cheap thrills.

Levi, one of Knox's sentinels, opened the rear door of the Bentley for them. He didn't look much happier with her than Knox did. "What the fuck happened to your face?" he growled, gun-metal gray eyes flaring with anger.

She gave the tall, powerfully built reaper a bright smile and slung her wet jacket at him. "Never say I don't give you any-thing." As she and Knox slid into the backseat, she turned to her mate and said, "You're back early from your trip."

His expression didn't alter at all, but his hesitation to answer her spoke volumes.

"Something happened. What is it?"

He took her hand in his. "It's Carla. She's missing."

Harper's stomach rolled. Carla Hayden was a sphinx and a member of their lair. She was also Harper's mother.

CHAPTER TWO

———◦◉◦———

Using a bottle of drinking water to wet a handkerchief, Knox then dabbed the healing wound on her cheek; wiping away the excess blood. He'd bitten her. The bastard had *bitten* her. Pointed a gun at her head. Slammed her into a wall. Tried to r—

The Bentley rattled a little, and she gave him a sideways glance. Knox took a deep breath to cool his anger, reminding himself that she was there with him, alive and safe. But it wasn't easy when his demon's rage heated his blood and buzzed through his veins. They'd seen through the human's memories *exactly* what he'd done to his mate.

Knox and his demon were doubly possessive and protective of Harper because in addition to being their mate she was their anchor. Demons came in pairs, but they didn't have soul mates. They had predestined psi-mates who would anchor their demon, make them stronger, and give them the stability that stopped them from turning rogue.

When a demon fused their psyche with their anchor's, it

forged a binding link between them. The link wasn't sexual or emotional; it was purely psychic. Still, anchors often become close friends since they found it mentally uncomfortable to be apart for long periods. They also instinctually protected and supported each other, and they were unswervingly loyal.

Being anchored didn't stop the inner demon from occasionally surfacing—nothing could completely control it—but it did stop the entity from taking over. And if a demon lost its anchor and the link between them broke, the demon often broke right along with it.

As his anchor and his mate, Harper was indispensable to Knox in more ways than one. He needed her alive and safe. He *didn't* need her being fucking shot at by a junkie. It didn't surprise Knox that she hadn't called out for help when the human attacked her. Harper was used to being alone and taking care of herself. He knew she was fully capable of doing so. He just didn't want her to have to. Knox wanted to be for her what she'd never had—someone to rely on, someone to turn to, someone who would deal with her problems for her. He wanted to make up for the things she'd never had. He definitely didn't want to find her injured and bleeding.

Knox very carefully slid his hand to the back of her head to check out the swelling. It wasn't so bad, which meant she was healing fast. Lost in her own thoughts, she didn't even seem aware that he was touching her.

He watched her closely, unsure what reaction his news would receive. He would wager that he knew Harper better than even she did, but he was never able to predict her responses. She was a guarded, complex, elusive creature who always managed to surprise him, which was an actual achievement considering he was someone who read people easily.

It was her ability to both surprise and intrigue him that had first drawn Knox to her. It made her different. Interesting. And that had intensified the raw need she sparked in him. Not even five and a half feet tall, she was small and feminine with delectably sinful curves and a mouth from every male's fantasy. She also had a natural grace and moved with an innate sensuality that enraptured his demon.

What Knox liked most about his pretty, shiny little mate were her eyes. Not simply because they were unusually glassy and reflective in a catlike way, but because they routinely changed color. Right now, however, they were annoyingly covered with contact lenses to hide her unique eyes from humans. And they showed absolutely no emotion. Whatever she was feeling about the Carla situation, he wasn't yet sure.

Mother and daughter had an extremely complicated . . . well, he wouldn't call it a relationship. There wasn't anything between them. When aborting Harper didn't work, Carla had wanted an incantor—a demon that could use magick—to bottle Harper's soul in order to punish her father, Lucian. That plan had also failed, at which point Harper's grandmother had paid Carla to carry the baby to term. Carla had then left Harper with the imps and never once played a part in her life.

It wasn't that Carla was evil. She'd just been too twisted up inside after Harper's father, who was both Carla's anchor and the demon she'd chosen for a mate, rejected her on both levels. A demon who lost its mate was both dangerous and unstable. Given that Knox would be just as hurt if he lost Harper, he could understand why Carla became so twisted. Nonetheless, he didn't see it as an excuse for anything Carla had done.

Harper had grown up believing the woman hated her just as she hated Lucian, and she'd come to terms with that in her own way. Months ago, however, they had discovered that Carla had actually watched Harper from afar when his mate came to Vegas—she'd even gone to Harper's graduation. Knox had sensed that a part of Carla wanted her only daughter in her life, but it simply wasn't a big enough part of her to make any difference. Learning these things had thrown Harper off-balance and forced her to re-evaluate what she'd grown up believing.

He suspected that too much had really happened for the two females to ever have a relationship of any kind. He strongly doubted that Carla's absence in her life bothered Harper that much, though. She wasn't bitter about it, and she didn't want anyone in her life who wouldn't be a positive influence.

In her position, Knox would have felt neither here nor there about the disappearance of a mother who had been anything *but* a mother to him. He certainly wouldn't feel sympathy for someone who had so drastically let him down. But unlike him, Harper had a huge soft spot. Beneath her hard exterior lay a marshmallow center that would no doubt feel bad for Carla.

"What do you mean by missing?" she finally asked.

Knox gently stroked her long sleek, dark hair that was tipped with gold—it was drying fast, since Levi had turned the heaters on full-blast. "Lawrence Crow, another demon from our lair who is also her neighbor, seems to have taken her."

"Against her will?"

"Yes," replied Knox. His demon wanted to nuzzle her. It had lost some of its anger now that she was safe, warm, and at its side.

Harper gave a soft shake of the head. "I don't get it. Why would someone take Carla?"

"In Crow's state of mind, it's not easy to say."

"He's the demon you told me about who was bordering on rogue, isn't he?"

"Yes." And that was a reason to worry, since it would mean the male's inner demon could soon have complete and utter control of him.

"Has he gone over the edge? Is he rogue now?"

"His partner, Delia, doesn't think he is yet, but he's close." Again, Knox watched Harper carefully. Again, her expression didn't change.

Harper exhaled heavily. "Then she's in big fucking trouble."

His mate was right. Sharing your soul with a dark, mostly psychopathic predator was no easy thing. It was a constant struggle to prevent the entity from taking over, and some didn't have the mental strength to be dominant over their inner demon. Those people either went insane, committed suicide, or turned rogue.

One thing could save a demon from ever breaking that way—finding and bonding with their anchor. Sometimes having a mate could keep a demon relatively stable, but although Crow was in a relationship with Delia, they hadn't claimed each other.

Seeing that Harper was pinching her lower lip, Knox tugged it free with his thumb and asked her, "What are you thinking?"

"I don't know what to think." On the one hand, Harper was angry that such a thing had happened to someone who, whether she liked it or not, was in fact her mother. But that made her feel almost hypocritical, given that Harper didn't want her around. "I can't pretend to care about her. I don't. But I never wished her dead." And if Carla was in the hands of a rogue, she could very well be exactly that.

"I know." Knox slid his hand from her hair to her nape. "Not that anyone would blame you if you had."

"When did this happen?"

"Four hours ago. That was why Tanner disappeared from outside your studio; he's trying to track Crow." Tanner was one of his sentinels who acted as Harper's bodyguard. As a hellhound, he was a very good tracker. "You don't have to come with me to see Delia. I can have Levi take you home so you can change out of those damp clothes."

"No, I want to hear from Delia what happened." She rubbed at her eyes, confused and off-balance. "I don't know what to make of it all."

"Look at me." Knox waited until she did before he said, "I can't promise you that Carla will get out of this situation unharmed, but I can promise you that I will find her and Crow."

She squeezed his hand. "I know you will."

That trust, that instant faith in him, made Knox swallow hard. He kissed her softly. Gently. He hadn't thought he had gentleness in him until Harper came along. She'd walked into his office, all shiny and unique and stubborn, and she'd lit his life right up—brought out plenty of emotions he hadn't thought himself capable of feeling.

But even feeling those emotions didn't make him "good." He'd never be that. There was a saying: "what's born in hell should stay in hell." Knox was an archdemon; a dark, cruel breed that was born of the flames of hell . . . meaning he didn't just call on the flames, he *was* the flames. Harper knew he was part of the fabric of hell, but she accepted him anyway. Loved him, even. If that wasn't a fucking miracle, he didn't know what was.

Harper stood at Knox's side in the center of the freakily tidy den, looking down at the woman who was huddled in an armchair and shaking with silent sobs. Delia kept her eyes on the floor, intimidated in the face of Knox's anger. Harper couldn't blame her. Oh, he didn't look or sound angry. It was rare that he ever did. But right then, the emotion pulsed around them like a live thing. He had every right to be pissed. Delia had admitted to knowing that Crow was getting worse, yet she'd done nothing.

Knox wasn't the only one radiating anger. Carla's mate, Bray, and their two sons, Roan and Kellen, were there too. Although Harper had no relationship with Roan, who was in his twenties and quite the momma's boy, she occasionally met with Kellen, which was something his parents and brother didn't know.

Unlike Roan, Kellen wasn't close to Carla. The teenager had remarked that she wasn't normal and believed that she found her demon hard to control. He'd also commented that though she could be kind at times, the oddest things riled her. Roan had cryptically told him that Carla was "twisted up inside" and not to blame, whatever that meant.

So far, Kellen had yet to acknowledge Harper. In fact, the hazel eyes he'd inherited from his father had looked everywhere but at her. He kept nervously shoving a hand through his dirty-blond hair, his lean build hunched over.

"You were supposed to tell me if he got worse," Knox said to Delia.

"I know, but I was afraid you would take him away from me," said Delia.

Harper could actually understand that, since she wouldn't want anyone taking Knox away from her whether he was hanging on some kind of edge or not. She'd want to be there for him and do whatever she could to help him.

"I would only have removed him from your home if there was a chance he was a danger to himself or others," Knox told her. "It would have been a temporary arrangement."

Delia looked up. "He wasn't dangerous."

"Clearly you're wrong," said Levi. "He kidnapped your neighbor."

She averted her eyes. "I know. But he was doing better. Really." Her brow furrowed. "Then he became a little depressed. I just thought it was a side-effect of the medication. I didn't realize until this morning that he hasn't been taking his pills lately."

Delia looked at a framed picture on the wall of her and a lean, barrel-chested male with gentle blue eyes and hair the same salt-and-pepper shade as his wiry mustache. Knox had told Harper a little about him during the drive here. Crow was a surgeon who loved his job, did charity runs, donated money to human causes, and helped the other demons within the lair who had come close to turning rogue.

Knox inhaled deeply. "What happened here earlier?"

"I walked into the bedroom to find him packing a suitcase," said Delia. "He said he had to leave. That he had a mission to complete."

"Mission?" echoed Knox.

Delia licked her lips. "See, Lawrence says he had a vision. A vision that you and Harper would eventually have a baby . . . and that the baby would be whatever you are and it would destroy us all."

Harper's stomach rolled and cold fingers scuttled down her spine. Everyone exchanged uneasy looks, except for her mate. Knox just stared back at Delia calmly, as if the woman hadn't just dropped a verbal bomb.

"So he's having paranoid delusions again," said Knox.

"Yes," replied Delia. "He's convinced that it's his responsibility to save the world by killing you before the baby can be born. I tried to make him see that it was all in his head. He wouldn't listen. He packed his things and was ready to leave, so I grabbed the car keys. He demanded I hand them over, but I refused. He yelled at me, angry that I wouldn't believe him. Then he . . . he hit me, and then he started draining me."

Harper frowned. Draining? No one else seemed confused, so she figured it was related to some kind of demonic ability Crow had.

"Carla must have heard us arguing," Delia went on, "because she charged inside to see what was going on and then . . . "

"And then?" prompted Knox.

"He started ranting at Carla that she put all this in motion by giving birth to Harper."

Bray growled and Roan spat a curse.

"He dragged her out of the house. I wanted to help her, but I was too weak to get up."

Confused that she'd been weak, Harper asked, "What is he?"

"A psi-demon," replied Knox.

Well, that explained a lot. Crow's breed fed from emotion like psychic vampires, draining them of energy. It also meant bad things for Carla.

"He'll kill her," Roan snapped out. His eyes slammed on Harper, hard and scornful. She'd seen that look on Carla's face in the past. Though he was tall like Bray, he looked a lot like Carla with his dark hair, brown almond-shaped eyes, high cheekbones, and golden skin "He'll kill her, and it'll be *your* fault."

Harper blinked. *Her* fault?

Roan made a beeline for her, but Levi stepped in his way. "Hold on there," he said, voice deadly. "You want to think hard before you try to harm Harper."

"It's her fault," Roan spat.

"How?" rumbled Knox, tone lethal. "Harper didn't take her. Harper didn't cause Crow's delusions. Harper doesn't even know him, and she has minimal contact with your mother. So explain to me how this could possibly be her fault."

"There's no saying he intends to kill your mom," Bray told Roan. "If that was what he wanted, he could have done that right here."

"But if he's hovering on the edge, it won't take much to drive him to do it," said Roan. Glaring at Harper, he stalked out of the house with Bray behind him. Kellen's eyes met hers, conflicted. But then he looked away with a frown and followed his father and brother. Ouch.

Knox put a supportive hand on Harper's lower back as he spoke to Delia. "If Lawrence comes into contact with you, call me. Don't try to lure him back here. Don't agree to meet him anywhere. Call me and tell me where he is. He's your partner and he cares for you, but he's also not himself right now."

Delia nodded miserably. "If he contacts me, I'll call you."

CHAPTER THREE

The black, heavy-metal gates swung open, and Levi steered the Bentley along the lengthy, circular drive toward the expansive, luxurious mansion. Harper loved the place. The contemporary piece of architecture was as spectacular as the guy who owned it. It was the kind of house you saw in magazines about the rich and famous, but there was nothing pretentious about it. The mansion had charm and a warm elegance. One of her favorite features was the bulletproof, blue-tinted windows that gave it a really modern look.

Ivy trailed along the high brick walls that framed the estate. Sprinklers were spraying the extensive lawn while landscapers were trimming the hedges that framed the security gatehouse. Levi dropped Harper and Knox off at the wide steps before heading to the garage that she knew stored several expensive cars.

Before she and Knox had even reached the top step, a tall male with graying hair opened the door and gave them a polite smile. "Mr. Thorne, Miss Wallis, welcome home."

"Hey, Dan," she said as she stepped into the marble foyer, where freshly cut flowers sat on a circular table.

Knox threaded his fingers through hers. "Come on."

He didn't lead her into the living area as she'd expected. Instead, he tugged her along the wide hallway and up the curved staircase. "You intend to have your wicked way with me already? We've only just walked through the door."

Mouth curving, he said, "That will come later."

He urged her into the lavish bedroom and along what she'd learned was rare, imported flooring. The room always seemed to smell of clean linen, Knox's cologne, and fragrant oils. It was as lush as the rest of the house with its quality wooden furnishings, super-soft bedding, electronic shades, and balcony. Well, Harper didn't really think "balcony" was the right word for what was more like a grand patio, complete with a small pool.

He led her into the private steamy bathroom. Her jasmine-scented candles had been lit and a glass of wine was waiting near the large circular, black-granite bath. And she knew he'd sent Meg, the housekeeper, a telepathic request to run her a bath. He did stuff like that a lot; took care of her in whatever ways he could. Since Harper was a self-sufficient person who had mostly raised herself, she didn't quite know what to do with that yet.

"You need to get out of those damp clothes and warm your bones." Knox kissed her. "I'll be back soon. I have some work to do." In truth, it was something that could wait, but Knox sensed she needed some time alone to assimilate everything. If he thought she'd talk to him, he'd ask her what was bothering her fascinating mind, but he'd quickly learned that his mate took time to think things through before she confided in anyone. "Relax and I'll see you in a while."

Harper hugged him. "Thank you for this," she said a little

awkwardly, still finding it difficult to accept … well, anything from anyone. "And thank you for getting me." Being alone was her default zone, but it couldn't be easy for someone as pushy and hyper-protective as Knox to not be all up in her business while she was stressing.

Hugging her just as tight, he pressed a light kiss to her neck. "I'll always give you what you need." She made him want to cosset her, spoil her, and surround her with whatever she wanted. Knox pulled back and squeezed her shoulders. "Enjoy." He closed the bathroom door and left the bedroom, heading to his office.

Knox, meet me in the living area, said Levi. *You should see this.*

Changing directions, Knox made his way downstairs and into the spacious, high-ceiling room. Levi was sat on one of the beige half-moon sofas, fingers tapping his touch-screen cell phone. The spotlights in the walls and mahogany ceiling illuminated the reaper's face; it was set into a mask of sheer exasperation.

"What do I need to see?" Knox asked, sitting on the other sofa.

Levi slid his cell phone across the coffee table positioned between them. "This."

Picking up the cell, Knox tapped the play button on the screen. What appeared to be outdoor CCTV footage coming from a house opposite Crow's showed him frantically dragging a yelling, kicking, squirming Carla to a red Toyota Corolla. He smacked her head hard on the window, knocking her unconscious, and then shoved her in the trunk. Raking a shaking hand through his hair, Crow looked in all directions, as if expecting someone to pounce at him. He then slung a suitcase onto the rear passenger seat before hopping inside the car and driving off.

As the footage ended, Knox swore under his breath. "His eyes are wild, but not black. He's not rogue."

"Yet," said Levi.

"Carla sure put up a hell of a fight." Just as Harper would have done, he thought.

"I've never known Crow to be violent."

Rising, Knox moved to the fireplace, looking up at the painting hung there without really seeing it. "Don't cancel his credit cards. Let him use them. They can help us track him."

"I'm not sure he will use them, no matter how desperate he is for money. He's so paranoid right now it will actually help him hide."

"It will be hard to track him any other way, given he knows how we hunt." In addition to being a surgeon, he'd been a member of the Force.

"He has no other properties, so I've no idea where he might hide."

"He won't go far," said Knox, leaning against the fireplace. The mantel had once been bare. Now it was lined with Harper's knickknacks from the years she'd spent traveling with her nomadic father. She'd added personal touches here and there to the room, giving it a homier feel. "He believes he must kill me. That means he'll stay local."

"There are so many cheap motels and B & Bs in Vegas, it's not even funny."

"Don't send the entire Force hunting. We know there is definitely one place he'll come: to wherever I am." Knox used his heel to smooth a small kink out of the blue Persian rug. "He won't try to penetrate this place when it would be so much easier for him to just walk right into one of my hotels."

"You think that's what he'll do?"

"Our kind hide in plain sight, right?"

Levi grabbed his phone and stood. "I'll send a high number of the Force on patrol around the rough areas. The other half will monitor your hotels and casinos; they'll watch out for any sign of him."

Knox nodded. "He'll show himself soon enough." They just had to hope that he didn't kill Carla in the meantime.

As the bathroom door opened, Harper opened her eyes to see Knox strolling inside, the top buttons of his white shirt open and his sleeves rolled up. Crouching beside the tub, he dipped his hand under the water and skimmed it over her leg. "You ready to talk about what's bothering you most right now?" he asked.

Not really. She turned off the Jacuzzi jets and sighed. "They all blame me."

Knox didn't have to ask who she meant. When they'd left Delia's house, Bray, Roan and Kellen were in their front yard, talking with their neighbors. Apart from Kellen—who had averted his gaze—each one of them looked at Harper like she herself had snatched Carla. "You know why."

She did know. "They feel guilty that they didn't help her and they need someone to blame to make themselves feel better. I get it. It doesn't mean I have to like it."

He stroked her leg soothingly. "I don't like it either." Which was why he'd been sorely tempted to hurl a ball of hellfire at them. Instead, he'd settled for shooting them a warning glare that made them look away.

"What do you think Crow will do?"

"It's hard to know for sure. No two near-rogues are the same. Generally, those on the edge suffer from delusions, paranoia, feelings of emptiness, and an irrepressible anger as their minds begin to splinter. Even then they're a threat, but once they cross over the edge, they're at their most dangerous. He already has a distorted notion of reality."

She sat up, biting her lower lip. "Knox . . . his vision—"

"Was the product of a disturbed, delusional mind." Knox cupped her cheek, glad to see the human's teeth marks were gone. "Harper, any child we have cannot be what I am. My kind is born from the flames of hell, not from a womb." But Crow didn't know that because he had no idea what Knox was. "Demons don't breed hybrids. That means any child we have will be a sphinx, just like you."

She took a long breath. "You're right. I didn't think of that."

Standing, Knox grabbed a towel from the radiator. "Up." After she twisted her hair to ring out the water, he lifted her out of the tub and wrapped the soft towel around her. He patted her dry while she used another towel to rub her hair. "I want you to take every precaution when you're out. People have used you to get to me before. You saw pictures of Crow at his house. You know what he looks like. If you see him, you call me. I know you're strong. You could cause his soul agonizing pain, but he can conjure weapons, which means he doesn't need to get close to you to hurt you."

"Does he have any other abilities?" Harper asked.

"A few minor ones. And he can conjure balls of hellfire."

"Delightful." It wasn't a rare ability, but it was substantial. Harper couldn't actually do it, though she could generate hellfire and infuse it into objects.

Knox guided her into the bedroom, where he grabbed her comb and began gently working it through her hair. "Be smart and be aware."

"How will you find him?"

"Half-rogue or full-rogue, they become worse stimulation seekers than before. They're drawn to drugs, alcohol, and danger, so we monitor the hot spots. The problem is that he was a member of my Force; he knows how we hunt and knows where we'll look."

"Do you think we should cancel the little shindig?"

"Stop calling it that." It was much more than a mere party; it was a noteworthy event that would take place in the Underground to celebrate the 150th anniversary of the day he created it.

"But Crow could take that opportunity to get to you," said Harper. "There would be so many people there, he could easily blend in with the crowd."

"The event takes place in six weeks. It's likely we'll have apprehended Crow by then."

"We can't be sure of that."

Knox's mouth curved. "Any excuse to get out of the celebration."

She sighed. "I don't like parties, big or small." She didn't like fuss or being on display. It wouldn't have been so bad if it was a private party. But no, it was to take place in the Underground on the "strip" and any demon could attend.

"Many people have put a lot of effort into organizing it. Anyway, I saved you from the party your friends tried throwing for you to celebrate our mating." He'd flew them both to Barcelona for the weekend on his private jet, wanting to celebrate their mating alone.

She turned when he'd finished combing her hair. "You didn't want that party any more than I did."

"The idea of the party didn't bother me. It was the idea of you being nervous and uncomfortable when it was supposed to be a joyous event that I didn't like."

"Yet, you have no problem with me being nervous or uncomfortable at *this* one."

Knox steered her to the foot of the bed and tipped her onto her back. "I get to show you off and see you in a dress. What's not to like?" He loomed over her to kiss and nibble on her mouth.

"It's also a good way to celebrate you becoming co-Prime of our lair."

Her eyes narrowed. "It was sneaky of you not to mention I'd be co-Prime before we agreed to take each other as mates."

"I knew you wouldn't want the position." His mate had no aspirations for power and was too individualistic to have any interests in leading others. It was rare for a demon. "I wasn't going to let it stand in my way of having you. Not that. Not anything."

She snorted. "Whatever."

Smiling, he kissed her. "I missed you while I was gone."

"You came to see me a few times," she reminded him.

Knox had occasionally pyroported home to see her. "That's not the same as having time with you." He kissed her again. "Now, about the mugger."

Using her elbows, Harper shuffled up the cool, silk sheets. "Don't start."

He followed her, crawling onto the bed and planting a hand either side of her head. "Harper—"

"I know where this is going. Really, just leave it."

"Look at me. You promised me you'd compromise on things. This is important to me. Did you even mention my proposal to your work colleagues?"

"Yes, I did. Like me, they're a little wary of relocating the business to the Underground." She co-owned the tattoo studio with her friend and fellow senior artist, Raini. Another close friend, Devon, was an apprentice who specialized in piercings. Harper's cousin, Khloë, also worked there as a receptionist. All three females belonged to her grandmother's lair.

He'd startled Harper when he'd first proposed relocating the studio, but really she should have seen it coming. He was an interfering bastard, after all. He had been from minute one.

"It's not based in a safe area, Harper. You could have been shot, raped, and killed today. Yes, you dealt with the human. Yes, you're very capable of protecting yourself. But a bullet to the heart could still kill you. He shot at the ground, granted, but he could have as easily aimed that gun right there." Knox laid a hand over her heart. "Then you'd be gone. Like it or not, you keep me stable—as my anchor and as my mate. If I lose you, if my demon loses you . . . I don't have to tell you how things will play out."

She slapped her hands over her face and groaned.

"I wish you didn't have to carry that weight, but you do."

Her hands fell away from her face. "I don't see it as carrying a weight. I anchor you just as you anchor me—that's how it's supposed to work with anchors and mates."

"It is a weight. I need you to be safe. Relocating to the Underground would make you safer. It would also benefit your business."

"I'd *lose* business. I have a lot of human clients."

"Yes, but you would get a lot of foot traffic to your studio if it was in the Underground. You'd lose human clients, but you would gain demon ones."

"Honestly, I'm not lacking in clients. I actually have a waiting list now, since so many demons are eager to say they have a tattoo from the mate of Knox Thorne."

"You have a waiting list because you're very good at what you do," he corrected. "Think of other ways moving to the Underground would benefit you. It would mean you won't have the costs that you have now, like rent, for instance. The Underground belongs to you as much as it belongs to me. Everything that's mine is also yours."

She didn't like thinking of it that way. It was hard to go from having little to having . . . well, most of Vegas. "I can't deny that it makes good business sense. It does. I'll talk to the girls about it when I go to work in the morning. I'll see what their outlook is on this now that they've had time to think about it."

Knox nodded, thinking they would agree to relocating if for no other reason than that they thought Harper would be safer that way. "There's a little building I think would be ideal for you. I hope you'll at least check it out before refusing." His brow furrowed. "Why are you smiling?"

The whole thing was just so typical of him. "You're such an opportunist. You see me get attacked and think, hey, I can use this to my advantage."

"This surprises you?" He'd warned her in advance that he was ruthless and would do whatever it took to get his own way.

"Not at all. Part of you is gloating that the incident has bitten into my 'I don't need to relocate the business' argument, isn't it?"

"The experience just proved what you already knew: it's not a safe area."

"Sure, but I grew up there. I'm a Wallis, Knox. That means that when it comes to crime, I'm not one who can judge."

"But you are mated to a demon that many fear and many would like to see dead. Just a few months ago, you were taken from me. I had no idea where you were, and I couldn't reach you. I don't want to experience that again. I proposed psychically tagging you so that I'd know where you were at all times, but you were against that. I agreed to drop it, but *you* agreed we would compromise on things. I'm asking you to compromise here."

He knew she found his overprotectiveness stifling, particularly since she also had to deal with his demon's overprotectiveness. She thought it was mostly Knox's need for control at work. Admittedly, he *did* need control. Not just to keep his demon and his abilities in check. He'd spent most of his childhood under the control of a sick, cult-like leader who'd dictated when he woke, what he ate, what he wore, when he slept, and where he slept.

The leader had insisted on complete submission, disallowing the others to make their own decisions, and punished any form of rebellion. Eventually Knox had joined the outside world, swearing to himself that he would never again be under the control of another. He'd seized all the things he'd previously been denied, including knowledge, independence, and possessions.

Now Knox took what he wanted when he wanted it. Now he lived by his own rules. Operated on his own schedule. He had a strong sense of self; it was something he'd worked hard for. He enjoyed the level of power, success, luxury, and decadence he had in his life. But nothing had ever been as important to him as Harper. She wasn't just important. She was *necessary* to him.

He'd explained to Harper that his overprotective behavior wasn't an attempt to control her, but she found it difficult to grasp that she could be indispensable to someone. He supposed that if your parents—the two people that were meant to love and care for you—didn't consider you essential to their lives, it would never be easy to accept that anybody else could or would. Lucian might care for her in his way, but he'd never put her first.

"Like I said, I'll talk to the girls about it."

"Fair enough." Done talking about others, Knox flipped open her towel and took a moment to drink in every inch of her. Satisfaction welled up in his demon at the sight of the possessive brands it had left on her breast and navel. Knox also liked to mark what was his, hence the many small bites on her ivory skin. Neither he nor his demon had been possessive of another being until Harper.

"It doesn't seem fair that I'm naked and you're not," said Harper. Dark eyes gleaming with a savage possession met hers as he shrugged out of his shirt. She swallowed at the sight of his powerful body. There wasn't a single ounce of fat; just pure hard, sculpted muscle. But she didn't have long to admire the view, because he then gave her his body weight. She'd never admit to the dominant fucker that she liked that feeling of being surrounded and trapped.

Harper slid her hands onto the solid bulk of his shoulders as his mouth consumed hers, feasting and dominating. His teeth raked down her throat, and then he was licking and biting her neck. Moaning, she arched into him. That was when one ice-cold, psychic finger slid between her folds. Harper gasped. She still didn't understand how something so cold could give off pure heat, but the sensation burned her flesh and made her pussy spasm.

He sucked on her pulse just as he shoved two psychic fingers inside her. Another moan slipped out of her as they expertly stroked, swirled, and thrust. They weren't just pleasuring her; they were building a need that only Knox could fulfill. If he was to walk away right now she'd stay like this—a sexual mess. No amount of touching herself would get her off. Only he could take away the ache once he put it there.

His hand shaped and squeezed her breast as those icy fingers continued torturing her. Her pussy no longer burned, it blazed and throbbed. Her thighs were tremoring and sweat beaded on her forehead. "Knox . . . "

"I know what you want, but—" Knox grazed his teeth over her pulse "—I haven't tasted you for two days." He'd fucked her, but he hadn't had time to explore and savor her. He kissed and nipped his way down her body, pausing to lick at the "So it goes" tattoo under the breast he hadn't branded; like her other two tattoos, it was easy to miss as it was white ink and mostly hidden.

He kissed his way down to the small raven tattoo in the hollow of her hipbone and swirled his tongue around it before heading further south. "I do love this brand," he said as he traced the triangle of intricate black, thorny swirls at the V of her thighs that looked just like a tattoo. "Spread your legs wide for me."

"Knox, I can't deal with anymore foreplay." She needed to be fucked. Badly.

He positioned himself comfortably between her thighs. "You'll deal with it."

She shook her head. He arched a reprimanding brow . . . and then the psychic fingers dissolved; the sensation fed the fire inside her. "No!"

He flicked her clit with the tip of his tongue, and she bucked. "Be still." He swiped his tongue between her slick folds, lapping up the sweet, honeyed taste of her. He groaned as it worked through his system, thickening his already rock-hard cock. "Fucking addictive."

Fisting the sheets, Harper shook and moaned as he licked and nipped and drove her insane. Then he was sucking on her folds, growling against her flesh. She cursed him. Threatened him. Demanded more.

He just chuckled, and then two ice-cold fingers began to pinch, tug, and tweak her nipples. So she cursed him again and tried to shift away from his mouth. But his hands held her thighs in place as his tongue then *finally* slid inside her. It eased the ache, but not enough. And he damn well knew it.

"You're evil," she fairly growled. "Totally, completely—" Her breath caught in her throat as he rose above her and blew over one cold nipple, making it painfully tight. "See, evil!"

"You like it." He sucked her nipple into his hot mouth and grazed it with his teeth. His mate liked a little pain, and he'd learned exactly what line between pain and pleasure she rode. Releasing her nipple with a pop, he traced the brand on her breast with his tongue. Like the one on her navel, it was an intricate swirl of thorns.

"Knox." It was almost a sob, to her utter annoyance.

He brushed his mouth against hers. "You hurting, baby?" he asked softly. She nodded. "Want me to take the hurt away?"

Harper nodded again, barely holding back a whimper. It almost slipped out when she heard a zip lowering.

Cupping her ass, he angled her hips. "Soft and slow? Or hard and fast?"

Harper knew a trick question when she heard one. "Whatever you want."

Knox's mouth curved. "Clever girl." He slammed home, and her scorching hot pussy clamped around him.

The breath exploded out of Harper's lungs as his long, thick cock drove deep; filling her to bursting, stretching her until it stung, and touching parts that had never before him been touched. As always, the psychic fingers had made her pussy so hypersensitive that she was aware of every ridge and vein. She wrapped her legs tight around him and dug her heels into the base of his spine. "Fuck me."

Knox powered into her at a merciless pace. Her pussy was so tight and wet that it drove him out of his mind. *She* drove him out of his mind. Her throaty little moans, the prick of her nails in his back, the scent of her need, the hot clasp of her inner muscles, and the taste of her in his mouth—all of it incited his senses. He thrust harder, faster. "My pussy."

As the tension built inside her, Harper clawed at his back. He always reduced her to this needy, restless creature that needed to come so bad she shook with it. "Knox—"

"Don't come yet."

Oh, the bastard. And to make it that much harder, he moved her legs to the crook of his elbows and angled her so that his cock brushed her clit with every brutal thrust. It was absolute torture. "Why do you hate me?"

"I don't hate you, baby. Far from it."

"I can't hold back."

"Yes, you can. You will." He upped his pace, claiming her with every territorial slam of his cock. Her pussy fluttered around him. "Hold it," he growled. She shook her head, but she didn't come. "Hold it." He rammed into her deeper, touching a spot that made her gasp. "Hold it." She swore at him and scratched his back. He bit her lip. "Come."

A blinding pleasure swept over and through Harper in a powerful wave. Her scream got caught in her throat as he brutally drove deep and his spine locked. Then he was growling her name, and she felt every hot splash of his come.

Shuddering, she blew out a long breath. All she could say was, "Damn, you're good."

He smiled against her neck.

Since demons could go for days without sleep, they spent a good portion of the night fucking and talking. After that, Knox did some work on his laptop while his mate lay beside him, watching TV. Before Harper, Knox had always preferred silence while he worked. Technically, she should have been a distraction. But there was just something about having his mate right there, where he could touch her whenever he wanted, that made him relax and focus better.

Of course, it was also a lot to do with the simple fact that his demon was better behaved when she was around. Harper charmed it, amused it, and delighted it. Without its only source of fulfillment close by, the demon became quickly bored and restless.

When breakfast time came around, the demon turned morose and sullen because it knew she'd be parting from them soon.

Harper smiled at Meg as the housekeeper placed a plate of food on the dining table in front of her. "Thank you."

The Hispanic she-demon nodded with a fond smile.

Knox arched his brows in surprise. "Toasted bagel with cream cheese for breakfast?" he said as he dug into his own meal of egg white omelet with toast. His mate usually stuck to cereal.

Harper shrugged one shoulder. "Meg says I don't have enough variety in my diet ... which basically means *you* think I don't have enough variety in my diet and you've expressed this to her."

Yes, that was exactly what it meant, which was why Meg was doing her best to stifle an amused smile as she left the room. As always, his mate's astuteness made his demon chuckle. "How are you feeling?"

"Better," Harper said, picking up her bagel.

She *looked* better. The lines of strain were gone from her face. "Good." He took a swig of his coffee. "Belinda left me another voicemail. You've been dodging her calls again?"

"She tried calling *once*," said Harper, sighing. "I was in the bath." But Harper hadn't returned the call because, to be frank, the she-demon in question pissed her off. Knox had hired the event planner to manage the shindig, and she was good at her job. Efficient. Prompt. Incredibly well-organized. But she also looked down on Harper in a major way and felt the need to repeatedly advise her on her relationship with Knox.

She also liked to call attention to how different Harper was from the females in his past—different in that they were elegant, well-groomed, and cultured whereas Harper was ... Harper. What Belinda wasn't grasping was that Harper was absolutely fine with who she was. She had no wish to change. Moreover, *Knox* didn't want her to change.

"She says you're refusing to work with the clothes designer she set you up with," Knox told her, mouth curved. He didn't care whether Harper bought a dress or had it designed as long as she was happy.

"I don't need someone to design and tailor-make a dress for me." Harper especially didn't want to work with *that* particular designer, who had rudely told Harper that it would be difficult to make her look elegant. "I can buy one like everyone else." The *real* reason the cambion called Knox was that she'd use any excuse to get his attention. She often ran to him if Harper gave her an answer she didn't like.

"Why can't *you* deal with the preparations?" Harper asked him.

"I've given my input. Now you need to give yours."

"But she's an event *planner*. Can't I leave it to her and her team to deal with?"

"No, baby. You're a Prime now. You can't hand anyone complete control of anything in your life."

Well, he had a point there. Dammit. "Did she happen to mention that she wanted to hold the event in the ballroom of one of the hotels?"

Knox frowned. "There isn't a ballroom big enough for hundreds of demons to fit inside."

"Oh, she's still happy for the whole stretch of the Underground's strip to be involved in the event. She wants each and every bar, club, restaurant, and other venue to take part, which is fine. But she just also wants all the Primes and VIPs to be separated from everyone else so they can have a fancy party—a party she doesn't want my relatives attending." Fuck that.

"She failed to mention all of that," replied Knox, face hardening.

"I told her that I didn't mind if she made the combat zone look fancy so it catered to anyone with that taste." It was no different than the clubs and bars throwing something casual, and she knew Knox would prefer the whole champagne and soft music scene. "But *only* if the space was open to anyone."

"That's more than fair," said Knox. Done with his meal, he pushed his plate aside. "If she complains to me about this, I'll be sure to make it clear that there will be no segregating anyone. I'm sorry she's being a problem for you, baby. If you want her fired, say the word."

"I don't want to fire her. In terms of her work, I have no complaints about her. Most of her suggestions have been really good, and her team is totally on the ball. I don't want to take care of all the stuff they're arranging. It's just that, well, she's a pain in the ass at times. But I can deal."

"All right." In truth, Knox would prefer to fire Belinda if she was causing his mate any frustration, but coddling Harper would only make her pissed at him. "If it comes to a point where it gets too much or she steps over any line, she's gone." Satisfied when Harper nodded, he stood and pulled on the jacket of his black suit. "Unfortunately, I have to go now. You'll find out your coworkers' opinion on my proposal?"

"I said I will, and I will."

Knox crossed to Harper and tugged her to her feet. "I have a busy day ahead," he began, nipping her lip, "but I won't be home too late."

Harper melted against him, inhaling his dark sensual cologne that drove her demon crazy. "The girls are taking me to the Underground after work. They want to help me pick out a dress for the little shindig."

"You say it like they're taking you for a walk down Death Row. And it's not a shindig."

"Hm."

He kissed her long and slow. "I'll meet you at the Underground tonight then." He breezed his thumb over her jaw. "Remember to be alert for any signs of Crow. You made me a promise yesterday and I expect you to keep it." He would give her the space to be self-reliant and he'd respect her need to fight her own battles, but not to a point that she wouldn't admit to needing his help.

"I will. Take care. A bullet to the heart could kill you too." Her brow furrowed. "Couldn't it?"

"Maybe." His mouth curved as he teased, "Then again, maybe not." With a gentle pat to her ass, he left.

CHAPTER FOUR

⸺◈⸺

An hour later, Tanner smoothly parked the Audi outside the tattoo studio, just as he did every morning. Her dark, broad shouldered bodyguard was also her chauffeur, and Harper didn't understand how the roles couldn't possibly bore the living shit out of him. He was a sentinel. He was trained in God knew how many different things and had plenty of adrenalin pumping stuff he could be doing, like tracking Crow.

She'd told Knox several times to give Tanner less demanding hours, but her mate wouldn't hear of it. And, considering stuff like almost getting raped happened when the hellhound wasn't around, she didn't really have a decent case to argue with.

"That's not nice," said Tanner, a smile in his voice.

Tracking his gaze, Harper saw Devon standing at the window flipping him off. Then, with a haughty glare, the hellcat flicked her long, ultraviolet curls over her shoulder and whirled back to face the jewelry display cabinet. Hellhounds and hellcats had an instinctive aversion to each other.

Twisting in his seat, Tanner held out a small paper bag, his wolf-gold eyes gleaming with mischief. "Give this to the kitty cat for me."

Harper raised her hands. "No way. I'm not getting involved in this weird little war you two are having."

"Oh come on, Harper."

Sliding out of the car, she shook her head. "You'll have to give it to her yourself. Though I wouldn't advise you to." Devon was by no means weak.

Pushing open the front door of the studio, Harper found Khloë sitting behind the curved, chrome reception desk. It was always kept obsessively neat, despite that the small, olive-skinned imp was literally the messiest person appearance-wise *ever*.

Khloë grinned. "Morning, sunshine. Donuts? I didn't steal these."

Such a little liar. Harper blew out a long breath and forced a smile. "Maybe later."

Sensing something was wrong, Devon quickly rounded the large L-shaped sofa and rushed to Harper's side—banging her leg on the coffee table in the process and almost knocking off the tattoo portfolios.

Harper winced. "Are you okay?"

She waved away the pain. "What happened? Raini, get out here, something's wrong!"

Raini rushed out of the office. "What is it?" In a blue vest and jeans, she couldn't have looked more casual. Nonetheless, any male would fall at her feet because, as a succubus, she exuded sex. There was no hiding her curves, flawless skin, or those piercing amber eyes.

Harper hung her jacket on the coat rack and then moved to her station, where she sank into her black leather chair. "Well, a demon from Knox's lair is close to rogue, the bastard's run off, and he's taken Carla with him."

Khloë blinked. "Huh. Didn't see that coming." She also didn't appear to care, which was no surprise given that she despised both of Harper's parents.

"Wait, why Carla?" asked Devon, her cat-green eyes clouded with confusion.

"It would seem that this demon, Lawrence Crow, has visions," replied Harper. "He claims he's had a vision that one day Knox and I will have a baby—a baby that will destroy us all. And no, I'm not kidding. He seems to feel that, by giving birth to me, Carla is partly at fault for this. Though I'm not sure he would have kidnapped her if she hadn't been right there when he chose to run. I think he was just being an opportunist."

Raini leaned back against her own chair. "Wow. That's ... wow."

Devon bit her lower lip. "Harper, I've been around someone who was close to rogue. They can be totally paranoid. They see threats and conspiracies everywhere."

Harper raised a reassuring hand. "I don't believe his vision was anything but a delusion."

The hellcat nodded. "Good."

"Oh, and I almost got mugged yesterday," Harper then announced. Yes, she was understating things, but only because she didn't want it to sway their decision to relocate. "Which Knox is of course using to support his case that we should move the studio to the Underground. He's even chosen a building he thinks will be ideal."

"Have you been to see it?" asked Khloë, to which Harper shook her head.

"I wasn't keen on the idea of moving at first," said Raini. "This is our baby. But there would be some benefits to moving. Let's face it; this isn't a good area. Our client base would be bigger if we moved to the Underground. We'd also be a lot safer there." She turned to Devon. "What do you think?"

"Part of me doesn't like the idea," replied the hellcat. "We built this up to what it is; we built up our reputation and our client base. And I like the location. It's near the sandwich shop and the bakery."

"But ... ?" prompted Raini.

"But moving makes good business sense," Devon went on. "We'd lose some clients, but we'd gain others. We wouldn't have to pay rent or bills because, hello, the Underground partly belongs to Harper now. Besides, there are bakeries and stuff down there too. What about you, Khloë?"

"I like the idea of working somewhere where we wouldn't have to pretend to be something we're not." Khloë gestured to the studio. "Here, we have to act human. Down there, we can be ourselves. There's a flipside to that, though. Demons will always look down on imps, especially Wallis imps. That will affect the business on some level and we might have to deal with a lot of rudeness."

"You're right," said Harper. "Our surname means nothing to humans, so we don't have that issue here. But we'd face it down there." Groaning, Harper rubbed at her eyes. "I know one thing. He's not going to let this go. So, what do we do? It has to be a unanimous decision."

"Despite the downsides of being there, I'm open to relocating," said Raini. "But I'd have to see the space he wants us to use. It would have to *feel* right to me."

Devon nodded. "Agree to take a look at it, Harper. If you think it's cool, call us. We'll come and check it out."

"If it meets all of our approval, I don't see why we can't move there," said Khloë. "People relocate their businesses all the time. I'd miss this place, though."

Looking around the studio, Harper couldn't help but smile. She really did love it. Loved its rock/art/Harley-Davidson vibe. Loved the metal wall art hanging on the white walls with framed photos of tattoos. Each piece of wall art was an enlarged copy of a tattoo. Some were simple, like bright flames and tribal swirls. Others were bolder, like the howling wolf, the flock of ravens, and the Chinese dragons.

Hearing the door open, Harper looked to see ... "Belinda." How wonderful. Her inner demon rolled its eyes; it deemed the woman rather pathetic. As a cambion, Belinda was half-human, but cambions were still classed as a breed of demon in their own right.

Belinda halted in front of her, hands on hips, long false nails tapping her pencil skirt. As ever, she looked the consummate professional. Her make-up was perfectly applied. There wasn't a single wrinkle in that gray suit tailor-made for her willowy figure. Her black heels were stylish, but sensible. And her wheat-blonde hair was pulled back in a severe French pleat with the help of a *lot* of gel. It looked a little painful, actually. Her scalp had to sting something awful.

Hazel eyes hard, Belinda spoke with a tone sharp enough to cut glass. "Really, Harper, you need to follow my schedule if this event is to go as it should."

Harper frowned. "What exactly have I missed?"

"Your appointment with the designer, of course. You were supposed to be there an hour ago."

"Oh, you mean the appointment I told you to cancel?"

Tapping one foot, Belinda sighed. "If you have an issue with the designer, there are others you can work with."

"There's no need. I'll pick up a dress from the mall."

Her face went slack. "You cannot be serious." She sounded utterly horrified.

"Why?"

"That would risk another person wearing the same dress as you at the event!"

Compared to the shit with Crow, it was such a petty thing to be concerned about. "If that happens, it happens."

Belinda's mouth tightened. "I emailed Knox a portfolio of the designer's work a few days ago. He approved of it."

"You were the kid in school that snitched on everyone to the principal, weren't you?" She really had that whiny, ass-kissing 'I'm telling Miss!' vibe about her.

One over-tweezed brow slid up. "Excuse me?"

"This might shock you, Belinda, but I make my own decisions. Knox might approve of something, but he would never tell me what or what not to wear." Especially since, thanks to his fucked-up past, he knew how that felt. Oh, he'd give his opinion, but he would never make the choice for her.

Belinda's smile dripped with condescension. "Knox Thorne is the type of demon who likes to have his own way. He makes no apologies for it. If you expect to keep him, you should learn that quickly and go along with his wishes."

Harper slowly pushed out of the chair and cocked her head. "Is that what you would have done? Given him whatever he wanted? *Become* whatever he wanted? Hmm. It's no wonder he never touched you." Belinda gasped, which made Harper's demon smile. "He'd have sensed that about you. His demon would have sensed it. Easy prey is no fun for a predator as powerful as Knox."

Cheeks almost as red as her lip gloss, Belinda jutted out her chin. "If you'll excuse me, I have things to do."

"Oh, you're excused," said Harper, sweeping an arm toward the door. Predictably, the she-demon marched out.

"She really doesn't think you're right for Knox, does she?" said Raini.

"She thinks she knows him. Probably also thinks she could be better for him." That was her mistake, Harper thought. "She's not alone in thinking either of those things." Many did.

Devon snorted. "You're *totally* right for Knox. She might not see that, but he does and you do. That's all that matters and—"

The door opened once more. This time, Harper smiled at the she-demon who strolled inside. "Grams, hi."

"Why didn't you tell me about Carla?" Jolene demanded, crossing the room with her anchor, Beck, and daughter, Martina, in tow. As always, Jolene was wearing a blouse and sleek skirt, emanating a natural veneer of elegance that didn't manage to hide the well-known fact that she was totally batshit. She was also a master manipulator who knew and insisted on pushing every hot button that Lucifer possessed, but that was off-topic.

"How did you find out?" Harper asked her. It was lair business.

"I have my ways," replied Jolene, patting her perfectly styled hair.

"Ways or spies?"

"You should have told me."

"I was going to, but I didn't want you to go and blow shit up." Her grandmother protected her family with a predatory fierceness. She also liked to destroy buildings when she was pissed off, referring to herself as a demolition expert.

"I'm tempted to," said Jolene. "Her eldest son is spreading

rumors. Little bastard is claiming that you probably took advantage of Crow's fragile state of mind and talked him into kidnapping Carla."

Khloë gaped. "You're not serious."

"What did you do?" Harper asked Jolene, because her grandmother would *never* let something like that go.

The image of innocence, Jolene said, "I didn't do anything."

Harper looked at Martina. "What did you do?"

Martina smiled. "What brings me joy in life." Which meant Roan's car was on fire. Great.

"Does the lair believe he's right?" Khloë asked, arms folded.

It was Beck who answered. "*That* we don't know."

"It wouldn't surprise me if they did," said Harper, rubbing the back of her neck. "They know Carla abandoned me as a baby and has no part in my life." There was a lot more to the story than that, but only a handful of people knew the whole of it. "Demons always get even, right?"

"Yeah," began Raini, "but you never felt the need to get revenge because you figured you were better off without someone like her in your life."

"But they don't know me like you guys do, so they could believe him."

Mouth tight, Khloë shook her head. "Knox is gonna be pissed when he finds out about Roan."

"He'll know about it by now," said Jolene.

Devon turned to Harper. "What do you think he'll do?"

"That all depends on just how pissed he is." In any case, it would be bad.

Lounging in his leather chair, Knox tapped his fingers on the office desk as he looked at the angry male in front of him. "What brings you all the way here? I'm assuming it's extremely important." Ordinarily, any demons from his lair with an issue came to him in the Underground. This particular demon had sought Knox out at one of his luxury hotels on the Las Vegas strip, risking interrupting his business day.

"The Wallis imps set my car on fire!" claimed Roan, face red.

Knox arched a brow. "Really?"

"I suppose they think there'll be no repercussions because they're related to your mate," he clipped tartly. "They seem to believe that gives them a free pass to do what they want."

Sliding his chair closer to the table, Knox leaned forward. "You saw them set the fire?"

"No, but it has to be them."

"Why?"

His brow furrowed. "Harper probably told them what I said when we were in Crow's house yesterday."

"You don't believe what you said was uncalled for?"

"Even if I did, the imps should have gone to you about it." He drew a line in the air as he added, "They had no right to do what they did."

Knox's mouth curved. "Since when do imps do what anyone thinks they should? They're protective of their families."

"It's not like I hurt Harper."

"That's true."

"So you'll deal with this?"

"I will." Knox slowly got to his feet. "I'm glad you came here today, Roan."

The male lifted his chin, seeming pleased by the comment.

Rounding the table, Knox said, "See, it has come to my attention that you've been making outlandish claims about my mate. I was about to have you escorted here when, as luck would have it, you appeared at the reception desk. Thank you for that."

It was taking everything Knox had not to wrap his hands around the fucker's neck. His demon bared his teeth, wanting to lunge and draw blood. The guy had some fucking nerve to come here whining about imps after what he'd done.

Roan's Adam's apple bobbed. "I didn't ..." But he trailed off, obviously conscious that to deny it would simply make the matter worse. If the male had assumed the lair wouldn't report his behavior to Knox, he had to be dumb. They were loyal to their Primes.

"I would have thought you were smarter than this, Roan." After all, Knox thought, the guy was allegedly a sharp and meticulous lawyer who ran a very successful private practice. "What's your true problem with Harper?"

"I don't have a problem with her. But I have a problem with my mother being kidnapped for doing nothing more than giving birth to her."

"Nothing more," Knox repeated. "Yes, it's true that Carla did nothing for Harper other than that."

Roan's mouth flattened. "That's not what I meant."

"It doesn't bother you whatsoever that your mother did what she did to Harper?" Because it bothered Knox a fuck of a lot. "You look down on my Harper, don't you?"

"She's a Wallis," Roan simply stated, as if that in itself was an explanation.

A lot of people looked down on Harper's family, though Knox didn't believe it bothered the imps much. They took a perverse delight in annoying people. "And you think you're so much better than her? Really? I suppose then that it must be eating at you that you now answer to her as you do me."

Roan's nostrils flared. "My mother made a mistake when she was young and depressed. She doesn't deserve to have that mistake paraded around her every day."

"I'm not so sure this is about Carla. I think you don't like that *you* have to face your mother's mistake every day. After all, the lair turned against Carla when they discovered what she did to Harper. I'm sure that has affected you. Maybe the lair treats you differently now. Maybe it's even affecting your business. If their hatred was redirected to Harper, your life would be easy once again."

Roan's eyelids flickered.

"If your aim is to cause dissension and turn the lair against Harper, I have to wonder ... " Knox cocked his head. "What kind of person does it make you that you would capitalize on your mother's disappearance that way? I will tell you, Roan, you may look down on Harper but that is something she would *never* do."

"I don't get it," Roan abruptly declared. "Women throw themselves at you all the time. I've seen them do it. You could have *anyone*."

"That's the life you want?" Knox sighed, disappointed in the male. "It's an empty life." Harper had taught Knox and his demon that.

"You never looked unhappy to me. You always had a gorgeous woman on your arm. You're successful and rich. Our lair worships you. Everyone always does their best to please you." Roan gestured to his surroundings. "You have everything you could ever want."

And living such a lifestyle meant that Knox was forever attracting the wrong type of people. Users. Manipulators. Gold diggers. The list went on. Harper was none of those things. But Knox had no wish to share his personal thoughts with this demon. "Are you purposely trying to redirect the topic of conversation?"

"I'm just saying she seems like an odd choice for you."

"Are you secretly worried that I'm not right for her?" he asked, mockingly. "Is this you being a protective brother, worried I might hurt her? I can assure you that will never happen. She will always be perfectly safe with me. It's other people who need to worry ... which is why it puzzles me that you would risk angering me." A little of that anger leaked into his voice, which was undoubtedly why Roan took a step back.

Knox glided into his personal space. "Let me make myself very clear. You are to stop making such claims. You are to cease attempting to stir trouble. And you are to have more respect for your Prime. If you have a problem answering to Harper, feel free to leave the lair."

"But—"

"But nothing. You are in no position to argue." His demon lunged to the surface and said, "It would be so effortless to kill you. And so very satisfying."

Roan blanched.

"I like the scent of your fear," the demon told him. "You should be scared. Others have died for causing harm to what's mine. You will too if you hurt her. Stay away from Harper."

Nodding, Roan quickly retreated.

Knox took back the reins. "Don't leave so soon, Roan. Maybe another Prime might give you some leeway for making such a grave mistake, given that your mother has disappeared. But I'm not one of those Primes. Harper is, which makes it rather ironic that you scorn her, doesn't it?"

Levi, take him.

The reaper immediately entered the room and seized Roan. The demon didn't pointlessly attempt to fight the sentinel as he dragged him out of the office, despite that his eyes were wide with fear.

Now Knox would need to make Harper aware of Roan's

rumors before someone else did. And he'd need to do it face to face. *Harper, meet me in the side alley.* He didn't like people knowing that he could pyroport—he preferred to keep them guessing about what he could and couldn't do—so he often met her outside the studio, where they could talk in private. *There's something you need to know.*

Roan's been spreading rumors about me.

He frowned. *How do you know?*

Jolene told me.

He didn't bother asking how Jolene knew. The woman was shrewd and crafty and seemed to have sources everywhere. *I've warned him to stop this behavior. I believe he'll listen.*

You'll still punish him though, she guessed, sounding a little saddened by the idea. There was that marshmallow center at work again.

Of course.

A pause. *What will you do?*

It's a standard punishment for a crime of that severity.

Harper must have decided she didn't want to know what that was, because she didn't ask. *He's going to hate me more than ever now.*

It's not you he hates. It's that his life suffered a hard blow when Carla's secret was exposed. As such, he resents answering to you. Knox slid his mind softly against hers, comforting her the only way he could right then. *Don't let this hurt you, Harper. He's not important. He may be your half-sibling by blood, but blood doesn't make family.*

Totally true, she replied. *Any news on Crow's location?*

Not yet. He'll be found. Knox was determined that it would be soon. *Unfortunately, I have to go. Remember, call me if you need me.*

I will. See you later.

His demon rose to the surface and said, *Be safe for me, little sphinx.* Then Knox resurfaced and reluctantly broke the connection just in time to start his conference call.

CHAPTER FIVE

———⊙———

As the Audi braked outside the club, Harper noticed the long lines of people waiting to enter. Even for a Friday evening, it was pretty busy. Then again, it was a very popular place within Vegas. It also happened to be an entrance to the Underground.

Tanner turned to Harper. "Keenan will be your escort tonight; he's waiting for you near the elevator."

"You joining the hunt for Crow?"

"Nah, I just have a couple of things I need to do."

"Like chase your tail and bury some bones?" said Devon.

Raini forced a smile. "Thanks for the ride, Tanner." She then dragged the hellcat out of the car saying, "Control that mouth." Khloë followed them, laughing.

Harper just rolled her eyes. "See you later, Tanner."

Sliding out of the car, she led the way to the front door. The humans waiting behind the red ropes tittered at their appearance. Yeah, well, they hadn't bothered changing out of their work clothes, since they were only planning to go to the mall.

The people in the VIP queue didn't bat an eyelid about it, since the line was solely for demons so they would understand.

Recognizing Harper, the doorman nodded respectfully and stepped aside. Giving him a grateful smile, Harper moved past him and walked straight to the stairs on their right. The girls stayed close behind her as she headed down to the basement and then over to the door at the back of the dark room. The brawny demons manning the door gave her a polite nod.

"This way, Miss Wallis," said one of the guards as he urged them through the door and then over to an elevator. After punching in a code, the polished metal doors slid open. He inclined his head at Harper and then returned to the other guard.

As the four girls stepped inside and the doors began to close, Devon grabbed onto the handrail and asked, "Are you used to being so easily recognized by our kind yet?"

"Nope," Harper replied. She found it a little uncomfortable. "It feels weird when they greet me by my name, like they know me."

"Well, people like the doormen kind of do," said Raini. "You co-own the Underground now, which makes you sort of their boss."

The elevator came to a stop with a chiming sound, and the metal doors slid open. And there was Keenan, flashing his adorable, boyish smile. One look from his hooded, blue eyes made her senses zing to life—it was beyond her control. The incubus, like Raini, oozed sex and could naturally stir lust in others whether he wished to or not. Nonetheless, no one made Harper's body react like Knox did, which was why it was easy for Keenan's effect to become background noise.

Behind Keenan was every demon's version of heaven. Kind of like the Vegas strip only ten times better. There were casinos, clubs, bars, hotels, restaurants, entertainment venues, and strip clubs. There were also things you wouldn't find on the Las Vegas strip, like combat circles where demons dueled for money, and dog racing stadiums where hellhounds competed.

"Hello ladies," greeted Keenan, flask in hand. It could be said that the sentinel had a drinking problem. It wasn't rare for demons, since their kind had addictive personalities. "I can't help but notice you aren't dressed for a night out." His shoulders slumped. "Tell me you're not here to shop."

Harper patted his shoulder. "If it makes you feel any better, I'd rather not go shopping."

Raini grabbed her arm and pulled her in the direction of the mall. "You need a new dress for the celebration, and we will find you one."

As they walked down the strip, Harper peeked into each of the buildings—none of which had a front wall, making it easy to see they were all heaving with demons. People were laughing, eating, drinking, and dancing. There was also a little brawling going on here and there, but that was pretty typical.

Reaching the mall, they walked through the automatic glass doors and right into a maze of retail stores, kiosks, coffeehouses, escalators, smoothie bars, hair salons, elevators, and stairways. The place echoed with the footsteps and conversations of the crowd. Bright and airy, it was well-kept and every surface and window seemed to glimmer. Harper's nose wrinkled at the smell of coffee, perfumes, floor wax, and meat grilling.

Raini pointed at the escalator. "Come on, the first floor has the best dresses."

Harper was more interested in following the scents coming from the food court. "Fine, but we have to eat before we leave here."

"Wait, I need to get some cash first," declared Devon, moving to the ATM with Raini. Keenan stayed with Harper near the fountain, watching Khloë expertly extract a plastic bubble from a coin machine with nothing more than a sharp punch to the side of the machine. She'd always been good at that.

Walking to them, Khloë cracked open the bubble and grinned as she pulled out a small pack of gum. "Yay, strawberry flavor!"

Keenan turned to Harper. "Is it wrong that, despite being a grown man, I want to learn how to do that?"

"No, it is kind of cool," Harper allowed, smiling as she saw that a group of kids who'd been watching Khloë were now trying the move for themselves. Sadly, they were having no luck getting a free bubble.

Raini sidled up to Harper and linked her arm through hers. "Let's go find you a dress."

The next few hours were spent browsing and trying on clothes and shoes. Keenan repeatedly sent Harper "please have mercy on me" looks, but she just shrugged each time. Raini and Devon were on a mission to help her find the perfect dress, and Harper preferred that to dealing with Belinda's designer-friend. Still, it was easy to feel claustrophobic when the mall was so busy. There wasn't much that it didn't sell. Clothing, books, electronics, jewelry, toys, music, shoes, purses, make-up, housewares, furniture—that was just the beginning.

Just as Harper was losing the will to live, Raini brought her to an abrupt halt and pointed to a dress in a window display. "That is perfect for you," declared the succubus.

Harper bit the inside of her cheek. "It's a little too . . . sophisticated for me."

"No, it's not," said Raini, urging her into the store.

A dark-skinned woman approached, smiling politely. "Hello, Miss Wallis. Can I be of any assistance?"

The amount of times Harper had heard that very sentence in

the last few hours was unreal. Before she could get a word out, Raini pointed at the peach dress on the mannequin and asked what sizes were available blah, blah, blah.

Harper browsed the rails while they chatted, sliding hangers back and forth on the racks. She paused as she came to a raspberry red, satin, strapless dress. Decorated with little gemstones, it was tight fitted down to mid-thigh, where it then flared out.

"You look great in red," said Devon. "This is perfect for you."

"Definitely," agreed Khloë. "But I'm not sure Raini will agree. She's got a hard-on for that peach dress."

It turned out that her cousin was right. The succubus insisted that it was the better choice.

"It's graceful, silk, and the shade suits your skin tone perfectly," stated Raini. "Right, Keenan?"

The incubus opened and closed his mouth several times. Then he grimaced. "Why are you involving *me?*"

"You're a guy; guys like seeing girls in dresses. This will look good on Harper, right?"

Again, his mouth bopped open and closed. "Stop. Enough. I can't handle the pressure."

Leaving them to argue, Harper went into the fitting rooms and tried on the dress. When picking clothes, she didn't really care about what they did for her bone structure or cleavage or ass. She just like to be comfortable and, well, feel *good* in whatever the item might be. This dress met her criteria perfectly, though it didn't manage to hide all of the brand Knox's demon had left on her breast. Not many dresses did.

When she came out of the fitting rooms, it was to find Raini and Keenan still arguing—this time about whether succubae or incubi were the better sex demon. Ignoring them, Harper went straight to the checkout.

With a bright smile, the shop assistant took the dress and did all the usual rigmarole. Carefully folding the dress and slipping it into a bag, she then said, "Have a great day."

"I haven't paid yet," said Harper, holding up her debit card.

"But ... you don't need to. You own the Underground."

"But I don't own this store, and it wouldn't be good for the store to be giving out free stuff." Harper knew from her own experience that it wasn't easy to run a business. The overheads in the mall had to be pretty high.

The shopkeeper inclined her head in respect and charged the dress to Harper's card.

"Now we just need to buy shoes," said Devon, but Harper shook her head.

"Another day. I'm tired." Harper wasn't the type of girl who could shop until she dropped. She was more of a "shop until you feel like punching random people for doing nothing more than bumping you with their bags" girl. "Time to eat."

As they were passing a shoe and purse store, Devon grinned. "Oh, I love that red purse. So shiny."

Scratching the back of his head, Keenan cleared his throat. "You probably shouldn't go in there."

"Why?" asked Devon.

"The manager once ... "

"Had a little fun with Knox," Harper finished.

He blinked at her. "How did you know?"

"I went in there a few weeks ago, and she bitterly congratulated me on my mating to Knox. With a sly smile, she said that she knows from personal experience how good in bed he is; she went on to paint a very vivid picture of their time together." She'd mentioned how good his psychic hands felt, how desperate he'd been for her, and repeated all the little compliments he'd made as he fucked her. "She then added just how comfy his bed is and asked how it feels to sleep in a bed that my mate had fucked so many other females in."

Devon gasped. "She didn't!"

Scowling, Keenan said, "You're the only female he's ever taken to the mansion. He took the others to his hotels, and he replaced the beds in all of his penthouses once he mated you."

"I know," said Harper. "Knox told me the same thing months ago, which is the reason I was able to laugh in her face and say I'd add all that to the list of other fictional concepts that I don't care about." But it had still been horrible to hear all that shit and be reminded of how ... eventful ... his sex life had been before she came along. "I would have dealt her some soul-deep pain, but then she'd have known just how much she'd pissed me off." Harper wouldn't give the heifer the satisfaction of seeing her hurt.

"Don't let her get to you," said Keenan. "She's no one. And I'm not saying she's a slut, but she's easier to pick up than a radio station."

Khloë licked her front teeth. "You know, Devon, I think we should take a closer look at that purse."

The hellcat smiled. "I think you're right."

Harper sighed. "Girls, let it be."

"I sure do like that blue scarf over there," said Raini.

Khloë gave Harper a pleading look. "Come on, let's have some fun. It's been a while since we tortured retailers."

Harper chuckled. "All right." Inside the store, they split up. Khloë and Devon checked out the purses and accessories, and Harper and Raini admired the shoes while Keenan kept a look-out.

Harper almost laughed when she noticed the manager's reflection in a mirror. The redhead's eyes went wide and she turned to one of her assistants and hissed, "Tell the guard to follow the tiny one and make sure she doesn't steal anything." By that, she clearly meant Khloë.

Raini cast Harper a "how petty" look.

The manager then appeared at their side. "Can I be of any assistance?" she asked stiffly, her smile brittle.

Harper read her name badge and smiled. "Well, hello again, Lora. I'm just here to find some shoes for the big event—Knox likes me in heels."

Lora's face hardened. "I see."

"You look surprised to see me."

"I didn't expect you to return, given that our last conversation didn't go so well," said Lora, touching her perfectly coifed hair. "I truly didn't mean to offend you." Glancing at Keenan, she cast him a sultry look that he completely ignored.

"How did she offend you?" Raini asked Harper, folding her arms.

"Lora felt compelled to share in great detail the fun she'd had with Knox," replied Harper.

Lora lifted one shoulder. "It was just a little girl-talk."

Ignoring that, Harper continued speaking to Raini. "And she claimed that she'd slept in my bed, which of course is pure bullshit."

The redhead licked her lower lip. "It is the truth. I didn't expect you to be sensitive about the subject. It's not as if it's a secret that Knox is highly sexual."

Glaring at Lora, Raini put her hands on her hips. "You're like summer. You have no class."

At Lora's gasp, Harper said, "Raini's right, you know. Sharing graphic details with me of your time with my mate was both petty and distasteful. I'll bet most of it was also pure bullshit, just like your little claim to have slept in my bed."

Lora sneered. "You want to believe it's a lie, but I know the truth."

"There you go again with your bullshit," said Harper. "God, your mouth must be full of it. Maybe you should do what you do best and swallow."

Lora's face flushed with rage. "I think you should leave."

"Why are you following me?" a familiar voice whined from behind them. They whirled to see Khloë pouting at the guard. "Are you some kind of weirdo?"

He gestured to his uniform. "I work here."

"You think I'm going to steal something, is that it?" Khloë sounded genuinely hurt. "Why? What did I ever do to you?"

The guard spluttered. "I'm not—"

"And why are you looming over me? Is it to intimidate me? Do you do that to all women?"

"I'm not—you're not—*she* asked me to follow you." He jabbed a finger in the direction of the manager.

At this point, they had the attention of everyone in the store.

The redhead lifted her chin and shrugged at Khloë. "You're an imp." As if that was all the explanation she needed.

"At least I'm not prejudiced against other demons," Khloë said, eyes wet. "I'll be outside, Harper." Lower lip trembling, the imp sharply turned to leave and crashed into a display rack, knocking all the purses over and even sending some sliding out of the store. The alarm started blaring and, cheeks flushed with embarrassment, Khloë marched out.

Harper turned to the redhead. "I'll have to go track down my cousin. First, I should probably let you know that it's very, very possible that the overheads for this unit might suddenly become much higher."

The managed gasped. "You can't do that!"

Her demon shoved its way to the surface. "And don't ever think you can dictate what we can or can't do."

As the demon withdrew, Harper spun on her heel and left the

store with Raini and Keenan; stepping over the assistants who were desperately trying to fix the display.

Glancing around, Harper spotted Khloë sitting next to Devon on a bench, head down, near the restrooms. The hellcat was rubbing her back soothingly.

As they reached them, Keenan crouched at Khloë's side, the image of concern. "You okay?"

The imp looked up and smiled. "Sure." She then fished a blue scarf out of her pocket and handed it to Raini. "Here."

The succubus took it with a delighted smile. "Ooh, it's so soft."

Keenan stared at Khloë for a good ten seconds. "You're good."

"First rule of stealing: make the alarm go off *before* you leave," said Khloë. "Then no one bats an eyelid when you walk out. Sometimes I make it go off a few times so it seems faulty." She stood, happy. Then she frowned at Harper. "Hey, what happened to your contact lenses?"

"My demon briefly surfaced to talk to the redhead," replied Harper. Whenever that happened, her contacts disintegrated. "Let's eat."

After having a Chinese meal at the food court, they finally stepped out of the mall. Harper was honestly surprised that Keenan didn't fall to the ground and kiss it in relief. She smiled at the sight of Larkin, Knox's fourth sentinel, waiting there. The stunning, slender harpy moved like a warrior; her gray-blue eyes missed nothing.

"Hey," greeted Larkin. "Keenan said you were done." Obviously they'd had a telepathic chat.

"Tell me you're here to say they've found Crow," Harper said.

Larkin's smile dimmed. "I wish. No, I'm here because Knox wants you to have two bodyguards while the place is so hectic."

Great. "That's not necessary," Harper told her as they began to walk. "I have Keenan, and none of my girls here are weak."

"No, but Primes need to keep themselves well-guarded," Larkin said. "You're a Prime now."

"I'm so looking forward to the celebration!" said Raini. "You could look a little excited, Harper. It's partly to celebrate you being Knox's co-Prime."

"You know me well enough to know that it's not something I'd ever want to celebrate," said Harper. She was getting a headache just thinking about it.

Larkin's mouth quirked. "I don't think I've met another demon who has no interest in power."

"Well, you'd better get used to it, Harper," began Keenan, "because you wield a shitload of it now. Being mated to Knox Thorne was never going to be a simple thing."

"Where *is* Knox?" Devon glanced around. "I thought he was meeting you here."

Harper shrugged. "He said he would."

"He's *in* the Underground," said Larkin, "but he's at his office. Jonas appeared as he was leaving and asked to speak with him." Jonas was another Prime. "He brought Alethea with him," Larkin told Keenan, whose brows flew up. The two sentinels exchanged some sort of meaningful look.

Harper halted. "What? What don't I know?" And who the hell was Alethea? Since it was pretty much impossible for any female to be around Knox without wanting him, Harper had to ask, "Is she an ex of his?"

"Ex?" Keenan stretched out the word.

"Ex-bed buddy," Harper amended.

"I wouldn't describe her as that," said Keenan. "More like they had the occasional one-night stand over the centuries."

"Centuries. Right." Harper's stomach rolled. She hated jealousy. It was a wasteful, pointless emotion. "What is she?"

Larkin bit her bottom lip. "She's an encantada."

Gut twisting, Harper blew out a breath. "He shook the sheets with the ultimate sex demon. Good to know." Encantadas and their male equivalent, encantados, were all exceptionally beautiful and well-known for their powers of seduction. They could also shapeshift into dolphins, which she thought was pretty random.

"Encantadas might be powerful, but they can only enchant humans. Succubae and incubi—we can enchant anyone." Keenan lowered his voice as he added, "Almost anyone."

That didn't make her feel better. Harper tried to shove the matter out of her mind but, dammit, it was hard not to be bothered by it. Just like it was hard not to be bothered by having two bodyguards; both of whom were now crowding her. And just like it was hard not to be bothered by her life suddenly changing in dozens of ways and how she was now co-running a freaking lair.

She didn't regret or resent any of it, but adjusting wasn't easy. What she'd love right then was a distraction. Something. Anything.

Hearing a loud, 'Yee-ha!' in the near distance, Harper looked to see a small rodeo arena. She looked at Khloë. And they both smiled.

Fingers steepled, Knox said, "Jonas, Alethea, what business brings you here?" His tone wasn't the least bit welcoming. He'd come to the Underground with the intention of finding his mate and taking her home. He wasn't in the mood for meetings, but Jonas was one of his business associates, so Knox had agreed.

He had no idea why Alethea was there, considering she didn't usually accompany her brother anywhere and she wasn't involved in any of Jonas's businesses. Knox didn't particularly care so long as the meeting was over with quickly.

Cordial smile in place, Jonas settled on the chair opposite Knox while Alethea sprawled on the sofa near the window that overlooked the combat circle.

"We heard about the problems within your lair," Jonas told him.

Knox arched a brow. "Problems?"

"Lawrence Crow," said Alethea, lips flat. She was a little miffed that Knox hadn't greeted her with a kiss on the cheek.

Knox narrowed his eyes. "And just how do you know about the problems within my lair?"

"I would imagine many people know," Jonas told him. "We were having drinks in a bar just now when one of your demons approached us. He's walking around the Underground with a photograph of a woman; says she's his mother and has been taken by a rogue, Lawrence Crow. He wants to know if anyone has seen her."

Fucking Roan. "Crow is *close* to rogue."

"If you need any help tracking him, I would be happy to spare some demons from my Force," said Jonas. "A demon in such a state on the loose affects our entire species."

"They tend to attract human attention," added Alethea. "We can't afford that, and we can't afford to overlook the danger they present. Thanks to what happened to our old Prime, we know from personal experience just how devastating and long-reaching the consequences can be when a rogue is on the loose."

Knox straightened in his seat. "As I said, he isn't rogue."

"He's still dangerous," Alethea insisted.

"I appreciate your offer of help, Jonas, but it won't be necessary."

Jonas inclined his head. "If you change your mind, don't

hesitate to contact me. On another subject, I'm sure you know that I'm hosting the annual meeting this year. It will take place on the last Saturday of this month at my home. I hope you will attend."

"I always do," said Knox. The Primes all met up once a year to address any potential issues.

Alethea pursed her lips. "I heard you've taken a mate since we last saw each other, Knox. That came as quite a surprise. In fact, I was fairly certain it had to be a joke."

"No joke," Knox told her.

"Shall I take it then that it's also true that she's a Wallis?" Her upper lip curled ever so slightly, but Knox noticed. His demon, who had never liked her, urged Knox to throw a pencil at her head. Maybe even the stapler.

"You should," replied Knox. "I would have thought you saw her on the video feed of the voting poll."

Months ago, some Primes had tried electing themselves as a US Monarch. Demons didn't have global leaders; they answered only to their Primes. The majority of demon kind voted to keep it that way. As the elections had been recorded live, every demon in the Underground had been able to watch the event—as such, they'd also seen him kill another Prime for attacking Harper, who dealt the she-demon a soul-deep blow before Knox stepped in.

"The whole thing held no interest for me. I was in Berlin at the time anyway." Alethea, like many of her breed, preferred to live closely with humans as they were easier for them to manipulate and control. "You didn't notice my absence?"

"No," replied Knox, rising to his feet. He spoke to Jonas. "Again, I thank you for your offer of aid."

One of Alethea's blonde brows arched. "Are you sure you don't need it?"

"Positive," said Knox as he began a slow walk around the desk. All he wanted to do now was find his mate. "Crow will be caught and given what medical help he needs."

"You intend to help him?" asked Alethea.

"Demons can be brought back from the edge," Knox pointed out.

"They can also do awful things while they're on that edge."

Knox couldn't argue with that. Absentmindedly, he ran his gaze along the security monitors. And he froze. No, he could not be seeing this. But he was. Unfuckingreal.

"Knox, what is it?"

Ignoring Jonas's question, Knox took a deep breath. It didn't help. He strode out of his office, sure that his mate wanted to drive him insane. It was really the only explanation he could think of that would explain why the hell she would put her safety on the line this way.

Levi fell into step behind him. *Knox, what's wrong?*

I'll kill her. He would. He'd ring her pretty little neck.

"Knox, wait!" shouted Alethea from somewhere behind him.

Knox didn't wait. He kept moving. Something about his expression must have given away his anger, because people scrambled to avoid him as he prowled down the strip. Finally, he reached the small rodeo showground, where he was immediately assaulted by the scents of dust, hay, rodeo fare, and animal dung. The loud audience was avidly watching a tall male trying to mount a huge bull.

Knox caught sight of Keenan, Larkin, and Harper's friends near the seven-foot high fence guarding the arena ... and they were all looking through the fence right at Harper, who was standing with Khloë near the bull pen. Slipping on a leather, protective glove, Harper patted her protective vest. She'd obviously borrowed both, along with the spurs and the cowboy boots.

"Not good," muttered Levi.

Charging at his sentinels, Knox growled. He'd trusted them with her safety. This wasn't safe. This was fucking crazy.

Keenan's head whipped around and his eyes widened. "Knox . . ."

"Why is my mate in there?" Knox ground out, fisting his hands against the urge to grab the incubus by his shirt and shove him against the fence. Losing control would be a mistake that could get a whole lot of people hurt. His demon wasn't so pissed; it liked a thrill just as much as the next demon and it respected her wish to pursue one.

Keenan scratched the back of his head. "Well, she wanted to ride a bull—"

"And you didn't think to stop her?"

"I would have done, but she snuck off!"

Not a surprise. "And you didn't save her from herself because . . . ?"

"The event is safer than it looks." Keenan winced as a demon bashed his face on the bucking bull's horns just before he hit the ground hard.

"If it makes you feel any better, it's not her first rodeo," said Devon. "No pun intended."

Levi turned to the hellcat. "She's done this before?"

"Imps love bull riding," said Devon. "Especially when they're drunk."

"When they're drunk?" repeated Knox. "They take part in this undeniably dangerous sport when they're drunk?"

Devon raised a brow. "You're really that surprised?"

Having spent a lot of time around imps recently . . . "Actually, no." Knox looked to see his mate being led toward the chute, where a white stomping bull waited. *Harper, do not get on that damn bull.*

Her head shot up, her eyes found his, and she waved with a huge smile. She. Waved.

Harper, I'm serious, he clipped.

Relax, I'll be fine, she assured him, like he was being melodramatic and this was merely a pony ride.

I will not allow you to put your safety at risk, Harper. They didn't call bull riding "the most dangerous eight seconds in sport" for nothing.

No one "allows" me to do anything, Knox.

His blood boiled. He wanted to yell at her, demand she come to him, forbid her from doing this ... but the reality was that he could order her around all he liked and it wouldn't make a damn bit of difference. In fact, it would make her even more determined to go through with this just to be contrary.

He'd known when he took her as his mate that he would *never* control her; that she had a mind of her own—a mind that didn't always operate the way he'd like it to. He'd known and accepted this. But *bull riding* ... yeah, he had a major fucking issue with that.

Trying a different approach, he softened his voice and said, *Baby, don't do this.*

Her shoulders stiffened and she looked at him, conflicted.

Come over here to me, he coaxed.

Alethea sidled up to him and put a hand on his arm. "She's really going to ride that bull?"

Harper's eyes cut to the female and narrowed slightly; then a blank mask settled over her face.

Fuck it all. He moved away from Alethea, but it was too late. *Harper, she's no one to me.*

Nothing.

"Look, all she has to do is hang on tight for eight seconds or more," said Devon.

Knox ground his teeth. "Yes, but she has to hold on to a two-thousand-pound bull." And as his mate looked the monstrously big, huffing, pissed-off bull right in the eye, Knox couldn't understand why she hadn't thought that, hey, maybe this wasn't the best idea.

"Honestly, I've never seen the imps suffer any major injuries," said Devon. "Sometimes they walked away with a concussion, a broken arm from an awkward fall, or a broken foot after being stomped on. But, really, that's it."

"That's it?" echoed Knox.

Devon pursed her lips. "Nothing I say is going to make you feel better, is it?"

"Not a thing." Knox looked back at his mate just in time to see her start to mount the bull. "Fuck."

Harper held onto each side of the chute as she slowly eased onto the bull's back. Beneath her, the bull snorted, no doubt angry and uncomfortable at the rope wrapped around its flank. Her demon was excited. It had always enjoyed the sport. Each pump of adrenalin increased the entity's excitement.

"The rules are pretty simple," the rodeo clown told Harper. "You've got to hang on for eight seconds. If you touch the bull, yourself, or the rope with your free hand, you'll be disqualified."

She nodded, already well aware of that.

"When you fall, get up and run because trust me when I say he'll come after you."

"Got it." With her gloved hand, she got a firm, solid grip on the flat, braided rope.

The rodeo clown sighed. "You sure about this? I have a feeling your mate won't be pleased."

Yeah, well, her mate was currently standing with an ex ...

whatever she was. And the bitch *touched* him. Not in the mood to be nice, she said, "You're in my way. Move."

He chuckled and stepped aside with an expression that said, 'It's your funeral.'

"You'll be fine," Khloë told her. "You always were the best at this."

"See you in about eight seconds." Harper nodded to signal she was ready, and then the bucking chute opened.

The bull stormed into the arena, and Knox's heart slammed against his ribs. There was no gentle build up, no moment of reprieve. The bull bucked. Kicked. Reared. Twisted. Spun in fast, tight circles. All the while, his mate clung on with her thighs—one arm in the air. The crowd hooted and hollered and cheered her on, including her friends and the sentinels.

He wanted to telepathically call out to her, but she didn't need a distraction right now. So all he could do was watch … and then it was over. It seemed like she'd no sooner shot into the arena than she deliberately threw herself to the ground and a loud whistle was blown.

The rodeo clown distracted the bull while Harper ran flat out for the exit, glancing up at the huge screen blazing "TEN SECONDS." She skidded to a stop near Khloë, threw her hands up high and yelled a battle cry worthy of any warrior. Everyone cheered with her, chanting her name, but she didn't seem to care about the attention. She was chatting excitedly with Khloë as the imp helped her remove the protective gear.

Levi sidled up to Knox. *You know why she did this, don't you?*

To give me a heart attack? Knox was pretty sure the organ came close to collapsing.

This wasn't about you. Before she became your mate, she had a completely different life. It was simple, but fun. Imps are wild and bold. Like every Wallis, she grew up doing risky, dangerous, and highly illegal shit—not taking life too seriously.

Yeah, Harper had told him about the many different "experiences" she'd had over the years, such as engaging in high-speed car chases and breaking into bank vaults.

Now everything's changed for her, Levi went on. *Things aren't so simple anymore. She gets to have fun, but not the same kind of fun. Instead of doing wild and dangerous things, she's walking around with bodyguards and dealing with an overprotective mate. She has to take life seriously now because she's a co-Prime—something, I'll remind you, she never wanted. Jolene raised her to take over from her, but she had no interest in the position.*

I know all this. He knew she probably worried she'd lose who she was. *I do, but bull riding—*

Is probably something she started to learn when she was a kid. Tonight, she needed fun, a distraction, something familiar that made things simple again just for a short time. She warned you at the very beginning that you'd never control her. Considering she's accepted all of you, it would be shitty of you not to accept all of her—even the parts that drive you crazy.

I don't want her to change. Knox wanted her exactly as she was.

Then don't give her a bucket load of shit for this. I'm not saying you have to be okay with it. I didn't like seeing her on the back of a bull either. But if you berate her for being who she is, you'll hurt her. I don't think you want that.

Knox exhaled a heavy breath, knowing Levi was right; resenting that Levi was right. He waited impatiently as she walked toward them, still talking animatedly with her cousin. Her cheeks were flushed and her eyes were gleaming. She looked happy. Exhilarated. Energized. And he found that he didn't have it in him to be pissed at her.

Raini, Devon, and Larkin crossed the space to her,

congratulating her and asking how the hell she'd managed to hold on for ten seconds. After a minute or so, Harper's gaze cut to him and turned wary and unsure. He hated that. Hated that wariness. *Come here, baby.* And she moved right to him.

Knox smoothed his hands up her arms, feeling for any injuries, as he said, "Imagine my surprise when I saw you on the monitor in my office."

Harper smiled at his concern. "Nothing is broken, don't worry. You should let go of me. I'm covered in dust." Some was even stuck in her throat. But Knox held her tighter.

A male approached them and smiled at her. "I'm Jonas. We met briefly during the elections, though I didn't have the pleasure of speaking with you."

She gave the Prime a polite smile and simply said, "Yeah, I remember." Tall, dark, and charming, he was a good-looking guy. But then his kind always were.

Jonas gestured to the female that then came forward. "This is my sister, Alethea."

Harper did her absolute best not to snarl, but it was kind of hard when her demon was urging her to pummel the little bitch. Alethea was almost painfully beautiful—a symmetrical face, perfect bone structure, exotic features, and one of those hourglass figures. Knowing that this female had touched Knox, kissed him, and had him inside her ... Yeah, Harper totally despised that *and* her. But she loved the bitter gleam in the encantada's eyes.

Alethea looked down her nose at her. "You're very small."

"But so shiny," said Jonas. "I've never seen eyes that color before. They're a sort of opal shade."

"Now they are." Knox breezed his thumb across her cheekbone. "Harper's eyes change color often."

Fascinated, Jonas said, "Really?"

"Change color?" Alethea sniffed. "How odd." She looked at Knox. "She's not your usual type. Far from it, in fact."

Harper gave her a winning smile. "Maybe that's why I got claimed and the others didn't."

Alethea's eyes flared and her mouth set into a hard line, which made Harper's demon laugh wickedly.

"Harper and I are done for the evening," declared Knox, taking her by the wrist and beginning to lead her away, but she dug her heels in to say a quick goodbye to her friends.

"Don't forget the meeting, Knox," Jonas called out. "It's important."

Harper shot him a questioning look, but Knox gave a quick shake of the head. They'd talk about it later. Now, he just wanted to take his mate home.

CHAPTER SIX

———◆———

Striding into the living area, Harper plonked herself on the sofa. She was tired, and her feet hurt after hours of walking around the mall, but she was also feeling pretty energized after the rodeo. "Are you finished brooding yet?" she asked Knox. "Because I'd like to know what meeting Jonas was referring to."

Knox stood in front of her. "I don't brood. But I am angry that you put yourself in danger like that."

"It's not like I threw myself in front of a bus."

"You were riding a bull."

"At least I didn't fuck a dolphin."

Knox double-blinked. "What?"

"You and Alethea." Harper raised a finger. "For the record, I don't like the way she looks at you. There's something proprietary about it. But I suppose it's natural that, given you've known each other for longer than I've been alive, she'd feel like she had some rights to you."

He frowned. "She doesn't have rights to me." The only person who had and ever would was Harper.

"I know that."

Knox sighed. "You're trying to distract me from the matter at hand."

"Of course I am. But you did fuck a dolphin."

"She *shifts* into a dolphin." Not that he'd ever seen it happen, but it was typical of her kind.

"Dolphins are seriously twisted, you know."

Knox's frown deepened. "Dolphins are twisted?"

"They're the only predators that kill their young for fun. And the males are rather fond of gang rape. Oh, they might look cute and seem charming, but that innocent exterior is quite an act. They're like the sea-world's version of Ted Bundy."

Knox closed his eyes and let out a long breath. His demon was laughing. "I'm not sure why we're having this conversation."

"Then maybe you can instead tell me what meeting Jonas was talking about."

He opened his eyes. "We'll talk about that once I've said what I have to say. I don't like that you mounted a two-thousand-pound bull, I don't like that you did something you knew full well could get you badly hurt, and I don't like that you dismissed my concern. But I do understand why you did it."

"You do?"

Knox pulled her to her feet and into his arms. "Your life is changing and you're finding it hard to emotionally keep up. That's natural. I want you to come to me when you're feeling overwhelmed. Talk to me. Let me help you. Don't jump on the back of a wild animal."

She smoothed her hands onto his shoulders. "Sorry if you

thought I was dismissing your concern. I genuinely wasn't trying to patronize you when I assured you that I'd be okay. I just didn't want you to worry. You're so extremely overprotective that you don't trust my judgement when it comes to my own safety."

"It's not that I don't trust your judgement. It's that I don't trust wild bulls."

She rolled her eyes. "You're deliberately missing the point, but whatever. Now tell me what Jonas was talking about."

Knox cupped her hips. "This year, he's hosting the annual meeting wherein the US Primes get together and discuss any issues. It takes place in two weeks. Tanner and Levi will come with us."

"Why did he come to your office?"

"He heard about Crow. Apparently Roan is walking through the Underground with a picture of Carla, asking if anyone has seen her."

She absentmindedly tapped her nails on his shoulders. "Even though I'm not totally comfortable with this co-Prime thing, I don't like that Jonas and the dolphin only asked to meet with *you* tonight ... like I don't count." Her demon was rather offended.

"If I had known it wasn't a standard business meeting, I would have included you."

"You know, it's probable that they don't truly see me as your mate. I mean, even *you're* shocked that you took a mate. It could be that they're also so shocked by it that they don't take it seriously. After all, it's rare for Primes to mate since demons didn't like to share power."

He thought about Alethea's belief that news of his mating was false. "You could be right."

"The rest of our kind are probably just as doubtful. Most saw you kill Isla to avenge me, but they could have decided to attribute that to me being your anchor."

"It could actually be that they don't *want* to take our mating seriously. A mated pair of Primes is far stronger than a demon ruling a lair alone. We're the only mated Primes in the world. The fact that we're both powerful makes us even scarier."

"I'm nowhere near as powerful as you." And she was totally okay with that, because she didn't think *anyone* should be expected to harness and control the kind of power he had.

"But you're by no means weak, and demons respect strength. It's well-known at this point that you can cause soul-deep pain."

"Yeah, but I'm a Wallis. They won't even take me seriously as a *person*." It was ridiculous, yet true.

"They'll learn to."

Hmm, she doubted it. The prejudice against imps, especially her family, was too deep-rooted.

Knox searched her eyes. "*You* take our mating seriously, don't you?"

"Of course," she said, surprised. "Why would you even ask that?"

"Because you expect people to leave you." The way her parents had. "I need to be sure that you trust I won't ever do that."

"I don't believe you'll leave me."

"But you don't trust that I won't," he sensed.

Yeah, but that wasn't anything he needed to worry about. "Knox, I never trust situations where I get what I want. It's not that I don't trust *you*."

"But you don't feel fully secure either, do you?"

She shrugged. "That's just me being me. It's not a reflection on what we have." But he didn't seem convinced. "A lot of people, like Belinda, just don't understand what you see in me. They don't understand how someone who could have pretty much anyone they wanted would choose me. Want to know why that pisses me off? Because that theory insinuates that you're shallow. You're not."

Melting against him, Harper admitted, "I do sometimes question how you could manage to be with someone who constantly tests your patience, but that's it. I know you're a person who doesn't make huge decisions without giving them careful thought. I know that you're someone who goes after what he wants. If you say I'm what you want, I believe you. My subconscious will take a while to accept that, since it's pretty much trained to believe people come and go like the wind. And I admit that a small part of me will always worry, but that's not a bad thing. It means I won't take what we have for granted."

"It also means I don't have every part of you. I want it all." He was greedy when it came to her. "I want that little part that eyes me warily."

"Give it time to get used to seeing you every day."

He tucked her hair behind her ear. "Before you learned what I was, I worried that you'd try to leave. But you accepted the truth of what I am. If I remember rightly, you said, 'big motherfucking deal.' You've seen me at my most dangerous. You know better than anyone else what I'm capable of. You know how far I'd go to protect you. And yet you're still here."

"That right there should make you see you don't have to worry. Actions speak louder than words."

Then Knox would have to think on what "action" he could take to assure her that he wasn't going anywhere. Putting that aside for now, he said, "It's your day off work tomorrow. How will you be spending it?"

"I have another flying lesson with Khloë." Not that they were helping much. Harper had spent most of her life unable to use her wings. Every sphinx had tattoo-like brands on their back that could become wings. But although Harper had the brands, her wings had never come to her when she called them. Or, at least, they hadn't until a few months ago when some of Knox's power had leaked into her mind and coursed through her system.

Knox's brow furrowed. "I can give you flying lessons. Why didn't you ask me to help?"

"You're a busy guy."

"I'll always make time for you. Khloë's wings are different than yours. They're gothic and bat-like."

"Yeah, and yours are made of magma energy so they're different than mine too."

"It doesn't mean I can't still teach you."

Realization dawned, and she tilted her head. "You don't like it when other people do things for me, do you?"

"Not always." All right, in truth, he wanted to selfishly be all she needed and wanted.

"Fine," she sighed. "You can give me flying lessons."

Satisfied, Knox kissed her. "We'll start tomorrow." Curling his arms around her waist, he lifted her. "Now let's go wash the smell of bull off your skin."

Harper locked her legs around him. Sounded good to her.

"Ready?" asked Knox.

Harper grimaced. "Not really."

"You've had flying lessons before."

Yeah, she thought, but she'd never had them near the border of a winding ravine before. It was making her nervous, even if the scenic views were divine. It also didn't help that she was baking in heat that was as dry as the breeze. "The lessons didn't amount to much. I don't know how easy it is for you to use your wings, but mine are a pain in the ass. I didn't realize how hard it would be just to call them."

"But they come to you on command now?"

"Yes, I have that part down." She batted at a bug that came too close. "It's the flying part that's the problem."

"Where do you *feel* the wings? Your back? Shoulders?"

"They feel like a weight extending from my shoulder blades right down to the center of my back. They feel more like another set of arms than a pair of wings. And *that's* just freaky."

Knox also "felt" his wings near his back and shoulders, but they didn't feel like an additional pair of arms. "Call them. I need to get a good look at them."

She nervously shifted from foot to foot on the uneven, gritty ground. "Are you sure we should be doing this here? The Grand Canyon is a pretty popular place." And extremely beautiful with the varied, vibrant colored rocks and the Colorado River flowing through the center.

"Baby, the park encompasses something like 1,904 square miles. The canyon itself is roughly 277 miles long. There is plenty of land for the tourists to explore; this particular spot is difficult to navigate and it's mostly left alone."

"Some tourists use helicopters," she reminded him.

"We'd hear them approaching and then I could pyroport us away from here." Just as he'd pyroported them there in the first place.

"Maybe we should reschedule. We have more important things to take care of. Like tracking Crow before he hurts Carla." If he hadn't already done so. They all knew there was a good chance she was dead.

The gravelly ground crunched beneath Knox's feet as he

moved to her. "I have many people tracking them, Harper. The Force is working night and day to locate them. They will be found eventually." He just couldn't promise Carla would be found alive. "Okay?"

Harper took a deep breath. "Okay."

"Good." He backed up a step and said gently, "Now stop delaying the lesson."

Inhaling deeply, Harper rolled back her shoulders and called on her wings. They snapped out, fanning around her and she bit out, "*Motherfucker*." It felt as if the skin of her back peeled away, but she knew it hadn't.

"Beautiful," said Knox. His demon agreed. They were huge gold, gossamer, eagle-like wings that had red and black streaks running through the feathers. He skimmed his fingers over one wing. "Hot. Silky. Soft. They look flimsy, but they're strong as steel."

"I doubt they're as strong as Larkin's wings, though."

"Her wings are heavy and strong, but they have bones; bones can be broken, and then she can't fly. Yours don't have bones or muscles, which means they won't break or feel any strain." She would only feel strain on the muscles of her back and shoulders. "They couldn't be snapped in half, but they do have some weaknesses."

Harper nodded. "They're so thin, they're very sensitive and especially vulnerable to sharp objects. They won't necessarily tear, but it'll still hurt."

"Yes, which means you need to be careful with them." He stroked her wing again. "You have an additional problem."

She knew what he meant. "Sphinxes are often hunted for their wings. They're considered a prize and they sell well."

"I don't want your wings to end up mounted on someone's wall. It's probably a good thing that you're keeping them secret.

They're very unique." While she was vulnerable in that she couldn't yet fly, a hunter would definitely take advantage and try to steal them. That was why Knox was so set on teaching her to control her wings.

"They share the same colors as the flames of hell." She bit down on her bottom lip. "What does that mean?" She'd never actually asked him outright before, wary of the answer.

"It could mean nothing."

"But it could mean something. What?"

"I truly don't know." He'd pondered over it many times, but he'd never come up with a satisfactory conclusion in his head. "It can't be that you now possess some of my power. That would have killed you."

"I'm not built to handle that level of power." Harper honestly didn't know how he did it. "When the shield between our minds dropped and your power poured into me . . . I've never felt pain like it. I really thought I was going to die."

He slipped his hand around her nape and gave it a comforting squeeze. "Maybe these colors simply represent that my power gave the wings a little push before it bounced straight back to me."

"That makes the most sense." Or, at least, it was an answer that didn't stress her out.

Knox released her and took a few steps back. "Now . . . on to the flying lesson. Flap your wings for me, but not hard enough to ascend."

Using her arm to wipe sweat and grit from her forehead, Harper flexed her back muscles, making the wings flap once.

"Good. That hurt?"

"No, but it will later."

"Try it again," he ordered. She did. "Again. Again. You're moving your arms at the same time."

"I know," she grumbled. "It's because the wings feel like another set. It's hard to keep my arms still."

"You need to learn, or it will massively affect your balance when you're in the air."

"Tell me something I don't know."

He swooped in and kissed her hard. "You're cute when you're agitated." She always made him think of a hissing, spitting kitten when she was in this mood. His sphinx muttered something under her breath, but Knox didn't hear it over the shriek of a predatory bird. "Flap your wings, but still don't lift from the ground. I want you to practice flapping them without moving your arms." She did extremely well . . . for all of twelve seconds. "You're moving your arms again."

She sighed. "I know."

Her little pout made his demon chuckle. Knox grabbed her fisted hands and held them at her sides. "Now try again. You need to be able to *feel* how separate the wings are from your arms." She gently beat her wings over and over, never looking away from him . . . as if drawing strength from him. "Good, you can stop now."

With a sigh of relief, she stopped. Her back and shoulder muscles were aching already, but she didn't complain.

"You did well. Now see if you can do it without me holding your hands."

Nodding, she stuffed her hands in her pockets.

"That's not much different from me holding your hands," he pointed out, amused.

"Don't care. I'm sick of flapping my arms like an idiot." Keeping her hands in her pockets, she flapped her wings several times until . . . "I can differentiate them from my arms now. The difference is subtle. Like one set is much lighter than the other. Who would have thought gossamer wings could feel heavy?"

"They might not feel so heavy once you get used to them. Now tell me the truth. When you practice with Khloë, do you fly or do you soar?"

"Soar," she admitted solemnly.

His mouth twitched. "Thought so." He moved closer, asking, "Out of interest, is there any grace about it?"

"None whatsoever."

He kissed her. "We'll fix that, but not today. A mistake a lot of people make when learning to fly is that they don't first learn to hover. If you fall, you'll be hurt. But if you know how to put on the brakes and hover, you'll be able to stop yourself from hitting the ground."

She cocked her head. "Huh. I never thought of it that way."

"Most demons don't, because they're not so much interested in learning the mechanics of flying; they just want to delve straight into the exciting part. Then they get hurt and wonder why. So, though it's not going to be at all exciting, I want you to learn to hover first."

"I'm good with that." Falling to her death did not sound fun.

"I need you to ascend a few feet off the ground. This time you're going to need to use a little force when you flap your wings or they're not going to lift you."

She closed her eyes, shutting out all other stimuli, and concentrated on that heavy weight she could feel extending from her back. She tensed the muscles there as hard as she could, and then she let them go—it was like pulling on an elastic band and then releasing it with a snap. Her wings lifted her nicely, but then she landed right back on her feet, almost slipping on the uneven ground.

"Good girl. That was a nice, neat ascent." The descent was clumsy, but not entirely her fault. "This time, don't pause in flapping your wings, but don't try to lift higher. Just beat them gently but fast."

"Okay." She did as he instructed. "Hey, I'm doing it." Then she lost her rhythm, and her feet touched the ground. "Well, I was."

"The point is that you *can* do it. Now, do it again. I know it's boring, but it's important. I'm not teaching you how to fly until I know you're not going to hit the ground like a dart." He kept her there for at least an hour, trying different exercises, until pain strained her features. "We'll end the lesson here. You've done enough."

Yawning, she did a very feline stretch and winced. "My back is killing me."

"I know, baby, but it will get easier. Tuck your wings back in. I know it'll hurt, but you have to learn to push past the pain so you can control them." Her wings folded and then sort of melted into her skin. "Good girl." He lifted her, and she lazily curled her arms around his neck. Flames erupted around them, licking at their skin, as he pyroported them home.

In their bedroom, he put her to bed and kissed her forehead. "Rest, baby. I'll be back soon." She mumbled something incoherent and rolled onto her stomach.

Knox walked through the house, going straight to the living area. His four sentinels were relaxing on the sofas; waiting for him, just as they'd been instructed to do.

"How did Harper do?" asked Larkin.

"Better than I did on my first real lesson," Knox replied truthfully. "Any sign of Crow?"

Tanner shook his head, legs crossed at the ankles. "But he has to be close. It's safe to say he'll come for you."

"What did Jonas and Alethea want?" Levi asked.

Knox slipped his hands in the pockets of his pants. "They

know about Crow. It would seem that Roan is strolling around the Underground with pictures of Carla, asking if anyone has seen her. He's also falsely claiming that Crow is rogue, which could very well have the demon killed on sight by someone who isn't aware of the truth. I need you to pay him a visit for me, Keenan. Express my displeasure and make him see reason."

The incubus nodded. "He and I will have a little chat."

Levi spoke then. "Jonas just wanted to ask you about Crow?"

"He came to my office to offer his help in tracking Crow," said Knox.

"So it wasn't a business meeting," began Keenan, "but he didn't invite Harper?"

Knox relaxed on one of the two half-moon sofas. "Harper has a theory that our mating isn't being taken seriously."

"I'd have to agree with her," said Tanner. "Don't get me wrong, the lair is happy for you and they want Harper as co-Prime. Not even Roan's little rumors changed that. I think they believe you *want* the mating to be a permanent thing; I think they just also have trouble believing it will be."

Levi nodded. "You've been a solitary creature for a very, very long time, Knox. They're not used to seeing someone so deeply enmeshed in your life. The longer you're with Harper, the more real it will seem to them."

"The shindig will go a long way to proving this is serious to you," said Tanner.

Knox gave him a put-out look. "Now *you're* calling it a shindig too?" And why did his demon find it so amusing?

"Sorry," said Tanner, though he didn't look it. "I'm used to hearing Harper call it that."

Leaning forward, Levi loosely clasped his hands. "There's

something you need to consider, Knox. Our lair wants this mating to be real, but I don't think the other Primes will."

"Neither do I," said Knox. "They feared me enough when I ruled alone. Having someone at my side will make me seem more of a threat."

Larkin toyed with her long braid. "It will shock them that you're prepared to share what power you have."

"But that's not a bad thing," said Levi. "Part of the reason people fear you is that they don't understand you or what motivates you. You're strong enough to rule our kind, but you have no wish to. That alone baffles them. People fear what they don't understand."

"I don't think they'll have any success understanding Harper, either." Keenan took a long swig from his flask. "I mean, she's not at all impressed at the benefits she has from being your mate."

Knox draped his arms over the back of the sofa. "Harper likes to earn what she has. Things that have been given to her—even the gifts she was born with—don't have as much value to her. She'll keep, use, and appreciate these things. But she gains more satisfaction in owning something if she somehow earned it."

"Ah," said Keenan. "I can respect that."

"You might want to know that Bray and Roan have told the rest of the lair about the vision Crow claimed to have," said Larkin. "Most are blowing it off—they've been around demons in Crow's state of mind before; they know that 'the end of the world' claims are pretty typical. Others are uneasy about it, but I don't think any of them truly believe there'll be an evil baby born to destroy us. Oh, and Bray and Roan are also calling for Crow to be shot down while he's shattering rather than given medical help."

That pissed Knox off. "Unless it's necessary to save the life of another, I have no wish to kill someone who's so ill they don't know what they're doing." Regardless of what some believed, Knox didn't like to kill for the mere sake of it. His demon … well, that was another matter.

CHAPTER SEVEN

⸺◈⸺

Pinching the bridge of his nose, Knox released a bored sigh. He glanced at his watch. Ten minutes, and then the meeting would be over. Still, he didn't want to spend another ten minutes of his life listening to a heated debate between two human business associates. He had better and more important things to do. His demon was becoming more and more restless by the minute.

He was thinking about reaching out to Harper, knowing the sound of her voice would settle his demon, when he felt Levi's mind slide against his.

Knox, you need to get out here, said the sentinel. *We have an emergency situation.*

Knox and his demon instantly went on high alert and a surge of adrenalin spiked through them. He quickly excused himself and left the conference room of the hotel to find Levi waiting outside. "Harper?" he asked, heart pounding.

Levi shook his head, lips tight. "Crow's in the building."

Son of a bitch. It had been merely five days since Crow disappeared with Carla. They had all been waiting impatiently for him to act. "Where exactly in the building?"

"Probably still in the lobby," replied Levi.

Knox turned toward the lobby, intent on tracking Crow down, but Levi grabbed his arm.

"You can't go out there, Knox. He'll conjure a weapon and start shooting at you—people could get caught in the crossfire. That's if he doesn't just conjure balls of hellfire and hurl them at you. I don't have to tell you that would be bad on a number of levels."

Grinding his teeth, Knox nodded. He wanted Crow badly, but exposing the existence of their kind to humans wasn't on Knox's agenda. Even his demon, eager to get a grip on Crow, understood the importance of discretion.

Knox did a U-turn and prowled to the security office. "When did he get here?"

"No more than a minute ago," said Levi, keeping pace with him. "He got out of a cab and walked right through the front door, bold as you please. The doormen recognized him, but they didn't stop him; they contacted me." Just as Knox had instructed them to do in the event that Crow ever showed up.

Inside the security office, Knox scanned the monitors as he asked the guard, "Where is Crow now?"

Matt, a demon from their lair, pointed at one of the monitors. "The lobby. Looks like he wants to use the private elevator."

Knox moved closer, watching as Crow—hair disheveled, clothes wrinkled, face set into a hard mask, and skin sweaty from the heatwave that had come out of nowhere—repeatedly jabbed the button for the elevator that headed to the penthouse. It was where Knox stayed whenever he spent the night at the hotel. "It's impossible to use that elevator without a keycard."

"Members of the Force are on standby. Want them to apprehend him?" asked Levi.

Knox nodded. "Tell them to take him down and to do it fast. Then they need to drag him out of sight of humans so he can be teleported away." As the sentinel telepathically repeated his orders, Knox frowned as Crow started punching the elevator doors in sheer frustration.

"His eyes aren't pure black," said Matt. "He's not rogue."

"But he's not entirely rational either," Levi pointed out. "Look at him. It's not even occurring to him that his actions could attract attention."

"That's because he's too focused on getting to me," said Knox. Crow had walked right into the hotel like he belonged here, a man on a mission. And that mission was clearly more important to him than being caught.

"Oh shit," muttered Matt as a female member of the human hotel staff tentatively approached Crow. Whatever she said made him whirl on her, every line of his body tense. Then he made a mad dash for the exit.

Knox swore. "She spooked him."

Before Crow could reach the door, a demon barreled into him from either side. They struggled to keep hold of Crow—he was manic and thrashing wildly, shouting obscenities. The humans recoiled from him, huddling against the walls and the reception desk. Then Crow stilled and inhaled deeply, and the demon holding him suddenly wilted.

"He's draining him," said Knox, jaw tight. Feeding on the psi-energy was not only weakening the demon; it was strengthening Crow. The moment the demon's grip loosened, Crow freed himself and pointed a hand at the other demon—a hand that was suddenly holding a revolver. And then he fired. The guard dived aside, dodging the bullet, and the humans all screamed and squatted on the ground. Crow raced out of the hotel.

"Someone needs to stop him *now*." Knox shifted his vision to the camera that monitored the entrance ... just in time to see Crow point the gun at a cab driver, yelling at him to get out the car. Four members of the Force appeared, but they instantly froze as they saw him aiming at a human. The cab driver obeyed, but Crow still shot him in the leg before leaping into the vehicle and disappearing with a screech of tires.

Shit. "Call an ambulance." Knox barely resisted slamming his hand on the desk. Clenching his fists, he took a deep breath. Control. He needed to maintain control. But it wasn't easy when his demon was growling and pressuring him to give into the urge to personally hunt the bastard down.

"Members of the Force are in pursuit of Crow," said Levi. "He made a mistake coming here today. He'll be caught."

Matt shook his head in disbelief as he slumped in his chair. "The Crow I know would *never* shoot an innocent bystander like that."

"He's not the Crow you know anymore." So close. They'd been so fucking close to detaining him.

"If he can shoot a human for no good reason," began Matt, "I don't think there's much hope for Carla Hayden."

Knox wished he could deny that, but she served no purpose for Crow. He had no reason to keep her alive and no issue at all with shooting people without cause. As such, it was entirely possible that Carla was already dead. If not, she probably would be soon enough.

"I was hoping I could speak with Harper."

She *had* to be hearing things. Or maybe the buzzing of the tattoo gun was affecting her hearing, because there was surely no way that bitch was here, at her place of work. But as Harper turned it was to find that, yep, the freaking dolphin was standing at the reception desk. Her demon curled her lip in distaste.

"She's busy right now," Khloë told her.

Alethea smiled pleasantly. "It'll just take a minute."

Turning, Khloë raised a questioning brow at Harper.

With an exasperated sigh, Harper turned to her client—a demon who was also Khloë's twin. "I'll be right back."

"I'm totally fine with having a break," said Ciaran, who was no doubt stiff after leaning forward for so long while she worked on the tattoo on his back. "Besides, this looks like it will be fun to watch."

It might be fun to watch, but it wouldn't be fun to have any part in. Putting down the tattoo gun, Harper removed her plastic gloves, put them in the trash can, and strode over to the reception desk. Raini and Devon moved to flank her, their expressions hard. Harper almost recoiled from the cloying rose perfume wafting from the dolphin.

Alethea gave her a beautiful smile. "Harper, how are you today?"

God, it was just too freaking hot for mind games. Although they had the air conditioning on full blast, there was really no escaping the heat. It made the air feel heavy and dry as a bone.

Alethea was also showing the effects of the heatwave—sweat beaded on her face, spoiling her make-up, and her sleek hair had a slight frizz to it. Harper was petty enough to find that amusing. Bluntly, she asked, "Why are you here?"

Alethea gave an innocent shrug. "I thought we could have lunch."

"I've already eaten." Actually, she hadn't, but she'd sooner starve than go anywhere with this particular she-demon.

"How about coffee, then?"

Harper narrowed her eyes. "Why?"

"I was just hoping we could have a little chat."

"I don't chat."

Alethea's smile faded. "This is important."

Harper folded her arms. "Then I guess you'll just have to spill it right here." There were no humans around, so neither of them would have to mind their words.

"Fine." Alethea lifted her chin. "I came here to ask you to be careful with Knox."

Okay, Harper didn't have a clue what that meant. "I'm sorry, what?"

"He's so tough that people don't realize it's possible to hurt him. They're not careful with his feelings. I just don't want you to make the same mistake I did."

"You're insinuating that you hurt Knox?"

"I didn't do it deliberately. I didn't think he cared about me. I didn't think he'd care what I did or didn't do, so I didn't think of it as cheating on him. That was when we broke up. We still got together from time to time, but ... I guess he just couldn't forgive me enough to give me a real second chance. I'd like to see him happy. It seems like you're capable of making him happy. So I wanted to give you some advice. I don't want to see him hurt again."

"So what you're saying is ... he was serious about you; he cared for you; and despite being hurt by you, he still wanted you so badly that he's fucked you on many occasions since your betrayal—he just couldn't help himself." Harper turned to Khloë, who was fanning her flushed face. "I wasn't aware before now that I looked gullible."

"I don't think you do," said the imp.

"And yet, she clearly thinks I'll believe that mound of bullshit." Her demon would be pissed if the whole thing wasn't so pitiful.

Alethea spluttered. "Excuse me?"

Raini snorted. "Oh come on, you didn't honestly think Harper would believe that, did you?"

"Were you hoping to make her feel jealous and insecure, or are you trying to cause some kind of divide between her and Knox?" asked Devon, sounding tired. The poor hellcat was so lethargic from the heat, she made Harper think of a wilting plant.

"What I said was the truth," Alethea stated. "His demon gets bored of females easily, but it never got bored of me. Knox came back to me time and time again. A lot of people thought he and I would one day finally get together for good."

"Let me ask you something." Harper leaned forward, elbows on the desk, and brought out the big guns. "Did his demon ever brand you?" Her tone said that it had sure branded her.

Alethea's eyes flared and every line of her body tensed.

"Did Knox want you as his mate?" Harper held up a hand when the she-demon went to answer. "There's really no sense in lying about either of those things. I already know the answers. And those answers tell me all I need to know about what Knox did or didn't feel for you. They should also tell *you* all you need to know."

Her beautiful face scrunched up into something bitter and hateful. "You think you can keep him?" she sneered. "You think this mating is real?"

"You do or you wouldn't be here trying to stir shit. You know it's real and you hate it."

"It's the way he looks at her, isn't it?" Devon said to Alethea. "His face softens and his eyes smile . . . like he's spent the whole day waiting to see her and his entire system relaxes as soon as he spots her. There's no way to deny how he feels about her, so it's sort of silly that you'd try, but whatever."

Alethea gave Harper a withering look. "The Knox I know

would never concern himself with a Wallis, let alone have one in his bed."

"Then clearly you don't know him at all," said Harper. Knox had an alliance with Jolene well before he and Harper met.

"You're not even his type," spat Alethea. "For that matter, he's not your type either. You prefer humans. In fact, Knox is the first demon you ever slept with. Before him, you were with the guy whose family owns the café over there."

Harper raised her brows. The dolphin had been doing her homework.

Devon looked at Harper. "I've always said that a crazy ex can do better research than law enforcement."

Alethea's eyes widened. "Crazy ex?"

Khloë patted the bitch's shoulder. "Don't beat yourself up about being a nut job. Facebook's made stalkers out of us all."

Upper lip curling, Alethea backed away. "You and Knox won't last."

"Maybe you're right," said Harper. "Maybe he'll decide he's better off alone. Maybe he'll then have you back in his bed. Maybe he'll even do something as surreal as take *you* as his mate. But I'll still be the first person his demon ever branded. I'll still be the first female he wanted to take as a mate. And I'll still be in his life because I'm his anchor. As he once said, he won't walk away from what's his. He'll always be in my life, and I'll always be in his. So no matter what you do, you can't get rid of me."

The front door swung open, and a wave of baking heat proceeded Tanner as he stalked inside. "Everything all right in here?"

Harper didn't move her eyes from Alethea. "Everything's fine, Tanner. The dolphin here just wanted to exercise her bitchy muscle. She's done now."

"Then it's high time she left," Tanner clipped, prowling to the desk.

Shooting glares at both him and Harper, Alethea spun on her heel and marched out of the studio. No one said a word until the bitch's car disappeared with a screech of tires.

"All day I stay out there and nothing happens," said Tanner. "The moment I leave to get a drink or something, a problem arises. What was that about?"

It was Ciaran who responded, moving to stand behind Khloë. "That was what Grams would call 'sizing up your enemy.'"

Harper nodded. "She wasn't so much trying to make me jealous as getting a feel for how easy I'd be to manipulate."

"What exactly did she say?" asked Tanner, so Harper told him. And he laughed. "I don't have to tell you she was talking out of her ass, do I?"

"Nope," replied Harper, "I worked out that much for myself."

"Good." He tugged on one of Devon's long ringlets, and she hissed. "Settle down, kitten," he chuckled. With a wave, he returned to the car.

Devon's hands curled. "Sometimes I just want to claw out his eyes."

"His eyes," began Khloë, "or the flesh of his back while your legs are wrapped around him and—"

"Don't make me hurt you," Devon snarled.

Innocence personified, Khloë said, "I was just asking. He is seriously hot. And he buys you gifts all the time."

Devon's mouth fell open. "You call balls of yarn, toy mice, a plush fishbone, and a catnip plant *gifts*?"

Khloë shrugged. "It's the thought that counts. And don't forget that pretty collar he got you with the little bell that—hey, there's no call for hissing."

Devon turned to Ciaran, waving a hand in Khloë's direction. "Deal with her. I can't."

Harper felt kind of sorry for her friend. There was definitely some sexual tension between Devon and Tanner, but nothing good could ever come of them acting on it. The fact was that hellcats and hellhounds had an instinctive aversion to each other. That meant that even if Devon and Tanner ignored it, their inner demons wouldn't.

A mind slid against hers. *Harper, meet me behind the studio.*

You really don't need to come here, she told Knox, guessing Tanner had informed him of what happened. *Honestly, the dolphin is long gone and I'm not upset or jealous or anything.*

She's no one to me.

I know. Really, her petty behavior didn't achieve anything. Apart from increase Harper's temptation to slice her from groin to sternum, that was.

You're sure you're fine?

Positive.

All right, baby. His mind once again slid against hers; this time softly and slowly. Then he was gone.

"I take it you and Knox were having a little chat," said Khloë. "You get this dazed, 'Harper is unavailable right now' expression on your face."

"Tanner told him what just happened," said Harper. "He was making sure I was okay."

Leaning her hip on the desk, Raini smiled. "I like that he takes care of you. You know what I like even better? That you let him."

"On another note, who keeps moving my stapler?" groused Khloë, as if it was a capital offense.

Harper looked at her cousin. "Sometimes I have to wonder if you have OCD."

"I do not have OCD. I just value order and precision."

Really? "When was the first time someone described you as OCD?"

"Eight years, six months, four days, and ninety minutes ago."

"Yeah," said Harper dryly. "Totally not OCD."

As they drove toward the tattoo studio later that day, Levi met Knox's eyes in the rearview mirror. "Tanner told me about Alethea. What was she thinking?"

"I believe Harper's theory is that Alethea was trying to get a sense of just how simple it would be to manipulate her," replied Knox. "One day, I am going to briefly run by a female from my past and she is *not* going to attempt to cause problems for my mate."

Levi snorted. "I wouldn't count on that. They see your claim on Harper as a personal insult to them."

"Personal insult?"

"Before Harper, your demon was lonely and could fixate on a female, but it quickly got bored with every one of them because it was the *challenge* the demon really liked. Even though you warned the females in advance that it would happen and the fling would be short-lived, they were still extremely pissed when you walked away so soon. But as long as you continued living your life that way, never committing to anyone, it was something they could accept—though it was often done begrudgingly and with a little drama thrown in."

A "little drama" was somewhat of an understatement.

"Now you've claimed a female as your mate, and they're wondering what she has that they don't. Harper isn't from a high-class family, she doesn't have a well-paid job, she wasn't born into a large or powerful lair, and—to top it all off—she's a Wallis. That you've chosen a female they believe is beneath them is something they feel insulted by and can't quite wrap their heads around."

"Harper isn't beneath them." It infuriated Knox that anyone could think differently.

"Not to us, no," said Levi. "Honestly, I don't think other breeds of demon truly look down on imps. I think they're wary of them. Imps are scary in their own way. They're cunning and daring and they can't be controlled. Nobody ever knows how an imp will retaliate; they just know that they will and that it won't be subtle. They're wild cards. Jolene is the ultimate wild card. That woman drives even the Devil himself insane."

According to Harper, Jolene had once fed Lucifer some drugged cookies; he'd later stripped down to his boxers and did a rendition of "Baby Got Back".

"The point I'm making is that they see Harper as beneath them, but they're also intimidated by her," said Levi. "That elusive, aloof 'I'm not interested and have better things to do with my time than talk to you' air . . . it's like she brushes people off before they've even spoken to her—which I find hilarious."

So did Knox and his demon.

"It's hard to approach someone like that. It's hard to offend someone who simply doesn't care what you think. And it's hard to manipulate a person who you can't understand. She's not driven by power, greed, addictions, or the need for an adrenalin rush. They don't get it, and they don't like that they don't get it. Nor do they like that she doesn't care that they exist. They want her to be darkly jealous that they 'had' you before she did. It will make them feel better."

"Even if Harper did feel any jealousy, she'd never let them see it."

"Which infuriates them." Levi paused as he shifted gears. "It's a good thing that you rarely got involved with females from our lair. It means she doesn't have to deal with bullshit from her own people. The few you were involved with are now mated and happily settled." And once a demon fully committed themselves to someone, they had no interest in others.

Glancing out of the window, Knox saw that they were almost at the studio. Just like that, his demon's agitation began to ease away. It had been in a bad mood all day, pissed that Crow had managed to evade the Force. Oh, the members of his Force had tracked down the cab quick enough, only to realize they had been following the wrong vehicle. There were just so many cabs around that Crow had found it simple enough to blend in and disappear.

The demon had wanted Harper; wanted to reach out to her telepathically and hear her voice. That alone would have helped both Knox and his demon calm, but Knox had resisted the urge. He hadn't wanted to spoil her day with talk of Crow; he'd decided he would tell her face-to-face later on. Then he'd heard from Tanner that fucking Alethea had confronted Harper and the news had only served to enrage him further. He'd briefly reached out to her, wanting to be sure she was fine. That small conversation had cooled his demon's anger a little, but not enough.

As Levi came to a stop outside the studio, he asked, "What are you going to do about Alethea?"

"That depends on Harper," said Knox. "She's been adamant since the beginning that it's important for her to fight her own battles. I don't like it. But I also know that Alethea is the type of person who finds bad attention better than no attention."

"So if you call Alethea and threaten her, a part of her will get a kick out of it."

"Exactly." And Knox had no urge to please that she-demon in any way. *Tanner, you can leave now. Harper's coming with me.*

Sliding out of the Bentley, Knox frowned under the weight of the dry heat. As the hellhound drove away, he pushed open the door of the studio and stepped into the air-conditioned building. He was instantly surrounded by the scents of paint, ink, coffee, and disinfectant. The receipt machine whirred as it printed a receipt for the human female standing at the desk, probing a bandage that was taped on her upper arm. Khloë gave Knox a brief salute, to which he nodded before turning his attention to his mate.

As if sensing him on some level, Harper paused over the tattoo she was working on and looked up. She smiled. "Hey, what brings you here?"

Crossing the space, he kissed her, and the stress of the day fell away. "I've come to take you to dinner."

Her smile widened. "Really?"

"Yes. How long will you be?"

"I'm almost done here. Then I just have to clean up. Wait in the car with Levi if you want."

Instead, Knox folded his arms and leaned his hip against the wall. "I'll wait here." He liked watching her work. And it would be best to make it blindingly clear to the human in her chair that she was taken, since the guy was looking at her with gooey eyes.

"All right." Harper turned back to the snake tattoo on the human's shoulder. Knox watched her, admiring her steady hand, fascinated by the sheer focus on her face. At those moments, her attention was centered solely on her work, and any red-blooded male would wonder what it would be like to be the focus of attention like that. Knox could tell them. It was heady. Arousing. Enlivening.

Finally, she was done and advised the human on aftercare as she attached a bandage to his shoulder. He nodded along, wearing an awe-filled expression that said he'd jump into the fires of hell if she told him to. Well, if the little shit continued to stare at her, he might find himself facing that problem.

When the guy headed to the reception desk, Harper said, "Now I just have to clean up."

"Do whatever it is you need to do. I'll wait." As she tidied the station and cleaned her equipment, Knox studied the various sketches and photos of tattoos that she'd tacked on the wall near her framed license. Pride swelled inside him. One glance at her work was enough to show that Harper had raw talent—there was no denying it. She had a true flair for design and a talent for putting a contemporary or inventive twist on the most original tattoos.

At last, she was slipping on her jacket. "Ready to go?"

Nodding, he shackled her wrist with his hand. "Come on."

Saying goodbye to the girls, Harper let him lead her outside. Her shoulders slumped under the baking heat as she crossed to where Levi was waiting; holding open the rear door. At his short nod, she smiled and said, "Hi, Levi." Sinking into the buttery smooth leather seat and escaping the merciless sun, she let out a happy sigh. She was tired and stiff, which was made worse by the fact that her muscles were still sore from her last flying lesson.

Knox sat close, combing his fingers through her hair. "How was your day?" he asked her as Levi pulled out onto the road.

"Good," she said. "Yours?"

"Busy." He kissed her. "Boring." Another kiss. "Better now." Also extremely frustrating, but he'd wait a little longer before he broke the bad news to her. He wanted them to enjoy some time together first.

"So, does taking me to dinner have anything to do with you wanting to make sure I was okay after the dolphin paid me a visit?"

"Must we refer to her as 'the dolphin'?" he asked; it made him feel like he'd partaken in bestiality or something.

"We? No. Me? Yes."

Sighing inwardly, he stroked her pulse with his thumb. "I'm angry at Alethea. I very nearly called her. But then I considered that I would be rewarding her behavior with attention. That could encourage her to do it again."

"Just ignore her. That will annoy her more than anything else could."

"There was never anything serious between me and Alethea. The picture she painted was very much false."

"I know that," Harper assured him.

"Good." He circled her pulse again, liking the way it spiked. "If your business was located in the Underground, you would have better security. Not only would that make it more difficult for people to bother you, it would mean I wouldn't have to rely solely on Tanner to inform me of any problems."

"Is that a fact?"

"I'm just pointing it out."

"Hm."

Resting his hand possessively on her thigh, he asked, "What are your co-workers' feelings on relocating the business?"

"They're *open* to the idea. At this point, it's just me who's unsure."

He rubbed her thigh. "What's holding you back?"

"You'll think it's weird."

"I often find your responses weird." It was something that didn't bother him, though. "Tell me. I want to understand."

"I lived in a shitty flat, and then I moved into a mansion. I used to get the subway to work, and now I get a ride there in a Bentley—by a chauffeur/bodyguard, no less. My wardrobe used to be small and filled with vintage stuff from thrift shops. Now

I have a walk-in closet that's bigger than my old room and is full of designer clothes that I pretend are from thrift shops. I have a housekeeper. And a butler. I co-run a lair. I'm adjusting as best I can to all this, but I worry I'll become ... "

"A snob?" he supplied.

"I worry I'll change and become someone who takes stuff for granted. My business has always grounded me."

"But now I ground you, just like you ground me," he said, watching as her face softened. "I understand the business is your baby and you're protective of it. But I'm not asking you to close it down. I'm just asking you to relocate it. In the Underground, it would be safer, it would have less costs, and it would gain more profits. Let me show you the little building I think would be ideal for you. Check out the location and see what you think of it. There's no harm in that."

She let out a long, put-out groan. "Okay."

"Good girl." He didn't bother to hide his satisfaction. "We'll take a look at it tomorrow."

"Fine." She crossed one leg over the other. "So, where are we going?"

"I told you, we're going for dinner."

CHAPTER EIGHT

———◦◦◦———

Harper wasn't exactly surprised when Levi stopped the car outside one of the classiest hotels on the Las Vegas strip—a hotel Knox owned, but not one she'd been to before.

Knox often took her to fancy places, not caring that she was only in jeans and a T-shirt and would stick out like a sore thumb. Harper didn't like to stand out, but the reality was that she'd stand out for the simple reason that she was with Knox Thorne—it wouldn't matter how she was dressed. So she figured she might as well be wearing comfortable clothes than an elegant get-up she didn't feel *right* in.

He kept his hand possessively locked around her wrist as they entered the grand, luxurious hotel and the cool air-conditioned air hit her face. A few of the staff rushed to him; he answered their questions without breaking stride. It was a usual thing, whichever of his hotels they went to. He led her past the elevator doors and toward the casino.

As the automatic doors swished open, the smells of tobacco,

perfume, cologne, and air deodorizer surrounded her. They walked along the soft, patterned carpet; passing roulette wheels, card tables, and people who were swearing or cursing at backlit gambling machines. Alarms dinged and players cheered, overriding the music filtering in from another room.

The security guards patrolling the floor nodded at Knox as he led her to the exit, through a boutique store, and over to a restaurant. He swung open the glass door and said, "After you, baby."

With a thankful smile, she stepped inside. Silverware clinked, ice tinkled in glasses, and diners murmured and laughed softly. The people queuing near the hostess station probably would have snarled at her for skipping the line if she wasn't with Knox, a guy moving with utter purpose like he had every right to be where he was; muscles flexing and bunching beneath his designer suit.

The hostess practically tripped over herself trying to get to him. "Mr. Thorne," she purred. "Such a pleasant surprise. I'm Trisha." The human's eyes cut to Harper and flickered with perplexity, and she knew what the hostess was thinking: what was such a gorgeous, successful, lethally sensual male doing with a small, average-looking, casually dressed nobody?

Harper had often asked herself the same thing until she'd come to know him and realized that, though he may have enjoyed the company of beautiful women, he wasn't at all shallow.

The hostess's attention returned to Knox. "I'm assuming you'd like to be shown to your usual private room?" He merely inclined his head. Grabbing two menus, Trisha said, "Please follow me."

The restaurant was just as elegant and tasteful as the hotel itself. Low-hanging lights. High-top tables. Soft music. Paintings lining the walls. And as always Harper felt out of place. It didn't matter that she lived in a home even more opulent than this. It was still hard to be among these people and walk in their world. That was what it often felt like—another world.

The elegant feel of the restaurant continued into the private room. Trisha stood aside while Knox and Harper settled at the tastefully arranged table that could easily seat four people. A middle-aged male entered and bowed slightly to Knox and Harper, quite obviously a demon.

Trisha seemed surprised by the courtly gesture but simply said to Knox, "Charles will be your waiter for the evening. If there are any problems, don't hesitate to ask for me." Handing the menus to Knox and Harper, Trisha then added, "Enjoy your meal."

Pen and pad in hand, Charles came forward. "Would you like to order a drink while you take time to read the menu?"

Knox looked at Harper. "Do you trust me?"

Without lifting her eyes from the menu, she replied, "In other words, will I let you pick the wine since I know nothing about it? Yes."

"Good."

Charles scribbled down the order Knox gave and left the room.

Knox then took out his cell phone and switched it off, wanting them to have uninterrupted time alone. "How's your back?"

"A little stiff," she replied. "Not as bad as it was this morning."

"The more natural flying comes to you, the less it will be a strain on your muscles."

"Can we have another lesson soon?"

"Sure. You impressed me with how hard you tried. I suppose I should have known how persistent you would be." She was a sphinx, after all. They had the fierceness of a lion. "Ready to order yet?"

She snapped the menu shut. "Yep."

"You want to skip starters and go straight for a steak," he guessed.

"You know me so well."

Moments later, Charles reappeared with the wine. Knox and Harper then placed their orders, and the waiter left. As Knox watched her fidget with the salt and pepper shakers, he said, "Something is bothering you. What is it?"

"I'm just tired."

"Don't lie to me."

"Kellen won't answer my calls." She slumped in her chair. "I didn't think he'd use me as a scapegoat the way Roan has."

"I don't think he's using you as a scapegoat. Nor do I think he blames himself for not helping Carla. He most likely feels guilty."

"For what?" she asked, smoothing her hands over the incredibly soft table cloth.

Knox picked up his glass and swished the wine. "He expressed to you on several occasions that he doesn't particularly like Carla. Now she's gone and she's quite possibly hurt; he could be feeling guilty for all the things he said about her."

"I never thought of that."

"He's young. Give him time. He'll call you back when he's ready."

She sipped at her drink. "Any news on Crow?"

Knox hesitated, wanting more quality time with her. Of course, the hesitation made her eyes narrow. "We almost had him earlier."

Harper leaned forward. "What happened?"

"He came to one of my other hotels. At the time, I was in a business meeting in one of the conference rooms. He tried to use the private elevator that headed to the penthouse, where I stay whenever I'm there overnight, but it's impossible to use that elevator without a keycard. One of the human hotel staff saw him punch the elevator door and approached him. He got spooked and ran. The guards tried to apprehend him, but he stole a wave of energy from them—which weakened them and strengthened him. Free, he conjured a gun, shot at one of the guards, and then ran outside where he shot a human and used his cab to make a quick getaway."

Fuck. "You're telling me he turned up at your hotel with the intention of killing you, went trigger-happy on the people around him ... and you're only sharing this with me *now*?" Unreal. "Why didn't you tell me straight away?"

Knox reached for her hand and tangled their fingers. "He didn't get anywhere near me. I waited to tell you because I'd hoped to quickly have him in custody; then I could have given you good news and bad news at the same time. Instead, I can only deliver you bad news."

Like Harper would believe that was all it was. "Keeping things from me doesn't protect me, you know."

He sighed. "If I had told you earlier, you'd have spent time needlessly stressing over it. I didn't want to ruin your day. I didn't want *Crow* to ruin your day."

"Which is sweet and all, but I would rather have known about it. Imagine if you were only now finding out what Alethea did earlier. Wouldn't that bother you?"

"It would bother me," he admitted.

"If Crow comes at you again, I don't want to find out *later*. I want you to tell me immediately. Can you do that?" At his nod, she settled a little. Not that it would surprise her much if he did delay telling her any future incidents. Knox Thorne did what Knox Thorne wanted to do. It was really as simple as that. She supposed she should just be grateful that Crow hadn't managed to reach him. Her chest tightened at the thought of what could have happened to him.

"And there you are stressing over what could have happened," said Knox. "This is why I didn't tell you earlier."

"I still would have preferred to know." She took a long swig of her wine. "The longer he has Carla, the less likely it is that he'll let her live."

He squeezed her hand. "I know, baby. We're doing everything we can to track him. We will find him."

At that moment, Charles entered with a steaming tray of food. The smells of spices, sauce, peppers, and meat made Harper's stomach rumble. As the waiter placed their plates in front of them, steam rushed up from the hot food. "I didn't realize how hungry I was until now."

Knox dismissed Charles, smiling to see that his mate had wasted no time digging into her meal. As he ate, he continued to watch her, enjoying her orgasmic expressions. "You haven't eaten much today, have you?"

"It was a busy day."

"I don't like it when you skip meals."

"I don't like it when I skip meals either. But sometimes the studio gets really busy, so I just quickly munch something small between tattoos."

That wasn't good enough for Knox. "You need to take better care of yourself or I'll send Tanner in each lunch hour to hand-feed you."

She froze with her fork halfway to her mouth. "You wouldn't."

"Wouldn't I?"

Probably. Harper just harrumphed and went back to her food. They talked about trivial things as they finished their meal: difficult tattoo clients, pompous businessmen, and funny little things that had happened through the day. He also relayed some lair issues, bouncing ideas off her, which she liked.

A little later, after Charles had brought their desserts, Knox told him, *No interruptions*. Charles left with a bow, closing the door firmly behind him. Knox then slid back his chair a little. "Come here, baby."

Harper blinked. He was using his deep, dominant, authoritative tone—she called it his "sex voice." "What?"

"Come here."

Curious about where this was going, she put her spoon back in her ice cream and moved to stand between his spread thighs. "What—" Her knees wobbled as a cold, psychic finger glided between her folds. "Shit."

"Watching you eat never fails to make me hard," he rumbled. "Eyes on mine, baby."

She kept her gaze locked with his as the icy finger stroked her and circled her clit again and again, building that all too familiar burning ache. She gasped as the finger suddenly drove inside her and swirled, making her pussy throb painfully.

Knox unbuttoned her fly and pushed down her jeans and panties. "Off," he ordered, tapping her thigh.

She kicked them aside, all the while feeling in a sensual daze as that psychic finger continued to stoke the fire.

"Now the rest, baby."

She whipped off her T-shirt and bra, so hot inside she was burning. The psychic finger dissipated, and then he lifted her and dropped her hard on his cock. She gasped into his mouth in shock and bliss as he stretched and filled her. She'd been so caught up in what that finger was doing, she hadn't even noticed he'd pulled out his cock. The psychic finger had left her so hypersensitive that it was almost painful to take him.

"That's better." Pulling her dessert closer, Knox scooped a little onto the spoon. "Open." He fed her the chocolate-sprinkled ice cream, loving to watch her cheeks hollow and her throat work. Then he kissed her, licking into her mouth, tasting cold vanilla. "You taste better." He slowly raised her, groaning as her hot, wet pussy squeezed him almost tight enough to hurt. Then he pulled her back down.

"We should stop," she rasped.

He lifted her again, until only the head of his cock was inside her. Then he roughly impaled her on him. "We should?"

"The waiter could come in."

No, he wouldn't, because Knox had telepathically ordered him not to interrupt them. But Knox couldn't resist teasing her. "You're right; he could." He gave her branded breast a possessive squeeze before pinching the nipple hard. "Then he'd see you sitting here, my cock buried deep in you."

"That's my point," said Harper. Her concern was ignored, however. He spooned more ice cream, but he didn't feed it to her; he put the spoon in his own mouth. Then he was kissing her, using his tongue to feed her the scoop of vanilla before once again impaling onto his cock.

Over and over he alternated between feeding and impaling her, driving her freaking insane. His hands were confident and sure as they touched her—squeezing her breasts, raking into her hair, cupping her ass. All the while, his mouth devoured her lips and neck.

"I want to lick and taste and mark every inch of you," he growled, eyes gleaming with pure masculine possession. Slamming her on his cock again, he bit her lip. "Mine."

Needing to come so bad she could cry, Harper tried to take over.

"No." His fingers dug hard into her hip to keep her still. "When I want you to fuck me, I'll tell you."

Bastard. She shook her head when he spooned yet more vanilla. "I'm done."

"This isn't for you. It's for me." He ate the ice cream. And then closed his cold mouth around her nipple and sucked hard. Her pussy contracted around his cock, and he groaned.

She tried pushing his head away. "That's cruel."

He licked his way from her nipple to the pulse beating in her throat. He gave it a sharp nip. "You're easily the most important thing to me. Do you know that?"

Harper closed her eyes. She wasn't good with hearing stuff like that.

Knox flexed his cock and sharply repeated, "Do you know that?"

Opening her eyes, she swallowed at the savage possessiveness stamped all over his face. "Yes." As if to reward her, he impaled her on him.

"You'll never be free of me." He slowly slid her up his cock, loving the way her pussy tried to hungrily suck him back in. "You'll always belong to me. And this pussy . . . " He yanked her back down, burying himself in her once again. "This pussy is all mine and it'll only ever be mine. Isn't that so?"

Frustrated at being so close yet so far to the edge, she snarled. "Yes. And that makes this cock mine. But if it doesn't do its job and make me come, I'm gonna snap it off."

Knox had to smile. There was his hissing, spitting kitten. "You're right, it's yours." He snaked his hands up her thighs. "But if you want to come, you'll have to work for it." He bucked his hips, giving her a short, shallow thrust. "Fuck me, Harper." She rode him hard, nails digging into his shoulders. "Your mouth . . . give it to me."

"Kind of busy here," she quipped.

Knox gave her ass a sharp slap; her pussy rippled around his cock, soaking him in cream. "Your mouth."

She kissed him, and Knox swallowed every moan as she frantically slammed herself down on him over and over. She was so fucking hot and slick, it drove him out of his mind. He fisted a hand in her hair. "Do you have any idea how hot it is watching you ride me like this? You know what I think? I think one touch to your clit will set you off like a rocket."

He wasn't wrong. So when his hand slipped between them, her whole system practically sighed in relief.

"But that won't be happening just yet," he said, his thumb hovering close to her clit.

Harper froze. "You motherfucking son of a bitch!" A chill washed over her as his eyes bled to black and the demon stared back at her. Crap. "Um . . ."

Its hand snapped around her throat. "Not nice, little sphinx."

Her eyes widened as the flesh beneath its grip began to heat and prickle. She knew what that meant. "Not my throat."

"I'll brand you anywhere I want," it growled.

Its free hand grabbed her hip and began yanking her down each time it thrust up. The demon was rougher than Knox. More demanding. The skin of her throat felt like it was on fire, yet the sensation sent pure pleasure rippling through her. "Fuck, I'm coming."

Knox lunged to the surface with a groan and licked along the fresh brand on her neck, knowing how sensitive it would be. "That's it, come." He thumbed her clit, and her head fell back as her mouth opened in a silent scream. Her pussy squeezed and contracted around him, milking him as he exploded inside her with a growl.

She collapsed against him, tremoring with little aftershocks. "How bold is it?" she slurred. His demon never did anything by halves.

Knowing she was referring to the brand, Knox lifted her face by her chin and examined it. "I think you'll like it." She didn't seem convinced.

"Snap a picture of it with your phone." He did, and Harper was surprised to see that it wasn't as conspicuous as the others. It was a black, thin choker that looked much like a branch of thorns.

"You like it."

"Well yeah, but . . . it would be really nice if it wasn't wrapped around my throat. Seriously, your demon might as well have just put 'All Rights Reserved' on my neck. It's not funny."

"I'm not laughing."

"Not out loud."

"I think, compared to the others, it's understated. Much like the tattoos Raini did for you." He cocked his head. "Why do you keep all your tattoos hidden?"

"People tend to ask what tattoos mean."

And his sphinx was an extremely private person who gave very few people peeks of her soul. "Will you tell me what yours mean?"

"I got 'So it Goes' from *Slaughterhouse Five* to remind myself not to dwell on anything I can't control—bad shit happens; it's part of life. I got the little raven on my hipbone because I can relate to ravens; they're tricksters, they think and strategize."

Like her family, Knox thought. "What about the dragonfly on the nape of your neck?"

"They have a short lifespan and they're very delicate, but neither of those things hold them back. I admire that. They're master fliers, which I also fully admire." And something she'd also envied until her own wings came to her. "What am I supposed to say when people ask why I have a thorny choker tattooed around my throat?"

"Only humans would need to ask. Demons will already know what it means." They would see the thorns and know immediately that it was his brand of possession.

"And you totally like that idea, don't you?" She gasped as he flexed his cock. "How are you still hard?"

"How can I be buried deep inside my mate and not be hard?"

Well, when he put it like that . . .

CHAPTER NINE

—————

The next day, Harper found herself in the Underground, standing outside a plain and clearly vacant building. "I can see why you chose this spot for the studio," she said to Knox. "As locations go, I will admit it's perfect." It was close to the mall and the best restaurants, and it even had a cute little coffeehouse next door. It also had top-notch security and, due to being a hotspot within the Underground, would get a lot of foot traffic.

"As a bonus, it's reasonably close to my main office," said Knox. He unlocked the door, but he didn't usher her inside. It had to be her choice. He'd pushed her far enough on the subject, and he knew his mate well enough to know that if he pushed any further she could object to moving here just to be contrary.

Promising herself that she would keep an open mind and try to imagine truly working there, Harper opened the glass door and stepped inside. The walls were a bright white, much like the walls in her studio. That was good. She'd need to get rid of the beige carpet if she took the place, though. A hardwood floor would be better.

"Take a look around," said Knox. "I'll wait here with Levi and Tanner."

Nodding, Harper took a turn around the reception area. It was bigger than her current one, and she was sure that Khloë would love that she could fit a large desk in here. Behind the reception area were a row of two office cubicles on either side of the space.

She walked behind the cubicles and over to the door on her left, which turned out to be an empty, nondescript room. It would be perfect space for Devon to do piercings, she thought.

Exiting the room, she went to the one adjacent to it that had a small metallic "Office" sign. Even with a large desk and filing cabinet, it was pretty spacious, unlike her current office.

There was one final door, which was against the back wall. Opening it, she found a very large space that contained a small kitchen and led to two other rooms; one door was labelled "restrooms" and the other had no label. Taking a quick peek at the latter space, she thought it would make a good stockroom.

"So many things would be simpler for you if you relocated here," said Knox.

Spinning, she found he'd followed her into the room. "Like what?"

He crossed to her. "Small things, like you wouldn't have to wear contact lenses. Big things, like you're close to all the places you often go and you wouldn't be restricted to daytime hours. But I'd ask that you leave at least most of your evenings free. I like spending them with you."

"Would you want Tanner sitting outside?" She didn't like that the hellhound had to do it, even though he claimed not to mind. He was a sentinel. He was made for better things.

"Only until Crow has been captured. After that, it wouldn't be necessary for Tanner to hang around. The reason I worry so much about you working among humans is that you and your friends have to be careful not to use your gifts against anyone who does you harm. Here, that wouldn't be an issue."

Valid point, and a good answer.

"There is much better security here." Knox combed his fingers through her hair. "And did you notice there's a coffeehouse next door?"

"I did." The smells of coffee and fresh donuts coming from the place were heavenly.

"We also have a penthouse suite in the hotel across the strip. That means if you ever feel like taking a long break or changing clothes before you go to a bar after work, you wouldn't have to go all the way back to the mansion."

And that really would be super convenient. "I'll admit, it's a great spot. Ideal for anyone. Which has me thinking that it couldn't *possibly* have been sitting here empty."

"It's been empty since I learned that you're my anchor."

"You were planning to relocate my business here even then, weren't you?" She shouldn't be at all surprised.

"I was hoping I'd be able to convince you to do so, yes." He curled his hand around her chin. "Your safety is vital to me. More important than anything else."

"What was this place originally?"

"One of my security offices. It was easily relocated without inconveniencing anyone."

Which meant no one had been put out of business; that was good. "I'm surprised you didn't immediately raise the issue when I accepted the anchor bond."

Knox rested his hands on her shoulders. "I'm not an easy anchor or an easy mate. I know that. I've pushed you on a lot of issues, including moving in with me. I don't want to overwhelm you, but it's hard to hold back. Moving at someone else's speed isn't in my nature."

Yeah, she'd long ago worked that out. "Thank you for giving me time." Grabbing the lapels of his jacket, Harper kissed him. "In terms of competition, how many tattoo studios are there in the Underground?"

"Two. One calls itself a parlor, not a studio. It takes itself very seriously. It's expensive, but people will pay the prices because the other place is run by a group of surfers that come and go all the time; sometimes it's closed for days on end." He paused to watch as her eyes swirled and became an entrancing ice-blue. "Both lost a lot of business to you after we bonded and demons became more aware of your studio."

"Neither place will like it if we move here."

"Probably not. But it won't be anything personal. That's the nature of business." He nipped her lip. "Of course, if they try to fuck with you in any way, they'll pay for it."

She smiled. "Sometimes, I get all tingly when you do that protective growl."

His demon chuckled. "Is that so?" Knox licked over the imprint of his teeth on her lower lip and then looked around. "Well?"

"I need to let the girls see it before I make a decision."

"I know that. But what do *you* think?"

A smile broke free. "I really, really like it."

Relieved, Knox kissed her, tracing the brand on her throat with his thumb. Now he just had to get her friends on board, which he didn't think would be too hard.

"You like that brand, don't you?"

"I do." He cupped her possessively over her jeans, sweeping his thumb where the brand on her navel was. "This will always be my favorite, though." It was also his demon's favorite. Knox kissed her once more and then released her. "Call your friends. Tell them to come." He was too impatient to have all this sorted.

Harper whipped out her phone and did just that. The girls must have been more eager to take a look at the place than she'd thought, because they arrived in record time. She waited in the reception area with Knox as the three of them took a turn about the building.

As predicted, Khloë loved the reception area—mostly because it would easily fit the desk she'd originally wanted. Oddly enough, Devon called dibs on the room that Harper had thought would be perfect her. Great minds thought alike. Raini, however . . . she didn't say a single word as she looked around. Nothing in her expression gave Harper a clue as to what the succubus was thinking.

"I think this place is awesome," said Khloë.

"Me, too," said Devon. "It's bigger, it has better security, the location is perfect, and it means the pooch won't have to sit outside like a stalker."

Tanner grinned. "Aw, kitten, we both know you adore me."

Devon's upper lip curled. "Don't you have a bone to go chew on?"

"You know that tone makes me want to bite you."

Harper raised a hand to shush them. "Raini, I can't take your silence anymore. What do you think?"

She slowly pivoted on her heel to face them and blew out a breath. And then her face broke into a bright smile that should have knocked them all on their asses. "When can we move in?"

"Whenever you want—it's yours," said Knox.

"We have to redecorate first," Khloë pointed out, fishing out her phone. "List. We need a list of what needs doing." Raini and Devon dashed over to her.

As the three girls chatted, Harper turned to Knox. "You're feeling really smug right now, aren't you?"

"Relieved," he said.

"Smug," she insisted.

Knox shrugged as he admitted unrepentantly, "I like to get my way." He dropped the keys for the building into her hand. "Now I have to go. Meet me at my office when you're done here." He kissed her. "Be good." With that, he and Levi left.

"You made the right decision, Harper," said Tanner.

She smiled, slipping her hands into her pockets. "Yeah, I think so too."

"Will you close the other place straight away?" he asked.

"Not until we've officially opened this one. A lot of people have booked in advance or need to come back for more sessions to finish their tattoos. I can delay demon clients, since they can simply come here later on, but not human clients." She didn't like to let people down.

Raini nodded. "We'll need to tell humans we're shutting down the business altogether or they'll ask where we're moving."

Tanner folded his arms. "How fast do you think you can get this place ready, bearing in mind that you can't spend a lot of time here while you're still working at the other studio?"

"Around three weeks, if we call on our lair," said Khloë, tapping her fingers on her iPhone.

Devon pointed to the carpet. "We need to get rid of that. In fact, it might be best to strip the place bare."

"In terms of furnishings and equipment, I think we should get all new stuff," announced Khloë.

"Yeah," agreed Raini. "We can afford to, since we won't have the costs here that we have in the other place."

Khloë looked up from her phone. "Okay, so, we list every single item."

"Let me guess," began Tanner, "you'll then hand over that list to your relatives. And they'll probably steal half of it so you're not waiting on delivery companies."

Khloë looked appropriately affronted. "Of course they won't. I can't believe you'd say that."

Tanner just snorted.

"The last grand opening we did was fun," said Devon. "We should make this fun, too."

Raini nodded, smiling. "We could do a street party. Maybe get a band from one of the bars to play outside. People love free food."

"And we could do a ribbon cutting," added Devon.

Harper pursed her lips. "Yeah, that would be fun. We could even get a celebrity to cut it." Everyone stared at her, and she frowned. "What?"

Tanner spoke. "Harper, you *are* a celeb."

She frowned. "No, I'm not."

"To our kind? Yeah you are," insisted Devon.

Harper just waved a dismissive hand.

"Can we please get a vending machine?" asked Khloë. "We didn't have room for one in the last place."

Harper blinked at the surprising request. "I guess."

Khloë brightened. "Score!"

"We're going to make this place look good," declared Devon. "Even better than our first studio."

Once they'd finished their list, they called in her family. The imps set about rolling up the carpet and getting rid of anything Harper didn't wish to keep—all of which her family would no doubt sell. Her uncle, Richie, claimed to have a van she could use to help transport the things they wished to bring from the old studio when she was ready, which was probably the same van he used to transport all the illegal shit her family got their hands on.

It was around 6.30 pm that everyone agreed to call it a day. As Harper and Tanner made their way to Knox's office, the sentinel walked just a little in front of her to protect her from being bumped or jarred by pedestrians. Most of the bars, restaurants, and clubs came alive in the evening, so it was fairly busy. Security shutters were being lifted and street vendors were setting up all over the place.

"Excuse me, have you seen this woman?"

Oh, God, she knew that voice. Up ahead, Roan was walking around with a photo of Carla, showing it to people. There was genuine worry in his expression, and she couldn't help feeling a little bad for him. Jolene was the closest thing she'd ever had to a mother, and Harper knew she'd be a wreck if something happened to—

He spotted Harper. Froze. Then he was shouldering his way through the pedestrians, heading right for her; eyes narrowed, nostrils flaring. *Shit*. Tanner obviously saw him too, because his shoulders stiffened and a low growl built in his throat. Harper grabbed his arm. "Let me deal with this, Tanner."

The hellhound slowed to match her pace and frowned at her. "You don't need to deal with him. That's what I'm here for. I'm your bodyguard."

"And I'm his Prime." She wanted to deal with this herself. Harper didn't hide behind anyone. What's more, she couldn't be *seen* to hide behind anyone. She was now a Prime, and there were plenty of demons around who would witness the little encounter.

As Roan came to a stop, she did the same. Tanner stayed at her side, vibrating with menace. Roan didn't even spare the hellhound a glance, too focused on her. His face twisted into a hostile scowl that both annoyed and saddened her. This was her half-brother, after all. Things could have been different if he didn't seem so determined to hate her.

Her demon wasn't sad about it. No. In its opinion, they'd dealt with enough hate over the years from the maternal side of their family. And, unlike Harper, the demon had happily accepted the position of co-Prime and picked up the torch. It demanded respect.

"You don't even care, do you?" Roan said through his teeth.

"About what exactly?" asked Harper, tone even.

"You don't care that he took her. You don't care that she could be *dead*." He was making sure his voice carried, obviously wanting people's attention. He easily got it. People stopped. Stared. A hush fell around them.

She spoke. "It wouldn't matter what answer I gave you to that question—you'd still snort at it."

"It was a rhetorical question," he spat. "You know what a rogue is capable of, but you haven't tried to find her. No. You're not interested, even though it's your fault she's gone."

"You think I'm to blame for Crow's actions?"

"He wouldn't have taken my mother if she wasn't related to *you*."

"Or maybe he would have, since she intervened when he was in the process of draining Delia. Did you ever think of that? Did you ever consider that he might have taken anyone who stepped in that day?"

Roan snorted. "Why would he take just anyone?"

"Why do demons bordering on rogue ever do any of the things they do?"

Hands fisted so tight his knuckles were white, he leaned forward a little as he snarled. "I'm sure the one thing she's wishing right now is that she never had you."

Harper almost laughed. "Roan, I'm sure she's been wishing that for many, many years." And Harper had accepted it, so if he thought that little comment would hurt her, he was wrong.

"And who could blame her after what your father did to her?"

Okay, that annoyed Harper. Lucian had shit on Carla, true, but the woman was responsible for her own actions. That was how life worked. "You need to move along now. You've had your moment in the spotlight. I'm sure everyone's impressed with the disrespect you show to your Prime."

"Prime?" he scoffed. "You're not and never will be Prime material. You're a Wallis, a sad excuse for a sphinx. Jesus, you don't even have wings."

Enough was enough. She lunged forward and fisted a hand in his T-shirt, making his eyes almost bug out of his head. "Now you listen to me, you snotty little fucker. We both know this isn't about Carla. You have a problem with me being your Prime and you're using your mother's disappearance as an excuse to vent, which pretty much makes you a prick."

Harper expected him to struggle. He didn't; he just looked at her warily through eyes flickering nervously. That anxiety pleased her demon. "Do you think dishing out bullshit to your Prime makes you seem big and bad to others? I got news for you, Roan. It just makes you look like a disrespectful asshole. Not strong. Not scary. Hell, compared to the people I've dealt with in the past you're a sweet little puppy that keeps stupidly rolling in its own shit. I don't have the time or patience for the stream of stupidity that flows through your head." She shoved him away from her, disappointing her demon, who wanted to snap his neck. "Go."

"But don't go far," Tanner growled. "Knox is going to want to see you."

Roan swallowed hard. To his credit, he tried to look dignified as he marched past them.

"You should have let me beat the shit out of him," rumbled Tanner as they carried on walking en route to Knox's office.

Harper shook her head. "I'm co-Prime, right? That means I've got to act like one."

Tanner blew out a breath. "Knox will be pissed. Roan was warned to leave you alone. He ignored that warning."

"Why would he dare?" Harper truly didn't get it. "He was punished for saying crap about me once before. Wasn't that enough?"

"Evidently not," replied Tanner. "Making sure you hurt is apparently more important to him than his own pain. News of this will get round fast. You need to tell Knox before someone else does."

Eventually they reached the large combat circle, beneath which Knox's office was located. She followed Tanner up the flight of stairs behind the dome and over to a door marked "Office"; as always, it seemed to pulse with Knox's power.

Stood there like a sentry, Levi inclined his head. "He's waiting for you, Harper."

"Thanks." She twisted the metal knob and pushed the door open. Inside the office, Knox was standing behind his desk, having what seemed to be a somewhat unpleasant conversation with someone on the phone. His dark eyes met hers, and the strain around his features fell away.

Closing the door behind her, she crossed to his desk.

"Just get it done," Knox ordered before ending the call. "Sorry, baby. There was a problem at one of the hotels. Apparently a fellow demon thought it was acceptable to fairly destroy a deluxe suite simply because he's a celebrity." He walked to her, drew her close, and kissed her soft and long. "You taste like coffee and caramel."

"That's because I had a caramel latte before I came here."

He cocked his head. "Something's wrong. What is it?"

She placed her hands on his upper arms. "Don't freak out or anything. I'm fine; I'm not upset, just annoyed."

Every muscle in his body tightened. "What happened?"

"Roan confronted me." Anger reverberated against her mind, but nothing in his expression gave away that anger.

"What exactly did he say to you?" Knox asked as her body softened against his; he knew she was trying to soothe him. "Shouldn't I be the one doing the comforting?"

She smiled, curling her arms around his waist. "I don't need comfort. I'm really not upset."

"Not upset," he agreed. "But this saddens you."

"It would be nice if things could be different," she admitted. "But it is what it is."

Knox tucked her hair behind her ear. "Tell me what he said to you." With a sigh, she did. And anger roared through him. His demon shot to the surface and stroked her hair, vowing, "It will be dealt with."

The lethal edge to its disembodied tone made Harper shiver. She nodded.

Knox reached for the surface, suppressing his demon, and cupped her neck. Brushing his thumb up and down the column of her throat, he said, "I'm sorry Roan said those things to you. You didn't deserve it. And he knows better than that." *Keenan, find Roan. Apprehend him. He and I need to have another talk. You know where to take him.*

Sure thing, Keenan replied. *Can I ask why?*

He confronted Harper and said some very unacceptable things.

A growl. *I'll get the little bastard.*

Harper smoothed her hands up his back. "Who you talking to?" As their psyches were bonded, she could feel echoes of any telepathic conversations he had; she just couldn't make out the words.

"Keenan," he replied.

It was easy enough to guess. "You sent him after Roan."

"He should have heeded my warning. I thought he had. Apparently not." And Knox would ensure the little bastard paid for it.

"His head is a mess right now."

"Not my problem. And it's certainly not yours. He shouldn't have tried to make it yours." But of course Harper would take pity on him.

"He didn't hurt me. Not physically or even emotionally."

"Because you don't care enough about him for anything he does to hurt you." In fact, Knox would be surprised if she cared for Roan at all. But she *did* care that things had to be this way. "He didn't know that, though. He set out to hurt you."

"I don't think he wanted to *hurt* me. I think he just wanted to vent."

"That's not the point. I warned him. My demon warned him. Apparently my last punishment didn't get through to him, so we'll have to try something else."

She resisted asking just what that punishment would be. "Can we go home now?"

He kissed her. "Whatever you want, baby."

CHAPTER TEN

———◆◆◆———

Driving through the fenced in property, Harper found herself frowning at the sight of Jonas's home. Oh, it was impressive with the expansive lawn, statues, and fountain. The mansion itself was certainly grand, and she did like the large windows and thick white columns. But it was too ... showy. Too snobbish. It had no personality and there was nothing welcoming about it.

The Bentley came to a stop near the front entrance, where a valet waited. Harper almost smiled at the extreme reluctance with which Levi handed over the keys. He and Tanner then stayed close behind Harper and Knox as they ascended the small set of slate steps.

The well-dressed demon at the door smiled. "Mr Thorne, Miss Wallis." He gave the briefest of nods to both Tanner and Levi. "If you would please follow me."

As they stepped into the open entryway, she was hit by the scents of polish and potpourri. With the crystal chandelier, painted high ceilings, and stone flooring, the interior was just as impressive on the inside. It was also just as soulless.

"Our home is better," she whispered to Knox, who gave her a lopsided grin that made her body perk up in all the right places.

The butler escorted them to a formal dining hall that was fit for royalty and seemed completely over-the-top. Still, Harper smiled as Jonas came forward, crystal tumbler in hand.

"Ah, Knox," greeted Jonas. "Glad you could make it. Harper, it's indeed a pleasure to see you again." He exchanged nods with both Tanner and Levi.

"Thanks," said Harper. She kind of liked Jonas. He seemed genuine and friendly, despite his apparent need for his home to be unnecessarily extravagant. Maybe he was compensating for something.

"We were so hoping you would come," said a voice that made Harper's demon sneer. And then Alethea sidled up to her brother, wearing that cloying rose perfume again.

"Were you now?" said Knox, expression hard.

Alethea's eyes cut to Harper and then hardened. "Sphinx."

"Dolphin," returned Harper. Her demon wanted her to smack the bitch who coveted its mate. Maybe later.

Jonas cleared his throat. "We'll be getting started soon. Please have a seat." He swept his hand toward the eternally long table. "I believe your designated seats are at the center."

Placing his hand on Harper's lower back, Knox guided her toward the table. The other demons nodded respectfully, fear and respect shimmering in their eyes. The fear pleased his demon, who hadn't wanted to come; it had no interest in politics.

"I see you've been seated near me, Knox," said Raul, a Prime who Knox respected. "And we're right near the floral centerpiece that smells so strong I'm getting a headache. Hi there, Harper."

Harper gave Raul a smile, but she ignored his anchor—the

uptight she-demon had flirted with Knox in the past. Not at all cool.

Finding his name card, Knox growled when he saw that Harper hadn't been seated next to him. *Alethea* had. He glanced around, searching for Harper's spot.

"Oh, she's been placed opposite you," announced a male demon on the other side of the table, holding up the name card near his.

Just as Knox had expected, Harper gave the demon a winning smile; she loved to toy with the guy because, well, that was what imps lived to do: fuck with people.

"Malcolm, hi," she greeted pleasantly.

As usual, a muscle in his cheek ticked. "It's Malden."

Harper blinked. "Isn't that what I said?"

Hiding his amusement, Knox reached over and grabbed her name card.

"You should swap mine with the dolphin's. Better yet ..." Harper tore up Alethea's card and threw the tattered pieces under the table.

"Could you stop referring to her as a mammal?" asked Knox with a reluctant smile as they took their seats. The sentinels stood behind them, on guard.

Harper pursed her lips. "I suppose I could instead call her 'that lying, skanky, soulless bitch.'"

"It has a nice ring to it," Tanner said.

Harper thought so too.

A server appeared with a trolley of bottles and then offered Knox and Harper a choice out of a variety of mostly foreign-sounding drinks. She only recognized scotch, brandy, and wine. She left the ordering to Knox.

"I like that you do that," said Knox when the server walked away.

Harper frowned. "What?"

"Let me choose your drink." It was a simple thing, really, but Knox liked that she trusted him with it; trusted he'd know what she'd like.

"Oh. Good."

"Jonas, it's always a pleasure," said a familiar voice that made Harper smile. *Jolene*. Behind her were Martina and Beck, staring at the furnishings and ornaments; most likely wondering what would be worth stealing.

"The three of you have been seated at the far end," Alethea told her.

Jolene frowned. "I can see my granddaughter in the center. We'll sit with her."

"There's no room for you there," said Alethea.

"There's an empty seat opposite Knox."

"That's Harper's chair."

"Really? Odd. Because she's sitting right next to Knox." Jolene walked to Harper, who stood and gladly accepted her one-armed hug. "Hello, sweetheart."

Harper patted her back. "Hey, Grams."

Pulling back, Jolene eyed the brand on Harper's throat and sighed. "Really, Knox, you need to get that demon of yours to ease up on the possessiveness before it writes your name on her forehead."

"Don't give it any ideas," Harper muttered.

Martina kissed her cheek. "Don't worry, I won't set any fires," she whispered.

Not sure she believed that, Harper nodded at Jolene's anchor. "Hey, Beck."

He winked. "Sweetheart, how are—"

Alethea shrugged past him and stopped in front of Harper. "That's my seat."

Blinking, Harper said, "I'm not sure why you'd think that."

"My name card is . . ." Alethea's voice trailed off as she read the name card she was pointing at. "It was here."

"I can't imagine why it would be here," said Harper. "I mean, the only she-demon that should be at his side is his mate. And that's just not you." *Knox, I can't promise I won't kill her at some point.* Both Harper and her demon felt it was only fair that he knew.

Knox stroked a hand down her hair. *Want me to deal with this?*

Nope. Harper smiled at the male fast approaching. "Jonas, I don't suppose you know why your sister's trying to push me into making a scene, do you?"

His face reddened. "Please give me a moment," he said to Harper before dragging Alethea aside. Twin spots of color on her cheeks, she hissed something at her brother. Whatever Jonas whispered made Alethea blanch. Chin up, she spun on her heel and stalked away.

Jonas then returned to Harper. "I apologize on my sister's behalf."

"No harm done," said Harper as she returned to her seat.

I didn't expect you to leave the matter to Jonas, Knox told her.

She'll be embarrassed to have her older brother reprimand her right in front of everyone.

Knox's mouth twitched into a smile. He'd expected Harper to threaten Alethea . . . maybe demonstrate just how much soul-deep pain could hurt. There would likely never be a day when he could predict her responses.

"Hello, Jolene," Malden greeted pleasantly, all charm, as Jolene sank into the chair meant for Harper. Male Primes were shuffling along to make room for Martina and Beck, obviously eager to please the astonishingly beautiful Martina who was sweet, kind, and—unbeknown to them—addicted to setting fires.

Jolene smiled. "Well, hello ... um ... "

Harper leaned forward and supplied, "Malc—"

"*Malden*," he quickly corrected.

Jolene nodded slowly. "Of course."

Tanner spoke into Harper's ear. "You two just can't help yourselves, can you?"

Harper shrugged. "It would be no fun if we did."

He just snorted.

A chair further down scraped against the floor as Alethea sharply pulled it out before none-too-gracefully settling into it, looking much like a spoilt child who was on strike. It was a wonder she didn't fold her arms across her chest.

Harper's demon grinned in satisfaction. "She's a bit of a brat, isn't she?" A faint vibe of amusement touched Harper's mind.

Knox lay a hand on his mate's thigh. "As she's used to living among humans—a race she finds easy to manipulate—she isn't used to people not falling in line with whatever she wants."

"The new studio is coming along very well," said Jolene.

"It is," agreed Harper. Her family had been a big help in stripping the place bare and then helping paint the walls, fit the flooring, gloss the doors, put up shelves, update the kitchen, ready the stockroom, and also set up the autoclaves and partitions, etc. Soon enough, they would be able to move in all the equipment and furnishings, and hang up the tattoo flash.

The space was pretty big, so getting it ready was no simple job. Sure, they could have hired a company to take care of it all, but there was some satisfaction in playing such a big part in setting everything up. They'd decided to keep the name "Urban Ink," and one of her cousins had created the most amazing sign with a font that was part calligraphy, part graffiti.

"How are your plans for the grand opening coming along?" Jolene asked.

"Pretty great. There are only a few last things to take care of." Belinda had been shocked that Harper didn't want her help planning the opening. She was also horrified that Harper was throwing a street party and stated that it would never be successful. Whatever.

"Several people have asked me when the new studio will open," said Knox. "I think it will do very well in the Underground."

"Did you know that a smug glint pops into your eyes whenever we talk about it?" asked Harper, amused. "You're still gloating that you got your way."

"Not gloating," lied Knox. "I'm just happy that you'll be somewhere safer."

She gave a soft snort. "You're totally gloating."

A hush fell as Jonas took his seat at the head of the table. "Let us have a light lunch before we begin."

Servers then entered the dining hall with platters. There were posh-looking salads, little fish-cake thingies, bruschetta, caviar, and a variety of small weird stuff. Harper wrinkled her nose. *What are they?*

A range of hot and cold canapés, Knox replied.

Oh.

Her glum tone made his mouth quirk. He flicked her earring gently and kissed her temple. *I'll take you to a restaurant of your choice after we're done here.*

Dude, you're so getting lucky later. Sipping at her red wine, she saw Alethea watching them with an inscrutable look on her face. The dolphin quickly looked away.

Harper tried the bruschetta, which was kind of nice but it sadly left her hungry. When the clink and clatter of tableware came to an end about an hour later, the servers removed the plates and cutlery.

Jonas cleared his throat. "Now, shall we begin?" Murmurs of agreement spread throughout the hall, and Jonas nodded in satisfaction. "Good. Is there anything in particular that anyone wishes to discuss?"

"Isla's lair has not yet agreed on a replacement for her," said a Prime at the far end of the table. "It is currently operating without a Prime."

The demon beside Beck spoke. "I heard there's a lot of arguing going on about who will rule it."

Another Prime frowned, confused. "I heard they simply don't intend to replace her until they've grieved her death. In any case, the fact that there's a lair operating without a Prime is concerning."

"It's also none of our business unless there's a reason for us to step in," said Raul. "Right now, the lair isn't being a problem for anyone."

"Onto another subject, Dario has gone off the grid," one Prime announced. "I don't suppose anyone knows why that is?"

Jolene's brow furrowed. "Gone off the grid?"

"He's become quite the recluse," said Alethea. "There are rumors that he's building an army."

There was a short silence. Harper broke it. "Our kind don't do war." Mostly because demons found it boring.

"Yes, but he'd hoped to be elected as a Monarch over us all," Alethea reminded her. "Perhaps he's angry that the elections didn't go in his favor. Perhaps he's so determined to be a ruler he intends to fight for that."

"I find it difficult to believe Dario would feel that way," said Raul, leaning back in his chair with his hands behind his head. "He didn't seem all that bothered by losing the election."

Harper happened to agree with that.

Apparently, Malden also did because he nodded. "He was

disappointed by the result of the voting poll, but not terribly angry. It was only Isla who reacted badly."

Alethea twisted her mouth. "In all honesty, I don't believe he's forming an army. But I still find his behavior odd. I don't like to say it, but it's possible that Dario's strange behavior is a result of him turning rogue."

Malden's jaw hardened. "I will not believe that."

"It was just a thought," she said with a shrug. "Maybe it's something we should investigate, just to be sure. I went to his home, hoping to see him for myself and put my mind at rest. He *refused* to see me."

"You say that like you're someone important," one Prime said to Alethea with a derogatory snort. "You're not a Prime. He's not obliged to see you. And you're certainly no friend of his."

Harper fought a smile as spots of color entered Alethea's cheeks.

Alethea's hand curled tight around her napkin. "Dario and I have history."

"Yes, *history*," said Malden. "As I recall it, you two didn't part on good terms. Unlike you, I *am* his friend. Until recently, I was in regular contact with him. He showed no signs of mental degradation."

Jonas spoke up. "I'm skeptical about him being rogue *and* about him forming an army. But I can't think of a reason why the man would lock himself up in his own home."

"Maybe he's found himself a nice woman and they're not inclined to leave the bedroom," joked the Prime beside Harper.

"It's more likely that than anything else." Raul took a sip of his scotch. "It's rare that Primes turn rogue."

"It's rare, but not impossible," Alethea pointed out.

Raul's mouth twisted. "You seem quite preoccupied with Dario."

"I merely don't wish to see another Prime turn rogue," she told him.

Raul sighed. "Look, I know what happened with your old Prime was bad—"

"No, you don't know," she clipped. "You didn't see what happened. You heard about it, but you didn't *see*. Let me tell you it is a frightening and painful experience. So many died—women, men, children, demons, humans, animals. A rogue will kill indiscriminately. It cares for nothing. It seeks only to cause pain and misery and destruction. In my opinion, every demon even bordering on rogue should be killed."

Wow, that was definitely going too far in Harper's opinion.

Alethea took a deep, centering breath. "I only wish to be sure that Dario is well."

"I'll contact him," Malden told her. "But I'm quite certain we have no reason to worry. I'm also very certain he is not forming an army."

"I would have dismissed the rumor if it wasn't for the unpredictable weather," said Alethea. "You know Dario can influence the weather. If he's out of control, his gift will be too."

"Raul can play with the weather too," one Prime pointed out with an accusatory tone that caused Raul to stiffen. He had bushy eyebrows that Harper badly want to pluck.

"Why would I do that?" asked Raul.

"You tell us," said Bushy Brows. "Maybe your anger keeps getting the better of you."

Frowning, Raul put down his glass. "Anger at what?"

"Your female. I heard she left you."

"The decision to separate was mutual and civil. My anchor can attest to that," Raul added, to which the she-demon nodded.

Bushy Brows shrugged one shoulder. "Not what I heard."

"Nor me," said Malden, a smile playing around the edges of his mouth.

Raul narrowed his eyes at Malden. "Personally, I find the rumor I heard about you much more interesting. Caught cheating on your woman with her two brothers, weren't you?"

Malden's cheeks flushed with outrage. "No, I was *not*."

Raul raised his hands, smirking. "Hey, I'm not judging. To each their own."

A lot of rumors going around lately, said Harper.

Knox put down his glass. *It would seem so.*

Bushy Brows looked at Knox. "I heard one of your demons turned rogue."

What's his name? she asked Knox. *It's annoying to call him Bushy Brows in my head.* A vibe of amusement touched her mind.

Thatcher. "Not rogue," corrected Knox. "He is, however, close to the edge."

"I also heard he had a strange vision," added Thatcher. "Is that correct?"

Knox tapped his fingers on his crystal tumbler. "Depends what you heard the vision was."

"That you and your mate would give birth to a soulless child that would demolish the universe itself," said Thatcher, a challenge in his tone.

Harper rolled her eyes. "The power of Chinese whispers . . ."

Knox spoke. "Crow claims to have had a vision that Harper and I would have a child and it would be powerful enough to destroy us."

"More apocalyptic visions," scoffed a Prime who hadn't spoken until then. "One of my near-rogue demons also claimed the end of the world was coming, though he didn't mention you."

"Maybe Crow really did have a vision that you would have a child capable of destroying us all," said a female Prime. "You and your mate are both powerful. It would be no surprise if you had a powerful child. Perhaps even so powerful that it can in fact annihilate us."

Jolene snickered. "You're making about as much sense as a demon on the edge, Mila." Raul and many others looked equally amused by Mila's theory.

"Any other issues?" Jonas asked, waving Mila's concern aside. A few minor things were raised and dealt with, and then Jonas planted his hands on the table and said, "Well, if no one has any other issues, I think we can agree to end the meeting here."

Knox nodded. Having exchanged farewells with Jonas and Raul, Knox cupped Harper's elbow and began to lead her out of the dining hall; Levi, Tanner, and the imps stayed close behind. As they reached the doorway, Alethea slipped in front of them.

"Harper, I'm sorry that I spoke so sharply to you." Alethea sounded sincerely regretful. "It was uncalled for."

Harper inwardly snorted. The bitch wasn't sorry at all. Still, Harper inclined her head ever so slightly.

Alethea then turned to Knox. "I hope none of the rumors about Dario are true. But I'm hoping that if the worst has happened and he's turned rogue, I will then have your support dealing with him."

"Why?" challenged Harper.

Alethea blinked. "Excuse me?"

"Why?" repeated Harper. "Jonas is powerful, right? There are plenty of other Primes who could have your back. So why do you so badly need Knox involved?"

"I don't badly need him to be involved—"

"That's right; you don't. But you think the easiest way to get this done would be to use Knox to do your dirty work. He's not a weapon to be used, and he's not a shield for you to hide behind."

"Shield?" echoed Alethea.

"You think there won't be any repercussions if Knox is involved. If you want to start shit with another Prime, you start it and end it on your own."

Alethea arched an imperious brow. "You speak for him now?"

"When I think someone is trying to use him like that? Damn fucking straight. And he'd do the same for me."

Knox stepped forward. "Which is why I'll address the little stunt you pulled at Harper's studio. You've never been *anyone* to me, Alethea; I know that, you know that. Most importantly, Harper knows it. You heard what happened to Isla, didn't you? It happened because she dared to hurt Harper. Think about that before you do anything else." Knox then guided Harper out of the hall, through the mansion, and out of the building.

On the steps, Jolene said, "Well, that went pretty much as I'd expected."

"I really don't like that little bitch," said Martina, rooting through a wallet that obviously wasn't hers. "I heard from Khloë that she appeared at the studio. Ooh, there are some nice credit cards in here." She pulled out a thin, silver box and opened it up with a bright smile. "Mint, anyone?"

Beck held out his hand. "I'll have one."

At the faint scent of smoke, Harper sighed at Martina. "I don't even want to know what you did."

Jolene kissed Harper on the cheek just as the valet pulled up in her Mustang. "I'll see you again soon, sweetheart."

As the imps drove away, Tanner grinned. "Your family has a way of spicing up politics."

Harper blew out a breath. "Imps don't take politics seriously."

The valet brought over the Bentley next, and they all hopped inside. As they drove through the gates, Levi said, "It surprised me that anyone would put any stock in Crow's vision, especially Mila. She never seemed the paranoid kind."

"She's not the only Prime who believes it's possible; she's just the only one willing to voice it," Knox told them.

"Seriously?" asked Harper. She knew he could pick up stray thoughts from people with weak shields.

"Yes." Knox tangled their fingers. "Some were even wondering if you could be pregnant. Did you notice that one of the other female Primes patted your arm as we were leaving?"

"Yeah," replied Harper.

"She can detect pregnancy," Knox told her. "She smiled in sheer relief when she sensed no baby."

"Do Alethea and Jonas think the vision could be real?" Levi asked.

"I don't know," said Knox, massaging Harper's palm with his thumb. "Their shields are strong. I'll have Larkin and Keenan look into the Dario situation. They should be able to find out if he has become a recluse and if maybe this rumor of him forming an army has any substance."

As Levi and Tanner began to discuss some sentinel-related business, Harper turned to Knox, intending to ask him just how many Primes had that dumb theory about her being pregnant. Instead, she frowned, because he had the weirdest look on his face. "What?"

"You defended me to Alethea," he said.

"And you find this amusing?" He sure sounded like he did.

"Touching," he corrected.

"And amusing," she pushed.

Knox's mouth curved. "A little."

"Just because you're, like, *super* powerful doesn't mean people shouldn't defend you." But he was looking at her like she was a cute harmless little bunny that was obviously on drugs. She sighed. "You're still not fearing my mighty wrath."

"I'm trying."

"One day I will unleash it and you will flee in terror. Why are you laughing? It's only the truth. A sphinx in full-on berserker-mode can wreak major destruction and instill fear into the hearts of all who ... *stop laughing!*"

CHAPTER ELEVEN

———◆———

Harper was just slipping on her shoes when Knox strolled into the walk-in closet a few mornings later. He was fully dressed and his hair was slightly damp from the shower—a shower they'd taken together during which he'd fucked her hard against the tiled wall. She took a moment to just drink him in. To admire his striking dark eyes, broad chest, solid shoulders, and purposeful stride. It was sometimes hard to believe he was hers.

Knox shackled both her wrists and kissed her gently. "I have news."

And she just knew . . . "Carla."

"They managed to track Crow to a motel room. He wasn't there, but Carla was."

Her stomach twisted at his grim tone. "She's alive?"

"Yes. But he hurt her."

"What did he do?" It was *bad*; she could feel it.

Knox didn't want to trouble her with the details, but he

understood that she needed to know. "He removed her reproductive organs."

All Harper could do was gape.

"Her cervix, ovaries, fallopian tubes, and her womb." Knox's voice vibrated with anger. He didn't like Carla, but she was still one of his demons and she'd suffered badly. That wasn't something he could be calm about. "Crow was a surgeon, so he knew exactly what he was doing. He purposely kept her alive. She's unconscious and weak, but she will recover."

Physically, maybe. But who could mentally recover from something as horrific as that? "I just ... I so didn't expect that. I mean ..."

Knox slid his hands up to her shoulders. "It's okay to have no words right now." When he'd first heard the news, he'd been lost for words himself. Lightly kneading her shoulders, he added, "We know Crow's still not rogue for the simple reason that she's alive." A rogue would kill without thought.

"But he's so far from stable it's not even funny." Harper shoved a hand through her hair. "And yet, he hasn't made another impulsive attempt to hurt you. Delia said he would target you; that he thinks he needs to kill you to save the world." Knox's mouth tightened, and she tensed. "He did try to get to you again, didn't he?"

"He tried to get into the penthouse of the same hotel again. The guards recognized and subdued him immediately, but during the struggle he conjured a gun and starting shooting at people. There were humans around, so the guards were restricted as to what they could do to detain him. He got away again."

"*What?* Why didn't you tell me?" she demanded.

He shrugged. "I wasn't even in the building at the time. It didn't seem worth mentioning."

"It didn't seem worth mentioning?" she echoed, incredulous.

"Compared to the dangerous situations I've known in my life, that was nothing."

Nothing? "It was an attempt on your life. It was something. You should have told me. You said that you would tell me immediately if he made another move to hurt you."

"Baby, I wasn't in the hotel. Even if I had been, it wouldn't have mattered because *he* didn't get into the hotel. The struggle happened on the steps. It barely counted as an incident."

"I don't care. You still should have told me."

Sighing, he smoothed his hand over his jaw. "I'm not used to this."

"What?"

"Having someone who cares." He liked it, but he didn't like being unsure in any situation. "Or having to explain myself to anyone." Settling his hands on her shoulders, he drew her close. "I'm sorry I didn't tell you straight away. If Crow makes another move, I'll tell you instantly."

"Even if it doesn't seem worth mentioning to you?"

"Even then."

After a moment, she nodded. "Fine. Back to the original subject . . . where's Carla?"

"At home. She's been checked out; she has no infections or major blood loss. Her body is healing at an accelerated rate. She's simply not awake yet. If you want to see her—"

"Her family aren't going to let me in their house." And Harper couldn't blame them for that.

"We're their Primes. They'll do what we tell them to do."

"But it's not fair of me to barge in there when they're worried about her. I'll wait until she's awake. If she asks to see me, I'll go." It needed to be Carla's decision, because Harper wasn't going to just walk into the woman's home like she had every right to be there. Not that she thought for even a second that Carla would ever request to see her, but still.

Knox kissed her forehead. "All right."

"Do you think she'll blame me?" Harper asked, not even sure she wanted the answer. It shouldn't even matter, but it did.

Not wanting to hurt her but not willing to lie, Knox said, "I'd like to say no, but I have no idea. It doesn't matter if or how many people blame you, it will *never* make it your fault."

"I know that."

"But you feel guilty."

"It doesn't take a genius to work out why the guy removed her reproductive organs. It was a punishment for giving birth to me, for 'putting things in motion.'"

"Because his mind is all kinds of fucked up right now. Not because of you."

Intellectually, she knew that, but the guilt was there all the same. Especially because ... "If he'd known that she tried to abort me, maybe he'd have taken pity on her."

The lair only knew the story that Harper had grown up believing: that Carla dumped Harper on Jolene's doorstep when she was just a baby. Harper, being such a private person, had chosen to keep the truth quiet. The only people within the lair who knew about it were Levi, who had uncovered most of it himself, and Carla's mate after she confessed it to him.

Harper tried to step back, but Knox's grip on her shoulders kept her in place. "I have to get to work," she told him. She hadn't yet closed what she was beginning to think of as "the old studio" and she had clients coming in.

"Maybe you should take the day off."

She shook her head. "I can't do that. I—"

"Baby, you've had a shock," he said, cupping her face. "A shock you're not sure how to process. Take the day off," he coaxed.

"No, really, I'll be fine."

"Take it off. I'll do the same." His demon really liked that idea, loathed to leave her. "I can work from home."

"I can't stay home. If I sit here all day, I'll think about it. Over and over. And I have no right to do that, Knox. It didn't happen to me. It happened to *her*. I'm not her family."

"But you get to feel how you feel."

"I don't know what I feel."

Seeing his usually decisive mate so unsure of herself ... it pissed Knox the fuck off. "If you need a distraction, fine." He could understand that. "Go to work. But if you need a break, take it." He kissed her. Softly. Gently. Thoroughly. "I love you."

She smiled, surprised. He didn't say the words often, because they didn't come easily to him, but he always seemed to know when she needed to hear them. "And I love you." Harper gave him one last kiss before grabbing her purse and heading outside, where she hopped into the Audi. His expression unusually soft, Tanner started to speak, but she shook her head. She didn't want to talk about Carla. Didn't have the right to worry or anything else. They didn't spend the journey in silence, though. They talked about general things, just like they did most mornings.

In the studio, Harper threw all her attention into her work. She smiled and talked and was glad of every distraction—hell, even Belinda's appearance later that day was a distraction she was happy to use.

Washing her equipment, Harper listened as the cambion chatted on and on about the shindig. Belinda had eventually admitted defeat and dropped the idea to separate the Primes and VIPs from the rest of the demons at the event. She'd also fallen in line with Harper's idea to jazz up the combat dome and use it as a large social area on the night. Now she was reading out the list of appetizers that would be served at the dome. Most of them sounded similar to the foods Jonas served at his mansion.

"What do you think?" asked Belinda, looking up from her clipboard.

"I think that's the most *un*appetizing list I've ever heard in my life," said Harper. "Can't we just serve normal food? I'll bet the people there would prefer that anyway."

Belinda gave her one of those condescending smiles. "The Primes and VIPs will surely head there. Canapés and hors d'oeuvres *are* normal for people of their class."

"Great, but it's not their shindig. How about little sticks with chunks of steak on and half a potato wedge? They'd make good appetizers."

Pausing in sweeping the floor, Devon hummed. "They sound good."

Mouth gaping open in horror, Belinda stared at Harper in dismay. "Steak? Wedges? You can't serve that at a black-tie event!"

"Why not?" It was *her* event.

Belinda spluttered. "It's not proper."

"But it means I won't starve."

Belinda sighed. "You're being dramatic."

"And you're being unprofessional by ignoring what your client wants. Your job is to ensure that what I want comes to life, right?"

The cambion lifted her chin. "Knox won't like it."

Harper snorted. "He'd prefer that to seeing me hungry. He gets pissed if I miss meals."

"Here are some alternative appetizers." Belinda detached a leaflet-type menu from the clipboard and offered it to Harper.

Drying her hands, Harper took the leaflet and quickly scanned it. "I don't even know what half this stuff is." And if she couldn't read the name of something, she wouldn't eat it. "These are no good."

Snatching back the menu, Belinda said, "We'll leave the choice to Knox."

"Yes, run to Knox." Harper wiggled her fingers. "Pester him. Then he'll come to me to work off his anger."

"I'm trying to *help* you. I've worked for Knox many times. I've organized several events for him. I know him. I know what he likes and what he doesn't like. You haven't known him long enough to know what he'll appreciate and what he will disapprove of. You hardly know him at all."

This bitch was *so* close to getting smacked around. She smiled inwardly as Belinda's eyes dropped to the brand on her throat. The cambion had looked at it a few times, but she'd said nothing. "Like it?" Harper asked.

"The artist has a steady hand," said Belinda. "How nice of you to mark yourself for Knox."

Yeah, like Harper believed for one second that the cambion really thought it was simply a tattoo. "You're insulting yourself by pretending you don't know what you're looking at." Oh, that comment got her a sneer.

"It will fade when he tires of you."

Her inner demon snarled. Harper arched a brow. "Is that a fact?"

"Yes. And he's bound to tire of you sooner or later."

"That tone ... it's almost like you're trying to goad me." Gently slipping one of the jeweled, metal hair sticks from her loose bun, Harper infused it with hellfire. The simple accessory was now not only ablaze, but absolutely lethal. Fear flashed in the cambion's eyes and she took a wary step back. "Don't start a fight you don't have a prayer of winning. Now go, Belinda, you're pissing me off and I have shit to do."

The cambion couldn't seem to get away quick enough.

As she was passing the reception desk, Khloë scowled at Belinda and demanded, "Is it you that keeps moving my stapler?"

Looking befuddled, the cambion just stormed out.

Khloë whirled to face Harper, Devon, and Raini. "Seriously, who is doing it?" The phone rang, and the imp answered it with her "receptionist tone." Then she called out, "Harper, Grams is on the phone! She wants to talk to you!"

Great. Easing the hellfire away, Harper returned the jeweled stick to her hair as she crossed to the desk. Taking the phone receiver from Khloë, Harper said, "I'm guessing you heard about Carla."

"Yes," replied Jolene. "Don't be feeling guilty. It did not happen at your hand. You wouldn't wish such a thing on anyone, not even her."

"I'm already under strict orders from Knox not to blame myself, so you can stop fretting."

A huff. "I'm your grandmother, it's my right to fret." The line went dead.

"Blame yourself for what?" asked Khloë, arms folded. "And what about Carla? Has she been found?"

Raini and Devon flanked the imp, looking just as worried.

Harper sighed, wanting to strangle her grandmother. Jolene could have spoken to her telepathically, but no. She'd wanted the girls to overhear the conversation so that Harper would have to tell them. Jolene didn't want her to bottle the whole thing up. Master. Manipulator.

Devon took a single step forward. "Harper, what's going on?"

Knowing they wouldn't stop pestering her, Harper told them. For a long moment, there was a stunned silence.

Khloë blew out a breath. "Well, fuckadoodledoo."

"You can't possibly think this is your fault, Harper," Devon said.

"I don't," Harper told her, returning to the sink. "And I don't want to talk about it."

Khloë sidled up to her. "Grams obviously wants you to."

Harper sighed. "Look, I have another client coming in soon."

"Not now you don't," said Raini.

Harper grit her teeth. "Raini—"

The succubus raised a hand. "We're officially closing for the day. In fact, it might be best to close for a few days."

For God's sake. "That's not necessary."

"Harper, news of Carla's condition will get around the demon community pretty fast," Raini pointed out. "Every demon who walks through that door is going to watch you carefully and report back to their friends whatever it is they think you're feeling. That's if they don't simply ask you outright and insist on talking about it. Is that how you want the rest of your day to go? Because I pointblank refuse to put you through it."

Shit, she was so right. "I know, but—" She paused because something ... something felt *off*. Looking into Khloë's coffee cup, Harper saw the liquid shaking just as she felt subtle vibrations beneath her feet. "Do you feel that?"

They all exchanged looks of alarm as the framed licenses and pictures shook against the wall. The items on the desk clattered on the wood, and pieces of equipment tumbled off the counters of their stations onto the floor. The ground no longer vibrated, it tremored. Harper's heart began to pound frantically, and her demon tensed.

"Did I ever mention how much I hate earthquakes?" groused Raini.

Devon winced as her shoulder crashed into the wall. Harper swayed, slamming her hand against the other wall for balance, while Raini and Khloë leaned against the desk for support.

Outside car alarms wailed, sirens blared, headlights flashed, and shingles tumbled off the roof and hit the sidewalk. People passing pressed themselves against the studio's window to support their weight, hands plastered to the glass.

Harper breathed in time with each bucking tremor. The glass of the jewelry display case shattered and the items inside rattled and jangled on the shelves. Coffee was sloshing out of the cups, spilling everywhere.

Then the tremors slowed until, finally, they eased away just as suddenly as they'd began.

Tanner came racing inside, face hard. "Everyone okay?"

Harper nodded. "But there was nothing natural about that earthquake."

Rubbing her sore shoulder, Devon declared, "That's it! We're getting out of here."

"I can't go home and just sit there," said Harper.

Raini slipped on her jacket. "Who said anything about you going home?"

Khloë picked up the phone. "I'll cancel the last two appointments for today and then we'll all get the fuck out of here."

"To go where?" asked Harper.

Devon grabbed her purse. "Where do you think?"

The human was good at bluffing; Knox would give him that. But he simply wasn't good enough. Knox had no interest in working with liars or people who believed they could manipulate him. This was why he preferred working with his own kind. They already knew these things and, as such, didn't waste his time with such bullshit. But in order to blend with humans, he had to work among them and—

Knox, said Tanner. *Sorry to interrupt, but I thought you might like to know that Harper and her friends are at the Xpress bar.*

They've been here for a few hours now and she's . . . well, she's blind drunk.

Drunk? I didn't expect her to go drinking. But he maybe he should have done.

I don't think anyone can ever expect anything when it comes to Harper. I have to admit, though, I didn't think she was the kind of person who would drown their sorrows.

She's not drowning her sorrows. She's distracting herself because she doesn't think she has the right to be upset.

I'm watching them from another table, since they wouldn't let me sit with them. Do you want me to take her home?

No. Knox got to his feet. *I'll go get her myself.* He quickly ended the business call, uncaring that he'd been rude. Opening his office door, Knox indicated for Levi to follow him. "Tanner just contacted me," said Knox. "Apparently Harper—" He cut off as a she-demon rounded the corner and came to a halt in front of him.

Belinda smiled. "Oh, Knox, I was hoping to catch you."

For fuck's sake. "What can I do for you, Miss Thacker?"

Her smile dimmed at his impatient tone. "It's about the appetizers for the event."

"I told you I want Harper to decide these things."

Belinda's mouth flattened. "She doesn't find any of my suggestions suitable."

"Then they're not suitable." Simple.

"Knox—"

"Miss Thacker, I didn't invite you to call me by my first name." Her cheeks reddened. "I gave you my orders when I hired you. They were not complicated. I specified all the details of the event that I wished to be left for Harper to decide."

"She wants steak and potato wedges on sticks!" Belinda took a deep breath and lowered her eyes. "I apologize for my outburst."

Steak and potato wedges on sticks? echoed Levi, a smile in his telepathic voice. *That actually sounds pretty good.*

"Do you remember the all-important order I gave you before sending you Harper's way, Miss Thacker?"

She swallowed. "Yes."

"What was it?"

Belinda met his gaze. "You told me to give her whatever she wants."

"Then do it. Now I have somewhere I need to be ..."

She straightened her blazer. "Thank you for your time, Mr Thorne," she said stiffly.

As the cambion strode off, Levi asked Knox, "Where are we going?"

"To the Xpress bar to collect my mate, who may or may not be conscious by the time we get there."

Raini clinked her glass against Harper's and loudly slurred, "Best. Night. Ever."

Harper nodded, smiling. "In the history of ever!" She couldn't understand how they weren't drunk. They'd been there for hours, drinking martinis, mojos, and shots. Harper could still feel the burn of the tequila in her throat ... though it was possible that the burn was more to do with the fun they'd had on the karaoke. Or maybe it was because of how loud they had to speak to be heard over the laughing, hooting, singing, and swearing.

Bopping her head to the thumping music, Khloë grabbed Harper's arm. "Dude, let's race."

Harper held up her blue martini; it glowed in the dim lighting. "I need to finish this first. Can you yodel?"

"Sure," replied Khloë, and went on to do just that.

"Yoo-hooing isn't yodeling," Raini told her.

Khloë frowned. "Oh. Then no, I can't yodel. We should learn. Is there a yodel school? We could go there. Or to a beatboxing school!"

"Ooh, yeah!" said Harper, eyes wide. "Dude, I will totally go with you."

"Me too." Raini adjusted her cleavage. "I always wanted to learn how to beatbox. And how to use a crossbow."

"He's not even that cute," Devon muttered to herself, playing with a cardboard coaster. "And he pulls my hair. *Pulls. My. Hair.*"

"Who?" asked Harper before she swallowed some of her martini; the cool liquid slid down her parched throat.

Devon looked up and straightened her shoulders. "I should call him. I should. Shouldn't I?"

"Are we talking about the hound?" asked Raini, reapplying her lipstick with a shaky hand.

"He has a girlfriend." Devon shook her head. "But I don't care. Why would I care? She's welcome to throw balls for him and scratch his belly."

Khloë puffed out a long breath and fanned herself. "Why do you think he has a girlfriend?"

"I heard someone talking about it. But it's fine. It really doesn't matter. Let's not talk about me." Devon turned to Harper. "Let's talk about you."

Harper pursed her lips. "Nah."

Devon grabbed her hand. "You can stop pretending you're not upset. This is *us*. We know you. We know when you're hurting. And what hurts you hurts us." The hellcat leaned forward, and Harper got a whiff of her hairspray. "Let us help you. We've got to stick together at times like this. We've got to be tight, like those sisters on *Charmed*. What do they say? Oh yeah, the power of three . . . something, something, free!"

"There are four of us," Harper pointed out.

Devon patted her arm. "Sweetie, a little miscounting never hurt anyone."

"I don't need help," said Harper. "I'm not the one who was hurt. And it's not like me and Carla are close or anything."

"That's not your fault," insisted Devon. "And it doesn't mean you can't feel bad for her."

Khloë pointed a finger at Devon. "Pure wisdom."

Raini tilted her head. "I wonder where things go when we delete them from our computers."

Harper frowned. "Huh?"

"At first, it goes to the recycle bin," said Raini. "But what about when we delete all our stuff from the recycle bin. Where does it go?"

"Maybe the FBI has it all in a secret database," suggested Harper.

Devon fluttered her fingers. "Or they could be just particles in the air."

"Who cares?" Khloë slammed down her empty glass on the table. "I need another Fuzzy Duck."

Raini grimaced. "I don't know how you drink them."

"Don't be a hater," said Khloë. "They have pineapple juice. That means I'm getting vitamins."

"Yeah, I really don't think it does," said a new voice that dripped with amusement. *Keenan.*

Harper looked up to see Knox and his sentinels. She smiled at her mate. "You're here. How did that happen?"

Knox slid his hand under her hair to cup her nape, surprised that her skin was cool considering how flushed her cheeks were. Looking into those languid, droopy eyes, he said, "I came to take you home."

"You should probably go with him," Raini advised. "The room's spinning. That can only mean bad things."

Tanner reached for Devon's arm. "Let's go, kitty."

The hellcat dodged his hand and jumped to her feet. Swaying, she pointed at him. "No touching, pooch. I mean it. I'm not scared to throw down right here, right now."

Khloë's shoulders shook. "Don't make me laugh. I might pee."

As the imp came to a stop in front of him, Keenan frowned and asked, "Why do you have your shoes on the wrong feet?"

"I don't feel that's important," said Khloë.

"Shit," hissed Raini as she stumbled into the table. "Who put this here?"

Laughing, Larkin said, "I am definitely going out with you girls next time."

"Ooh, yeah, you should!" Raini told her, casting Levi a frown as he urged her away from the table and tried grabbing her hand.

Knox squeezed his mate's nape. "Up, baby. Time to go."

Harper stood upright, smiling at him. "You're adorable."

"And you're wasted," he said, amused. No one ever had, or ever again would, call him adorable.

She frowned. "Wasted?"

"Completely wasted," Knox insisted.

"I'm not," she objected, affronted.

Knox just smiled. "Yes, baby, you are."

"If I was wasted, I wouldn't be able to put on my jacket."

Knox watched as she struggled to put it on. Honestly, it was painful to watch. "Give me the jacket."

"Okay." She leaned into him as he slipped an arm around her and guided her out of the bar. "I missed you," she slurred. "Can you get drunk?"

"Yes. It's just not a good idea."

Because he needed control at all times, she realized. "Gotcha." As they walked to the elevator, she told him, "I think pirates are cool. They drink rum. Do we have rum at home?"

"No."

"None? But you have that big wine cellar."

"For wine."

"You should think about adding a little variety."

Knox just shook his head, helplessly amused. "Do you really think it was a good idea to go drinking?"

"It was a better idea than fucking a dolphin."

He closed his eyes, resisting the urge to comment.

She looked up at him. "You're judging me right now, aren't you? I can see it. You think I'm awful and pathetic now. Don't. I'll be an awesome mate. Promise."

"You already are," he said, chuckling.

"I love you, you know. Really. Seriously. Totally. You know right, that?"

He punched the button for the elevator. "I know."

She took in a deep breath. "I'm completely blitzed, aren't I?"

"Yes. And yet, you're somehow cute at the same time."

"Well, that's what's important."

CHAPTER TWELVE

———◉———

Harper woke to the feel of warm lips kissing her back. She swallowed. Her throat felt dry and rough, and there was an icky taste in her mouth.

"Morning, baby," Knox said against the back of her shoulder. "You smell like a bar." He'd showered her before he put her to bed, but the alcohol was seeping from her pores.

"I feel like I've been in a car wreck," she mumbled into the silk pillow, voice hoarse. A human probably would have been fighting against a splitting headache and a queasy stomach. One good thing about being a demon was that their hangovers weren't too bad and they wore off pretty fast. She was damn tired, though.

Knox trailed the tip of his finger down her spine. "I heard all about your version of Aretha Franklin's 'Respect.'" Tanner had been only too glad to fill him in on everything.

Tensing, she frowned at the smile in his voice. "Go away."

"Apparently you sang pretty well . . . until you stopped to save

Khloë from falling off the speaker where she'd been dancing like a Hawaiian stripper."

Oh shit, she remembered that. It had seemed hilarious at the time.

"Want to know what else I heard you did at the bar?"

"I don't think I do."

"You used your red lipstick to scribble 'Alethea is a skanky hoe' on the bathroom mirror."

In her opinion, truer words had never been spoken—well, scribbled. Her demon agreed.

"You almost yacked in the Bentley."

Oh, God. She squeezed her eyes tightly shut. "Stop."

"We had to pull over so you could vomit in a bush."

"Stop."

"Then you got back in the car and said, 'Taco Bell, anyone?'"

"*Stop.*"

Knox chuckled. "But I haven't told you what you did when you got home yet."

She buried her face deeper into the pillow. "I don't want to hear it."

He spoke into her ear. "You told me you love me, you'd always love me, and that you even love my demon . . . which would have been really sweet if you weren't bent over the toilet with vomit in your hair."

She groaned. "I can't listen to anymore. Leave me to sleep." Instead, she was gently rolled onto her back. And there he was, fully dressed, looming over her on all fours.

"You've been asleep for seven hours." It was a long time, for a demon. Considering she'd been absolutely smashed last night, Knox figured that she should, by all rights, look a mess. She just looked sleepy and flushed. "I'd kiss you if I didn't think you'd taste like a bag of fries." She'd brushed her teeth before bed, almost poking herself in the eye in the process, but still . . .

"Good call."

"I might have let you sleep a little longer, but I have news that you should hear. Carla's awake."

It was more of a relief than Harper had anticipated it would be. "You need to visit her," she said, understanding the next expected step. Carla was one of his demons; he was responsible for her. As Prime, he would—at the very least—need to pay her a courtesy visit. And as co-Prime, Harper would be expected to do the same. *Shit.*

"Yes, but you don't have to come along if you don't want to. Honestly, I'd much rather you didn't." The woman had hurt his mate enough. It was possible that, like Roan, she blamed Harper for what she'd endured. If that was the case and Carla felt the need to hurl accusations at her, she'd then hurt Harper once again.

"I know I should go with you. Part of me wants to. But it doesn't feel right to go there." It was Carla's home; her sanctuary and safe place. Harper was far from her favorite person, so it would feel like she was intruding on that. "I'm not welcome in that house."

"You don't know that for sure."

"If she asks to see me, I'll visit her." It was doubtful that Carla would want that, however.

Knox rubbed his nose against hers. "Okay, baby."

"You're relieved I'm not going with you," she sensed.

"Yes, I am."

It was only then that she noticed he was wearing the same shirt and pants he'd worn the day before. "Have you been up all night?"

"Yes. I had a lot of work to do. Speaking of work . . . why did you close early yesterday?"

She smoothed her hands over his blue shirt. "Raini pointed out that demons would be curious about my reaction to what happened to Carla. People rarely approach me. But if they were sitting in my chair, they'd use the opportunity to—under the pretense of being friendly—ask me questions. So we all agreed we'd close the studio for a few days. I'm not happy about it, but I can't argue with Raini's logic."

Knox was glad she hadn't. "You working on the new studio again today?"

"Yes." She had nothing else to do anyway. "First, I need coffee, breakfast, and a shower . . . and not necessarily in that order."

Two hours later, they were both ready to leave and Knox walked her to the foyer with his arm around her waist. "I'm glad you'll be at the new studio today. Crow will have a hard time getting to you there."

"It's not me he's after. He'll probably be in a panic after he was almost tracked. He might strike at you. I know you want him to do that so you can grab him but . . . just be careful, okay?"

"I will if you will," said Knox, helping her slip on her jacket.

Flicking her hair out of her collar, Harper grabbed the lapels of his suit jacket and kissed him. "Then it looks like we'll both be fine."

They then parted ways; she slid into the Audi, and Knox hopped into the Bentley.

"Where to?" asked Levi as he put the car in gear.

Knox fixed his cuffs. "Carla's house."

Soon enough, they were driving into a small cul-de-sac. The children playing in the road quickly moved onto the sidewalk; the ones from his lair quieted at the sight of the Bentley. Levi parked outside the semi-detached suburban house that Carla and Bray had lived in since their sons were young boys.

"I'll be no more than ten minutes," Knox told Levi. "Wait here." Exiting the car, he nodded at the demons from his Force who were parked behind them, watching over Carla. As he strolled up the path, he noticed Delia peeking out of the venetian blinds of the neighboring house. Before Knox could even press the doorbell, the door opened.

"Knox," said Bray a little stiffly. "I'm guessing you're here to see Carla. Come in." Bray guided him through the house into the kitchen. "Would you like a drink?"

"No, thank you."

Bray quickly prepared one for Carla and then led Knox out of the patio doors. The decking boards creaked beneath Knox's feet as he walked with Bray to the table in the middle of the backyard. Feet tucked underneath her, Carla sat on a wrought iron chair with her face angled to the sun, seeming to bask in the warmth. She looked tired yet serene. Personally, Knox didn't know how she could look so relaxed while those damn wind chimes were clinking together and pop music was filtering through a neighbor's window.

Bray handed her a glass. "Here's your ice tea." He then fussed with the umbrella attached to the table, trying to put her in the shade.

"No, Bray," she complained. "It seems like months since I felt the sun on my skin."

He ignored her. "It's hot. You'll burn."

She turned to Knox with a weak smile. The small she-demon didn't look like Harper at all, apart from the dark hair and slightly pointed chin. "Bray hasn't stopped fussing since I woke up. He'd keep me in bed if he could. I needed air. I don't like having to stay in one place too long."

"You look better than I thought you would." Pale and exhausted, but otherwise fine. Knox took the empty seat opposite her. With the exception of the rickety-looking tree house, the backyard was well-tended. The rose bushes were neatly trimmed, the lawn was freshly-mown, and the pool was clean. The lantern patio lights weren't unlike the ones in Jolene's yard. He wondered how both women would feel, knowing they had similar tastes in . . . well, anything. "How do you feel?"

"Lucky to be alive." She sighed. "Crow's far from well."

"I'm still surprised he let you live," said Bray, standing protectively at her side.

"He said killing me wasn't part of his mission." Carla licked her bottom lip as she told Knox. "He doesn't want to kill anyone except you. He's utterly paranoid and his thought processes are all messed up. He's convinced you'll have a powerful child that's pure evil. A child of flames, he kept calling it. He said he saw it in a vision."

"He told Delia something similar," said Knox.

"Nothing I said could convince him that it was all in his head. Nothing." She sipped at her drink. "I wish I could tell you something that would help you find him, but I have no idea where he could be."

"How did he stop you from telepathically calling for help?" Knox asked.

"He did something. It was the strangest feeling. Like he inhaled my psychic energy—not sips of it to drain me, but one huge gulp that made my vision go black and my head pound. I passed out after that. When I woke up, I had this awful pain in my head. Whenever I tried to call for help, the pain got worse. He kept me low on psi-energy so I couldn't recover from it. The worst part was that I could hear Bray and the boys call for me, and I knew how worried they were, but I couldn't answer them."

Bray put a hand on her shoulder. "It's all right. You're home now. You're safe."

Carla took a steadying breath and patted his hand. "I know." She looked at Knox and awkwardly asked, "How is Harper?"

"She's fine," replied Knox. "She was going to come with me to see you, but she believes she won't be welcome here."

"I don't blame her for what happened," said Carla, brow furrowing. "I know Roan does, and I heard what he did. He was just angry and looking for someone to blame. That doesn't make it right, I know."

"No, it doesn't." Which was exactly why he'd been punished for it. "I assume you've noticed your protection detail?"

Carla licked her lips. "You think he'll come back for me?" Her voice shook.

"No. The security measure is more for your peace of mind than anything else."

She swallowed. "I appreciate that."

"You will catch Crow, won't you?" said Bray.

Knox nodded. "Of course."

"And you will punish him?" pressed Bray.

"What I do or don't do will depend on several things." But Knox wasn't going to get into that here and now. He rose to his feet. "I'll leave you to rest, Carla. Take care." He retraced his steps, taking him back inside the house. He'd just reached the front door when he heard shuffling. Turning, he saw Kellen sitting on the stairs.

The teen rubbed the back of his head. "How's Harper?"

Knox raised a brow. "Why not find that out for yourself?"

Kellen lowered his eyes. "She won't want to speak to me."

"Why would you think that?" Knox asked, but Kellen just shook his head and disappeared up the stairs. All right then.

Outside, Knox strolled down the path to the Bentley only to find a nervous-looking Delia standing with Levi.

She offered Knox a quick, half-hearted smile. "I saw your car parked outside. I just wanted to ask if you'd had any luck finding Lawrence."

"It's only a matter of time before we have him, Delia," said Knox. "He can't run forever."

"He's not running, he's hunting," she reminded him.

"True, but I'm nobody's prey."

She nervously rubbed at her thigh. "When you do catch him, you won't hurt him, will you? I know lots of people think he should be killed for what he did to Carla, and I share their anger at what he did. But he's not well. He can be helped, I'm sure he can."

"We won't know what needs to be done until we have him in custody."

"Let's all hope that happens sometime soon." She turned away and headed back to her house.

In the car, Levi switched on the engine. "What time is your business meeting in New York?"

"Soon, so we need to head for the jet." As they drove out of the cul-de-sac, Knox spoke again. "Has the lair been giving Delia a hard time?"

"Yes," replied Levi. "She's been vocal, though not insensitive, about the fact that she thinks Crow's entitled to the same help as other near-rogues get. Not many agree with her."

"It's to her credit that she's not willing to give up on him," said Knox. He'd never give up on Harper, no matter what. Nor would his demon, who was currently sulking about the upcoming business meeting; it found them boring and mundane. The sulking would no doubt continue during the meeting itself. The entity wanted Harper. Wanted to be with her, touch her, breathe her in. It wasn't placated by the knowledge that Knox intended to collect her for dinner.

"We're being followed," announced Levi a few minutes later.

Knox tensed. "Crow?"

"It's not his Corolla; it's an SUV. But he could have stolen another vehicle easily enough."

Knox twisted in his seat to glance out of the blackened rear window, knowing Crow would be unable to see him. The metallic silver SUV was two car spaces behind them. It was hard to get a good look at the driver, especially since he was wearing sunglasses and his cap was pulled low. "Let him get a little closer." He wasn't worried about Crow shooting at them. The windows were bulletproof.

"What are you going to do?" asked Levi.

He wasn't yet sure. His choices were limited while so many humans were around. To take out Crow in the middle of busy traffic would cause a number of accidents, not to mention that Knox would be restricted as to what gifts he could use. Calling on the flames of hell was definitely a no-go.

"We need to lead him away from the main traffic," said Levi.

"I don't think he'll follow. So far, all his attacks have happened in plain view of humans. He did that knowing our demons wouldn't be able to use their most powerful gifts to take him down."

"If he believes he's safer in public, it's likely that he'll conjure a gun any minute now."

"Yes," Knox agreed. Up to now, Crow hadn't used hellfire, just weapons. Each time he'd conjured a gun, humans simply figured he'd had one tucked into his waist. "But it won't do him much good against bulletproof windows. If we try leading him into a less populated area, it's unlikely that he'll follow. Our best chance of grabbing him is if we head to a public place."

"Like where?"

"The very hotel where he's already tried to reach me twice." Knox then telepathed both Keenan and Larkin to inform them of the situation. Having ordered them to linger outside the hotel, ready to take Crow down, he turned to look out the rear window. "He's still with us."

Each time Levi took a turning, Knox checked to be sure that Crow was still following them. At no point did the psi-demon slow down or hesitate as he followed them to the strip.

"The moment I pull up outside the hotel and you step out of the Bentley, he's going to conjure a gun, lower the window, and take a shot at you," said Levi.

"I know. But Keenan positioned snipers on the roof, and Larkin and some of the Force are close. They'll apprehend him."

"Yeah, but will that be before or after he starts shooting?"

"We'll find out soon enough."

Turning the car up the winding road leading to the entrance of the hotel, Levi warned, "Harper will be pissed if you get shot."

Yes, she would. "But she'll be happy that it's over." The Bentley slowed as it reached the entrance.

Suddenly there was a horrible screech of tires.

Knox twisted in his seat to see Crow doing a sharp U-turn and speeding away.

"Fuck, he must have noticed the others or spotted one of the snipers," said Levi.

Jumping out of the Bentley, Knox ordered, *Keenan, Larkin—pursue.* Through his teeth, he cursed, "Dammit. We almost fucking had him."

"It's always that we 'almost' had him, and I'm getting real tired of that," said Levi.

Yeah, so was Knox.

The sentinels and most of the Force spent the rest of the day tracking Crow, but he managed to evade them once again; clearly pre-empting their moves. As such, Knox was pissed and beyond exasperated, especially since he hadn't been able to take his mate to dinner.

Coming home to Harper later on went a long way to improving his mood. Strolling into the living area, he found that she wasn't alone. Jolene and Ciaran were on one sofa while Harper was on the other, legs crossed yoga-style. She was also "revamping" her designer jeans again. The box at her side was filled with lots of appliqués, such as gems, sequins, rhinestones, crystals, beads, sash, and lace—things she often sewed on her clothes.

She'd once told him that it was something she began doing when traveling the world with Lucian, since they were occasionally strapped for money and unable to afford new clothes. It was something she had continued to do because she found enjoyment in personalizing things. He'd noticed that it also seemed to relax her.

She smiled at him. "You're home earlier than I expected."

Yeah, well, he hadn't been able to focus on his work while the Crow incident replayed in his mind over and over.

A furrow appeared between her brows. "Everything okay?"

Holding her by her ponytail, Knox said, "It is now." He bent and gave her a hard kiss.

He got away again, didn't he? she asked.

Yes. Knox had told her about the incident earlier, keeping his promise to contact her immediately if Crow made another move. Standing upright, he nodded at the imps relaxing on the other sofa. "Jolene, Ciaran."

Khloë's brother gave him a brief salute before his eyes quickly slid back to the game he was watching.

"Knox, it's always a pleasure," said Jolene. "I heard that Carla's awake now."

It wasn't me that told her, said Harper.

"You heard correctly," said Knox as he poured himself a gin and tonic at the small bar. "Just where *did* you hear it?"

Jolene gave him an enigmatic smile, but he didn't bother pushing the matter. There was little point in him demanding an answer. Expecting cooperation from an imp would be a pointless and exasperating exercise.

Settling on the sofa beside Harper, he asked Jolene, "Any luck tracking Crow?" She looked surprised by the question. "I didn't think for one minute that you wouldn't attempt to find him, given that he could be a danger to Harper."

Jolene didn't bother denying it, which he respected. "He's elusive. I'd admire it if I wasn't so intent on getting hold of him."

"He's mine, Jolene," Knox told her, voice hard. "If you find him before I do, you hand him over to me."

"Knox, there's no helping him now. Even if you pulled him back from the edge of madness, your lair would still despise him for what he did and Carla's family would demand vengeance. Contrary to popular belief, I don't think you like to kill for killing's sake. Let us deal with this."

"In many ways you're right. But he's one of my demons. That makes him my responsibility."

She sniffed. "And you call my granddaughter stubborn."

"She *is* stubborn."

Jolene grinned. "I know. It makes me so proud." *She'll tell you that she's fine, but she's not. She still feels bad for Carla.*

I know. And he hated that there was nothing he could do about it.

She'll also pretend it doesn't hurt her that Kellen isn't speaking with her, but it does.

I know that, too.

Yes, I suppose you do. She'll fight you on it, but be here for her. And don't let Roan take it out on her any more than he already has.

You know better than to think you need to tell me these things.
He knew Harper well.

Harper sighed at her grandmother. "Let me guess . . . you told
him to be here for me and to keep Roan at bay."

Knox nearly burst out laughing. His mate was even more
astute than the woman opposite her.

Jolene looked at her steadily. "Actually, no, I told him just
how many weird and wonderful methods of torture I will use on
Carla if she blames you for her ordeal."

Harper smiled. "You're like the best liar *ever*."

"Well, thank you." Jolene got to her feet. "I have to leave now.
Don't forget dinner at my house on Sunday."

Knox nodded. Family dinner at Jolene Wallis's house was a
hectic experience. Lots of people were always clustered around
the table on stools and mismatched chairs. There wasn't a single
bit of order, but Knox didn't mind that because there was also
no pretentiousness. Just a large number of people talking, joking,
and laughing.

Looking reluctant to leave while the game was still on, Ciaran
nonetheless said his goodbyes to Harper and Knox and then
teleported Jolene out of the house.

Harper turned to Knox. "What do you think spooked Crow
and made him race off in a hurry?"

"I don't know. Maybe he saw a member of the Force. Or maybe
he's just so paranoid that the whole thing felt wrong to him." He
took a swig of his gin and tonic. "We almost had him, Harper.
Almost. Again," he added, unable to keep the agitation out of
his tone.

Thinking a change of subject might help calm him, Harper
asked, "How's Carla?"

"Better than I'd expected her to be." He recited his conversation with Carla.

"It's nice to know she doesn't blame me," said Harper. "Knox, he called the baby a child of flames."

"That doesn't have to mean anything."

She frowned. "How can you say that?"

Knox curled his hand around her chin. "Plenty of demons speculate that I can call on the flames of hell. He could have simply meant a child that can *call* on the flames. Don't make the mistake of expecting anything Crow says to make sense. It won't. He's living in a complete fantasy world right now."

Harper nodded. "I still say it's spooky."

"I also spoke briefly with Kellen." He quickly relayed the short conversation. "Why would he believe you won't wish to speak with him?"

She shrugged. "I haven't a clue. But for him to say that, it has me wondering . . . what did he do?"

CHAPTER THIRTEEN

———◦◉◦———

A few days later, Harper was unlocking the door of what was effectively her old studio, despite that she wouldn't be opening the new one until two days' time. Most of the things they wanted to take with them had already been moved to the new Urban Ink. As for—

"Harper! Harper!"

Recognizing the voice of her ex, she rolled her eyes.

"Harper, what the hell's happening?" demanded Royce.

She glanced around, confused. "You'll need to be more specific."

"I heard you're closing this place down. Why? It's a successful business. You love your job."

"Well, I don't really need to work now that I've shacked up with a billionaire."

He snorted. "I'm not buying that. I know you. Part of our problem when we were dating is that you're too independent. I don't believe for one second that you'd live off another person. No way."

He was right, of course. "Royce, go home."

"Has someone bought it from under you? Are you having money problems?"

She shot him an incredulous look. "While living with a billionaire?"

"I doubt you let him pay for much or that you're comfortable accepting anything expensive from him."

Again, he was right. "Is there a point to this conversation? Because try as a might, I can't find one. None of this is your concern."

Tanner got out of the car, expression sober. "Harper, would it bother you if I slapped him around a little?"

"Nope." Stepping inside, she closed the door on Royce's face and gave him a cheery wave. Confident that Tanner would chase him away, she grabbed the pile of mail from the floor and flipped through the envelopes as she headed to her office. Bills. Bills. Shit-mail. Inside the office, she placed the envelopes on the desk and opened one of the drawers. She needed to pick up a few things and—

The breath exploded out of her lungs as a large body crashed into her back and thick arms locked around her. Before she could even think about reacting, a long piece of cloth was wrapped around her hands—binding them together and covering her palms.

"I wouldn't think about using that hypnotic tone you have to manipulate me," said a scratchy voice. "I'd hate to have to conjure a gun and shoot your brains out."

Crow. Well, shit. Her demon went frantic and a dark, protective power gathered inside her and rushed to her hands, prickling the pads of her fingers. Sadly, she wasn't able to use it right then.

She went to telepathically call Knox for help, but then she

paused with an inward frown. Crow *had* to know there was a strong possibility she could send out a telepathic call for help, considering telepathy was a pretty standard ability for demons, but he hadn't warned her not to do it.

Of course it was worth noting that the guy wasn't exactly firing on all cylinders, so he might not have thought of that. But what if he *wanted* her to call Knox for help? What if he was using her to get to Knox? After all, Crow's attempts to get to him had failed, so maybe he figured he'd get *Knox* to come to *him*.

Well, Harper would be damned if she'd help Crow spring a trap, but she did need a little assistance here. She could call Tanner, but he'd most likely summon Knox irrespective of her wishes. She needed to keep Crow distracted while she figured out what to do. "I heard about your vision."

"Did you?"

"I also heard you're bordering on rogue."

"So you think I'm suffering from delusions?" He sounded amused by that.

"You have to admit, even if only to yourself, that it's possible."

"I know what I saw," he snapped. "Killing you won't stop it from happening. If you die, he will just have the child with another. The only safe future is one without Knox."

Well, that wasn't a future Harper or her demon was interested in letting happen.

"I can't let that child be born. I won't fail my mission. I was chosen for a reason."

She frowned at the word "chosen." "Someone told you to do this?"

"They believe me. They've seen the future too; they've seen the child. A child of flames."

Her skin chilled at that.

"Evil. Conscienceless. None of us would stand a chance against it. Even Knox wouldn't be able to control it. This future cannot come to fruition."

Conscious that she needed to act fast, Harper glanced around the room, searching for inspiration. Nothing. *Fuck.*

"Call to Knox."

So she'd been right; this was a trap. "I can't use the phone without my hands."

He chuckled. The sound grated on her nerves. "Don't insult my intelligence. Call to him. It shouldn't take him long to arrive in the Bentley. In the meantime, we'll stay right here."

Not a chance. "Why did you hurt Delia? She just wanted to help you."

His hold on her wrists tightened. "Stop trying to distract me and do what I told you to do. And don't think about lying to me. I'll know if you don't call him. Want to know how? Because the moment Knox realizes you're in danger, he'll send Tanner inside. But it's okay, I'm ready for the hellhound. I have an arsenal of weapons at all times."

Meaning he'd conjure whatever weapon he wanted and take Tanner out of the equation. Not gonna happen. "If I call Knox, he'll kill you."

"No, he'll trade his life for yours."

"Knox wouldn't do that. He's your Prime; you know how merciless he is."

"Yes, he's merciless. But you're his mate. He cares for you. *Now call to—*"

Harper snapped out her wings, taking him off-guard and making him stumble backwards. She shook off the T-shirt binding her hands and whirled on him. He shackled her wrists before she could touch him . . . and then there was a tug inside her chest and a dizzy feeling swept over her. *Oh, the bastard.*

"Call to him!"

"Fuck you!"

Squeezing her wrists so hard she wouldn't be surprised if something snapped, he shook her. "Call to him!"

Her demon lunged to the fore. "Release me."

He sucked in more psi-energy, startling her demon into retreating. *"Do it."*

"Fuck. You." Harper's voice was now as unsteady as her legs. Lethargy swept over her, leaving her feeling weak. No, she wasn't going to go out like this. Harper sharply twisted one wrist and freed her hand.

"No—"

She slammed her palm on his forehead. And as the power poured out of her and into him, she fell to her knees. The darkness gathering around her vision was closing in on her, but she forced her eyes to stay open; watching as Crow shook and howled.

Tanner! The strain of the telepathic cry made her collapse onto her stomach. Darkness beckoned. She fought it hard.

Tanner burst into the room just as Crow conjured a gun. The first shot went wide, but the second made Tanner stagger back with a grunt.

She tried to crawl toward him, but her body went limp and she felt herself fading away. Using the last bit of psi-energy she could muster, she called out, *Knox . . . my old office.* Then it all went dark.

It was pain that woke her. A draining, excruciating, white-hot pain lancing through her head. God, it felt like someone was using a sword to carve her skull in two. Nauseous, she clamped her lips shut, afraid she'd balk.

Harper knew she wasn't alone. She could smell Knox. Could

feel his eyes on her. She could also feel his rage brushing the edges of her consciousness. The same rage was thickening the air and weighing on her chest. It made her demon stiffen, wary.

Harper forced her eyes open, wincing as the light stung her eyes and sent more pain knifing through her head. She gritted her teeth against the urge to cry out. At that moment, pain was the least of her worries. Over six feet of raw power was standing over the bed, hands casually stuffed in his pockets . . . and exuding a soul-gripping fury that made her hackles rise.

His face was blank, but his dark eyes were diamond hard and sparked with anger. A frisson of fear scuttled down her spine. It always spooked her when he was so unnaturally composed. Mate or not, she *never* allowed herself to forget that she was dealing with the ultimate predator; an archdemon, a creature born to cause havoc and destruction.

Clearing her throat, she sat upright, distantly noting that her wings had melted into her back. "Is Tanner okay?"

For a moment, Knox was silent. "He's healing." His tone was even, but she wasn't mistaking that for calmness.

"And Crow?"

"We've detained him." Knox's eyes narrowed. "This is the second time you failed to call me while you were in danger." The words were as lethal as any blade.

"I *did* call you . . . eventually."

"Yes, but by then Tanner had already called me."

Refusing to back down in the face of his anger or power, she lifted her chin. "Look—"

"You *promised* me that if you ever needed my help, you would call."

"You're right, I did."

"But you didn't do it."

Nope, and she didn't regret it. "Crow wasn't interested in hurting me. He wanted to hurt you. It was a trap."

His nostrils flared. "You think I don't know that?"

She frowned. "If you know that, why are you mad at me?"

"He. Could. Have. Killed. You."

She almost shivered at the silken menace in those softly spoken words. "He didn't want me dead, he wanted *you* dead."

"But he'd have had no problem killing you."

"Not until I'd served my purpose, which was to call *you*. By not doing that, I saved us both." The air cooled as his eyes bled to black. And she saw that the demon was exponentially pissed.

"You were drained to the point of unconsciousness," said the demon, its tone cold and detached as always. Still, she could sense its rage. "How is that saving yourself?" it challenged.

"Drained, but not dead," she pointed out.

"Drained, dead—neither is acceptable to me." The demon then retreated, and Knox was glaring at her yet again. "Nor are they acceptable to me."

"Well, *your* death isn't acceptable to *me*." He wasn't the only one in their relationship who got to be protective. "He didn't want me dead, he only wanted *you* dead."

"And yet, he shot Tanner ... and he shot to kill. Or did you forget that?"

"Tell me, if I'd done as he asked, what do you think would have happened? Huh? Do you think you would have just destroyed him on the spot and we'd have walked away with a carefree whistle? He had hold of me. That alone would have made you hesitate to act—something he was counting on and had planned for. That hesitation would have gotten you killed."

"It might not have happened that way."

"I wasn't going to risk it."

"Which almost got you killed."

She shoved a hand through her hair. He just wasn't hearing her at all. "What do you want me to say? That I'm sorry? That I'll never do it again?"

He scoffed. "Why would I ask you to promise me you'll never do it again? Apparently you don't keep your word."

She shot to her feet so fast she swayed. "You motherfucking son of a bitch."

"Sit down before you fall down."

Ignoring that, she scowled. "You're honestly saying that bullshit to me?" He would actually question her sense of integrity?

"You made me a promise. You didn't keep it."

"Oh yes, I'm just the worst mate ever for wanting to protect you. How dare I," she mocked.

He took an aggressive step toward her. "I don't need you to protect me. I don't *want* you to protect me. I want you to live."

"Do I look like a fucking apparition to you? I *am* alive, asshole! And if you don't want me to protect you, ask me if I give a shit! I'm your mate! That's what mates do! And protecting the people I care about is who I am!"

"And that protective streak makes you reckless," he snapped.

"Says the person who called on the flames of fucking hell and destroyed a house of dark practitioners to protect their mate! Yeah, you don't get to judge me on this one, Thorne."

"I do get to be pissed that you made me a promise but didn't keep it."

"You're pissed because I won't fall in line with what you want. I'm my own person and I've never pretended to be anything else. People like Belinda would change to suit someone, but that's not me. It will *never* be me. I protected you tonight and, if necessary,

I'll do it again. If you can't accept that, then you're not accepting *me*. And if that's how it is, say so now and end what we have before we drive each other completely insane."

He closed his eyes and released a frustrated breath.

"Well? Can you accept it or not?" Because she wasn't going to have this argument every time she did what she had to do to protect him. He had to understand that she wouldn't change, and he had to make peace with it.

A few moments later, he opened his eyes. "I have to speak to the sentinels."

Her stomach rolled. His failure to answer her question told her all she needed to know.

"You should rest and—"

"Get out," she snarled.

His brows shot up. "Excuse me?"

"Get the fuck *out*." Instead, the cheeky fucker moved toward her. Her demon leapt to the surface and hissed, "Don't." He wisely halted. "You won't get an apology," it told him. "Neither she nor I are sorry for what we did or who we are." Harper took back the reins and scowled at him. "And if you don't like it, fuck you!"

With that, she stormed into the bathroom and slammed the door shut. Breathing hard, she leaned back against it. Footsteps headed her way . . . but then the sound of them faded as he left the bedroom.

Grams, I need to get out of here.

Knox prowled out of the bedroom, more enraged than he'd been in a long while. He'd been in a meeting with Levi, Keenan, and Larkin when he'd received Tanner's frantic call. Fear clogging his throat, he'd pyroported himself and his sentinels to the reception area of the studio. He hadn't needed to hear Harper call out to him; he'd been able to hear the struggle coming from the office. Barging inside to find her on the floor; eyes closed, not moving ...

Dead.

The word had bounced around his skull until he felt her pulse with his fingers. Relief had rushed through his veins, but it hadn't eased the fear and rage heating his blood and sending his demon into a frenzy. The insidious emotions lingered even now. It all curdled in his stomach, twisting and tugging at his gut, and tormenting his demon.

All Knox wanted was for her to be safe. He *needed* her to be safe. He'd trusted that she'd keep her promise and call him if necessary. Trusted that her need to take care of herself wouldn't drive her to put herself in too much danger.

He'd been wrong to do so, apparently. And, yes, it hurt that she'd broken her promise. That pain was keeping the bubbling rage alive.

Striding into the living area, he found Levi, Keenan, and Larkin sat on the sofas, looking the epitome of awkward. They'd obviously overheard the argument. "Tanner still recovering well?" Knox asked.

Levi nodded. "He'll be fully healed soon."

"Good." Knox crossed his arms. "What did Crow have to say?" He had every intention of speaking to him when he could be sure his inner demon wouldn't rise and destroy Crow and whatever stood in its way.

Not that Knox would regret the kill. He wouldn't at all. In fact, answering the need for vengeance that was hammering at him would go a long way into making him feel a whole lot better. But when Bray and others had called for Crow's death to avenge Carla, Knox had refused; had argued that Crow deserved the same help that any near-rogue was entitled to.

He'd lose the respect of his lair if he acted differently to avenge his mate.

"Plenty," replied Keenan. "He was more than happy to share his belief that you needed to be destroyed. He didn't shut up about it until Doc injected him with the liquid form of his medication. Now he's sitting in the corner of his cell, rocking and muttering to himself."

"He's refusing to take his pills," Levi added. "He said we're trying to poison him. He's quite sure the Doc is part of some conspiracy to see him dead."

"He's not afraid," said Larkin. "He says he was chosen for this mission; he's positive that the person who selected him to do their work will ensure he's freed. Obviously he's deluded himself into believing someone 'sent' him." She sighed. "I'm not sure he can be helped. He seems too far gone to me."

"Bray and Roan want to confront him," began Levi, "but I denied them access until you okay it. Roan, being the obstinate little bastard that he is, probably would have pushed it if he wasn't still in pain after his last punishment."

"Well, now Roan can vent at the true person at fault for his mother's suffering instead of blaming Harper," said Keenan.

"Onto another important subject," began Knox, "what did you learn about Dario?"

"Exactly what you heard," said Larkin. "He's walled himself up in his castle and he hasn't left it for months. We spoke to plenty of demons from his lair. Most believe he's genuinely grieving the death of someone, though they're not sure who."

"There's nothing to suggest he's building an army," said Keenan. "It just seems to be conjecture, but no one knows where the rumor started, just like no one knows where the rumor began that he's turning rogue."

"Most don't believe either rumor," added Larkin.

Without proof, Knox wouldn't believe them either.

Levi got to his feet. "Unless you need anything else, we'll take off."

"We'll talk again tomorrow," Knox told them.

Keenan and Larkin left the room, but Levi lingered at the doorway and turned to Knox. "I couldn't help but overhear what got said upstairs . . . go easy on Harper."

"Easy?" Knox echoed in disbelief.

"There are many things you'll get Harper to compromise on," said Levi. "But ignoring the urge to protect people she cares about is *not* something she'll agree to do—not even for you."

Jaw tight, Knox said, "You were right there in that office with me, Levi. You saw her on that floor." Pale. Unmoving. His demon had lost its fucking mind.

"Yeah. And like you, I panicked. And I was angry with her," Levi admitted. "So fucking angry. But then I reminded myself who I was dealing with. You know her better than anyone. You know that underneath that hard shell is a soft heart that feels deeply."

He did know that. He loved that about her.

"She's protective to the core. You can't expect a person like that to put someone they care for in danger."

"I can expect her to value her own life."

"She does value it. But she also values yours, and clearly she values your safety more than she does her own. That's a special thing, Knox."

Yes, it was, but it didn't change one very simple fact. "Her safety is more important than mine."

"To you, but not to her. Tonight, she only did what *you* would have done in her position."

Fuck if he wasn't right.

"She's the best thing that ever happened to you, Knox. Don't fuck this up," Levi called over his shoulder as he left.

Raking a hand through his hair, Knox sighed. He'd messed up. Royally. And now he needed to fix it. He headed upstairs and into the bedroom. Harper still hadn't come out of the bathroom.

He wrapped his knuckles on the door. "Open up, Harper." Nothing. "Baby, we need to talk." Still nothing. Knowing that barging in wouldn't earn him any points, he said, "You have until the count of five to open the door or I'm coming in, baby. One. Two. Three. Four. Five."

But she didn't come out. *Stubborn through and through.* It had to make him weird that he liked that about her. He turned the knob and walked inside . . . only to freeze as he found the room empty. "Fuck."

Jolene placed two steaming mugs on the square coasters of the mahogany coffee table. "Drink your tea, sweetheart. It'll relax you." She then sat on the couch beside Martina and crossed her legs. "Feeling any calmer?"

Holding a soft cushion to her chest, Harper settled deeper into the overstuffed armchair. "Not really." She'd tucked a fleecy blanket around her legs, just as she'd often done as a child. When she'd visited Jolene over the years, she'd curled up in that chair many times—sometimes with a book, sometimes snacks, while she watched a movie with her cousins.

She loved her grandmother's house. Loved the welcoming feel of it. It always smelled of cookies, coffee, and lavender. Tonight, there were also a hint of the light rain coming through a partially open window.

It wasn't a quiet house, since her relatives were always waltzing in and out for one reason or another. The kids in particular showed up a lot, hoping Jolene had made her famous cookies.

But even though it was a constant hub of activity, it was relaxing. Maybe because it was so homey with all the throw cushions, blankets, and the earthy colors. There were framed photos, keepsakes, and knickknacks everywhere. Like Harper, Jolene treasured memories.

"You know why he's angry," said Jolene.

"Sure I do. But I'll be damned if I apologize for what I did." Or for being who she was.

"I wouldn't expect you to. But imagine being in his position." Jolene picked up her coffee. "Imagine you received a weak telepathic call from him. Imagine you then arrived at his office to find him sprawled on the floor, not moving. Tanner's been shot, and Crow has a gun. How would you react?"

In a word, badly.

"Knox was scared, sweetheart." Jolene blew over the rim of her mug. "Now, sure, he knew you were alive because the anchor bond was still in place. But I'll bet he wasn't thinking of that when he saw you lying there. Panic and fear probably took over."

Harper could understand that, could even sympathize. But it didn't erase how much his words hurt. Her demon was imagining lots of wonderful ways it could make him suffer. "It still doesn't give him or his demon the right to be an asshole."

"No, it doesn't," Jolene agreed. "Which was why I sent Ciaran to teleport you here. That comment about you not being someone who keeps their word was a shitty thing to say."

Martina nodded, painting her long acrylic nails red. "People say things they don't mean when they're angry, but that's no excuse."

"It pisses me off that he said that," Ciaran told Harper, his eyes glued to the TV as he lounged on the reclining chair; beer in hand, remote controls on his lap. "But I don't believe he really thinks that of you."

"Neither do I," said Jolene.

Harper tightened her hold on the cushion. "Maybe. Maybe not. But if he can't accept that I'll do what I have to do to protect him, consequences be damned, then he doesn't accept me."

Jolene sipped at her coffee. "He accepts you, Harper. He just doesn't know what to do with you. He's used to things and people being under his control."

Yeah, she knew that. "I warned him over and over that he'd never control me."

"Maybe some really, really dumb part of him thought it wasn't true," suggested Ciaran.

"Men," scoffed Martina. "You're attacked, but does he hug you? Kiss you? Reassure you that you're fine? No, he behaves like a dick."

Ciaran tore his eyes away from the wall-mounted TV. "That's not because he's a man," he said, offended on behalf of his gender. "It's because he isn't good at handling fear."

Whatever. Harper sighed. "Let's just talk about something else."

Jolene patted her hand. "Of course."

Harper leaned her head on the cushion, listening to the kids laughing as they jumped in the puddles in the front yard. Each time she heard a car approaching, she panicked; wondering if Knox had come for her. But then the car would drive by, and her heart rate would slow down.

"I'm glad they've caught Crow," said Jolene.

That had Harper thinking. "Something he said bothered me."

"Knox or Crow?" asked Martina.

"Crow," Harper replied.

Martina blew on her nails to dry the paint. "You mean the demon baby thing?" She said it with no concern whatsoever.

"No. He said he was on a mission; that someone told him to do this."

"He's suffering from delusions, sweetheart," said Jolene.

"I know." Harper lifted her mug and took a sip of her tea. "It was just something about the way he said it. What if he didn't have a true vision? What if someone manipulated his mental state and put the idea in his head?"

"Crow isn't even close to a real match for Knox," said Ciaran, frowning. "It doesn't make sense that someone would try to kill Knox using a mentally unstable demon who's not powerful enough to really be a threat."

Martina nodded. "It does seem like a rather bad plan."

"So poor it wouldn't be worth trying," added Jolene. "Believing he was 'given' the mission is part of his delusion."

That made sense. And yet, Harper wasn't convinced.

She tensed as she heard another car approaching. Not just approaching, slowing down. *Please, no, don't be him.* It could just be a neighbor's car, she thought as it came to a stop. Or it could be someone visiting one of the neighbors. There was really no need to panic . . . even though the sound of a door slamming shut was followed by footsteps coming up the gravelly path. It could be Beck. Or one of her cousins. Or—

The doorbell peeled.

"That's probably Knox," said Jolene. "I take it you don't wish to see him."

Harper shook her head. "I'm too tired for him, Grams." A girl needed to be at her sharpest when dealing with someone like Knox Thorne. Right then, she was emotionally drained and way too angry to have an actual conversation with him.

"Sending him away won't be easy," Ciaran warned.

Jolene rose from the couch, determination etched into every line of her face. "No, but it will be done." Her heels click-clacked on the hardwood floor as she strode out into the hallway and to the front door. "Well, hello, Knox."

Even from the living area, Harper could hear his response perfectly.

"Jolene," he greeted. "I've come for Harper."

"Yes," said Jolene, "I gathered that."

A sigh. "If you're not going to invite me in, send her out."

"She said she'd follow me to the door, but it seems she hasn't. Maybe we shouldn't be surprised, since she's not a woman of her word."

Harper's mouth quirked, in spite of her dull mood.

Jolene spoke again. "It might be a good idea if you give her some space." It wasn't a suggestion; it was an instruction. And it no doubt made him bristle.

"I'm not leaving without her, Jolene."

"Well, I can assure you right now that you won't leave *with* her," stated Jolene, voice hardening. "You promised me she would be safe with you. You promised that you wouldn't hurt her."

"I'd never hurt her," Knox immediately responded. *Harper, come to me.*

Harper snorted. He couldn't be serious.

"There are different types of pain, Knox," said Jolene. "You didn't hurt her physically, which is the only reason you're breathing. But you hurt her heart—something you should have protected with everything in you."

A pause. "Jolene, this is between me and Harper."

"No, it isn't, because she doesn't want to see you."

Harper, unless you want your grandmother and me fighting, come to the door.

Cursing to herself, Harper stalked out of the room and down the hallway.

"It would seem she does keep her word after all," Jolene said to him.

Harper came to a stop behind Jolene, and his gaze boldly locked with hers. Her chest hurt just looking at him. He was so achingly good-looking. Living, breathing seduction. And a total asshole. Her demon glared at him, upper lip curled.

He held out his hand. "Come on."

She shook her head. "Go home." Looking at him was pissing her off all over again.

Harper—

Just. Leave.

Knox inwardly cursed. His mate was a lot of things, but not cold or distant. At that moment, she seemed both those things. The short physical distance between them might as well have been an ocean. She was lost to him right then. And he didn't know how to bring her back.

He *did* know that it would be a lot fucking easier if her family backed off and let them deal with it. Jolene, however, still stood there like a sentry. Martina and Ciaran were at Harper's back, scowling at him. What's more, other demons were gathering in the yard, watching with shrewd eyes.

That was the thing about imps. You took on one; you took on them all.

Not that Knox was worried. He could kill them all with minimal effort. He wouldn't, of course, since they were Harper's family. But a display of power would serve as a decent enough warning to make them back off. And he would have made such a display if two little girls hadn't dashed into the house and coiled themselves around Harper's legs ... which was no doubt *why* they'd done that. Imps of all ages were as cunning as they came.

His demon growled at the scene. It wanted its mate. Wanted to smash down the wall she'd erected between them. Wanted to grab her and haul her home. But Knox knew better than to even attempt to touch her right then. Besides, he'd messed up enough already. So he sighed and said to her, "I'll be back in the morning. Be ready."

Harper stayed where she was as Knox prowled to the Bentley, where Levi was waiting. The reaper gave her a "take pity on him" look, but she ignored it.

"I really didn't expect him to leave," said Martina as the car disappeared down the street.

"He's respecting her wishes," said Jolene. "There's hope for him yet."

CHAPTER FOURTEEN

———◆———

Silky, fiery heat licked at Harper's skin. It shocked a gasp out of her and tugged at her consciousness, pulling her out of her sleep.

"Shush, baby."

Her demon snarled at the sound of his voice, making the memory of the argument blast to the front of Harper's mind. Her eyes snapped open, and she glared at the fucking asshole holding her possessively against him on their—no, *his*—bed. "Are you kidding me?" He had to be. Or he'd lost all sense of self-preservation, whichever.

"You didn't think I'd really spend the night away from you, did you?" Knox had waited until she was asleep before taking her from Jolene's spare bedroom.

"If I'd wanted to come here, I'd have left with you!" Growling, she struggled against him. She was getting out of there. She was going back to Jolene's house. She was—

Knox rolled her onto her back and used his psychic hands to

pin her wrists above her head. "I fucked up." She stilled, so he continued. "I know that. But you didn't call me, baby. You didn't trust me to protect us both."

"You should have just stuck with 'I fucked up.'" The rest canceled out his admission and made Harper want to punch him in the face, which would be mega hard while she couldn't move her hands. And, seriously, who would ever be dumb enough to subdue someone they had *majorly* pissed off?

"I fucked up," he repeated.

"Yeah, you did," she clipped. And he needn't think that was enough to make her forgive him.

"You weren't moving, Harper. You didn't look like you were breathing. For a few seconds, I thought you were dead. My demon went ape-shit. If I hadn't felt your pulse beating against my fingers, everyone in that office would have been dead within seconds." He would have lost every ounce of control.

The pain in his tone took a tiny bit of the wind from Harper's sails. Her demon, however, had no sympathy for him whatsoever.

"Even when I realized you *were* alive, I was still so frantic that I would have killed Crow right then if my priority hadn't been getting you someplace safe, far away from him." Knox combed his fingers through her hair. "At that point, it didn't matter to me that killing him would be the wrong thing to do; that I would have been undermining myself to my own lair if I'd done for you what I wouldn't do for another. All I could think was that you could have died."

"I get that you were scared. I do. But if you think that gives you a free pass to be a shithead and question my integrity, you're out of your mind."

The stubborn jut of her chin almost made him laugh. She was just plain cute when she was mad. "When you first asked me to tell you immediately if Crow made any moves, I assured you that I would. But I didn't. I waited until later that day to tell you. I saw that as protecting you—I didn't want to fuck up your day by delivering shitty news smack bam in the middle of it. Even though you understood my intentions were good, you were pissed that I didn't tell you straight away, weren't you?"

Harper could see what he was getting at: although he knew her intentions were good when she didn't call out to him, he couldn't help being hurt that she'd gone back on her word. "Okay, so I didn't keep my promise. I regret that I was *in* a situation where I chose to do that, but I don't regret that I chose to do it." She wasn't going to lure him into a trap.

"Just as I couldn't regret that I'd delayed giving you bad news. In that sense, neither of us were in the wrong. We both had good intentions when we made those decisions, but we still hurt each other when we did."

Yeah, okay, that was true. "You didn't answer my question earlier."

Knowing she was referring to what she'd asked him just before she left, Knox said, "Of course I accept you as you are. I *want* you exactly as you are. You seem to think I want to control you. I like that I don't. I like that I can't. I like that you have your own mind and you demand that I respect that. And I *do* respect it. But, baby, that doesn't mean I'll always like your choices. I'm certain that works both ways."

Harper sighed. He was right again, which was unfortunate because he was taking major chunks out of her "you're an ass-hole" argument.

"We both have very strong personalities," Knox continued. "Neither of us are the type to bend to please others. That means we'll sometimes butt heads. It means I'll hurt you when I don't mean to, and vice versa. We have to learn to move past things, Harper."

"I don't know *how* we move past this. I will never change."

"I know that, but you're missing that I don't want you to." He lightly traced her collarbone with his fingers. "I'll have to accept that you're willing to put yourself in danger to protect me. And you'll have to accept that I'll be pissed and react badly if you do."

"Reacting so badly that you say mean shit—"

"Was wrong," he finished. "I apologized for that."

"Actually, you didn't."

Realizing she was right, Knox curled his hand under her chin as he spoke. "I said things I didn't mean, I hurt you, and for that I'm sorry. But I can't be sorry for being angry that you took Crow on without me." He wasn't going to insult them both by saying otherwise just to placate her.

"And I can't be sorry for not luring you into a trap."

His mouth quirked a little. "So very stubborn."

"And so very proud of it."

Knox swept his thumb over her bottom lip. "I was angrier at myself than I was at you."

She frowned. "Why?"

"I'm your mate and your anchor. I'm supposed to protect you." He rested his forehead on hers. "I hate that I was sat in a meeting with my sentinels, having no idea that you were somewhere in pain, being attacked." He placed his hand over her heart and let the beat of it soothe him. "You underestimate what you mean to me. You always have. I need you safe. Well. With me."

That was sort of sweet. She wasn't good with "sweet." "If I'm ever attacked again, I'd rather have a comforting hug and a 'how are you feeling' than be yelled at."

Knox slipped his arms under her back and hugged her to him. "How are you feeling?"

"Less pissed at you."

Knox didn't relax, knowing he wasn't out of the woods yet. "How about your demon?"

"It wants to bitch slap you. And I mean, like, *really* hard."

He'd thought as much. "My demon wants to snuggle you and make you feel better."

Okay, that softened her demon a little.

He kissed the hollow of her throat. "We've never had a major argument before. It was bound to happen at some point. And now we deal with it. We start as we mean to go on. When I fuck up, I'll admit it. I'll apologize. If you need space while you work through some of your anger, fine. It won't be easy to give it to you, but I will. In return, you don't leave in a huff. And you don't sleep anywhere but right beside me, where you belong."

"I'm not sure you're in a position to use that demanding tone with me."

His mouth curved at her haughty look. "How would you have felt if I walked out on you, baby? How would you feel if you came to find me, hoping to work things out, and you saw that I was gone?"

Like utter shit. She blew out a long breath and then agreed, "I won't walk out next time. I'm not saying I won't walk away to cool down, but I won't leave."

He nodded, satisfied. "That's my girl."

"Can you free my hands now?" The wicked curve to his mouth made Harper tense. "What?"

He fingered the bobbly white T-shirt she was wearing. It smelled of her. "This an old shirt of yours?"

Harper nodded. "Jolene kept it for me." He hummed against

her neck as he gathered the ends of it. "Now wait a minute, Thorne—"

"It needs to come off. I want to be able to touch and taste every part of you."

"I'm still mad at you." Well, only a little.

"I know that." He rubbed his nose against hers. "But you're holding onto that anger just for the sake of holding onto it."

Damn him for being right.

"Let it go," he whispered into the hollow beneath her ear. "I know I hurt you. I know I messed up. But now I'm going to make it up to you."

"Oh yeah?" she said as he peeled up the shirt. He released her hands to whip it off, and then her wrists were once more pinned above her head. "Hey, no—" She cut herself off when he rose from the bed and shed his own shirt, exposing broad shoulders and a solid very lick-able chest. She loved the ripples of his abs. Loved tracing them with her fingers and tongue. But, yeah, that wouldn't be happening until he freed her hands.

He removed the rest of his clothes, and she clenched her thighs at the sight of his cock, hard and ready. His body hummed with raw power, and it was a total aphrodisiac for her demon, who had let go of its anger; placated by his apology. So Harper did the same. He'd made a mistake, but he'd apologized. And she could tell that he meant it. And, hello, he was really hot.

Naked, Knox loomed over her with his hands braced either side of her head. He swiped his tongue over her bottom lip. "When I first met you, I wondered if your mouth was really this shade or if you were wearing cherry lipstick." The shade was as natural as her coal-black lashes. She raised her mouth to his, lips parted. He wanted to delve and taste and take. He would. But not yet.

He traced the outline of her mouth with the tip of his tongue. He loved the shape of it, loved how plush and soft it was. Loved the feel of it wrapped tight around his cock. "All mine." He kissed the curve of her mouth. Suckled on her upper lip. Tugged on the fleshy part of her lower lip with his teeth just hard enough to leave a mark. She licked over it, soothing the sting. He let the tip of his tongue slide out and briefly glide against hers.

She growled. "Getting cranky here, Thorne."

He smiled. "Ah, my kitten's back."

She was about to ask what the hell that meant when his mouth closed over hers. His tongue sank inside and tangled with hers. He didn't just kiss her, he consumed her. Licking, biting, sucking ... pretty much taking possession of her entire mouth. His hand slid into her hair and his fingers kneaded her scalp. Oh God, that shouldn't have felt so good, but it did. She pretty much melted into the mattress.

"Silk has nothing on your hair."

Harper shivered at that deep, almost rumbly whisper. She struggled to free her arms, but those psychic hands just held her tighter. Her pussy clenched. A part of her liked being held down, but she wanted to touch him. "Free my hands." He slowly shook his head, and an icy thumb circled her pulse on her wrist.

"I think I'll leave them where they are for now." Knox sucked on the hollow beneath her ear, right where he'd left the small mark that said she was anchored; that there was a demon out there who would kill to protect her. She'd left a similar mark on him. Knowing she loved it, he spoke into her ear. "Don't ever think I don't accept all of you."

His warm breath blew over her ear, making the hairs on her nape stand on end. "Knox—"

"I'll always want you exactly as you are." He massaged her inner thighs, making her slick folds open and close. The scent of her need rose up and filled his lungs, and he growled. His cock throbbed painfully. He needed to be in her, but he also needed to drum something into her pretty little head. So he repeated, "Exactly as you are."

Harper inhaled sharply as he spread her legs wide and the cool air hit her pussy. He gave her his weight, settling his cock over her slick folds, just as his tongue curled around her nipple. She arched into his mouth and ground her clit against his cock, needing *some* measure of relief. She was wet and restless, and he seemed happy to ignore that.

"So many times I've been in a business meeting or on a conference call, and all I've been able to think about is getting home and pinning you against the wall while I take you." He bit into the side of her breast, renewing a mark that had faded.

"We can totally do that now," she said hopefully.

"I want to explore first."

Harper didn't have the patience for that, but she knew better than to argue with him. He was sadistic enough to deny her an orgasm if she didn't let him have his way. His hands were firm but his fingers were feather-light as they moved over her skin, playing with all kinds of nerve endings and sending feel-good chemicals racing through her. When he touched her, it always felt like he was tracing her, committing every line and curve to memory.

All she could do was gasp and moan as he stroked. Licked. Kissed. Left suckling little bites that he soothed with a swirl of his tongue. Then his mouth clamped around her pussy, making her breath catch in her throat. He didn't tease her, he drove her hard and fast into an orgasm that left her shaking from head to toe and burning inside.

Releasing her hands, Knox flipped her onto her stomach. He

licked along the lines of her wings, knowing how sensitive the marks were. She writhed and arched beneath him, moaning for more. "I want to shield you. Protect you. Fucking possess you." He pulled her to her knees. "But never change you." He slammed home. Her pussy was swollen, but he forced his cock deep; groaning at how inferno-hot and slick she was. "My favorite place to be."

Harper pushed herself up, bracing her weight on her hands. "Fuck me," she rasped. She thought he might make her beg. He didn't. Wrapping her hair around his fist, he snatched her head back and powered into her at a frantic pace, hitting her g-spot with every perfect, territorial slam of his cock. She fisted the sheets, pushing back to meet each thrust.

Knox fucked her harder, knowing she was close; he could feel her getting hotter and tighter around him. "Come when you're ready, baby." He wouldn't make her wait. This, here and now, this was about her. As her pussy began to quake, he said, "You're fucking everything to me. Don't ever think differently."

It was the words that threw her over. Harper arched like a bow as white-hot pleasure tore through her body, fragmenting every cell and muscle and bone. Her pussy clamped down on Knox, who stiffened above her with a growl of her name. She felt his cock pulse inside her, felt every hot splash of his come. And then the energy left her body in a rush, and she slumped onto the mattress.

"Am I forgiven yet?" he asked, kissing her back.

She snorted. "That wasn't you making it up to me. That was you using orgasms to soften me up so I'd more easily forgive you. Sometimes I wonder how you live with yourself."

He smiled against her skin. "But you love me anyway."

She exhaled heavily. "Yeah, I do."

* * *

The guard pressed the button, and a large buzzer sounded just as the iron, mechanical door slid open. The scents of sweat, mildew, and bleach hit Knox hard. At first glance, the cell looked empty. The thin mattress didn't appear to have been slept on, and the chair was neatly tucked under the steel table. There wasn't a single sound except for the guards' footsteps echoing down the corridor. But Knox didn't fail to notice the toes of lace-less shoes near the dented metal locker. Levi also noticed them and rolled his eyes.

Knox strolled further into the room. Crow was crouched against the cement wall, hands shackled, eyes fearful. He might not have been afraid when talking to the sentinels the previous night, but he was sure afraid now. And the scent of his fear made his demon bare its teeth in a feral smile. The entity's rage had calmed after time with its mate, but the emotion still bubbled beneath the surface.

Knox didn't say anything. He let the silence stretch until Crow began to fidget nervously. If Knox was a better person, he might have felt a twinge of sadness at the situation. Crow had always seemed good and righteous. He'd never given Knox any trouble. He'd been loyal to Delia and his lair. The man he'd once been would be horrified by the things he'd done. But Knox didn't feel bad for him. After what the bastard had done to Harper, Knox would gladly peel off his skin like an onion and then cover him with pepper and wrap him in barbed wire.

"I knew you'd come," Crow boasted.

"It doesn't take a vision to know that."

Crow swallowed. "Have you come to kill me?"

"What do you think?"

"You could try to kill me. It wouldn't work."

"Why is that?"

"My fate is to kill you in order to save our world." His shoes squeaked on the cement floor as he struggled to his feet. "As long as you're alive, I'm protected so I can fulfill my duty."

"I see." Knox scraped his jaw with his hand. "Sounds like an honorable mission."

Crow lifted his chin, proud. "It is."

"Tell me, was hurting Harper part of this mission? Was shooting Tanner part of it? How about hurting Delia, butchering Carla, or shooting a cab driver? None of those things seem 'honorable' to me."

A tiny hint of regret flickered in Crow's eyes. "Collateral damage."

"Harper is not collateral damage." His voice was like a whip. "She's my mate and your Prime. Tanner is a sentinel; one who has protected you and the rest of our lair many times. I don't think a single person would agree that repaying that devotion to your safety with a bullet is 'honorable.'"

"You don't understand because you didn't see what I saw."

"I don't think *you* saw it either. It's all in your head."

"I saw that future," he stated, adamant. "I'm not alone in that."

Knox slowly arched a brow, unconvinced. "And who else shares this belief?"

"That is not something I intend to reveal."

"Why not? Why be loyal to whoever who sent you on a dangerous mission without any help or protection?"

Crow's confidence faltered for a few moments, but then he jutted out his chin once again. "They trust in my ability to see this through."

"Of course," said Knox dryly, exchanging a look with Levi.

"You can't hide the truth from me," Crow claimed. "I know what you are now."

Knox couldn't help smiling. He'd heard that statement over the years more times than he could count; none had ever guessed correctly. "And what is that?" No answer, which was no surprise. "You know nothing, Crow. You saw nothing. You hurt people who didn't deserve it while on a non-existent quest. If you were sound of mind, I would kill you right now."

Crow backed into the wall, swallowing hard.

"Would you like to know what I'm going to do instead? I'm going to get you well. I'm going to bring you back from the edge. And then you'll have to live with what you've done—that's if you *can* live with knowing you hurt so many people, including your own partner. Personally, I don't think I would ever forgive myself if I hurt mine." Knox spun on his heel and left with Levi close behind him.

The guard punched the button to lock the door. It slid shut with a clang. "You really think we can bring him back?"

"I fully intend to try," replied Knox. "If I was to punish him now, it would mean nothing to him—it would just feed his fantasy of me as the big, bad wolf."

The guard nodded in understanding. "He'd become a martyr in his own mind."

"Exactly." Knox then continued down the corridor.

"I've got to say," began Levi quietly, "I'm ... well, proud of how you handled that. I didn't think you'd be rational enough about the situation to do anything but kill him on the spot. I guess we have Harper to thank for that. She keeps you stable in more ways than one."

"She does." Which was good for the world in general.

It wasn't until they were inside the Bentley that Levi spoke again. "He was very adamant that someone assigned him this mission. Do you think it's possible that someone else is involved?"

Knox smoothed a hand down his tie. "According to Keenan, he was also very adamant that Doc wants to poison him."

Levi inclined his head. "True. We'll know for sure when he gets well and starts thinking straight. If there are others involved, he'll give them up."

And then they'd be dealt with, one way or another.

Being bold and expressive creatures, imps didn't bother themselves with passive-aggressive behavior. If they had a problem, they had absolutely no issue with letting you know about it. Not out of spite, but because they simply didn't believe in stewing on bullshit. And that was why Harper was listening to a full-on rant from a concerned and pissed-off Khloë.

Harper had known it was coming because she knew her family; knew how Khloë would react to the Crow vs Harper event. As such, she did what she always did when her family felt the need to let it rip: she continued with whatever she was doing and let them get on with it. And so she squatted near Khloë's new reception desk that also doubled as a display cabinet, carefully placing jewelry and other products on the glass shelf, while her ranting cousin stood over her.

Slapping the half-price tattoo certificates on the desk, Raini growled. "Let it go, Khloë."

The tiny imp folded her arms. "I'll let it go when Harper apologizes for not telling me last night that Crow attacked her. I had to learn it from Ciaran."

With a sigh, Devon slipped an arm around Khloë's shoulders. "Sweetie, the sooner you accept that your cousin is not the 'I'll call my friends and offload my anger and pain onto them' kind of person, the happier you'll be."

Raini nodded, leaning over the desk. "Our Harper's not the confiding type."

Khloë didn't seem at all appeased. "A heads-up that she'd been hurt would have been nice. That's all I'm saying."

Harper stood. "So freaking dramatic."

Khloë snorted. "Duh. Imp."

She gave her cousin a patronizing pat on the back. "How about you sit down and chill? You've had a hard day," she mocked. The imp hadn't done anything but rant while the rest of them had worked on the preparations for the grand opening the following day.

Khloë narrowed her eyes. "Did you forgive Knox?"

And like that, the atmosphere in the room changed.

Devon's spine snapped straight. "Why would you need to forgive Knox? What did he do?"

"Did he hurt you?" demanded Raini, eyes briefly flashing demon. "He did, didn't he? Devon, where's the bat?"

Harper glared at her cousin, who no doubt knew perfectly well that Harper hadn't wanted to share the argument with her friends because they were so overprotective they might do something dumb. "You're such a bitch."

Khloë lifted a single brow. "Is this brand-new information?"

Devon elbowed the imp aside, planting herself in front of Harper. "What. Happened. What did the rich motherfucker do to you?"

Harper raised her hands. "Let's just calm down, shall we? There's no need for any rash actions."

Devon covered her ears. "Don't use your therapist voice, I hate that."

"For the last time, what did he do to you?" asked Raini, though she sounded calmer.

"He didn't do anything to me," replied Harper. "We had a fight. Not a physical fight, but an argument. That's what couples do. We moved past it."

Raini drummed her nails on the glass surface. "Why did you argue?"

"He was angry about me being attacked and not calling him for help immediately and, well, he dealt with that anger in the wrong fashion." She didn't want to go into specifics; it was between her and Knox.

"He said she wasn't a woman of her word," said Khloë.

Harper shot her smirking cousin another hard glare. "I will kill you. I will. I'm not afraid to go to jail."

"He really said that?" asked a shocked Devon.

"He apologized for saying it and assured me that he didn't mean it," said Harper. "He thought I was dead. He got a shock and he was scared. To be fair, I *had* promised I would call out to him if I was in danger. I broke that promise to protect him, but I still broke it. No, it doesn't make what he said right. But we've all said crap we don't mean when we're mad."

The girls exchanged looks with each other as a silence fell. Finally, Devon spoke. "Well, if you can forgive him, I'll forgive him."

Raini nodded. "But I'll be watching him."

"Me too," said Devon. "That's not something I'll forget in a hurry."

Harper turned to her cousin, head tilted. "Now about your little habit of blurting out people's personal business . . . maybe I should return the favor. Maybe I should share what you did to Keenan the night he took you home when you were blitzed."

Khloë's eyes widened. "He told you?"

"He told Knox some of it," said Harper. "Knox told me. And I wasn't sure whether to laugh or cringe."

Devon skidded to the imp's side, curious as ever. "What did you do?"

"Tell them," Harper urged, smirking. "The truth shall set you free."

Khloë sighed. "I was just joking around."

"Oh God," Raini groaned, because so many of Khloë's stories began with that sentence.

"I snapped a picture of him with my phone while he was carrying me to my front door—I can't remember why." Khloë scratched her hand. "Anyway, Keenan freaked on me. It turns out that the incubus hates having his photo taken. And I mean *really* hates it. Said he's camera-phobic or something. So I started taking some selfies of the two of us."

"Of course you did," sighed Raini, rubbing her forehead.

"And then ..."

"And then?" prodded Devon.

Khloë put her hands on her hips. "He snatched my phone, dumped me on my ass on the doorstep, and started deleting all the photos. I was not okay with any of that, but I couldn't stand up to grab my phone because my legs were shaky. So I started pulling on his jeans to drag him down to me. Then there was this really loud tear—"

"Oh Lord," muttered Devon.

"—his jeans were near his ankles—"

"Oh Khloë," said Raini.

"—and I was staring at this monster cock."

And since her cousin had no problem saying exactly what she was thinking, Harper guessed, "You told him he had a monster cock, didn't you?"

"I thought it only fair that he knew." Khloë pursed her lips. "He seemed to think that was funny and he gave me back my phone. But he stopped smiling when I snapped a picture of his cock."

Raini gaped at her. "You thought taking a photo of it was okay?"

"I also thought that my ex would be the best person to call for no apparent reason," said Khloë. "I was smashed."

Twirling her hair around her finger, Devon asked a little too casually, "Did Keenan delete the photo?"

Harper shook her head at her friend. "You're such a perv."

"I'm just curious," the hellcat defended.

Raini leaned into Khloë. "Well, did he?"

The imp sighed, shoulders slumping. "Yeah. I don't think he trusted that I wouldn't share it on Facebook or something."

"That was pretty wise of him," said Harper.

The imp sighed again and admitted, "Yeah."

"What was wise of who?"

Harper twirled on the spot and gave Tanner a bright smile, relieved to see him fully recovered. "Good to see you up and about."

The hellhound glanced around. "This place looks great."

It totally did. Since they'd kept the name "Urban Ink," they'd kept the rock/art/Harley-Davidson feel. There was tattoo flash on the ceiling and metal art on the walls. The furnishings were now all inside, including the new lighted tracing tables that were gifts from Jolene. The stations were separated with checkered glass partitions—a nice idea from Raini. Also, at Devon's suggestion, they had a wall-mounted TV in the reception area, near the vending machine that Khloë had requested.

"You officially open tomorrow, right?" asked Tanner.

Harper nodded. "Yep."

"We're super excited about it," said Raini, eyes twinkling.

"So, I take it you're relieving the demons out there of their temporary guard duty?" Harper said to him. Knox had assigned two members of the Force to stand outside the studio and keep watch.

At the hellhound's nod, Devon groaned. "Lucky us."

"Admit it, kitty," said Tanner with a smile. "You were worried about me."

Devon gave him a haughty "you're delusional" look, but Harper knew the hellcat had in fact been concerned for him.

"So, what's the plan for tomorrow?" Tanner asked.

Harper smiled. "Well, it'll go a little something like this."

CHAPTER FIFTEEN

———◦———

Reaching into one of the drawers of the walk-in closet, Knox
pulled out his navy-blue, pin-striped tie. He straightened it out,
ready to hook it around his neck. And then he sighed. He wasn't
seeing this. He wasn't.

But he was.

Not sharing even an ounce of his demon's amusement, Knox
walked into the bedroom. His mate was sitting on the edge of
the bed, slipping on heels that were the same turquoise shade
as her lacy stop. She also wore the black slim-fitting pants that
never failed to draw attention to that pert little ass.

Seeing the silver earrings that he'd given her dangling from
her ears, satisfaction bloomed in his gut. He liked when she wore
something he gave her; they branded her as his, in a sense. But
that didn't mollify him right now.

Clearing his throat, Knox held up the tie. "I thought I was
forgiven." But apparently not, because she'd sown pink sequins
to one of his favorite ties.

Smiling at him, Harper shrugged. "You are. I always forgive." Slyly, she added, "I just never forget."

Knox sighed again. Really, he shouldn't be surprised. Demons always got even, one way or another. "I like this tie." Mostly because she'd bought it for him.

"I happen to think the sequins are a nice touch," said Harper. "They give it some color."

"You can't be serious."

Of course she wasn't, which was why she smiled.

He rubbed his temple. "I don't suppose there's any way you can remove the sequins without fucking up the tie?"

Sure there was. "Nope." She wanted to laugh at the tic going crazy in his cheek.

"If sometime in the future you feel the need to do such a thing again, choose something that wasn't a gift from you." He narrowed his eyes at her noncommittal sound. "Harper."

"Cool your engines, I can fix the damn tie." Standing upright, Harper straightened her shoulders. "Well, I'm ready. And you're not, I see. Get moving, we have an opening to attend."

He cocked his head. "Why do I get the feeling that you're so eager to leave because you're so eager to have the whole thing over with?"

"Um, because that's exactly it."

Moving to her, Knox loosely curled an arm around her waist. "Everything will be fine. The day will run smoothly. You don't need to be nervous."

"I'm not." At his arched brow, she said, "Okay, maybe I'm a little nervous. But not *bad* nervous."

"So what has you so keen on getting it over with?"

Wasn't it obvious? "I'll have to talk to people. Like *really* talk to people. I'll have to sell myself and my co-workers. It feels awkward and false doing that when I'm not the type of person who seeks to impress people. I also don't have any charm to dazzle them with, which will make it harder. Mingling is just not my thing." It annoyed her.

"You charm people all the time. You just don't realize it." Many found her openness and lack of façade refreshing. "You have my demon completely charmed." He kissed her, resting his hands on her ass. "You have no need at all to stress."

She wasn't so sure about that. "I predict I'll offend quite a few people."

"If it looks like it could happen, I'll step in," said Knox. "But I don't think it will come to that."

However, it did come to that. Many times, in fact. Especially since a lot of the people were damn chatty, which irritated her demon. Thankfully Knox would sense Harper's discomfort and smoothly step in; oozing charisma. He sure was handy to have around at times.

Though colorful banners, flyers, and balloons were plastered around the Underground to advertise the opening, Harper hadn't expected so many people to turn up. She supposed most were probably lured there by the scents of meat grilling, corn boiling, hot peppers, and smoke coming from the grill. But they hadn't simply grabbed some food and gone on their merry way. They'd stuck around and checked out the studio, sure to take a half-price certificate when they left, which was encouraging.

There was lots of free food on tables lined in front of the studio and the nearby businesses on this side of the strip. The deli, coffeehouse, bakery, ice cream parlor, and diner had all agreed to get involved in the opening. Lots of people stood around, talking and eating and drinking, while listening to the live band that was set up across from the studio. Kids, several of whom were her cousins, were squealing and laughing on the bouncy castle.

"It was a good idea to keep the food and entertainment out-side," said Levi. "It means everyone's not crammed in the studio and there won't be plates and cups all over the place."

It also meant Harper could stand outside to take a break and *breathe*.

"You'd be surprised by how many people have swiped a business card from the desk." Khloë tipped her chin toward the flow of demons moving in and out of the studio. "I think a lot of them were just being nosy when they went inside."

"But if they were impressed enough to take a card, that's good," said Keenan, staring at a completely casual Khloë with a furrow between his brows—something he'd been doing for a while.

Harper figured he expected her cousin to feel awkward after her drunken behavior. If so, he was wrong. Khloë didn't do "awkward."

"This is a *way* bigger turn-out than we had at the first open-ing, which isn't at all surprising given we have a good reputation and you're now a Prime," said Devon, eating off a flimsy paper plate. She hissed when Tanner snatched a chicken wing from it, but the hellhound just ignored her.

"Roan walked by earlier." Khloë paused to pop open a can of soda. "I half-expected him to come over and be a dick to you again," she told Harper. "But he seemed to think better of it because you had this tower of terror and sex appeal at your side."

Knox blinked, unsure if he was offended or not. "Tower of terror and sex appeal?"

Khloë lifted one shoulder. "Am I wrong?"

Chuckling, Harper shook her head. "No, you're not." Her demon was in complete agreement that its mate was both hot and terrifying at the same time.

"Have you noticed that a lot of people are staring at you, looking puzzled?" Devon asked Harper.

She glanced around. Huh. Devon was right. "Weird." But whatever.

Knox understood why they were looking puzzled, because he'd been playing close attention. It was interesting to see people's reaction to Harper. She didn't talk or act like a typical Prime, demanding respect and acknowledgment and submission. She never rubbed her status in people's faces. Never spoke like she was above them or like they owed her anything. She smiled and laughed and ate junk food, and he could see that most just didn't know what to make of her.

She hadn't simply opened the studio with that "build it and they will come" attitude, relying on her status to reel curious demons in. It was a technique that would have worked, after all. No, she'd been professional about it and shown that she took pride in her business. It was something they'd admire and respect.

Splaying a hand on her lower back, Knox asked, "How are you doing?"

Harper's mouth twitched. "In other words, have I hit my 'dealing with people limit'? I'm close." It had been a long, loud, busy day. She was glad it was almost over. *Thank you for staying with me. I know you have an endless amount of stuff to do.*

He gave her a soft kiss. *You're more important than any of that. This is a big day for you; of course I'd be here.*

Even though I sowed pink sequins on your tie? Her lower stomach clenched at the lopsided smile he gave her.

Even though, he replied. *Am I going to find any appliqués on my other clothes?*

Not unless you piss me off again.

"Look who's here," drawled Devon, gesturing at someone behind Harper.

Curious, Harper turned. And groaned.

Devon, however, flashed the she-demon a bright smile. "Belinda, it's always good to see you." The hellcat held out her plate. "Fries?"

Belinda jerked back, nose scrunched up, like she'd been offered a roasted rat. "No, thank you." She cleared her throat and flashed Knox a gracious smile. "You look a little out of place here."

Okay, that pissed Harper off. "I know you might have meant that as a compliment to him, but it was a shitty and most decidedly snotty thing to say."

Belinda lightly patted her bun. "I just meant that, well, this isn't his usual scene. Really, Harper, it's not the sort of party a Prime would throw."

"It's not a party, it's an opening," Harper told her. "Now, is there something you wanted?"

Belinda went to open her briefcase. "Well—"

"No, no, no," Devon interrupted, slinging her empty plate in the garbage can that Raini had artfully painted. "Today is about the studio, not the shindig."

Knox sighed. "It's not a shindig."

"I just needed you to sign a few forms," Belinda said to Harper.

"That can be done tomorrow, Miss Thacker, I'm sure," said Knox, a hard edge to his voice.

Belinda's smile was brittle. "Of course." She looked around, taking in the big crowd of people. "Well, it would seem the free food did the trick."

Knox stiffened at the bitchy insinuation that the success of the opening was owed to the free food. "Careful, Miss Thacker."

Belinda swallowed hard. "I simply meant that it was a good idea. I was praising Harper."

No, she wasn't. He went to say as much, but then Harper's elbow jabbed his side.

"I appreciate the compliment," said Harper.

Straightening her blouse, Belinda said, "Well, I'll be on my way."

As the cambion click-clacked away on those heels, Khloë turned to Knox. "You thought it would be a good idea to hire her? Really?"

"She's good at her job and hasn't given me any problems in the past," he said. "She was always polite and helpful."

Khloë snorted. "That's because you weren't mated in the past." Crushing her empty soda can, she said, "I'm going to get a burger."

"I'll go with you, keep you out of trouble," said Keenan.

Khloë frowned. "*No one* could keep me out of trouble."

So true.

As they walked off, Raini stepped out of the studio and asked, "Was that Belinda I just saw?"

"Yep," replied Devon. "She was being her usual snotty self. Well, I say 'usual' . . . according to Knox, she was always nice and helpful in the past."

"Yeah?" said Raini. "She was probably eager to impress him, thinking she had a chance with him. Now she's eager to stress Harper out and make her feel like she doesn't suit him or his lifestyle."

Knox frowned at his mate. "What did she say to you?" He'd known Belinda was annoying her, but he hadn't been aware that she'd been making sly personal comments.

Raini blinked. "You haven't told him?"

No, because Harper wasn't like Belinda—she didn't go whining to people about stuff, expecting them to deal with her problems for her. She'd blow the whole thing off if she didn't know for sure that Knox wouldn't let this go until he knew everything. "I'll tell you later," she said to him. "But only if you promise not to intervene."

"Harper, I hired her to *help* you. She's supposed to be making things easier for you, not harder. You can't expect me to overlook this."

"You call me your co-Prime, but do you really mean that?"

"You know I do," he fairly growled. How could she even ask him that?

"Then you can't fight my battles for me. It would undermine my authority. Besides, it's kind of fun to make her do all these things for the shindig that make her gasp in horror."

Raini nodded, smirking. "It really is."

"You mean like the sticks with chunks of steak on?" asked Levi, mouth twitching.

Harper snorted. "I'm not surprised she ran off to whine about it."

Knox tilted his head. "A part of you finds it amusing that I have to deal with her complaints, doesn't it?"

Harper put a hand on her chest. "I would never be so selfish as to not share with you the wonder that is Belinda."

Tanner snickered. "She's right. Mates should share everything."

Harper's chuckle faded as she caught sight of none other than Carla approaching, arm in arm with Bray. Well, wonderful. Her inner demon tensed, baring its teeth.

"What's *she* doing here?" asked Devon.

"We'll soon find out," said Harper. Tanner sidled up to her protectively so that she was flanked by him and Knox.

Moments later, the couple came to a stop in front of them. The guards at their back nodded respectfully at both Harper and Knox. Bray stiffly inclined his head, and Carla ... well, for a while, she and Harper just stared at each other. The moment stretched until it was painfully awkward.

Finally, Harper greeted, "Carla, Bray."

Carla glanced through the window. "The place looks good. Even better than your old studio." Which would suggest she'd actually *seen* the old studio, but that could be a lie. "I'm sure it will do well." Her eyes slid back to Harper. "I just wanted you to know that I don't blame you for anything Crow did. He's responsible for his own actions." She gave a humorless chuckle. "Well, considering he's far from sane, it might be fair to say we can't really hold him responsible. In any case, I don't blame you."

And if Carla hadn't said the latter like it made her considerate and merciful and she deserved some praise, Harper's inner demon might not have wanted to pop her right in the face.

Face hard, Raini said, "*Of course* it's not Harper's fault. No one should ever think otherwise."

"I hear you're treating Crow with drugs," Bray said to Knox, a note of anger in his voice.

"I know you probably want him dead," said Knox. "It's perfectly understandable."

"Surely *you* want him dead after what he did to your mate." Bray's gaze cut to Harper. "You should want him dead too. He deserves to be punished."

"Yes, he does," Knox easily agreed. "But to punish him while he believes I'm evil incarnate would only feed his fantasy and make him a martyr in his own mind. Then it wouldn't be a punishment, would it?"

Bray swallowed. "Well, I suppose that's true." Movement on their right seemed to catch his attention. His eyes hardened. Following his gaze, Harper saw Delia standing with a small group of women, looking pale and harried.

"*She* thinks Crow can be helped," said Bray sharply.

"It's natural that she doesn't want to give up on him," said Harper. "No one can judge her for that."

"I damn well can," snapped Bray. "She's supposed to be Carla's friend."

"I'm sure Delia is, but she's also Crow's partner," Harper pointed out. "I wouldn't want to give up on Knox, and I'd imagine you wouldn't want to give up on Carla, so how can we be mad at her for standing by him?"

Bray's eyes narrowed. "You weren't so understanding when it came to Roan."

Knox stiffened. "Be very cautious about what you say next, Bray."

Harper almost shivered at the silken menace in his voice. Her demon hissed at Bray, backing up its mate.

Carla spoke. "Roan didn't mean the things he said. He was angry and scared for me. He's always been an emotional boy. If he does or says anything else, please bear that in mind."

"If he steps wrong again," began Knox, "he'll be punished again. Nothing will get him a free pass, Carla." His eyes cut to Bray. "And you should seriously rethink ever using that sharp tone with my mate again."

Bray's Adam's apple bobbed and he lowered his eyes submissively.

"There's plenty of food, feel free to grab some," said Devon. It was a subtle attempt to make them move along. It worked. They nodded and headed for the grill with their guards.

"As much as I feel bad for her after what she went through, I could happily slap her right now," said Raini. "I can't *believe* she said she doesn't blame you for what Crow did like that made her a good and kindhearted person. I mean she genuinely seemed to be expecting gratitude from you for it."

Devon nodded. "Not holding you responsible for Crow's

actions should be *natural*, not a kindness. That woman is not, and has never been, kind. She's just ..."

"She's just Carla," Harper finished, having long ago realized that her birth mother simply wasn't normal. "And she's not important right now. This day is about the studio, nothing and no one can spoil it."

Raini gave a curt nod. "Right. It really has been a productive day. I took a *lot* of bookings. Some were from people who wanted us to fix badly-done tattoos they got from the other places round here. Oh, I almost forgot to tell you. Our local competition tried to recruit me."

Harper gaped. "You're kidding!"

Devon hissed. "Motherfucker. Who exactly was it?"

"A tall guy with dreadlocks and lots of piercings," replied Raini, smiling. "He said he owns the Sleepy Hollow Parlor and he wanted me to come work for him. Can you believe that?"

"What did you say?" asked Levi.

"I told him to go fuck himself with a blow torch, obviously," replied Raini.

"Obviously," said Levi.

"I could kill the cheeky fucker." Harper glanced around, looking for him. "He needs to—" She frowned as a red-faced Keenan stumbled past with Khloë on his back, doing his best to buck her off. But the imp held tight, pulling lots of weird expressions as she took selfie after selfie of the two of them.

Devon sighed at the spectacle. "You know ... I sometimes look at how well-organized, precise, and fearless Khloë can be and think, 'Wow, she'd make an excellent army general.' But then I remember it would only be a matter of time before she'd be shot by her own troops."

It was sad because it was true.

"What's his deal with cameras?" Raini asked Levi.

The reaper shrugged. "He just hates having his picture taken."

Devon sighed again. "I guess we better dislodge her from him."

Harper went to follow both Devon and Raini, but then she froze as anger seemed to suddenly blast from the archdemon at her side. His eyes briefly bled to black. She grabbed his arm. "What is it? What's wrong?"

Knox's nostrils flared. *I've just spoken with Larkin.*

And?

Crow is gone.

Gone? What the fuck?

Harper watched as Knox paced up and down in front of the fireplace, muscles rippling beneath his suit, looking much like a caged tiger. To say he was pissed would be a massive understatement. Hell, they were all pissed. No one could work out how Crow could possibly have escaped his cell.

The prison was well-guarded and had several, complicated security measures in place. In addition, the building was safeguarded by a myriad of spells that also prevented anyone from teleporting inside. Each individual spell was actually covered with a protective spell to stop them from being unraveled.

They'd initially suspected that dark practitioners had somehow miraculously managed to find a way to undo the spells, but an incantor had visited the prison and assured them that no one had even attempted to tamper with the spells.

Yet, Crow was gone.

None of the cameras showed him leaving the building. He'd simply disappeared from his cell somehow. As Harper sat on the sofa with her feet tucked under her, she couldn't think of any possible explanation for that. She had, however, thought of something else—a theory that Knox wasn't going to like at all.

Keenan leaned back on the sofa, crossing his legs at the

ankles. "Well, I think we can safely say that Crow was telling the truth and he's not alone in this little mission. Someone's been helping him all along. That might have been why he was so hard to track. They could have given him money and even a place to hide."

Larkin fidgeted with her braid, brows pulled together. "But why? Is it someone who believes Crow's vision was real and they want to help him?"

"Crow told me he was 'chosen' for this mission," said Harper. "I think this person has been *using* Crow, not helping him. He may not have even had a vision at all. They could have planted that idea in his head to manipulate him." Just as she'd suspected after he attacked her, only she'd dismissed the idea too easily. And that made her want to slap herself in the face. She should have trusted her instincts.

"But it makes no sense that someone would use a demon bordering on rogue as an attack dog," said Larkin.

"Sure it does," said Harper, having given it some real thought. "To use Crow is a risk-free and highly devious move. He can actually conjure guns and knives and all kinds of shit. In that sense, he is, literally, a loaded weapon. A loaded weapon that's absolutely and fanatically *obsessed* with its mission; nothing could deviate Crow from it. That makes him very, very dangerous. Add in that even if he *did* mention that someone else was involved it would be dismissed as the ramblings of a demon on the edge" —which all six of them had done— "that makes Crow a pretty good attack dog."

"Okay, yeah, so there was a sneaky sort of wisdom in recruiting Crow," Larkin conceded. "But only to an extent. He's no match for Knox."

"No, but he's a match for me."

Knox came to an abrupt halt at Harper's words. "What?"

Ah, well, here was the theory he'd undoubtedly hate. "I've been thinking," said Harper. "He told me that killing me wouldn't be enough to stop this evil child being born because you could then meet another she-demon and have it with her. He thinks that ending *your* life is the answer."

"But you think the puppeteer actually wanted him to kill *you*," sensed Levi.

"I think that, at the very least, they wanted me in danger," said Harper. "Crow's a match for me because he's good at taking people down fast. Like a Taser. But I'm well-protected and I have pretty substantial abilities, so it's not like anyone could rely on him to kill me."

"What are you getting at, Harper?" Knox asked. But he was quite sure he already knew.

"I think the puppeteer's plans were simple: send Crow on a mission after me," she told him. "I mean, look at the way Crow went after you again and again, determined and undaunted. I think that was what they were hoping he'd do to *me*. Only no one can truly control a demon so close to rogue, so their plan fucked up and Crow instead targeted you."

Harper straightened her legs as she went on. "But let's say their plan *had* worked. Let's say Crow had honed in on me the way he did on you; coming at me over and over, but getting away each and every time. You'd have been frustrated, anxious, and even a little scared. You'd also have felt helpless and angry with yourself because you believe it's your responsibility to protect me. What happens when a demon is stressed and their anger is building and building like a pressure cooker?"

It was Keenan who answered. "Their dominance over their demon slips. The entity starts to surface more and more."

"Yes, their control falters," said Harper. "I think someone wants you to lose control of your demon, Knox. I think they're trying to find out what you are, because they think if they know what you are then they'll know how to kill you."

There was utter silence for a moment as everyone digested that, exchanging grim looks.

Levi finally broke the silence. "I hate to say it, but I think she's right, Knox. Sending Crow after you makes no sense, but I can see someone thinking he'd be strong enough to take on Harper. Maybe not strong enough to kill her, but strong enough to be a threat which—as she pointed out—is all they'd really need to peck at your control."

Knox scraped his hand over his jaw, anger pulsing inside him. He wished he could argue with Harper's theory, but it made too much sense. That meant his mate had been the real target all along. Not the main target, no, since her death would have been a means to an end; a way to rid him of his control. But someone had still purposely set out to harm her, wielding Crow like a weapon. Flames flickered from his fingertips, making everyone but Harper stiffen.

Her mind slid against his—a soothing touch. It settled him just enough for him to bury the rage, and the flames blazing from his fingers then puffed into smoke. He rolled back his shoulders and cricked his neck. Every muscle was stiff with tension and anger. "Now that we know the puppeteer's end game, it's a matter of identifying just who they are."

"Maybe this is payback from Isla's lair," suggested Larkin.

"Or maybe Alethea's somehow involved," said Keenan. "It's possible that she'd been bitching at Harper for the simple reason that pissing her off pisses you off."

Tanner twisted his mouth. "You need to talk to Dario, Knox. I was skeptical about the rumors, but maybe he really is building an army. Maybe he plans to go up against you once he believes he knows how to kill you."

"It doesn't necessarily have to be a Prime," said Knox. "They may not even be particularly powerful. So far, they've hidden behind someone else."

"But they *did* somehow find a way to get into the prison and retrieve Crow," Keenan pointed out.

"Yes, but they could have hired others to do that," said Knox. "That would make them smart and resourceful, not necessarily powerful."

Keenan tilted his head, conceding that.

"You know," began Levi, "it occurred to me that someone might not necessarily have *taken* Crow from the cell. He could in fact be dead. They could have implanted some sort of trigger in his body or mind that allowed them to kill him from afar. It's not an easy thing to do, but it is possible. If he vaporized after his death, there would have been no remains to find."

Knox nodded. "You could be right, but I won't allow myself to believe it and drop my guard." He'd been too dismissive of Crow, and it had backfired on them. Knox wouldn't make that mistake again.

"Now that I've really thought about, I have to agree that using Crow really was a risk-free plan," Larkin mused, looking at Harper. "From their perspective, if it works and you die and Knox loses his shit, great. If it doesn't, only Crow dies and they get to try something else."

Neither of those scenarios were acceptable to Harper. She folded her arms as she spoke to Knox. "Does Dario have an anchor?"

"Why?" he asked.

"Because one thing we know about the person behind all this is that they don't," she replied.

Knox cocked his head. "Why do you say that?"

"The idea of me hurt, stressed, or in danger makes you want to lose your shit, right?"

"Absolutely. But as my anchor, you also keep me stable enough *not* to do that."

"Exactly. But this person didn't think of that, which means they don't have an anchor." Otherwise, they'd have *known* how much stability an anchor could provide and, as such, they would have also known that just putting her in danger wouldn't be enough to crack his control.

Levi nodded. "*Does* Dario have an anchor?"

"He's never brought one with him to any meetings," said Knox. "Which means he either doesn't have an anchor or he hasn't publically declared it. Many Primes choose not to, especially if their anchor doesn't want to be under a spotlight. I'll need to make a call to find out for sure."

Harper hadn't wanted to share Knox's spotlight, but he'd been adamant that she would be safer if demons knew her to be his anchor. Although being in his life did bring a certain danger to her own, she'd been more vulnerable when she'd been a she-demon of a small lair. Jolene was powerful and scary, but it didn't stop demons from bringing shit to her door for the simple reason that small lairs were considered easy prey.

"Look more into this rumor about Dario and find out *where* it came from," Knox told Larkin and Keenan. He then turned to the other two sentinels and said, "Announce to the lair that they need to once again be on the lookout for Crow. If he is alive, he'll be even more determined than before to finish his mission." After giving a few final orders to his sentinels, Knox sent them away. Alone with his mate, he framed her face with his hands. "I should have seen it. I should have seen that the intended target was you."

She shook her head. "None of us saw it. The situation didn't make sense, but no one would expect 'sense' from someone in Crow's state."

"You have to be extremely careful, Harper. It's clear that we aren't just dealing with Crow. Someone is behind this. Possibly more than one person. They might decide to take the matter into their own hands, though I doubt it because they appear to prefer to hide behind others. In any case, be safe. *Nothing* can happen to you."

"You be careful, too." She toyed with his collar. "You're mega powerful, but anything that's born can die. We will find out who it is that's manipulating Crow."

He rested his forehead against hers. "We will." Whoever they were, however many of them were involved, Knox would fucking destroy them.

CHAPTER SIXTEEN

———◆———

The following morning, Harper stood outside Knox's office, debating whether to knock or just barge right in. It wasn't unusual for him to spend a fair portion of the night in his home office, making or taking calls. What was unusual was that he hadn't spent a little time with her first. Literally ten minutes after the sentinels left the previous night, he'd retreated to his office. And he was still in there.

Harper knew he was pissed about the Crow thing, so she'd let him be. After all, she liked time alone to think shit through; she could understand why he'd need it. And since he gave her space when she needed it, it would have been shitty of her not to afford him the same.

As such, she hadn't bothered him all night. She'd even showered, dressed, and had breakfast alone. Still, though, he was holed up in there. She was due to meet with the girls in an hour to do some shopping, since the studio didn't open until seven that evening. She wasn't going to leave without first checking that he was okay.

Knocking would be the polite thing to do. But then, Harper wasn't polite. So she turned the knob and swung open the door, unsurprised to find him on the phone. She didn't enter the room, however. He'd either invite her in or he wouldn't.

His dark gaze locked with hers, unreadable. Her demon's mood lifted a little. It had missed him and consistently harassed Harper to go find him. For a long moment, Knox just stared at her. She considered walking away, but then he gestured for her to enter.

"I simply wish to know if he has an anchor," he told the person on the other end of the call.

He was talking to someone about Dario, apparently. Harper stood admiring the three abstract art canvases of mechanical clockwork hanging on the gray wall, but she was *totally* listening to every word. She liked his office. It was way cooler than hers with the sleek black, U-shaped executive desk and lush leather chair. He had an almost futuristic computer with multiple monitors that she wouldn't have a clue how to use.

"No major question," said Knox. "I'd just like to know. Really? All right. Thank you. I will." He sighed heavily as he ended the call.

She turned to face him. "I take it that was about Dario?"

"Yes," Knox replied, slowly moving to her. "According to Raul, Dario doesn't have an anchor."

She bit her lower lip. "I see."

Cupping her hips, he added, "That doesn't necessarily mean he's Crow's puppeteer, of course." But it didn't look good for Dario. Knox kissed her gently, none too surprised when she didn't react as enthusiastically as usual. "I neglected you." He sorely regretted it now.

"To brood." Her tone dared him to deny it.

"I had a lot of calls to make."

Ha. "You were brooding."

"I was trying to find out if there was a spell that could teleport people into secure places."

"You were brooding."

"No one was able to help with that."

"So the brooding continued."

Mouth twitching into an involuntary smile, he framed her face with his hands and kissed her. Hard. Long. Tasting and taking what was his and only his. Letting the feel and scent of her soothe the chaos in his head.

He slid one hand under her T-shirt and closed it possessively around her breast. "I missed you." So had his demon. It had sulked all damn night, wanting to seek her out.

Harper stepped back, pushing his arm down and out of her shirt. "Nu-uh. I have to leave."

He stalked her as she backed up. "The studio doesn't open until much later."

"Yes, but I agreed to meet the girls to go shopping. I can't just cancel on them because my mate has decided he regrets spending so long br—"

"I wasn't brooding."

Harper snorted. "Whatever."

"Before you go, you can tell me what Belinda has been saying to upset you."

"First you have to promise that you won't interfere."

Grinding his teeth, he nodded.

"Yeah, I'm gonna need the words, Knox." Because she wasn't an idiot.

His demon chuckled. "I promise I will let you deal with this matter yourself." Though it would gall Knox to do so. It went against the grain for him not to defend her against anything or anyone.

"Belinda has basically set out to make me feel like I don't compare to the females in your past. Maybe she'll eventually realize I am totally fine with not being like any of them, maybe she won't. Who knows?" Harper shrugged. "But she likes to constantly remind me that I don't behave like other Primes, and she feels pretty certain that we won't last. It's annoying, but it doesn't hurt me."

Knox shook his head, anger rising inside him sharp and fast. His demon wanted to track the bitch and force a ball of hellfire down her throat. "I wish you had told me, Harper. I would have fired her immediately." And he'd do exactly that very soon, his promise be damned. His mate didn't deserve this shit.

"That's part of why I didn't tell you. I don't want you to fire her. Tell me you won't."

He said nothing, not prepared to lie to her.

"I mean it, Knox. You swore you'd let me deal with this in my own way."

"I can't sit back and allow this to happen," he clipped. "Belinda is purposely trying to hurt you and *no one* has the right to do that."

"Stop with the protective growl. You know it makes me tingly." Harper curled her arms around his neck. "Anyway, she annoys me, but her opinion isn't relevant to me—something I think she's finally beginning to sense. Which is making her crazy, and that's just awesome."

"I hired her, baby. It was clearly a mistake on my part. Now I need to fix that mistake."

"You don't need to do anything. I'm handling this. It really is fun knowing I'm making her organize an event that will make her die a little inside. All those pretentious people will check out her work, see skewered steak and wedges, and gasp in the same horror that she's dwelling in. Her reputation will take a huge hit."

Sometimes he forgot that his mate was ruthless in her own way. "You fight half her suggestions on principle, don't you?"

"Of course. If she was nice, I'd be much more accommodating." Harper gave him a quick kiss. "See you later. Have a good day."

Knox grabbed her wrist before she could leave. He felt like a bastard for not spending any time with her. She was right; he'd been brooding. Brooding when he should have been with her, making up for the fact that her grand opening had been tainted by this mess. "You know you're my priority, don't you?" No matter how much time he spent in his office or anywhere else, she came first. Always would.

"I'm not judging you for wanting some time alone," Harper said truthfully. "Everybody needs that sometimes. And I know you're feeling helpless now that Crow could be on the loose once again and that we have no idea who's pulling his strings. You hate not being in total control. I can completely understand you wanting to address that helplessness and take back the control by being proactive. I really do get it, which is why I'm not mad. I just wanted to check that you were okay before I left."

He swallowed. She got him. Understood him better than anyone else and let him be exactly who he was without judgement. "What would I do without you?"

"Kill lots of people?" she quipped.

He chuckled and kissed her again. The kicker was ... she was right. If he lost her, many would die in the destruction that followed. He broke the kiss as his office phone rang. "I'll see you later tonight."

"Tonight," she agreed. Harper headed for the door, but she

came to an abrupt halt when she heard Knox say, "Morning, Dario." Brows flying up, she pivoted on her heel just as Knox pressed a button that put him on speakerphone.

"Ah, Knox, I hear that your sentinels have been asking questions about me and the rumors that are currently circulating." There was a lazy amusement in the Prime's voice.

"Should I be concerned by what I heard?" Knox asked, planting his hands on the desk.

"Concerned about which rumor exactly? The one that I'm turning rogue or the one that I'm building an army?" His tone said he found each of them ridiculous.

"Both," replied Knox, eyes on Harper as she approached the desk.

"Neither are true. I simply wish to be left alone to grieve in peace," Dario added, a note of emotional weariness in his voice.

"Strange that such an innocent thing would be twisted." Which was why Knox wasn't convinced that was all there was to it.

"I thought so. That's why I had my sentinels work to find out where exactly the rumors came from."

"And?" prompted Knox.

"They were unable to find out. But I at least know why the rumors were started."

"And why is that?" he asked Dario, watching as Harper slid half her delectable ass up on to the desk.

"For the same reason that a rumor is now circulating about you."

Knox stiffened. "What rumor might that be?"

"That you accused a psi-demon of being close to rogue in order to discredit his claim that he foresaw you fathering a child that could obliterate us."

"Motherfucker," Harper mouthed. It was one thing for the Primes to speculate on it at a meeting. It was another to spread it around when it could potentially cause panic among the demon population.

"Who is claiming this?" Knox asked, forcing himself to unlock his jaw.

"You need not worry," Dario assured him. "The rumor is not being taken seriously, since the psi-demon butchered a member of your lair and attacked your mate. It is clear his mental state is not what it should be."

That didn't placate Knox much. "Who began the rumor?"

"Come visit my home today. Bring your mate with you, since she is your co-Prime. We should all talk."

"You expect us to visit you when we've heard you're building an army?" Knox asked in surprise.

"I expect nothing. I am simply inviting you. Whether or not you take me up on that invitation is entirely up to you." The line went dead.

Looking at the phone, Harper spoke. "He sounded ... like himself. I don't think he's near-rogue. Do you?"

Knox shook his head. "He was too calm." There were no short, choppy sentences. No notes of agitation in his tone. "I can't say for certain whether or not he's building an army, but my gut tells me he isn't close to rogue. And if that rumor isn't true, maybe the other isn't either."

"Maybe. After all, the one about you isn't true." Harper slid off the desk. "I'm coming with you."

Knox's jaw tightened. He didn't want her around Dario when he couldn't be sure that the demon wasn't a threat to her. "Harper ..."

"This is Prime business." She lifted her chin. "I'm your co-Prime."

"A position you don't like, as I recall. You can't play that card when it suits you."

She gave him a bright smile. "Sure I can."

"You have a shopping trip to attend, remember?"

"This is way more important than shopping. Look, I know you're wary about me being in Dario's company. I'm just as worried about *you* being around him. But we've agreed it's unlikely that he's near-rogue, and I don't think you believe he's building an army any more than I do."

She was right about that. "You're asking me to risk you."

"And you're asking me to stay at home while you risk yourself." She shook her head. Not going to happen. "If it's too dangerous for me, it's too dangerous for you."

Knox shoved a hand through his hair. On the one hand, he liked that she was so protective of him. On the other hand, it could be pretty inconvenient at times. "Stay by my side while we're there. Just because my gut says Dario isn't near-rogue doesn't mean I trust it's safe for you there."

Harper saluted him. "When do we leave?"

"No time like the present."

A few hours later, they parked the jet at a landing spot near Dario's home, which turned out to be a cute little castle that sat smack bam in the middle of a privately owned island. Though the building wasn't huge, it was regal and stately. Harper kind of liked it. It had real character.

With Levi and Tanner close behind them, she and Knox walked across a wooden bridge to where a bearded demon stood, wearing a long, leather jacket. He had "bad-ass" written all over him.

"Reece," greeted Knox.

Harper didn't recognize him, but she nodded all the same.

He inclined his head in greeting. "Follow me." Apparently he wasn't the conversational type.

He didn't lead them inside the castle itself. Instead, he led them through the courtyard to a glass building at the side of the castle that Harper quickly realized was a greenhouse.

Reece stopped near the door and gestured for them to enter. "Regardless of what you may have heard, Dario is not near-rogue."

Yeah, Harper would believe that for certain once she'd seen Dario for herself. Knox entered the glass structure first, keeping her hand in his. It was hot and moist and smelled strongly of damp soil, sun-warmed earth, fresh flowers, and sweet herbs. Among the sounds of insects buzzing and a hose spraying mist was the precise snipping of scissors.

They followed the snipping; passing potted plants, hanging baskets, bags of compost, and trowels. She tucked her arms tight into her body, but leaves still brushed her skin as they walked deeper into the greenhouse. Soon enough, they found Dario. He was pruning dead leaves from a plant. The sun streaming through the glass roof illuminated his expression. It was one of total serenity.

"I wasn't sure if you would come," said Dario, eyes on the plant. "After all, the rumors about me have been quite serious."

Knox stopped a few feet away from him, keeping Harper slightly behind him. "I'm willing to hear you out."

"But if I make a wrong move, you will kill me," said Dario, a smile in his voice. He turned to face them, his close-set blue eyes pink-rimmed. He looked tired and drawn. She'd never before seen his lean figure in anything but a suit. Today, he was wearing old jeans and a V-neck T-shirt. "How are you finding being a Prime, Harper?"

"It has its challenges," she said vaguely.

Dario nodded his agreement. "Indeed it does. Many times I've wondered if the power is worth those challenges. Are you satisfied that I'm far from rogue, Knox?"

"Yes," replied Knox. There was no way Dario could manage to look so very calm otherwise. Act calm, sure. But he *looked* it. There were no twitchy movements, no turmoil in his gaze, and no dark vibes coming from him. "But it doesn't look good to others that you've become a recluse. It gives weight to the rumors."

"I know." Dario's brow furrowed and pain etched his features. "My concubine of fifty years died recently."

Harper bit her lip. *Fuck.* "I'm sorry to hear that."

Dario shot her a sad smile. "I was not in control, and I did not trust myself not to act irrationally while I was so deep in grief. I locked myself away for the safety of myself and others. My control has improved enough for me to leave the castle, but I want solitude while I do my best to find some peace. Without it, my control could splinter again."

"Understandable," said Knox. And sensible. Near-rogues didn't make sensible decisions.

"But you do not fully trust it is true." Dario put down the scissors. "There is another reason I invited you here. Come to my garden. There is someone you should see."

Knox slowly lifted one brow. "Someone?"

"Yes. They are hoping to speak with you and your mate, but it is of course your choice whether or not you come along."

Harper stayed at Knox's side as he followed Dario out of the rear exit of the greenhouse and down a long stepping stone path. At the end was a pretty floral arch with vines twined around it. They walked through the arch into a maze-like garden of carefully plucked bushes. They made a serious of short, sharp turns until eventually they came to a small opening.

Harper arched her brows, impressed. It was like a little oasis with patches of herbs, colorful fragrant flowers, and the soothing trickle of the fountain. The chirping of the birds splashing in the bird bath added to the relaxing feel. The breeze rustled the leaves and flowering trees, and bees and butterflies swooped from bloom to bloom. What held Harper's attention was the small old woman on the wooden bench, knitting what looked like a scarf, which was a little odd, considering the heat.

Dario gestured to the woman. "Meet my grandmother, Nora."

Pausing in her knitting, Nora studied all of them. She spoke to Harper. "You're smaller than I thought you would be. People often underestimate those who are short. I do enjoy shocking people by showing them what a mistake that would be."

Harper couldn't help but smile, since she could fully relate to that.

Nora's eyes danced from Harper to Knox. "Your emotional bond is very strong. That is good. You will need each other if you are to face what is coming."

"Nora has premonitions," Dario told them. "She sees the future, but she does not have visions. She *knows* and *feels* things about the future."

"I knew Dario wouldn't win the election, but he didn't listen to me." Nora shook her head. "It's rare that he ever does," she muttered.

Dario looked close to rolling his eyes. "Can you not just get to the point?"

"I could." The woman cackled at his exasperated expression.

She makes me think of Jolene, Harper told Knox. Harper kind of liked her already.

Nora resumed knitting as she spoke. "I'm sure all of you have heard the rumors about Dario, just as we have heard the rumors about you and the other Primes. So many rumors," she mused. "Rather odd, don't you think? Obviously someone started them, but it seems such a petty thing to do ... unless their aim is to cause discord among the Primes, of course."

It wasn't a theory that Knox hadn't already considered. It held merit, but ... "Who would want such a thing?"

"I did not see their faces, nor do I know their names. But they call themselves 'the Four Horsemen.'"

Harper frowned. "Like the Four Horsemen of the Apocalypse?"

Nora placed her knitting beside her and smoothed the creases out of her long gypsy-like dress. "Yes, only they do not want to see the end of the world. They want to see the fall of the US Primes. They want domination of the entire country. But they're having to use underhanded methods to achieve that because they cannot destroy all of the Primes by themselves."

"They need the Primes to destroy each other," said Levi.

Nora nodded. "They believe that causing a political war will lead to a physical one. As such, they are trying to cause arguments amongst Primes and make them distrust each other in the hope that they will turn on each other."

Harper recalled the tension and distrust at the annual meeting; the rumors were certainly having some effect, even for those who didn't fully believe them. "I don't think Crow is one of the Horsemen."

"He is merely a tool," Nora confirmed. "A tool his manipulator is having difficulty controlling. But, really, they should have thought of that."

Knox spoke. "He was sent after Harper, not me."

Nora smiled. "Very good. I wasn't sure if you would see that for yourself. This person planted the idea of the vision in Crow's head, so you need not worry that there's any substance in it. But there will be a child one day. And others will come for it. You will both need to be prepared for that."

Harper swallowed, anxious at the idea of not only being a mother—after all, what did she know about parenthood? —but also at the idea of people seeking to take the child.

"What about the unpredictable weather?" asked Knox.

Dario cleared his throat. "I will accept the blame for that, but not publically. It would be used against me to support the 'I'm turning rogue' rumor. I was grieving, and my control over my gifts was not at its best."

Given that Knox had lost his mind when he'd almost lost Harper, he could understand. "Why trust us with this when you don't trust the other Primes?"

"Because I believed you, as a mated couple, would understand the depth of pain that would come with losing someone you treasure," said Dario. "And because Nora felt you should hear her premonition."

"You have already killed one of the Horsemen," said Nora.

Shocked, Knox stiffened. He didn't want to believe it, but he had to wonder if she meant . . . "Isla?"

Nora gave a slow nod.

"Well, shit," muttered Levi.

Tanner cursed under his breath. "Why would she want to see the fall of all the US Primes if she was one of them?"

"She wanted more power. It was her addiction," said Nora. "There are three Horsemen left. As I said, I do not know their names and I did not see their faces. But I *know*—I *feel*—that the one manipulating Crow is not a Prime. There is so much greed in their cold heart. They want power. They want people to envy them as they envy others. They do not see it, but nothing will ever make them feel happy or satisfied. There is a void inside them that will never be filled."

Well, don't they sound like a freaking treasure? said Harper.

Nora pointed at her. "Be warned that you and your demon will face a trial. You do not like to accept help, but you will need your mate's aid when the time comes. Accept it, because nobody else will be able to help you."

Cold invaded Harper's limbs. It wasn't so much *what* Nora said as the way she said it; that ominous tone was spooky. *Okay, this woman is kind of scary.*

"There's nothing else you can tell us about the Horsemen?" Knox asked Nora, who shook her head.

Harper turned to Dario. "Will you tell the other Primes about the premonition and the Horsemen?"

Dario lifted a single brow. "If I was to tell them that four demons were plotting to see the fall of the Primes, how do you think they would react?"

"They'd think you were deluded and paranoid, and that the rumors are true," said Harper. All right, point taken.

"Yes. I am hoping none of you will speak of this to the other Primes," Dario added.

For a moment, Knox said nothing. "It would be best if they knew not to take all the rumors seriously. They have a right to know where they're originating from and that they're being played. But you're right. Your words would be mistaken for paranoia. We will not repeat what you've told us." For now, at least.

Dario's shoulders relaxed slightly. "I appreciate that."

Knox inclined his head. "We'll leave now."

After they said their goodbyes to Nora, Dario led them out of the garden, through the courtyard, and to the bridge. "Thank you for accepting my invitation," Dario said, graciously. "It was good to see you again. Be sure to take care."

Nodding, Knox urged Harper forward as Levi and Tanner

stayed behind them. No one spoke a single word until they were fully across the bridge.

"Of all the things I expected to hear," said Tanner, "it wasn't that."

He wasn't alone in his shock. Harper still hadn't quite processed it all yet. "I feel really bad for the guy. Losing his partner of fifty years had to be a seriously hard hit." She wasn't sure she'd emotionally survive a loss like that.

Knox nodded, draping an arm around her shoulders. "He did the right thing to isolate himself while his control was weak. It protected him and his lair. And he has every right to take the time to heal in peace." Or to heal as much as anyone in his position could be expected to heal.

"Now that we know about the Horsemen, Isla's push for a US Monarch makes a lot more sense," said Levi, moving to Knox's side. "If she'd been Monarch, she'd have had the power to crush the other Primes and to give the other Horsemen whatever power they wanted. That must have been their plan 'A'. It failed, so now they've moved onto plan 'B'—sic the Primes on each other."

"Anyone have any suspicions as to who the other three Horsemen could be?" asked Tanner as he sidled up to Harper.

"We should probably bear in mind that Malden also pushed to be the US Monarch," said Knox. He could have had the same motivation as Isla. "But then, so did Dario."

"Can we be sure Dario isn't one of them?" asked Levi.

"If he was, surely he wouldn't have shared all that information with us," said Tanner.

"Unless none of it is true and we're all being set up somehow," said Knox. It was possible that Dario was playing a very intricate, dangerous game, but Knox's gut told him that wasn't the case.

"Just because Isla was a Prime doesn't mean the other

Horsemen are," said Harper. "Nora told us that the person who sent Crow on his 'mission' wasn't a Prime. That might mean the others aren't one either."

Knox nodded. "Which means they could be anyone." He looked at Harper. "It stands to reason that if they sent Crow after you and it hasn't worked, they would try to target you in other ways."

Harper twisted her mouth. "Alethea, Belinda, and Roan seem to have made it their mission to piss me off. None of them are Primes."

"Crow said that Delia was poisoning him," said Tanner. "Can we be sure she wasn't somehow involved in trying to pull his strings?"

"We can't be sure of anything," replied Knox. "But people heard Delia and Crow arguing. If Delia is involved, I don't see what reason she'd have for staging a fight. And if we're operating on the theory that this person wants to cause Harper upset, telling Crow to kidnap Carla makes no sense. Everyone knows Harper doesn't have a relationship with her."

Tanner tipped his head to the side, conceding that Knox had a valid point. "Then our most likely suspects are Alethea, Belinda, and Roan."

"We'll have some members of the Force watch them," said Levi. "But we can't spare many, what with Crow being on the loose."

In Harper's opinion, the person they should be watching was Alethea. Belinda was an annoyance, but she didn't come across as someone ambitious enough to seek control of the US. Roan was a prick most of the time, but he was also a momma's boy. He would surely kill Crow for harming Carla.

Soon enough, they reached the jet. Once inside, Levi and Tanner headed to the front cabin as per usual, giving Knox and

Harper privacy in the rear cabin. The stewardess served them both drinks before disappearing to the front of the craft.

Harper clicked on her seatbelt. "You know, I never thought of having kids until Delia told us about Crow's vision. I know most women wonder about it at some point—even if only when they're kids themselves—but I never did." Which was probably weird, but *she* was weird, so she shouldn't really expect anything else of herself.

Opposite her, his legs bracketing hers, Knox rested one hand on the armrest and balanced his glass on his thigh with the other. "You don't want kids, baby?"

"It's not that." Though she'd never asked herself that question before. "I guess I just worry that I wouldn't make a good parent."

He frowned at the ridiculous idea. "Of course you would."

Harper blinked, surprised at the surety in his statement. "Knox, I don't know anything about parenthood. And although Lucian has plenty of other offspring and Carla has Roan and Kellen, I never grew up with any of them. I never had to be responsible for anyone."

"Sure you did," said Knox, taking a swig of his gin and tonic. "You took care of Lucian. He didn't raise you, Harper. He relied on you. Like you've often said in his defense, he can't meet his own needs. One conversation with him was enough for me to see that he's a grown spoilt, self-centered child. You were the parent in that relationship. And you somehow coped with him."

She could admit that her father hadn't been . . . well, a father. And she could admit she'd taken care of him in a lot of ways, but Knox was missing something. "That's not the same as taking care of a baby. As raising it and teaching it right from wrong and all that stuff."

His grip tightened on the armrest as the craft started to

move. "I have every confidence that you would make a great mother."

She cocked her head. "Why?"

"You're protective. Responsible. Caring. You have your priorities in the right order, and you're good at whatever you put your mind to." He nudged her leg with his. "Don't worry so much, baby. I never had siblings either. I'll be just as out of my element as you'll be. But we're two very capable people. I'm sure we can manage."

She had to smile. It had to be great to be so utterly confident. She envied him that. "Do you ever doubt yourself in any situation?" she asked, curious.

"To do that would be to hold me back in life. I don't see the sense in doing that. Self-belief is a powerful thing."

He had a point there, she thought.

"Nora said there would be a child one day. She didn't sound as if she meant someday soon," Knox pointed out. "Let's just cross that bridge when we come to it."

Harper sipped at her Coke. "What bothers me most of all was that Nora also said people would come for the baby." She stilled as his eyes very briefly bled to black. That idea clearly riled his demon.

Knox spoke, menace in every syllable. "If we ever have a child and someone comes for it, they'll suffer so horribly they'll beg for death." Only that reprieve wouldn't come until Knox was ready to give it to them, which could very well be never. His parents hadn't protected him when he'd needed it. He'd be damned if he failed his child the way they failed him.

"Can I watch you torture them?"

His mouth curved. "Bloodthirsty little thing."

"Surely this is not new information to you."

His smile widened. "No, it's not. And I like that you're

bloodthirsty." She was a good person, but not innocent. "Innocent" would never be able to handle him or accept him. "Now stop worrying about things that haven't even happened, get over here, and give me your mouth."

She sniffed, though she did unclip her seatbelt. "Bossy."

"Surely this is not new information to you."

Straddling him, Harper laughed. "No, not new at all."

CHAPTER SEVENTEEN

———◆———

Harper looked up from her sketchpad as the door swung open and Raini strolled inside their office with a Deli takeout bag. The scent of fresh bread, mayonnaise, smoky meat, and hot peppers wafted over Harper, making her stomach rumble.

"Time for lunch," said Raini.

"Good, I'm starving." Standing, Harper did a long, languid stretch.

Raini leaned over the desk to take a closer look at one of the sketches of an owl tattoo. "That's cool."

"The client doesn't like it."

The succubus frowned. "Really? Why not?"

"She has lots of grand ideas, but she doesn't know how she wants the tattoo to look. So we sat down and discussed it in length. I did a few rough sketches of different styles, and she agreed that something like this would be great. However, every time she came back to look at what should be the final design, there was something minor that she didn't like about it. The one you're looking at is the initial design." Harper held up another sketch. "This is the seventh revision. I'm hoping that she's happy with this one."

Harper understood the need to be completely sure about the design; a tattoo was permanent and, in many cases, had senti-mental value. The client *should* be totally happy with it. But there was being cautious and there was being a nit-picker. This particular client was the latter, though not in a bitchy way ... just in a very time-consuming way that plucked at Harper's impatient nature.

"You have another client coming after lunch and then we're closing early today so we can go to the BBQ," Raini reminded her. A family from Jolene's lair was throwing the BBQ to cele-brate someone's birthday.

"I know. I told the client she'd have to either make another appointment or come back on our walk-in day." Harper rounded the desk as she added, "I just hope the next one isn't as chatty as the others." They'd all peppered her with questions.

Was she excited about the upcoming event?

Did she have a nice outfit?

Would it be delayed until Crow was found?

A few had actually been ballsy enough to ask what she thought about Crow's vision, though she'd sensed fear behind the question. It was a rational fear, to be fair.

Each time, she'd simply snorted and said, *"Why is it that all rogues believe the end of the world is coming? Why don't they ever think anything nice will happen?"*

Praise the Lord that it was Friday. They could all use the weekend to unwind after how hectic things had been of late.

Knox, the sentinels, and the Force had invested a lot of time, energy, and emotion into finding Crow over the past week—so much, in fact, that Knox spent many nights in his office making calls, checking camera feeds for signs of Crow, and also catching up on the amount of work he'd had to put on hold. And, yes, he'd done a lot of brooding.

They hadn't had much quality time together lately, but she got why and she let him be. Feeding his frustration was that Crow was doing an extremely good job of hiding. He hadn't once tried to get to Knox. Hadn't appeared at any of the hotels or showed up on any security cameras anywhere. He was either lying low or Levi's theory was right and it was quite possible that Crow was dead. The "not knowing" bugged them all.

Harper agreed with Knox that it would be a mistake to assume he was dead and drop their guard, particularly since that could be what Crow wanted. Knox had become more hyper-protective than usual, making her demon feel stifled and exasperated. Harper was a little more understanding, though it sometimes grated on her nerves too.

They still had no way of even guessing the identities of the Horsemen. It had made Harper a little paranoid, really. After all, they could literally be anyone—even someone she knew and liked.

"Did your new shoes for the shindig arrive?" Raini asked, pulling her out of her thoughts.

"Yep. They fit fine." And they matched her dress perfectly.

"I still say we should have gone shoe-shopping."

"Of course you do." Harper preferred shopping online, where there were no crowds. As she reached the door, the phone in her pocket vibrated. Retrieving it, she frowned at the unfamiliar number. "Hello?"

"Hey, baby girl," drawled a familiar deep voice.

"Lucian, hi," said Harper.

Raini's mouth set into a flat line.

He spoke again, but Harper couldn't hear him over the music

blaring in the background. "I can't hear you. Where exactly are you?"

"Thailand," he replied loudly—so loud that Raini was able to hear him and mouthed, "Thailand?"

"I found myself a nice little bar where I can drown my sorrows," he added, glum.

Sorrows? "What's wrong?"

"He died," said Lucian, a hitch in his voice.

Her frown deepened. "What? Who?" There was a slurping sound that told her he'd just downed a good deal of whatever he was drinking.

"Elvis."

She scratched the back of her head. "Um, Lucian, Elvis Presley died a *long* time ago."

"Not him," he said, impatient. "My Elvis. My emu."

Raini crossed her eyes, but Harper said, "I'm sorry to hear that. What happened to him?"

A sniffle. "I can't talk about it, baby girl. It hurts too bad."

"Of course. I understand." She considered telling him about the Crow situation, but she didn't for the exact same reason that she didn't tell him about the shindig. Lucian would probably turn up, and having him and Knox in close proximity was not a good idea. Especially when Knox's current basic emotional setting recently was "irritated."

"So ... have you broken up with that psychopathic bastard yet?" he asked.

Harper placed a hand on her hip. "He's not a psychopath."

"That's what you think, but they're good at blending. They show you what they want you to see and tell you what you want to hear. Then they carve you up and bury you under the patio."

She closed her eyes. "Lucian, I can't have this conversation. I just can't."

"Fine," he said, petulant. "When he murders you in your sleep, don't come crying to me." The line went dead.

Raini shook her head. "I don't have words where he's concerned."

Harper slipped her cell back into her pocket. "Yeah, most people don't." Swinging open the door, she strolled into the working area with Raini. Harper then signaled for Khloë and Devon to join them in the back room.

Devon, who was sweeping the floor, said, "Give me two seconds."

Phone to her ear, Khloë raised her forefinger at Harper as she spoke to whoever was on the other end of the call. "I can assure you that your tattoo is not washing off. It's just a little excess ink. Some will wash or flake out as your body heals. Try your hardest not to pick at the scabs. If after the tattoo is fully healed it still seems to have breaks in the lines, come back and we'll patch it right up."

The doorbell chimed, and Harper tensed as Kellen walked inside. His shoulders were hunched and his gaze was wary as he scanned the studio until he spotted her. He offered a sheepish smile that made her chest twinge.

Tanner, who'd followed him inside, raised a questioning brow at Harper. *He says he wants to talk to you. I can throw him out if you want.*

I'll talk to him. She was interested to hear what he had to say. Tanner nodded but didn't leave, eyes boring into Kellen's back.

Harper slowly made her way to him, unsurprised when Raini and Devon followed. Harper waited until her cousin ended her call before she said, "Hey."

Rubbing the back of his nape, Kellen spoke. "Harper . . ." His face was a mask of regret.

She took pity on the kid. "It's okay."

"No, it's not," Kellen insisted, his expression downcast. "But I didn't know what to do."

She tilted her head. "About what? Why did you think I wouldn't want to see you?"

He licked his lips. "Roan ... it was my fault he yelled at you."

Harper blinked at the unexpected answer. "How could it be your fault?"

"He found out that I meet with you sometimes. I don't know how; he wouldn't tell me. Anyway, he was really pissed ... " He trailed off, cheeks reddening.

"It's okay, you can use bad words," she told him with a smile. "So he was upset with you?"

"He said I was betraying Mom by seeing you. He told me if I didn't swear to stay away from you, I'd be sorry. I told him it was my life and my decision. Then he ... I really am sorry. I didn't think he'd stay bad stuff about you to the lair and then yell at you, I thought he'd yell at *me*. Then when he got punished by Knox, Dad was really mad at me. He said I should have just left well enough alone."

"Why would Bray blame you for what Roan did?" asked Devon, folding her arms. "That's shitty."

"Roan flies into rages sometimes," said Kellen. "I get blamed for 'setting him off.'" His eyes cut to Harper. "I wasn't sure if you'd blame me too."

Harper exhaled heavily. "Roan did what he did because he's an ass, not because of anything you did or didn't do. I do not blame you. Got me?"

Swallowing, he nodded curtly. "Yeah. Bray and Roan won't like that I've come here, but I heard that Mom spoke to you. I figured if she could, I should be able to, right?" He jutted out his chin.

"Right," said Harper, "so come tell me what you've been doing with yourself lately."

Tanner then returned outside so Khloë could lock the front door and flip the sign to "Closed for Lunch."

Harper led Kellen into the back room, where all five of them took a seat at the table and dug into the deli takeout. As they ate, he and Harper caught up on what had been happening in their lives. She hadn't realized how much she'd liked their little talks until he stopped answering her calls. Over the years, she'd seen Roan and Kellen from afar. Had wondered what they were like. Roan might be an ass, but Kellen was a sweet kid who didn't bother with swagger to try to fit in. He just was who he was, and she respected that.

It was shortly after they had finished lunch that there was a knock at the front door.

"I'll get it," announced Devon, disappearing out of the room. She returned moments later with Knox, who looked as hot and tempting as ever.

Harper smiled at him, and her demon practically rubbed its hands with glee. "Hey there."

Knox stroked a hand over her hair and nodded at her brother, surprised to see him. "Kellen. I trust you won't shut Harper out like that again." It was a pressing suggestion that carried a threat.

Kellen swallowed nervously. "I won't."

"Good." Knox suspected the teenager didn't realize how much it had hurt Harper when he cut contact with her, but Knox knew. And he had no intention of allowing it to happen again. Turning back to Harper, Knox asked, "How long before you're done here?"

Rising from her seat, Harper started clearing the table. "We're closing at two today so we can go to the BBQ, remember. You're invited too."

"Ah, yes," said Knox. He'd forgotten about that, what with all that was going on. "I'm afraid you won't be going to the BBQ."

She slowly lifted a brow. "I won't."

"No, because I need you to come with me somewhere."

"Yeah? Where?" she asked, intrigued and wary at the same time. He just gave a crooked, enigmatic smile.

"Don't worry, you'll like it."

"So this is a surprise for her?" Raini asked Knox, looking excited on Harper's behalf.

"Yes," replied Knox, amused to see that his mate was looking at him suspiciously. He wondered if she'd ever like surprises. He doubted it. "Meet me at my office after you're done here."

"Seriously, where are we going? Where are you taking me?" Harper couldn't keep the impatience out of her voice. The truth was that she wasn't a fan of surprises or delayed gratification. And he damn well knew it.

His mouth curved. "You'll see."

CHAPTER EIGHTEEN

———◦◦◉◦◦———

After a short flight on the private jet, Harper found herself standing on a pier where a line of boats rocked gently as their owners waxed, cleaned, or hauled on supplies. The sun sparkled off the exteriors, seeming to somehow illuminate them. That same sun beat down on her, prickling her cheeks and nose. The seagulls flying overhead cawed and screeched.

None of that held her attention.

She was too busy staring at the breath-taking, four-decked, gleaming white mega yacht in front of her. All sleek fiberglass and polished wood, it was a sight to behold. "That's pretty impressive."

"Thank you," said the demon at her side.

She blinked up at Knox. "It's yours? Of course it's yours. Dumb question." She should be used to his level of luxury by now.

"Ours," he corrected. What was his was hers, as far as Knox were concerned.

"We're going to spend the weekend on the yacht?" The only

clue he'd given her as to where they were going was that she'd need bikinis.

"I want us to have some uninterrupted time together." They hadn't had enough of it recently; he'd neglected her again, and he hated that. Although Tanner and Levi were coming along, they would give them space. "It will be good for us."

"I accepted your apology for all the brooding. I'm honestly not mad about it." He didn't need to do nice things for her.

"I know, which I appreciate because I am nowhere near as understanding as you are." Knox would have lost his patience and demanded her attention because, well, he was that selfish. He placed a hand on her lower back. "Come on." Knox guided her along the pier, across the bridge, and onto the main deck. "I want to introduce you to the crew."

Having met the rather charming, uniformed crew—all of whom were demons—Harper tangled her fingers with his as Knox took her on a tour of the yacht. The bright and spacious interior was as impressive as the exterior. The lower deck featured a home theater, gym, guest cabins, crew quarters, engine room, and also an exterior platform with outdoor showers and plenty of "toys," including kayaks and motor boats.

The sun terrace of the main deck led into a salon—a place to escape the sun that had comfy looking couches, a wide-screen TV, and a bar. The dining salon was just as spacious, and the galley was every chef's wet dream. Large windows were everywhere, allowing in plenty of light.

The upper deck featured a sun terrace for outdoor dining and also Knox and Harper's extremely decadent bedroom suite—or stateroom, as he called it, whatever. The sun deck was probably the coolest of all, though, with its Jacuzzi, wet bar, and cozy little seating area.

After the tour was over, Harper slipped on a hot-pink bikini and settled on a rattan lounger on the main deck. Smearing on sunscreen, she peeked at Knox, who was sprawled on the lounger beside hers in just swim shorts, drinking wine. He was also closely watching the movements of her hands, and she had to smile.

He looked more relaxed than she'd seen him in a while. But then, it was pretty impossible to be anything but relaxed right then. The heat of the sun, the cool spray of the ocean water, and the light, salt-scented breeze—it all created a deliciously lazy atmosphere. The only sounds were that of the engine, the hull slicing through the water, and the soft laughter of Levi and Tanner who were on the above deck. They were giving her and Knox privacy, bless them.

"I'm not sure whether this bothers me or not," said Knox.

Confused, she frowned. "What?"

"The brand on your breast is slightly visible through the thin material of your bikini. I like that I can see it." It was sexy as hell. "But I don't like that it's eye-catching enough to draw people's attention to your breasts." They were for his eyes alone.

She snickered. "Take the matter up with your demon."

"Baby, that put-out tone isn't fooling me for a second—you like that brand."

Yeah, she did. She liked the others too, for that matter. "Whatever." Putting down the bottle of sunscreen, she lay back.

"Did Kellen tell you why he thought you wouldn't want to see him?"

"Yes." Harper repeated the conversation she'd had with Kellen. "I'm surprised Bray wasn't supportive of Kellen being in contact with me. I mean, he was upset with Carla for the way she abandoned me. He's all about family."

"Bray's had it hard lately, what with Carla disappearing," said Knox. "He probably just wanted to keep Roan calm so that he didn't do anything else that would earn him a punishment from me." That didn't mean Knox could or would excuse Bray's behavior.

"Well, his plan failed."

Knox put his empty glass on the small table between them. "I don't want to talk about him or anything else that could ruin the mood."

"So I probably shouldn't tell you that Lucian called me earlier, huh?" she said with a smile.

Knox's demon snarled. "What did he want?"

"His emu died. He's devastated."

Emu? Knox's demon rolled its eyes. "Is he coming back to Vegas any time soon?"

"No. It'll probably be another few months before he does. Besides, he's still sulking over my refusal to leave 'that psychopathic bastard.'"

"He's a waste of skin, Harper, and a sad excuse for a parent." The only reason Knox hadn't beat the shit out of him was that Lucian did actually care for her in his own way. She was the only person he had an attachment to, in fact.

"He's not so bad."

"You deserve a better father than he could ever be."

"Your parents let you down, but you still cared for them right up until the end, right?"

"Hmm." His parents hadn't been biologically related to him, since his kind were born from the flames of hell, but they had cared for him. Loved him, even. They'd also fell victim to the lies and manipulation of a demon cult-like leader and failed to protect Knox from him.

Eventually they'd stood up for him. And then the leader had slit their throats as punishment. At that point, Knox lost control of his demon for the first time in his life. And the demon avenged his parents in a very painful and final way.

"What were your parents like, if you don't mind me asking?" asked Harper.

"Of course I don't mind you asking. They were idealists. Not always grounded in reality. They didn't like what they were. It wasn't that they were ashamed of being archdemons; it was that they hadn't liked living a life in which they had to hide what they were from their friends. My mother liked to cook, but she wasn't very good at it. My father liked to build things. He was full of ideas, but he never finished any project that he started unless he was ordered to do so by the leader."

Then they were very unlike Knox, thought Harper. He saw things through to the end. "I don't think they purposely failed you, Knox. I don't think they meant to hurt you."

"Their intentions were good when they helped form the group." For that reason, he could forgive them for their mistakes. But Lucian? His motivations were always selfish, and Knox would never make allowances for that.

"This may seem like a really dumb question," began Harper, "but do you remember anything about being born from the flames?"

"No, I don't. My earliest memories are of when I was a toddler."

"Tell me a little about the children's home you stayed at." He'd only ever mentioned that in vague terms, so all she really knew was that it was where he met the sentinels.

"It wasn't good. It wasn't bad." But at least he'd been safe there. "It was cold. Dull. There was no real color there. Everything was plain, including the food. The staff were strict, but they had to be in order to deal with a group of demon orphans. I liked the library. I spent most of my time there; absorbed every bit of knowledge I could find."

"Is the place still standing?"

"Yes. It's a hotel now."

"You bought it," she guessed.

"Someone needed to save it."

Like it had saved him, Harper thought. The ice clinked against the glass as she sipped at her soda. "What drew you and the sentinels together?"

He thought about it for a moment. "Rage, maybe."

She hadn't expected that answer. "Rage?"

"All five of us carry it, each for our own reasons. Isla had it too."

"For what it's worth, I'm sorry that she put you in a position where you had to kill her—she was once your friend, so it had to have hurt on some level."

Knox looked at his mate, amazed she could feel that way when the person in question had wanted her dead and, in temporarily stealing some of Harper's power, made her vulnerable to the dark practitioners that had then kidnapped her. That night had been awful for her in more ways than one, but she could still speak Isla's name without anger. "Come here."

Harper slid off her lounger and straddled him. "What?"

He smoothed his hands up her back, breathing in the coconut scent of her sunscreen. "It's a very good thing that I was the first demon to ever possess you. Not just because I would have been tempted to hunt down and destroy the others, but because if another demon had had you, he wouldn't have let you go. Then I'd have had to kill him to take you from him."

Harper snorted, amused. "You wouldn't have done any such thing."

"As I once told you, I'd started to feel numb to everything. Then there was you. And it all changed. You surprise me. Defy me. Frustrate me. Amuse me. Tease me. Having someone do those things . . . it was like waking up after a long yet unfulfilling sleep. So, yes, I'd have done whatever it took to have you."

"You'd have had me as your anchor," she reminded him.

"That wouldn't have been enough." He slipped one bikini strap aside and kissed her shoulder. Her petal-soft skin was hot from the sun. "I was always sure I wouldn't need an anchor. It wasn't until our psyches connected that I realized that, for all my power, you're truly the only thing that could stop me turning rogue."

"Sometimes I think, given my personality, I'm also the most likely thing to drive you to the brink of insanity."

Pulling back, he smiled. "It's true that you can get to me in a way that no one else can."

"That's just what it means to love someone. They can hurt you worse than anyone, but they can also make you happier than another person ever could."

"Which is why I'm never letting you go."

They spent the next two days sunbathing, swimming, scuba diving, and doing other watersports that he convinced her to try. Her favorite was scuba diving. She'd done it a few times before, so she already knew how to use the equipment. Still, it felt weird breathing through a regulator, and it took a while before she could tune out the bubbling and whooshing of air as she breathed underwater. Having her peripheral vision obstructed by the face mask annoyed her, because Harper didn't like blind spots. Still, scuba diving itself was awesome.

She loved the underwater paradise with the colorful fish, amazing coral displays, and the rock formations. Loved the freeing feeling of weightlessness—of being able to fly up, down, left and right. As always, she was exhausted by the end of it.

Her evenings with Knox included a seriously delicious meal followed by either a dip in the Jacuzzi, a movie in the theater, or simply having drinks at the wet bar with the sentinels. On

their last night, after she'd showered and—exhausted by watersports—pretty much fell face first on bed wearing only a towel,
she felt Knox's warmth breath on the back of her shoulder.

"Wake up for me," he whispered.

"In a minute," she sleepily mumbled into the pillow.

"Come on, wake up."

"I just need a minute. Or an hour."

He kissed and licked her shoulder. "This is important."

"What?"

"I have something for you."

She groaned. Not more gifts. They were always super expensive and it still felt weird to accept stuff from him.

Knox chuckled. "Such gratitude." Not that he'd expected a
different response. He actually found her awkwardness at receiv-
ing gifts kind of endearing.

"What is it?" She rolled onto her back to find him sitting on
the edge of the bed, a towel around his waist. And he was holding
a small, black velvet box. "Not more jewelry," she whined with a
playful smile. Her demon was excited. It liked shiny things.

He chuckled again and handed it to her. "Open the box."

"Do I have to?"

"No, but I'd like you to."

She sat up. "Okay." She carefully opened the box. And
swallowed hard. It wasn't a ring. It was two rings. One was a
black-gold band that was dotted with small diamonds. The
second was also a smooth black gold and it looped twice, crossing
just beneath where a black diamond was set.

Harper cleared her suddenly dry throat. A demon only bought
a black diamond for their mate; it was a symbol of their com-
mitment, the ultimate brand. Couples often waited years—even
centuries—before exchanging them, as demons didn't make any
commitments lightly.

"You're that sure of me?" she asked him, astonished. "I thought it would have taken you a long, long time to get to this point." She knew that he was so used to being alone.

"I want you to wear these. I want you to be able to look at them and remember you're very important to someone." Knox hated that her emotional reflex was to expect people to leave her, but who could blame her for that? Both parents had abandoned her as a child. Although she eventually went to live with her completely useless father, she'd then lived a nomadic lifestyle, always leaving things and people behind.

Knox needed her to believe he wasn't going anywhere. He needed her to understand that it wasn't because she was his anchor, it was because he fucking adored her. "I want you to always have these reminders that you belong to someone—me. And I want others to see them and know you're off-limits." Even humans would understand the rings symbolized she was taken.

Feeling a little choked up, Harper said nothing. She just stared at the rings, moved and warmed by what they meant. She just . . . she wouldn't have expected . . . she just . . . wow. The whole thing was just surreal. She had no words.

"I was originally going to wait until the night of the event to give them to you. But I knew there was a possibility that you wouldn't feel ready to wear them yet. I would have understood. Still, you'd have felt bad about it. The whole thing would have made an awkward start to what I want to be a pleasant evening for us." Knox would like to think she was ready, but there was really never any knowing how his mate would react to anything. He'd bet she was unpredictable even to herself. "So I'm choosing to give them to you early."

Knox studied her expression, trying to guess what was going through her head. He had no clue. "If you're not ready, I'll accept that. No pressure." But if she didn't say something soon, he was going to snap. The silence stretched on. Just when he opened his mouth to demand to know what she was thinking, she carefully plucked the two rings from the box and slid them on the third finger of her left hand. Relief rushed through him and his demon. Until amusement flashed across her face. "What's funny?"

She somehow managed to speak past the frog in her throat. "I'm just surprised you didn't have 'Property of Knox Thorne' inscribed on the rings."

"I thought about it."

Still stunned, Harper just stared at the diamond. Her demon was smirking, thrilled that its mate had committed so fully to it. "They're a perfect fit. How did you guess what size I'd need?"

Knox brushed his mouth over hers. "Baby, I know every inch of that body." It was imprinted on his brain.

Harper skimmed her finger over the black diamond. "Did they come as a set?" Mating rings usually came as a set: the diamond ring, the "her" ring, and the "his" band.

Knox took her hand and kissed her palm. "Yes, but I don't have to wear a ring just because you're wearing them."

She frowned. "I want you to wear it. Not because you gave me these, but because I love you. And because it'll warn off all those flirty heifers that flock around you."

He curled his hand around her neck and said against her mouth, "Then that's what I'll do." He kissed her. Hard. Long. Deep.

"Where's the third band?" she asked when he broke the kiss with a nip to her lip.

"In a box in my bag."

"Then go get it."

"You're sure?"

She sighed. "Would I say it if I wasn't?"

No, she wouldn't. Mouth quirking, he did as she requested. It was a thicker version of her black gold band and was dotted with silver diamonds. The diamond in the center, however, was black. Sliding the band on his third finger, Knox closed his fist. "Never thought I'd ever wear one of these. Or that I'd be proud to." Or that his demon would be smug about such a thing.

Moving to the bed, Knox flipped open their towels and gave her his weight. "No psychic hands tonight, baby. Just you and me."

He linked their fingers, feeling her rings, and pinned her hands above her head as he fucked her soft, slow, and deep. Fucked her until she screamed into his mouth and came apart around him. With two slams of his cock, he followed her right over the edge.

CHAPTER NINETEEN

⬥⬥⬥

"Oh my God! I will kill you!"

At Harper's angry cry, Knox rushed out of his office, down the staircase, and into the dining room ... and there was his mate, arguing with the Devil himself. Pinching the bridge of his nose, Knox sighed. "Lou, what are you doing here?"

Lucifer turned to look at him. He was dressed in faded jeans, sneakers, a baseball cap, and a Bob Marley T-shirt that read "Why Drink and Drive When You Can Smoke and Fly?". With an innocent expression he said, "I just wanted to ask if she'd sew some skeleton heads on my new jacket. She started yelling at me, which I feel was unnecessary."

Harper's mouth tightened. "Look at me, I'm *soaked*." Her white shirt had a huge brown stain. "You shocked me on purpose."

"No use crying over spilt coffee," Lou told her with a huff.

Knox sighed again as the two proceeded to argue. Lucifer actually visited her regularly. If Knox didn't know any better, he'd think Lou liked her. But the psychotic, abrasive, sarcastic, and irritatingly mercurial male disliked everyone.

Contrary to what several human religions upheld, Lucifer was not the ruler of hell. He did have a major dispute with God, though, after which he moved to hell and brought some order to it. His laws were short and straightforward: demons must protect knowledge of their existence from humans, they must not get caught breaking human laws, and they must never harm a child of any species.

"I will send you a chain letter—don't think I won't," Harper warned. It was a threat that worked, since the guy was OCD.

Lou gaped. "That's just mean. No, that goes beyond mean. That's—"

"I don't care," said Harper.

Knox stepped forward. "Why are you here?"

Lou looked at him. "I told you, I want her to jazz up my new jacket." He slung the denim coat on the table before sinking into a chair with a happy sigh. Noticing the rings that they had exchanged the previous night, he whistled. "Black diamonds, huh. Who would have thought you'd ever be so tangled up in a female, Knox? It's quite nauseating actually."

"It is not nauseating," said Harper, plucking at her wet shirt. Her skin burned from the scalding splash of the coffee.

"Hey, I heard about what happened to Carla. This Crow-guy is *warped*." Looking at Knox, Lou smiled and added, "I also heard that he claims to have had a *fascinating* vision that Harper will have a baby that's the same breed as you."

"Not a vision, a delusion," said Harper. "It was planted in his head."

"It's still fascinating," Lou insisted. An excited glint to his eyes, he went on, "I can just imagine a tiny bundle of chaos, death, and cosmic power. Think of the destruction it could cause."

"Yes, because that's exactly what I would want my child to do," Harper said in a deadpan voice.

Lou's smile widened. "Me too. I will totally babysit. Hey, you could name it after me!"

And Knox knew he wasn't kidding. He exhaled heavily, seeking patience. "Any child Harper and I have will be a sphinx and you know it."

Lou's brow furrowed. "That doesn't mean it can't be pure evil and carry an innate wish to indiscriminately wipe out everything in its path."

Harper's hands clenched into little fists. "If and when I have a baby, it will not be evil."

Lou clasped his hands behind his head. "You say that now, but you might think differently when you catch it choking chickens for the pure joy of it."

Harper made a guttural noise in the back of her throat. The guy could not be real.

Lou studied her. "You sure you're not pregnant now? It might explain why you're all flushed and in a mood."

"I'm not in a mood, I'm pissed because I'm *soaked in coffee.*"

"Are we still on that?"

Harper raised a hand. "I need to go change. First, who's pulling Crow's strings?"

Lou shrugged, seeming surprised by the question. "How would I know?"

"You're the Devil. Don't you keep a close watch on our kind?"

"I have a life, you know," he replied, affronted. "Hell is filled with things to do. Besides, people aren't very interesting to watch. All they really do is eat, sleep, and shit. But a baby with the power to decimate the universe—now that would be entertaining. And you really should call it Lucifer." He pounded his fist on his chest. "It's a good, strong name."

Harper looked at Knox. "He really is serious about that, isn't he?"

"Deadly," Knox confirmed, surreal as it was.

"Evil kids can be real cute, you know," said Lou. "Haven't you seen Stephen King's *Pet Sematary*? When that little boy goes after his mother with a scalpel ... wow, totally cute. You can't help but want to hug him." He tilted his head. "I wonder why King deliberately spelled 'Sematary' wrong. I'll Google it later."

Harper shook her head in exasperation. The guy was wacked. "Off the topic of babies, you must know about the demons calling themselves the Four Horsemen. Well, *three* Horsemen now that Isla's dead. Who are the others?"

Lou's brows pulled together. "There are demons genuinely calling themselves the Four Horsemen? How uninventive. And why would they want the apocalypse to come calling?"

"They don't," she told him. "They want to see the US Primes fall."

"Well, that's not very ambitious."

"So you have no idea who they are?"

"Nope." And Lou clearly wasn't concerned about it either.

Harper's shoulders slumped. "What about Crow? Do you know where he is?"

"Like I said, I have a life. I'm not like the big G," Lou added, pointing to the sky. "I'm not interested in keeping tabs on people."

"You just like appearing at their side and startling the shit out of them, making them soak themselves in coffee," said Harper dryly.

"Are we back to that again?"

"We never left it."

Knox moved closer to Lou, arms folded. "I have a question for you. How could someone have got inside my prison and taken Crow?"

"They couldn't have," replied Lou. "But they could have extracted him by magickal means. It wouldn't have been easy. Probably would have taken blood magick."

Knox narrowed his eyes. "So the person responsible is either an incantor or a dark practitioner." One that was powerful, since blood magick was no simple thing to perform.

Harper planted her hands on her hips. "The question is . . . were they hired by the Horsemen, or *are* they one of the Horsemen?"

The answer was . . . Knox had no idea.

She plucked at her wet shirt again, lip curled in distaste. "I really need to change out of this shirt."

Lou stood upright. "Before you start riding my ass about that again I'm off. Got stuff to do. People to torment. Harper, don't forget to jazz up my jacket. I'll see you both at the big party."

Knox frowned. "Who invited you?"

"I did," said Lou. He pointed at Harper. "Be safe. We don't want anything to stop Baby Lucifer's conception."

Harper looked at Knox. "If you don't kill him, I will."

But Lou was already gone; the echo of his laughter was in the air.

Knox crossed to her and sank his fingers into her hair. "There are times when I wonder if he might actually like you." He kissed the pout right off her face. "You're going to sow pink sequins on his jacket, aren't you?"

She placed her hands on his chest. "Yep. But considering he's an absolute nut job, it really wouldn't surprise me if the weird bastard liked them."

Knox twisted his mouth. "Yeah, it wouldn't surprise me much either."

*　　*　　*

Since she had to change her shirt, Harper was a little late walking into the coffeehouse. The door chimed as she pushed it open, and the girls somehow heard it over the whirr of machines, the chatter of customers, the dishes clattering, and the staff calling out orders. It had become a regular routine for them to meet there before heading into their new studio. She liked it.

As Harper crossed to the bistro table near the large window with Tanner in tow, Devon pointed to a steaming mug and said, "We ordered your usual caramel latte. I even drizzled chocolate all over the froth for you."

"And that's why I love you." Harper really didn't feel like joining that eternally long queue.

Tanner's brow furrowed. "Hey, what about my cappuccino?"

Devon gave him a blank look. "What about it?"

Raini gestured to the mug near the free seat between her and Harper. "It's right here. Before you ask, no, I will not move so you can sit next to Devon and torture her."

"You're no fun," complained Tanner.

Fairly plonking herself on the padded seat, Harper sighed happily. She loved coffeehouses. Loved the scent of fresh-brewed coffee, warm caramel, and the pastries in the glass case beneath the cash register.

"So, today we need to—" Devon cut herself off, eyes widening, and grabbed Harper's hand. "A black diamond? Knox gave you a *black diamond?*"

Harper smiled, admiring the rings once more. Her demon loved how shiny and twinkly they were. Most of all, her demon loved what they represented. "Yeah."

Devon flopped back into her seat, a smile curling her mouth. "Oh. My. God. I'm floored. Not that I didn't think he was utterly devoted to you."

Raini leaned forward to get a good look at the rings. "They're so beautiful. Is he wearing one too?"

Harper cradled the warm, porcelain mug with her hands. "Yep. He let it be my decision, though. He said he didn't have to wear one just because I was wearing these."

"The guy has good taste," said Khloë, swirling her smoothie. "I'll bet his demon is smug as fuck. Does Grams know yet?"

"Yes, I told her this morning." Harper sipped at her latte and hummed in appreciation. "She said that if I'm happy, she's happy." She also hadn't been at all surprised by the news.

"How did Knox give the rings to you?" asked Raini.

"He woke me up, handed me a box, and then told me he wanted me to wear them so I'd have a constant reminder that I was important to someone."

Devon put a hand on her heart. "It's hard not to like the scary son of a bitch."

Tanner snorted a laugh before grabbing a newspaper from a neighboring table.

"I'm so happy for you, Harper," said Raini with an excited smile.

"Me, too." Khloë slurped some of her smoothie. "And I predict it's going to be really fun to watch people's expressions when they notice the rings."

"So far, it kind of has been." Some had looked shocked, others had appeared pleasantly surprised, and— in the case of several females—some had seemed severely disappointed. Harper's demon enjoyed the latter.

"As immature as this sounds, I am so looking forward to seeing Belinda's expression when she sees them," said Raini, stirring her tea.

"You should get your wish soon enough." Harper took another sip of her latte. "She wanted to see me, so I asked her to meet me here."

Raini did a little clap. "I do love a good show. Where have you and Knox been for the last few days anyway?"

"On his yacht," replied Harper.

"Well, of course he has a yacht," Devon said dryly.

A chiming sound was followed by the quick arrival of Larkin and Keenan. Harper smiled at them. "Hey, what brings you two here?"

"I heard about the rings from Levi and I really wanted to see them." Larkin looked at them as Harper held out her hand. "I'm not a girly girl but I'm actually squealing in my head."

"Some people are going to shit a brick, especially Alethea," said Keenan.

"We should celebrate," Devon announced.

Khloë nodded, excited. "We could go to the Xpress Bar tonight."

"You really want to get smashed again?" Keenan asked the imp.

Confused, Khloë said, "Why wouldn't I?"

Keenan folded his arms. "I'm not taking you home this time."

At his snippy tone, Khloë cocked her head. "Is this about me telling you that you have a monster cock?"

Raini nearly spat her tea all over the table. Larkin, shaking with silent laughter, patted the succubus' back. People turned at the word "cock," as if it had snapped them out of their own conversations. And why wouldn't it?

"No," Keenan ground out. "It's about the photograph you took that night."

Khloë sighed, rolling her eyes. "I don't know why you got so upset about it. It was a lousy picture anyway, since I couldn't fit your whole cock on it." That comment had plenty of brows raising. "On a serious note, did you have it surgically enlarged or are you just gifted in that department?" It was a genuine question.

With a groan, Devon buried her face in her hands.

Keenan looked at Harper, cheeks flushing with self-consciousness. "Make her stop."

Khloë snorted. "You're just mad because your incubus mojo has no effect on me."

Larkin blinked at him. "It doesn't? Really?"

"It's rare that people are immune to incubi allure, but it happens," said Keenan.

Hearing another chime, Harper swerved to see her favorite cambion enter the coffeehouse. Anticipation thrummed through her inner demon, who wanted to punch the bitch hard enough to leave an imprint of the rings so the cambion could never forget who Knox belonged to. "Well hello, Belinda."

Belinda's hand tightened around the strap of her purse. "I have been trying to get hold of you for *three days*. Why have you been ignoring my calls?"

"I wasn't ignoring them . . . per se." All right, she totally was. "Knox whisked me away for the weekend, so I was sort of busy."

Lips flat, Belinda said, "You couldn't take two minutes to answer at least one of my calls?"

"Now, let me see." Harper held out one hand, palm up. "Spend quality time with Knox." She held up her other hand, palm up. "Talk to you." Harper moved each hand up and down. "Knox was always going to win that one." Honestly, the cambion looked close to whacking Harper with her clipboard. Awesome. "So, what is it you want?"

"I took the liberty of writing you a speech. I need to know if there are any changes you wish to make or—"

"Whoa, hold on a minute. Speech?" Who said anything about a speech?

"Well, yes, of course."

Harper frowned. "Yeah, I'm not understanding the need for a speech."

"You'll need to thank the attendees for coming and express your gratitude to all those who helped to organize the event," said Belinda in an "obviously" tone. "You'll also need to say a few words of romance to Knox."

"I don't do speeches. Not my thing. Knox is the one who has a way with words. If there's anything that needs to be said, he'll do that." Harper would just trip over her own words or blush several shades of red.

"You can't leave everything to Knox."

"You're right, and I don't. But speeches are more his thing, and I can't recite something that somebody else wrote for me." It would make her feel phony. Harper prided herself on not being fake. "Besides, who really wants to hear from a Wallis?" she mocked.

Belinda's nostrils flared. "Fine. There are a few more things I need to run past you."

Harper finished off her latte as the cambion read out a list of things from her clipboard. When she abruptly stopped speaking, Harper looked up. And saw that Belinda was staring at the rings. Harper wiggled her fingers. "Like them?"

Belinda swallowed. "That's a black diamond."

"I know. So pretty and shiny."

"He gave you a black diamond?"

Harper grinned. "You're ecstatic for me. I can tell."

Spluttering, Belinda turned to Tanner. "Doesn't it worry you that your Prime isn't acting like himself?"

Tanner lifted his mug. "It would worry me if it were true."

Belinda ground her teeth. "He gave her—someone he barely knows—a *black diamond*."

The hellhound nodded. "Yeah, I can see that."

"Let me reiterate, he barely knows her."

"He clearly feels he knows all he needs to know." Tanner went back to his newspaper.

Lips pinched together, Belinda turned to Keenan. "Would *you* commit yourself so completely to someone you had only known a few months?"

"That's a human question," said Harper.

Belinda blinked. "Pardon?"

"Since you're half-human, I can understand why you'd have such an issue," said Harper. "See, humans need everything to make sense. But not everything can be seen, or heard, or felt, or explained. Some things just *are*."

Face flushing, Belinda spoke. "Knox is—"

"Uninterested in you, so get over your-fucking-self."

"Yeah, it really is about time you gave up the dream of being with Knox," Khloë told her. "There are plenty of other guys out there. You should consider Keenan. He's got a monster cock."

Keenan's cheeks turned fire engine red. "Khloë!"

"Am I wrong?" the imp challenged, raising one shoulder.

Trying not to laugh, Harper turned back to Belinda. "Are we done here?"

"We're done," she said, mouth tight around the edges. "Thank you for your time." Spinning on her high heel, she left.

A mind slid against Harper's—comforting and familiar. *You sure you don't want me to fire her, baby?* asked Knox. *I'd take great pleasure in doing it.*

Guessing one of his sentinels had alerted him about Belinda's little tantrum, Harper said, *That would spoil my fun.*

All right. His disappointment was evident in his telepathic tone. *Don't forget your flying session later.*

I won't. She was actually looking forward to it.

"Ready to get to work?" asked Devon.

"Yes. Later on, before we close for the day, I need you to do something for me."

The hellcat smiled. "Gladly. Just what might that be?"

CHAPTER TWENTY

———◦◦◦◦———

Once again standing near the border of a winding ravine, Harper moaned, "My back is *killing* me."

"I know, but you need to master this. It has to be second nature for you." Knox planted his feet, resisting the urge to go to his mate and comfort her. He was proud of how well she'd done and how very little she'd complained. He was pushing her hard, giving her no breaks. "Now ascend, and hold yourself in position until I tell you to drop."

So Harper did, just as she'd done at least eighty times in the past half hour. She was aching, sweating, and tired. The light breeze would have been welcome if it wasn't as hot as the day itself. Seriously, it was like having someone point a hairdryer at your face while it was on its hottest setting. As if that wasn't bad enough, the breeze brought plenty of dirt with it. She hated the gritty feel of it on her skin.

"Okay, drop." He nodded in satisfaction at her clean descent. "Again, Harper."

Biting back a curse, she did it again. And again. And again. And a-fucking-gain.

"Better. Much better. Now, do it once more. This time, I'm going to ask you to go higher and hold it a lot longer." When she slumped, Knox arched a brow. "Do you want to try flying or not? We'll do it today, but only if you master this move."

Harper rolled back her shoulders. "I'll do it," she bit out. She wanted to punch him square in the face for grinning at her. "What's so funny?"

"I'm not laughing."

"Not out loud."

"You're just cute when you're agitated." She was back to being a hissing, spitting kitten that amused the hell out of Knox and his demon.

"Let's just do this."

"All right, ascend." Knox felt another swell of pride as she made a perfect ascent and balanced effortlessly midair; she'd massively improved since the very first lesson. He kept her there for a good minute or so before allowing her to drop. "Very good. Ready to try flying?"

"More than."

"Good. Let's get started."

Harper gave a silent gasp of sheer awe as he snapped out his large wings. "Yours are so much cooler than mine." There were not only made of magma energy, the feathers were ablaze.

He lifted her hand to admire the rings; they looked good there, looked *right*. "Has anyone commented on these yet?"

"Pretty much every person who walked into the studio. They were all shocked. The demons from our lair seemed happy about it. Anyone ask about yours?"

"I've been in my office most of the day, so I've barely seen anyone. They'll no doubt be as surprised as the yacht's cabin crew."

Harper couldn't help but smile at the memory of the steward dropping the drinks in utter shock. "Probably." He kissed her and then pulled her to the edge of the ravine. Harper peered down, noticing the dry bed at the bottom. "That's a hell of a drop."

"It is, but it's also a good place to practice flying. In the sky, you have to contend with the wind and you'll be distracted by the view. Down there, the wind can't throw you around and there's nothing at all pretty to look at. The only thing to see is a drop that reminds you just how careful you have to be. Sometimes fear is the best motivator. You have to be positive that—"

"I can hover just fine," she clipped.

Knox's mouth curved. "I agree."

Good. "Now what?"

"Now you show us that we're both right." And he shoved her right over the edge.

Harper screamed and her stomach did some kind of dive as she hurtled at top speed toward the ground. The wind whipped up her hair and stole her breath, cutting off her scream. She flapped her wings like crazy, but it didn't seem to help. She was falling and falling.

Remembering what he taught her, she threw her weight backwards, making her body vertical. Harper then dug her heels down as she beat her wings harder and harder. And she some-fuckinghow came to a smooth stop a couple of inches above the bed of the ravine.

And there was her mate, leaning against the rock wall, looking impressed. She guessed he'd pyroported there—she didn't care. All she cared about doing was beating the ever-loving shit out of him.

Letting her feet touch the ground, she bore down on him. "You insane motherfucker! I could have died on impact!" Before she could smack the bastard, flames roared around him, pyro-porting him away.

"But you didn't," he said from behind her, a smile in his voice.

She whirled on him. "Sheer luck saved me!"

"Technique and muscle memory saved you," Knox corrected. "You came to a perfect stop. Well done, baby." She'd done better than he'd expected.

"You frightened the shit out of me!"

"I did, but are you scared of falling anymore?"

Her mouth opened, but no words came out . . . because no, she wasn't. "That was sneaky," she said, narrowing her eyes.

"But effective."

Harper couldn't deny that, and his smirk said he knew it. "Don't be smug."

"Don't sulk," he said.

"You're supposed to be teaching me how to fly, remember?"

He moved to her and cupped her neck. "I would have caught you if necessary; you know that." She was never at any risk.

"That's not the point."

He held out his hand, and she reluctantly placed hers in his. "I'm going to hold onto you until you're comfortable in the air. Even though you've mastered ascending, flying is somewhat different. You associate being balanced with standing upright and having your feet on the ground. You're not used to moving horizontally or relying on wings to move your body. Try not to kick your legs."

"Why would I kick my legs?"

"Because you've always relied on your legs to get you where you want to go—even swimming, you use your legs. It's instinctive to move them, but it will affect your balance." He squeezed her hand. "Ready?"

She took a preparatory breath. "Yeah."

"Ascend." Together, they gracefully moved upwards until they were a quarter of the way up the ravine. "Good. Now tip forward, but beat your wings at the same time. Forget your legs, they're not going to move you. Only your wings will." She wobbled a little at first, but soon enough she was in position. "That's it."

Following his every instruction, Harper focused on moving only her wings as they flew hand-in-hand in loose circles, going higher and higher. She was enjoying herself . . . until she quickly glanced down and swore. She hadn't realized they were *that* high.

"You'll be fine."

"Okay, but don't let go."

"Tuck your legs up to your stomach."

She frowned. "Why?"

"Do it."

So she did, and then she was squealing because he made her do a forward flip. But she wasn't angry. In fact, she was laughing. Her demon was having the time of its life, what with all the adrenalin pumping around Harper's system.

"Baby, look."

"What?" That was when she realized he'd let go of her hand. And, of course, she dropped like a lead weight. Cursing, she slowed her descent and came to a sharp halt in the air. She scowled at her mate as he flew in circles around her. "I should have known you'd let go."

"How will you learn if I'm always holding your hand?" Curling an arm around her waist, Knox pulled her close. "You're tired. Come on, we'll fly to the top and then we'll go home." Once they reached the top of the cliff, he pyroported them straight to the bathroom. "We both need a shower. Then we can go over all the security measures for Saturday."

"You think Crow will strike at the shindig, don't you?"

"The Underground will be packed with people, which makes it the perfect time for him to make his move."

"The doormen of the club can watch out for him."

"Yes, but he could have another demon teleport him to the Underground for a price." It was what the dark practitioners had done when they'd snatched Harper. Knox wasn't going to overlook the possibility of it happening a second time. "If one of the Horsemen can teleport, they could sneak him inside." Like Harper, Knox's money was on Alethea being Crow's puppeteer. "The point is we have to be ready for anything."

"We know he likes guns, so there's a strong possibility he'll just open fire." She helped him shove down her jeans and panties before kicking them and her shoes aside.

"Which is why we'll be surrounded by the sentinels and members of the Force. But guards or no guards, you don't leave my side." Knox whipped off her shirt and bra. And froze. "Fuck."

Harper smiled a little shyly as he stared at her new nipple ring. "Devon did it for me. You approve?"

Knox gently thumbed the ring on her unbranded breast, and her soft moan shot straight to his thickening cock. "You know I don't like rhetorical questions." He flicked the ring again, watching her face carefully. "Does it hurt?"

"It did until a few hours ago." Demons thankfully healed fast.

"Good." So unbelievably turned on it wasn't even funny, Knox swooped down and curled his tongue around her pierced nipple. Her fingers pulled at his hair—a demand for more. He gently tugged on the ring with his teeth, and her body curved into his with a breathy little moan. Knox quickly shed his own clothes and then tapped her ass. "Shower."

Harper stepped into the walk-in shower first, and he turned on the water. The LED ocean-blue lights came on just as the twelve-inch square rain shower sprayed down on them. Then his mouth was on hers, greedy and possessive; kissing her so fiercely that her head spun. He tasted of him and wine and the water raining down on them. His hands stroked and squeezed her ass as his tongue and teeth devastated her senses.

Her breasts seemed to swell and her pussy clenched, needing to be filled. Needing *him*. A kiss shouldn't have this much power over her body, but it did. *He* did. His knowing, confident fingers traced and shaped her. She shivered and goosebumps rose on her skin.

Knox broke the kiss and sat on the bench. "Come here." As she moved to stand between his legs, he scooped up her breasts and held them to his mouth. "All for me."

He feasted on her breasts—there was no other way Harper could describe it. His teeth grazed and bit. His tongue licked and swirled. Each tug on her nipple ring caused a jolt of pleasure in her pussy. And when he drew her unpierced nipple deep into his mouth and sucked hard . . . oh, that got him some bonus points. All she could do was cling to his solid shoulders.

Finally, he lifted his head and his mouth once more took total command of hers, swallowing every sigh and moan. "In me." She hated how needy she sounded, but she was so desperate to be fucked, she was shaking with it.

Knox tapped her full lower lip. "First, I want this mouth wrapped tight around my cock." Defiance glittered in her sapphire eyes, and he slowly arched a brow. "It's mine. Mine to fuck whenever I want to." Her jaw tightened, but she slowly got to her knees. "Good girl."

Good girl? Since Harper was seriously considering slapping his face, she wasn't sure the word "good" was the right choice. She needed him in her, dammit. Her nipples were tight and throbbing, and her pussy felt hot and painfully empty.

"Harper."

It was a warning and it vibrated with power and authority. Curling one hand around the base of the long, full cock bopping in front of her face, Harper took it into her mouth. She sucked and licked for all she was worth, knowing exactly what drove him to the edge. His hand held the back of her head, controlling her pace, and he whispered little compliments in a thickly possessive voice—told her she was perfect for him, made for him, would only ever belong to him.

Harper jerked as an ice-cold fingertip circled her clit, sending a tremor quaking through her. Instantly, that all too familiar burn began to sizzle her nerve endings. *Motherfucker*. The psychic finger expertly rubbed and flicked and plucked at her clit. She moaned around his cock as she bucked her hips, seeking more. Then two cold fingers abruptly drove deep inside her. She gasped in both shock and pleasure.

"Shush. Take it." Knox worked the psychic fingers in and out of her, fueling the fiery ache he'd sparked inside her pussy. Her mouth was sheer fucking heaven and he couldn't help but savor it. He'd taught her what he liked, and she always gave it to him. But when he felt the telling tingle at the base of his spine, he knew he had to stop her. "Enough, baby."

Harper almost sobbed as the psychic fingers dissipated, making her pussy tingle and throb. If he didn't get inside her soon, he really was going to get bitch slapped.

"Up," Knox ordered. The sight of her gorgeous mouth all red and swollen made his cock pulse. "Do you want my cock in you, baby?"

She swallowed against the urge to tell him to fuck her now or go fuck himself. She knew one word would get her exactly what she wanted. "Please."

Knox shot to his feet, lifted her, and pinned her against the tiled wall. She wrapped her legs around his waist, and he slammed home; burying himself balls-deep in one smooth, possessive thrust. Her pussy—blazing hot and deliciously slick—clamped and rippled around his cock, and what little control he had left simply went.

Harper dug her nails into his back as he pounded in and out of her, stretching her hypersensitive walls. His dark eyes bore into hers, blazing with raw need. He was brutal and relentless. He was also parting her slick folds so he hit her clit with every feral thrust. *Bastard*. She was wound so tight, she could burst. "Fuck, I'm gonna come."

"Not yet," growled Knox. Her eyes bled to black, and the flesh on his back beneath her hands heated and prickled, but the pain instantly became pleasure. He was being branded, he instantly realized. Fuck, fuck, fuck. Fingers digging into her thighs, he hammered into her harder. Faster. Deeper. Those black eyes blinked, turning sapphire blue once again. "Make me come, Harper," he rumbled against her mouth.

The words were like a trigger. Harper shattered with a scream, tightening her legs around him just as her pussy squeezed and milked his cock. She felt him swell inside her, and then his spine snapped straight as he exploded. Harper sagged over him, quaking with little aftershocks.

Knox kissed her neck as she came down from her orgasm. "We need to get to the mirror so I can find out what it looks like."

It was only then she recalled that her demon had branded him. "I'm curious myself." Their demons were bold and very possessive, so she doubted it would be at all understated.

Knox gently set her on her feet and turned off the spray. He wrapped a towel around her before grabbing one for myself. Then he angled his back to the mirror so he could see the brand. It was more like an extension of the one on his nape and expanded across both shoulders. It was masculine and tribal with solid black lines and pointed curves.

Rubbing her hair with a small towel, Harper said, "It makes you look even more like a bad-ass than you already do." It was pretty hot, in her opinion. "Like it?"

Sensing that she was a little nervous about his answer, Knox turned to her and drew her close. "What do you think?"

Judging by the rock-hard cock now digging into her stomach … "I think you kind of like it. Or, at least, you like that the demon branded you."

He brushed his mouth across hers. "I like both. And I really like this nipple ring." He thumbed it through the towel. "I'm going to enjoy playing with it. Often."

"As long as those psychic hands don't start playing with it in public." Her eyes narrowed as a lopsided smile curved his mouth. And she knew she'd just stupidly planted that idea in his head. She should just slap herself. Really.

CHAPTER TWENTY-ONE

———◆———

For Harper, everything about this particular spa created a serene, peaceful, and deliciously restful atmosphere. Not just the warm and cozy décor, but the incense burners, the relaxing soundtracks, the herbal aromas, the low lighting, and the snug fluffy robes. But right then, she wasn't feeling restful. In fact, as Belinda stood at her side reading out the itinerary for the next day, Harper just wanted to whack the she-demon around the room with her own clipboard.

Harper was at the spa for a *reason*—a surely perfectly obvious reason: to relax. Simple.

Of course, it wasn't an easy thing when she was extremely conscious that the shindig would begin the following evening. By some miracle, though, Harper *had* been relaxing. As the massage therapist had kneaded and stretched her skin with fingers coated in a tingling oil, her body had loosened until she was like melted wax against the padded table.

Now she was clasping the edges of said table to stop herself from taking a swipe at the cambion, who had barged into the private room with her little clipboard firing out reminders . . . as if there weren't four half-naked women being massaged right in front of her.

She wouldn't let Belinda get to her. She wouldn't. Inhaling a deep breath that was filled with citrus, Harper concentrated on the hands that were working magic on her muscles and the feel of the warm stones on her back. Her muscles were a little sore, thanks to her last flying lesson. God bless spas and—

"Are you even listening to me?" asked Belinda.

Harper sighed. "Honestly? No."

Belinda planted one balled up hand on her hip. "The event takes place tomorrow evening. There is still a lot that needs to be done."

Devon groaned in annoyance. "You do realize we brought Harper here to get her mind off all that stuff, right?"

Belinda gave Devon a haughty look. "This is much more important than a massage. These things need to be addressed now if the event is to run smoothly." She turned back to Harper, but her gaze was on her clipboard. "A beauty team will arrive in the afternoon to take care of your hair, make-up, and other such things."

"Not necessary. I can deal with all that myself."

Belinda gaped. "You can't seriously prefer to do this yourself. For heaven's sake, you *can't* do this yourself."

Khloë looked up from her magazine. "Why can't she?"

Belinda ignored the imp. "Harper, surely you want to look your best for Knox. You don't wear much make-up; you would have no idea how to—"

"If I covered my face with layers upon layers of make-up and did my hair in some fancy twist, it would piss him off," said Harper. "He doesn't want a fake version of me."

Belinda's lips flattered. "I'll speak with Knox about it."

"Snitches get stitches, you know," Khloë told her.

Glaring at the imp, Belinda spoke. "My job—"

"Is not to hang around him like a bad smell," said Khloë. "But you use every little opportunity to call him or go knocking on his office door." Khloë flipped her page extra hard. "Just so you know, he thinks it's pathetic. We laugh about you, like, a *lot*."

Cheeks flushing, Belinda turned back to Harper. "I'll cancel the team."

"Wasn't so hard, was it?" said Harper.

Belinda flapped her arms, almost knocking over the tray of oils and lotions. "I'm trying to help you, Harper. If you go to that event looking like nothing but a warmed-up version of yourself, you will embarrass him in front of the other guests. Is that really what you want?"

Harper arched a brow. "What, pray tell, about me is so embarrassing?"

"Yeah, tell us," said Devon, her eyes narrowed dangerously.

Belinda straightened her shirt. "I just mean that you want to look like you've made an effort."

Khloë smiled. "Ooh, good save."

"I thought so," said Raini a little drowsily, head leaning on her folded arms.

Eyes gleaming with exasperation, Belinda said to Harper, "The other guests will be elegantly groomed."

"Not all of them."

"You'll stand out like a wet lemon," said Belinda. "If you see people tittering at your appearance, how will it make you feel?"

Was that a trick question? Harper puffed out a breath and answered honestly, "I can't say I'll care." That seemed to *really* piss off Belinda.

Devon's massage therapist chuckled and looked Belinda up

and down. "You don't know anything about the Wallis family, do you?"

"They're not people pleasers," said Raini.

Belinda's mouth tightened. "Harper, I really must insist that you reconsider—"

Harper sighed. "You might be the sort of person who'll change for a guy and show him only what you think he wants to see, but I'm not. I'm just me. People can like it or they can lump it, but they won't change me. I will not go to that event looking like someone I'm not. I will not act soft and genteel. I will be me. You don't have to approve of that. It isn't your job to care. Now, how about you walk on out of here and take your clipboard with you."

The cambion jutted out her chin. "I have a job to do and I will—"

"Do you really want to take me the fuck on, Belinda? I honestly hope you do. I have a lot of tension to work off. Smacking the shit out of you would really help with that." Harper truly wasn't kidding.

Hugging her clipboard to her chest, Belinda cleared her throat and backed away. "I'll leave you to your massage." She stomped off, but the carpet was so plush that it kind of ruined the effect.

As the door closed behind her, Devon muttered, "She needs a good bitch slap."

Yeah, she damn well did. It was at times like this when Harper wondered if just maybe she was wrong and it was *Belinda* who was one of the Horsemen. But, honestly, she couldn't see that uptight bitch who truly had a major thing for Knox wanting any part in trying to expose him for what he was. Belinda was just too much of a goody-goody.

"Hey, you and Knox are in a magazine again. A reporter took a picture of you together getting out of the Bentley, and they've added another photo that zoomed in on your rings."

Khloë angled the magazine so that Harper could see it. "They say 'sources told them' that you and Knox got married in a Vegas chapel."

Harper had figured that the human reporters would come to that conclusion. She and Knox were only hot news because in the past he was so rarely seen with the same woman more than a handful of times.

"I'll bet Knox will be happy to know that humans think you're married and unavailable," said Devon.

Harper nodded. After all, he'd said as much when he gave her the rings.

"Call me evil," began Khloë, "but I like how much this is eating Belinda alive." That made the therapists chuckle.

Raini lifted her head. "Ladies, we're supposed to be relaxing. Belinda is not a relaxing subject, so let's move on from that."

Harper did her best to clear her mind and enjoy what was left of the massage. After that, each of them had both a manicure and a pedicure before finally leaving the spa. Keenan was waiting outside, ready to escort her out of the Underground and to the car. As the girls were off to the mall, Harper said her goodbyes to them and then left with Keenan. He radiated menace as they walked, on high alert for any signs of Crow.

Fortunately, there were none.

Exiting the club that doubled as the entrance to the Underground, Keenan walked her to the car and opened the rear door. "See you later, sphinx."

"Sure thing," she said, reading the message on her phone from Martina. She slid into the car, and Keenan shut the door. "Hey, Tanner," she greeted.

It wasn't until he pulled away from the curb that he spoke. "Not Tanner."

Harper's head snapped up from the cell phone . . . and she met

manic blue eyes in the rear-view mirror. *Fuck.* Stunned, she froze
for a short moment. Then panic set in and she went to lunge
at Crow. That was when his hand whipped back and grabbed
her leg—there was no tug inside her chest this time; there was
a sharp and incredibly painful yank that stole her breath and,
with it, so much psi-energy that white-hot pain blasted through
her skull. It was a struggle to stay conscious. A struggle she was
losing.

Frantic, she telepathically reached out to Knox. More pain
tore through her skull, and her agonized cry seemed to echo
in her mind. And now she could feel herself fading. Her vision
dimmed and blurred.

"I know it hurts, but it was necessary," said Crow, sounding
very far away. "Just sleep. Everything will be fine. You'll see."

Then the lights went out.

Pulling his chiming cell phone out of his pocket, Knox sighed at
the name on the screen. He sorely regretted promising Harper
he wouldn't involve himself in her little problem with Belinda,
because he sure would love to fire her right that very second.
He'd gathered with Levi and Larkin in his home office to discuss
the security measures for the event; he didn't have time for this
shit.

"Yes?" Knox clipped on answering the call, hand clenching
around his pen.

"Oh, um, Mr Thorne," she said, spluttering, "sorry if this is
a bad time."

It was always a bad time. "What is it?"

"I, well, I thought you should know that Harper is refusing
the help of a professional beauty team."

If that surprised Belinda, she'd clearly learned nothing about
his mate. "Is that so?"

"Yes. I have explained that this will make her stand out compared to others—"

"Harper will always stand out, Miss Thacker. And always in a good way." It was the truth. "Now, if there's nothing else, I'm a busy man."

"Of course," she said, tone curt. "I apologize for disturbing you."

Ending the call, Knox turned back to his sentinels with a sigh.

Levi seemed to be fighting a smile. "Belinda telling tales again?"

Knox placed his cell on the desk. "Yes."

"After all the stuff she's done and said, I'm surprised you haven't fired her," said Larkin.

"I promised Harper I would let her deal with the matter herself. I won't lie, I've come close to breaking that promise many times. But if I do, she'll never confide in me like that again because she won't trust me not to interfere." And it was possible that she would sow sequins on more of his clothes. "Now let's get back to—"

Knox. The pain in Tanner's tone brought Knox up short and made everything in him tense.

What is it? demanded Knox.

Fucking Crow got the drop on me. He took the car. I've tried to call Harper, but she's not answering me.

The pen in his hand snapped and his heart slammed against his ribcage. Knox broke his connection with his sentinel and reached out to his mate. *Harper? Harper?*

Nothing. Nothing at all. Not even a brush of her mind against his.

Harper, baby, you need to answer me right now and tell me you're safe.

But she didn't. Panic ripped through him and his demon,

sending his pulse racing. Breaths coming hard and fast, he asked Keenan, *Did you walk Harper to the car?*

Of course, Keenan instantly replied. *I watched her get in.*

Fuck. *How long ago was that?*

Around half an hour ago, why?

So, Crow had had her for thirty minutes. Thirty fucking minutes. *Harper, talk to me.* Nothing. Not a damn thing.

A red haze fell over Knox's vision, heat rushed to his head, and a strange roaring sound filled his ears. He shook his head, jaw clenched. Not again. Not. Fucking. Again. This just couldn't be happening again. But it was. Someone had taken Harper from him.

Panic. Dread. Fear. Ice-cold fury. It all exploded inside his gut, stealing his breath, and flared through every part of him from his head to his toes. His demon rose up sharp and fast with an animalistic snarl, seething and raring to destroy. "He. Took. Her," rumbled the demon.

Levi stiffened. "Crow?"

Digging deep for control, Knox shoved his demon back down. His sentinels were eying him warily, and he realized his body was so tense he looked on the verge of springing. He took a long breath to center himself, to *think*. He needed to plan, but it was hard to do that when everything in him roared, fumed, and ached. "Crow has Harper," he told them, throat thick.

Levi swore and shot to his feet.

Anxiety bloomed in Larkin's eyes, but that anxiety was quickly replaced by a fierce determination as she stood. "We'll find her."

Yes, they would, because Knox wasn't fucking losing her. "He's had her for approximately thirty minutes." Knox didn't want to think what the bastard might have done to her in that time.

"The anchor bond still intact?" asked Larkin.

"Yes, which means she's alive." And Knox clung tight to that, using it to keep his focus. "He made a mistake; he took the Audi. Unless he knows it has several GPS trackers and has managed to remove them all, he'll lead us right to him and Harper. *Find the Audi*." And then Knox would find them and rain fresh hell on the bastard who dared to take his mate.

I'm coming for you, baby. Just hold on for me. Hold on.

She wasn't sure if it was the splitting headache, the nausea, or the voice in her head calling to her that woke her. She was cold. Stiff. Worse, she found it hard to breathe while there was a tight, constricting weight on her chest—a weight that was also around her lower legs.

Harper forced her heavy eyelids open, wincing at the brightness of the bulb directly above her. Following the sounds of muttering, she saw Crow near a black countertop of what seemed to be a kitchenette, messing with something she couldn't quite see. His beard was as scraggly and dirty as his clothes.

Glancing around, she realized she was in a trailer that was set up as an office. It stank of grease and oil, and there were toolboxes, car radios, and other vehicle parts lying around.

She also realized she was bound to a desk. Well, this was familiar.

Unlike when the dark practitioners took her, however, Harper's arms were pinned to her sides as opposed to pinned above her head. That posed a problem, since it meant she couldn't twist her hands to infuse hellfire into the thick, heavy ropes.

She'd also been stripped of her jeans, socks, and boots, leaving her in only her bra, T-shirt, and boy shorts.

Harper, baby, you need to answer me.

Knox's panic brushed at her consciousness. She recalled

Nora's warning: *"You and your demon will face a trial. You do not like to accept help, but you will need your mate's aid when the time comes. Accept it, because nobody else will be able to help you."*

The old woman hadn't been fucking kidding. And while part of Harper loathed the idea of calling him here, she truly needed his help. Nobody else would be able to find her so fast, so she would have to do what she hadn't done the last time that Crow came for her: she'd have to trust that Knox could protect them both.

Harper? Harper, answer me.

She reached out to him and—

Pain sliced through her head, and a moan slipped out before she could stop it.

"Telepathy will be a problem for a while." The voice lacked any compassion.

Crow turned away from the counter, eyes glinting with something that was far from rational. He was wearing an apron and trying to fit a surgical mask over the lower half of his face.

Her gaze slid to the tray of surgical instruments on the counter, and she knew then exactly what he intended to do. Dread shot through her. "No."

"I have no other choice." He ripped open a packet and pulled out a clean syringe. "Even if you could call out to Knox, you wouldn't. I can't get to him." He rubbed the back of his hand against his forehead in what seemed to be a restless, irritable movement. "A hysterectomy will stop him from having the child with you."

No motherfucking way was he performing any fucked-up surgery on her. "You want to let me go," she told him, but her compulsion was weak while she was low on psi-energy. Nonetheless, she tried again. "You don't want to hurt me."

He shook his head, shaking off the compulsion with ease. "This has to happen—"

A cell phone rang, and he bit out a curse. Placing the syringe on the tray, he stalked through the trailer to a coat he'd slung on a filing cabinet. Fishing a phone out of his pocket, he tugged down his face mask and gruffly answered, "What?" A pause. "Yeah, well, I've been busy."

Harper figured it was the person pulling his strings, but just in case she shouted, "I've been kidnapped! Tell Knox Thorne—" She cut off when Crow rolled his eyes at her. Damn.

"Yes, I took her," snapped Crow. "I had to act quickly. The security will be too tight for me to touch them at the event." His back went ramrod straight. "No. *No.*" He shook his head so fast she was surprised it didn't make him dizzy. "Killing her is *not* part of my mission."

Harper strained to hear what was being said on the other end of the phone, but she couldn't even make out a voice. She flicked her gaze to the rusted door. Out. She needed to get out, out, out.

She struggled against her bindings, ignoring the burn of the rope as it chafed the bare flesh of her chilled legs. But even with adrenalin rushing through her system, enhancing her strength, her struggles came to nothing. A knot of fear lodged in her throat and left a jittery sensation in her stomach.

Crow started jabbing his closed fist against his temple. "*No.* If I kill her, it frees him to find another she-demon and have a baby with her. He won't cheat on Harp—" Crow growled. "Forgetting about the baby would mean abandoning my mission! I won't do that!" He ended the call.

"Who's trying to use you like a puppet?" she asked when he returned to her.

"I'm no one's puppet."

"They think you are. They're trying to use you, trying to divert you from your true path," she added, wondering if playing along with his little fantasy might buy her some time. Knox obviously knew she was missing. He'd find her. Somehow. Right? "Who is it?"

A muscle below his eye ticked. "They don't matter."

"Tell me why I'm strapped to this table. I need to understand." She didn't need to understand. She needed her *blade*. But it was no doubt wherever her jeans and boots were, dammit. She scanned her surroundings in search of something, *anything*, that could help—

A gun. It was on the far end of the counter. If she could just get to that . . . which, of course, she couldn't do since she could barely move at all.

"I told you about my vision, I gave you the chance to call him to me so I could destroy him. You should have listened to me, you should have helped me, but you didn't." His tone said that she only had herself to blame for what he was about to do.

"Everyone told me not to listen to you; that you're so close to rogue you don't know what you're saying."

"Oh, I know what I'm doing, and I know what I'm saying. More importantly, I know what needs to be done."

"Explain it to me."

"You're going to pretend you believe me?" he scoffed. "We both know you don't." Crow picked up a small bottle of clear liquid and shook it. "This should help with the pain."

She shook her head and tried once more to call to Knox. Another explosion of pain rattled her skull. Her pulse was now racing a mile a minute. "Don't do this."

"It has to be done."

"No, it doesn't."

"A hysterectomy won't stop the child being born—he'll just have it with another she-demon. But he won't do that as long as you're alive. This surgery will buy me some time."

"It's not surgery, it's butchery!"

He settled his surgical mask back into place. "You had the chance to help me stop that child from being born. You didn't take it. You've left me no choice."

"There's always a choice. But you haven't been making your own choices lately. You're being manipulated!"

He ignored that. "You should have chosen a safer mate. You can't get in bed with the Devil and not pay the price."

She frowned. "You think he's Lucifer?"

"I was speaking metaphorically," he replied, impatient. "Now be quiet while I prepare everything."

She kept quiet, but she didn't keep still. An imp for all intents and purposes, no one could keep her anywhere she didn't want to be. But after a hard, lengthy struggle, she had to accept that this twisted son of a bitch was managing to do just that. All the while he rambled to himself, flushed, jerky, and agitated.

Harper was no stranger to life or death situations, but she'd never experienced this sense of utter powerlessness before. She was used to dueling. Would face a challenge head-on and, if need be, she'd fight until someone was dead. But this wasn't a duel. She couldn't fight. She was trapped. Powerless. Vulnerable. And she hated it. Hated it even more than the metallic taste of fear coating her tongue.

Why the fuck hadn't she checked that Tanner was in the driver's seat before she got in the damn car? Granted, she wouldn't have been able to see him through the blackened windows, but she could have checked before sliding inside the—

Harper stilled as Crow came to her. "You don't want to do this," she told him. Again, he ignored the compulsion with ease.

"I can't knock you out for the op—I don't have the drugs or equipment for that," he said, sounding a little apologetic. He held up a syringe. "But this will help with the pain. Not a lot, but a little. You might feel a bit drowsy. That's normal."

She cringed away from him, but it did her no good while she was all tied up.

He sighed at her. "I hope you're not going to wriggle around while I'm operating. If you do, the incision will be jagged and you'll have an ugly scar."

He thought she cared about a fucking scar? The second he came close, she lifted her upper body as much as she could and rammed her head into his nose. There was a nauseating crack as blood poured from his nose and soaked the surgical mask.

He roared and dropped the syringe. Cupping his nose with both hands, he glared at her with such malice that it made her shiver. Spitting insults that she couldn't quite understand while his nose was broken, he quickly removed the mask and used some padding to absorb the blood. He snapped his nose back into place and snarled, "You bitch!"

He slapped her hard across the face. Pain exploded beneath her cheekbone and a ringing sound filled her ears. Her demon lunged to the surface and hissed at him. "I will kill you. That is a promise."

Crow just sneered as he picked up a scalpel from the tray and moved to her abdomen.

Harper retook control of her body, wrestling her demon into submission. A wave of pure dread washed over her as he rolled her boy shorts down a little. *"Don't fucking do this, Crow!"*

But he did. The scalpel sliced through her skin like butter, and she bit her bottom lip. No way would she give him the satisfaction of hearing her cry out in pain. She needed to stop him, needed to do something, but there wasn't a goddamn—

They both froze at the sound of footsteps outside. Hope raced through her so fast, her breath caught in her throat. Crow cursed, and Harper screamed for all she was worth. The door swung open, and there was Delia. Her eyes widened as they danced from Crow to Harper.

His hand clenched around the scalpel. "Delia ... "

"Lawrence, what are you doing?" Her voice shook.

No, Harper thought with a shake of her head. Delia couldn't possibly be involved. No way. No motherfucking way.

"I'm doing what needs to be done," Crow told Delia.

Harper struggled against the rope. "Delia, untie me!"

But she didn't. She took slow steps toward him. "You think Harper's pregnant?"

"Not yet."

Delia took in the slice on Harper's abdomen. "You're going to operate on her like you did Carla?" She shook her head. "Lawrence, no—"

"I have to. The child's birth won't happen for a while, but it *will* happen."

"Listen to me for a minute."

"No, this child cannot be born! It will unless I stop it. And that's what I have to do."

"Your mission is—"

"*Leave, Delia.*"

"No, you need to listen to me," she insisted, but he pointed at the door.

"You can't possibly be one of the freaking Horsemen!" Harper declared. "No way!"

"You're right," said another voice as footsteps approached. A voice she *knew*. A tall figure entered the trailer as he went on. "She isn't. But I am."

Harper glared at Roan. *Motherfucker.*

Delia looked from Crow to Roan, eyes wide.

Crow scowled at him. "How did you find me? You weren't supposed to find me."

"I followed Delia, though she didn't know it." Roan arched a brow at Crow. "You told her about our partnership?"

Crow shook his head. "I wouldn't tell the bitch anything; she was trying to poison me. I don't know how she found me."

Roan turned to Delia. "Do I need to punish him or is that true?"

"It's true," replied Delia. "I was looking for him, and I remembered he used to come here as a kid with his dad."

"I'm glad you remembered," Roan told her. "I was counting on you to find him for me. You led me right to him. Thank you for that."

She backed up as Roan moved toward her. "I'll leave. I won't tell anyone what I saw, I swear."

"No, you won't," agreed Roan. He snatched the gun off the counter and shot her right between the eyes.

Harper jumped, despite the fact that there was a silencer on the weapon. He'd just . . . the bastard had . . . What. The. Fuck? And Crow just stood there, expression blank. "You don't care that he just killed Delia?"

Crow frowned. "She was poisoning me with those pills. I wouldn't have known if it wasn't for Roan."

"No, he told you to stop taking them because he didn't want you to get better! He wanted to use you!"

As Delia slumped to the floor, Roan whirled on Crow and gestured at Harper. "I told you to kill her."

"And I told *you*, killing her isn't part of my mission," snapped Crow. "My goal is to stop that child being born. Knox is loyal to Harper. He would never betray her. But if she's dead, it frees him to be with another. That means we can't kill her."

Roan growled at him. "Forget your damn mission for one minute and look at the bigger picture! If she dies, it will *weaken* him. He will be distracted. Vulnerable. Too angry to think straight or keep control of his demon. It will rise; then you'll know what he is and know how to end him! Killing her will *help* your mission, idiot."

But Crow shook his head. "No. I won't do it."

"You don't need to." Roan pointed the gun at her. "I'll do it."

Crow blocked his path. "No! You'll ruin everything!"

"You're not the only one with a mission."

Crow tensed. "What does that mean?"

Roan rolled his eyes. "You really think you and me are in this alone? How do you think you got out of that cell?"

"Fate got me out."

"Blood magick got you out."

"You're working with dark practitioners?" Crow asked, horrified.

The sick bastard wasn't really in a position to be judging others, in Harper's opinion.

"No, but a dear friend of mine knows how to use it," replied Roan. "Now step aside. I've helped you with your 'mission.' Here's where you back off so I can do mine."

Crow grabbed the gun in Roan's hand … and then it disappeared.

Rather than looking pissed, Roan seemed impressed. "You can make any weapons you conjure disappear, huh? Interesting." He shoved Crow so hard, the guy stumbled. "Out of my fucking way."

"If you want to know what Knox is, just *ask* her."

Roan looked at Harper. "You'd never tell me. Would you? Even now, when you know death is close, there's defiance in your eyes."

And while he stood there, glaring down at her with malicious intent in his gaze, she couldn't help but feel a twinge of pain in her chest. He was still her half-fucking-brother, dammit. That made no difference to her demon; it bore a soul-deep hatred for him and wanted nothing more than to end his life. "Why do you want Knox dead so badly?"

"He's the only real thing that stands in our way," replied Roan. "Even if we caused all the Primes to turn against him, it's doubtful they would unite to kill him. Not unless they knew *how* to kill him." Roan snickered. "He thinks he's so smart and powerful. But look at the life he leads. He doesn't take advantage of his power or success. He hasn't sought global domination. There is an endless amount of women out there he could have, but he chose *you*."

"If you hate me so much for not showing any concern for Carla, why haven't you killed Crow for hurting her?"

Roan's eyes hardened. "She deserved it. She's no mother. She's twisted. Sick." He tapped his earlobe. "She cut mine right open once. I can't even remember why."

That made Carla a sick bitch, sure, but ... "*You're* just as fucking twisted."

"Oh, yes. And you and I ... we both have her tainted blood inside us. I don't hate you. I don't feel anything for you. Except for disgust, of course. You're a Wallis, after all." He tilted his head. "Just where did you hear about the Horsemen?"

She didn't answer, just stared at him defiantly.

"I'll bet you didn't know that Isla recruited me." Her surprise must have shown on her face, because he smiled. "There were originally only three demons working on the fall of the Primes, but then I was brought into the fold. They needed someone from Knox's lair to report back to them—an insider who was smart and manipulative. And I think Isla liked that the person she had recruited was related to you by blood. She really did hate you, but I suppose you guessed that." Grabbing a pair of surgical scissors, he moved closer. "Now, Harper ... I doubt you'll tell me just what Knox is. But, to be a good sport, I'll give you one chance to tell me. If you do, I won't make this hurt. But if you don't, we'll play a little before you die."

She snorted. He was going to hurt her no matter what she did or didn't say, and he was going to enjoy it—they both knew that.

"Just think of how much fun it will be when you die, big sister. He'll feel it. He'll feel that exact moment when it happens. Your anchor bond will break, and his control will break right along with it."

"Maybe." Harper bared her teeth. "But then you'll die too."

Anxiety flashed in Roan's eyes, but it disappeared just as fast as it came. "He has no idea I'm involved and, since he has no idea where you are, he isn't going to find out. But he is going to reveal his demon in all its glory, whether he wants to or not."

Bastard. "If you kill me, we'll all die." Maybe it should have brought Harper some comfort that at least the bastards wouldn't get away with what they'd done, but it didn't. She didn't want Knox to suffer. She didn't want his demon to rage.

"I'll give you the count of ten," said Roan.

Well, wasn't he a sweetheart.

"Ten."

Fuck. Harper was going to die; there were no two ways about it. Not even in a fight where she could at least have a chance of defending herself; no, she was going to die while tied up and helpless.

"Nine."

Her ribs felt tight around a heart that was beating so fast she was surprised it hadn't exploded. She *hated* being afraid. She *hated* being helpless.

"Eight."

Worse than the knowledge that she'd die tonight was the knowledge of what it would do to Knox; of how he'd blame and torment himself, especially if he learned Roan had "played" with her first.

"Seven."

Her demon turned frantic; her rage built and built until it pumped through Harper just as fast as the adrenalin streaming through her body.

"Six."

The warmth and smell of her blood, the sour taste of fear, the rope biting into her flesh, the burn of the slice on her stomach, the pounding pain in her skull—it all amplified her demon's rage until the emotion inflated inside her chest like a balloon.

"Five."

Another spike of adrenalin rushed through her, along with the inescapable truth that no one was coming to help her. And then those scissors cut into her earlobe. Her demon lunged to the surface again. It hissed. Struggled. Snarled. Writhed. Screeched in fury.

Roan laughed. "Four."

That laugh ... oh, that intensified the fury that was *demanding* release. Harper's heartbeat thrashed in her ears almost as fast and loud as the soul-searing anger roaring through her. And as Harper's anger and her demon's fury mingled, something inside them both snapped.

"Three."

The demon charged to the surface and let it all go—the rage, the dread, the panic, the powerlessness, the need for vengeance. Its wings snapped out, blazing with a fire that burned right through the rope. The entity bolted upright and snapped both hands around each of its opponents' throat. At the same time, the ground shook and flames roared and crackled to life around them. Flames that were gold, red, and black.

The demon spoke through gritted teeth as it glared at Crow. "I told you I would kill you." It tossed them both across the trailer. The back of Crow's head hit the edge of the top kitchen cupboard and he slid to the floor with a weak groan. Roan crashed into the filing cabinet so hard the drawers flew open.

Grabbing the tie binding its legs, the demon infused hellfire into the rope, burning its way free. Roan coughed as he staggered to his feet, glancing around; taking in the flames spreading across the walls and ceiling, boxing them in.

"You have nowhere to go," the demon told the two males as it slipped off the desk.

Crow's eyes widened in fear and panic. "There's no smoke. They're the flames of hell."

The demon smirked. "And now you are trapped, just as Harper was. For that, you will pay."

Eyes wide, Roan swept out his hand, and the tool box flew at the demon's head. It ducked, but the edge of the metal box clipped the demon's temple hard enough to slice into flesh.

"That is something else you will pay for," it told him.

"You don't want to hurt me," said Roan.

Oh, but it did. The demon gave an evil grin. "You cannot compel me." Not right then, when the raw power it wielded over the flames was trickling through its veins; hot as hellfire, thick as syrup, bubbly as sparkling champagne. It sent sparks of electricity shooting to every nerve ending and filled the demon from head to toe, smoothing into every extremity.

The demon felt Harper reach for dominance. It ignored her. The demon would keep control. It would have vengeance. It would kill these people for daring to harm Harper.

It could compel its prey to surrender, but it didn't want to defeat them that way. It wanted to fight them, to make them bleed, to show them it was far from helpless. Wanted them to be the ones who were trapped and afraid, knowing no help would come.

"If I'm dying, you're dying too," snarled Roan.

One item after another went flying at the demon. Furniture, tools, a sparkplug, a kettle, a toaster. Crow curled up against the kitchen cupboards, leaving Roan to fight the battle. All the while, the trailer creaked and shook as the flames ate at the walls.

The desk tipped up, smashing into the demon's shoulder, sending pain radiating down its arm, but the demon didn't move to stop Roan. It wanted him to see that no matter how powerful he was, he was also completely helpless right then. He was at the demon's mercy . . . and it had no mercy.

Spotting its boot under the table, the demon snatched it and whipped out its blade. "You will bleed soon, just as I do." The demon infused hellfire into the knife, enjoying the glint of fear in Roan's eyes. Harper pushed for dominance again. The demon fought her easily while it was filled with so much power.

Roan hurled a succession of balls of hellfire—one, two, three, four. The demon ducked, dodged, stooped, and sidestepped, evading each one. The tray of surgical implements flew off the counter and at the demon's face. As it batted them away, a fifth ball of hellfire hit its chest. Skin sizzled and blistered, but the adrenalin dimmed the pain.

Roan's gaze darted around as he searched for something else to throw. The trailer no longer had walls or a ceiling and the flames had consumed most of the objects. All that was left was the fire-free patch that the three of them now stood on.

The demon bared its teeth in a feral smile. "You have nothing—" It squinted as a white unnatural light shined in its eyes. Crow rushed out of the light, scalpel ready. The demon slashed at his arm with the blade, making Crow stumble back in alarm. "Like to cut people, don't you? Now you'll feel the burn of my blade." The demon plunged it into Crow's gut. His eyes bulged and he stilled, looking at the blade with disbelief. Done with him, the demon called to the fire. A golden flame hooked around his neck and yanked him into the fire.

Roan's demon rose to the fore with a growl and charged, scissors in hand. The she-demon wrestled them out of its hand, fisted its shirt, and slammed it against the broken desk. "An ear for an ear." The she-demon cut into the lobe, enjoying its scream. "If it's death you seek you may have it."

The demon slung its prey into the fire.

CHAPTER TWENTY-TWO

Standing in front of the busted-open gates of the chain link fence that was capped with barbed wire, Larkin asked, "Why would he take her to an old salvage yard?"

Levi looked down at the guard dogs that had both been dealt a gunshot wound to the head, probably courtesy of Crow. "He could have simply come here because it's local and isolated."

"I think his dad used to work at a salvage yard," said Tanner. "Maybe this was the one."

Knox rolled back his shoulders; his muscles felt tight and cramped. "Maybe." He didn't give a flying fuck why Crow had taken Harper there. All he cared about was finding them, and he needed to do it fast. His chest was cold and tight with fear. That emotion was fueling the clawing, hissing, spitting rage in his gut.

His demon was fighting Knox for control. It wanted to be free to do what it did best. To hurt. To maim. To rage and destroy those who would dare take its mate from it.

Honestly, it was tempting. So fucking tempting to surrender

control to his demon and let it demolish whatever stood between them and their mate. He didn't care that this could be a trap or that someone could be trying to goad his demon into surfacing—he just wanted Harper. But what Knox *didn't* want was for Crow to know they were there, and his inner demon wouldn't be even the slightest bit discreet.

"Tanner, release your demon," clipped Knox, voice guttural. "Find her."

The moment they had the Audi's location, Knox had pyroported there with Levi and Larkin—collecting his other two sentinels on the way. He needed the help of Tanner's hellhound to track Harper, since the GPS signal could only give them the car's general location. There were no better hunters than hellhounds.

As Tanner stripped and handed each piece of clothing to Keenan, Levi turned to Knox and said, "I don't think Crow means to kill her. If that was what he wanted, he'd have done it by now."

True, but if that was supposed to comfort Knox, it didn't. Not even a little bit. "She's still not responding to my calls," Knox said between his teeth. His jaw ached from how hard he clenched it.

"Which suggests she could be unconscious or that he's done to her what he did to Carla so that she can't use telepathy," said Levi. "But we know Harper *is* alive. Hang on to that."

He was. It was the only thing keeping him and his demon stable. Or, at least, as stable as they could ever be in a situation like this.

"We also know from prior experience that you can't keep a Wallis anywhere that they don't want to be," said Keenan, voice grim. He was still beating himself up about not checking that Tanner was in the driver's seat, despite being assured by the other sentinels that they wouldn't have thought to check either. But Knox wasn't in the right frame of mind to deal with Keenan's turmoil. His focus was purely on finding Harper.

Fully naked, Tanner asked, "Ready?" At Knox's nod, the sentinel released his demon. Bones cracked and popped as he shifted shape. Hellhounds were much bigger and more muscular than normal wolves with coal-black fur and blood-red eyes. They were also fast, strong, vicious, and smelled of burning brimstone.

The hellhound shook its head and snorted, probably agitated by the strong scents of motor oil, dirt, grease, and rusted metal. It raked the ground with the claws of its front paw, making Knox think of a bull scraping its hooves on the floor.

"Find Harper," Knox ordered, urgency in every syllable.

The hellhound snorted again and got moving. They stalked after the hound as it prowled along the dusty road that weaved through rows of cars, cabs, buses, and trucks. Even through the thickening shadows, Knox could see that most of the vehicles were rusted and dented. Some had shattered windshields while others were missing doors or had been stripped of the seats and front wheel.

Knox strained to hear voices, but the only sounds were that of glass crunching beneath their feet and the whistling breeze rattling open doors or raised hoods. "Where are they?" he growled, stepping over a stray sparkplug. "She's got to be here fucking somewhere." But all he could see ahead of him were more vehicles, stacks of tires, and a rusted forklift.

They kept on walking for what quickly began to feel like hours. With every moment that passed, his panic grew and his control started to fray around the edges. The longer she was with Crow, the more likely it was that Knox wouldn't get to her before Crow could kill her. He could be hurting her right now. Chest squeezing at the idea, Knox closed his eyes. The bastard would pay for whatever he did. And he'd pay in blood.

The hellhound came to an abrupt halt. Growled. And then headed east at a fast pace. Adrenalin shot through Knox as they trailed after the hellhound, ready to—

In the distance, a loud, banshee-like screech of fury split the air. Instinct sent Knox charging toward the sound, even as the ground began to shake beneath him, causing the debris at his feet to rattle. Then flames seemed to explode out of the ground bordering a trailer far ahead, making him and the sentinels jerk to a halt. They were high, ferocious, blinding ... and all too familiar to Knox.

"The flames of hell," Levi said in utter shock.

Keenan stumbled backwards, almost tripping over the hellhound. "Holy fuck."

Larkin gaped. "Knox, what ... I mean, did you—"

"I didn't call them," Knox told her, breath coming fast.

"*Harper* called them?" asked Levi.

Apparently so. And just how the fuck did that happen?

Later. He'd work that out later. Now, he needed to get to her. They rushed toward the fire, only stopping when the blistering heat emanating from it became too much for the sentinels to bear. He urged the flames to ease away, but they flickered only slightly. Frowning, he tried again. They still didn't calm. Instead, they leapt, danced, swayed, and consumed whatever they touched.

Levi raised a hand to shield his reddening face from the searing heat. "Make them die down."

"I can't," clipped Knox. "They won't answer to me."

Larkin's brow pulled together. "Why?"

"Because they're answering to *Harper.*" She was the one who'd somehow managed to conjure them and her emotions were, literally, feeding the fire. By the way the fire was raging, so was she.

It hissed. Popped. Spat. Crackled. Sizzled. Snapped. Heat waves shimmered in the air—air that now seemed heavy and thick. Thick with power.

"I have to get to her," said Knox. He was the only one who could walk through the flames.

"The fire's starting to spread," warned Tanner, pulling on his clothes now that he'd shifted once more.

The sentinel was right. The ragged line of the flames moved slowly but steadily closer to them. Metal creaked and glass shattered. Vehicles toppled and crashed onto others. The scent of hot metal and burned rubber filled the air. Hell, the heat itself was melting the cars. It was a good thing the flames of hell didn't operate like normal fire or there'd be several explosions going on around them, given how much gas was in the yard.

He tensed at what could have been the sound of a male crying out in pain, but Knox couldn't be sure he'd truly heard it while the fire roared so loudly around them. "I'm going in," said Knox.

Levi grabbed his arm. "Bury your anger, Knox. Those flames are wild and furious, which means she is too. A demon that out of control can be an extremely dangerous thing. Harper needs you to be calm right now."

Well aware of that, Knox nodded. He had no chance of easing Harper's anger if he wasn't calm himself. And if he didn't manage to calm her, the flames would keep on blazing and consuming whatever they touched. No pressure. "I'll bring her back."

Taking a deep breath, he walked through the shimmering waves of hot air and right into the vivid, glowing tri-colored flames. A scorching, prickling heat engulfed him as the flames lashed and whipped at his skin, but they didn't scald him; they couldn't.

The ground itself was so hot, he could feel the baking heat through the soles of his shoes as he walked deeper into the fire, searching for any sign of his mate. All he could see were melting cars and tires being swallowed by the fire. He stepped over a partially consumed forklift, glancing around while his demon frantically urged him to hurry and find her.

A *male scream.*

Knox whirled toward the sound, tracking it through the flames. He heard the very familiar sound of his mate's voice, but it was her demon speaking.

"If it's death you seek you may have it."

Another male scream, this one closer, rang through the air.

Knox hastened his steps, edging his way toward the—

And there she was. Standing with her back to him on a fire-free patch of metal that was covered with a dirty carpet—all that was left of the trailer. Her wings were blazing and surrounded by a strange kind of faint magma aura.

He stepped out of the fire and up onto the carpet, making the metal base creak and rock slightly. "Harper?"

She slowly turned her head to glance over her shoulder, and pure black eyes bore into his. He went absolutely still. Her demon was in control, and that wasn't good; not if the demon was as furious as the fire. A need for vengeance could be riding it hard, even if the threats were now nothing but ashes. And a demon in that state was almost as bad as a rogue.

It didn't react to his presence. Didn't say anything. Just stared at him through chillingly cold eyes, its expression completely blank. He wasn't sure if it even recognized him. That would be bad, since he didn't want to end up having to defend himself against his own mate. "Do you know who I am?"

The demon slowly turned to face him, and he sucked in a sharp breath. There was a shiny silver and black bruise on one side of her face, as if something big and hard had smashed into it. Blood was dripping from a thin, deep slash on her temple. The skin of her upper chest was raw, blistered, and peeling. There was a clump of blood so dark it was almost black crusted around her earlobe. As if all that wasn't bad enough, blood was dripping from a slice just above her blood-soaked boy shorts. *Son of a bitch.*

His demon roared in his head and lunged to the surface, but Knox beat him back just in time. She needed a calm influence, not his demon. Still, it was hard to subdue the entity when he himself was boiling with the same ice-cold rage. "Baby ... I should have got here sooner, I'm sorry."

If the apology meant anything to the demon, it didn't show it. Just continued to stare at him, face blank. A full-body tremor ran through its body—a jerky movement that made him think of a junkie. It was totally bloated on the power it was wielding over the flames. Knox could completely understand why. He knew how it felt for his own demon: energizing, intoxicating, a rush like no other. And very, very hard to come down from, especially for a demon in a rage. *Shit.*

Forcing his tone to stay smooth as he spoke over the roaring fire, he repeated, "Do you know who I am?"

It gave a slow nod.

Despite his relief, he didn't cross the space between them. He wasn't sure how his proximity would be received at that moment. Mate or not, the demon could be angry with him for not coming sooner and saving it from Crow. "You're safe now."

"They hurt her," it told him in a disembodied voice that had a cutting edge to it. Incredibly protective of Harper, the demon was as mightily and righteously pissed as he'd expected.

Fuck, so was he—especially when he could see and smell her blood. But he put his own emotions on lockdown; this was about his mate now. Harper had once brought him back when his demon took over, and now he needed to do the same for her. He also needed to find out who "they" were. One was obviously Crow, but the other . . . he wasn't sure.

"They can't hurt her again," said Knox, taking a slow and risky step forward. Thankfully, the demon didn't warn him off.

"They would have killed her," it added, hand twitching slightly.

"I know, but they're gone." No doubt consumed by the flames.

"Dead," it confirmed. "They deserved it."

"They did. You're safe now," he said once again, but the demon still didn't appear at all appeased by that fact. *Come back to me, Harper*, he coaxed.

"They wanted to kill you."

"But they didn't." He risked taking another step forward. "You stopped them." His demon wanted Knox to give it control and let it speak to the entity. It was a good idea but, honestly, he didn't trust his demon not to join in on the fun. "You need to calm the flames."

Another fine tremor worked through the demon. "I like them."

Fuck. It was only right then that Knox really understood how hard it must have been for Harper to bring him back when he'd been in the same state; how scared she must have felt that she wouldn't be enough to tempt him and his demon away from the power and the rush. And for the first time in as long as he could remember, he found himself beset by self-doubt.

Harper, baby, you need to fight your demon and you need to fight her hard. I'm not sure I can do this on my own. He felt her mind brush his. It was a slow, drowsy touch. He guessed she was exhausted from trying to force her raging demon to retreat. If so, he'd have no help with this.

"You'll destroy everything and everyone if you don't calm the flames," he told it.

"Yes, but then nothing would hurt her again."

Which was clearly all the demon cared about while it was still so hung up on what had happened to Harper and too high on power. There would be no reasoning with the entity. His only real hope of easing those flames was if he got the demon to pull back and let Harper resurface. Easier said than done, of course.

He took another step forward, but he froze when the demon flapped its wings. Shit, he knew how fast and adept those wings were; it would be a nightmare to catch the demon—not to mention a sight that would attract human attention—if it flew off. "I need Harper right now."

"They hurt her," it rumbled, as if he just wasn't getting the point. "Tied her down. Slapped her. Cut her with scissors. Sliced her open."

Barely managing not to snarl at what had happened, he reminded it, "And you killed them. You protected her. She's safe. You're both safe. You don't need the flames anymore."

It blinked.

Feeling a little desperate now, he said, "I need her." In more ways than he'd ever imagined it was possible to need someone.

The demon cocked its head.

"Let Harper come to me. I know you want her safe. She's safe with me. You know that." He slowly covered the small space between them. Just as slowly, he took a chance and reached out to curl a hand around its chin. "She's tired. Don't make her keep fighting you. Just let the power go. You don't need it anymore. Trust me to keep her safe."

For a moment, it did nothing. Then the entity did a slow blink, and he had glassy forest-green eyes staring back at him.

Thank fuck. He quickly looped an arm around Harper as the power left her system in a rush, causing her knees to buckle. She gave a drowsy moan. "Shush, baby, I got you." Almost dizzy from relief, he lifted her up, careful of her injuries. She weakly curled her legs around his waist. "Good girl."

Closing his eyes, he kissed her temple. He had her. She was alive. Injured but healing. His heart was still thundering, and his chest was still tight with fear. The demon inside him shot to the surface just long enough to rub its cheek against hers.

The moment his demon retreated, Knox turned and retraced his steps through a fire that was now beginning to ease. The flames were thinning out and lowering, though the heat was still a bitch. Walking out of the flames, he found his sentinels waiting, their expressions anxious. All four of them rushed forward.

"Is she all right?" asked Larkin, panicked. Her face tightened as she saw some of Harper's wounds. "Fuck, what did the bastard do to her?"

Knox suspected that Crow, the son of a bitch, had intended to operate on her. "It looks like she fought him hard. She has some injuries, but nothing she won't heal from."

"The flames have eased," Keenan pointed out.

So had the flames on her feathers. "Her emotions were feeding the fire. She's unconscious now." Which meant that the storm inside her was over, but it had left a fair amount of damage. Most of the salvage yard was gone, and the ground looked like a blackened, dry riverbed. It was also sprinkled with red ashes—residue of the flames of hell.

Knox tightened his hold on Harper. "Let's get her home."

He knew by the tensing of her shoulders that she was waking—finally. After Knox had brought her home, he'd carefully cleaned and checked out her wounds before giving her a quick shower. She'd been so wiped out that she hadn't once stirred. He'd then put her to bed and lay beside her.

For the past six hours while she'd slept like a log, he'd stayed with her. Listened to her breathe. Watched the rise and fall of her chest, assuring himself that she was fine until the fear taunting him began to ebb away. It still lingered, but it didn't have a tight hold on him anymore.

Now that she was finally awake, he wanted to hold her, taste her, and soothe her, but she couldn't even look at him. He understood why, because he understood her. She didn't like that she'd lost total control of her demon, and she was embarrassed that she'd been unable to fight it into submitting.

Knox brushed his thumb over her bruised cheek. The bruise was now yellow and fading fast. "Do you judge me for the times I've lost control?"

After a moment, she mumbled, "No."

"Then don't judge yourself." But she still didn't look at him. "Come on, let me see those eyes." Finally, her lids flickered open. Shadowed gold eyes met his. He smiled. "Hey, baby."

"My demon . . . it's not usually like that." She licked her lips. "It's protective of me and it's vicious and cold, but it doesn't get a kick out of destruction. Earlier, it would have happily watched everything around it burn to the ground." And it wasn't feeling in the least bit apologetic about it, to Harper's utter annoyance. It felt fully justified in its actions.

"Your demon was bloated on a power it's never before tasted." Knox tucked her hair behind her uninjured ear. The other was healing but would probably be sensitive. "It got a little carried away."

She shot him an incredulous look. "Carried away?"

"I thought your demon handled it pretty well, all things considered," he said, paraphrasing something she'd once said to him after he'd been the one to lose control. Her mouth kicked into a reluctant smile. "That's my girl." He kissed her, greedy for a long, thorough taste of his mate. He breathed her in, filling his lungs were her scent. Something in him settled, and his demon relaxed a little. "You scared me when you disappeared."

"I was kind of scared too," Harper admitted in a whisper, biting on her lower lip. She detested that those bastards had made her afraid.

"Why didn't you answer my telepathic calls?"

"I couldn't. It hurt whenever I tried." The headache was thankfully long gone, so Harper reached out to touch his mind with hers, glad to feel no pain slicing through her head. "The bastard sucked so much psi-energy out of me that I couldn't even use a compulsion on him." Her stomach churned as she remembered the helplessness and terror that she'd felt as—

"Hey, come back to me," said Knox, tracing the shell of her ear.

Snapping herself out of the memories, she took a deep breath. "I'm okay."

Knox would be the judge of that. He rolled her onto her back and gently opened her towel. The blisters on her chest were gone and, as he danced his fingers over the unmarred skin, he found that it was petal-soft once more. He slid down her body to examine the healed slice on her stomach. Like the one on her temple, it was now a thin, pink line. "Crow was going to perform a hysterectomy on you, wasn't he?"

Sensing his anger, she sifted her fingers through his hair. "Yes, he saw it as a way of 'buying time' before he could get to you."

Knox pressed a kiss to the pink line. "If he wasn't already dead, I'd kill him." And he'd be sure to make it a long, slow and agonizing death.

"Delia walked in and interrupted him—"

Knox's head snapped up. "Delia?"

"She wasn't one of the Horsemen. She turned up at . . . where were we?" All she remembered was the trailer.

"A salvage yard. Tanner said Crow's father used to work there."

"That explains what she meant when she said Crow used to go there as a kid with his dad. How did you find me?"

"The Audi has several GPS trackers. Before you ask, no, I was not secretly keeping tabs on you. All my vehicles have trackers."

Harper wasn't entirely convinced, but since the trackers had led Knox to her, she had no intention of complaining. "Anyway, Delia walked in. Moments later, someone came up behind her." Harper licked her lips, hating to say it. "It was Roan." A growl rumbled out of Knox, so she stroked his hair again. "He was one of the Horsemen. He killed Delia. Shot her." And Harper was still finding the whole thing a little surreal.

"He tried to kill you," Knox guessed.

She nodded. "He wanted Crow to do it, but he refused. So Roan decided to take the matter into his own hands. Only Crow made the gun poof away—it was weird. And that was when Roan picked up the surgical scissors."

Realization hit Knox. "That's what happened to your ear."

She nodded again. "He said Carla once did that to him. I think he talked Crow into hurting her. He called her twisted. Said both me and him were twisted too because we share her blood—"

"Not fucking true." There was nothing at all twisted about Harper.

She snorted. "If you'd seen my demon at work last night, you might not be so sure. It was merciless."

"It had every right to be, baby. They hurt you." He kissed the healing wound again, tempted to go lower, but she was tired and needed care. "I don't suppose Roan gave the names of the other Horsemen, did he?"

Harper shook her head. "He was just as Nora described. Cold. Envious. Greedy for power. And I never saw any of that in him before. I thought he was an asshole, but not someone who would plot to see you and me dead." Or maybe she hadn't wanted to see that potential in him.

Knox slid his arms underneath her back to hug her. "I hadn't suspected him either. I sensed he was envious of the kind of social and preternatural power I had, and I knew he looked down on you in many ways. But even though I considered him a suspect, I hadn't really thought it was him. I was leaning more toward Alethea."

Hearing self-condemnation in his tone, she narrowed her eyes. "Don't be mad at yourself for not seeing Roan in all his fucked-up glory. He was responsible for his own actions, just as Crow was. And we should probably consider that although Alethea wasn't the one pulling Crow's strings, it doesn't mean she isn't one of the Horsemen."

That was the one thing that stopped the last bit of tension leaving Knox's system: the knowledge that this wasn't over. Two of the Horsemen were dead, but there were two more to find and destroy. He doubted such a thing would be easy, but it *would* be done—he wouldn't accept anything less.

"We were right about one thing," said Harper. "They want to know what you are so they'll know how to kill you. They see you as the obstacle between them and the success of their plan." She slid her fingers through his hair. "I won't let them hurt or kill you. I'll annihilate them if they try. Why are you looking at me like that again?"

"Like what?" he asked, unable to keep the smile out of his voice.

"Like I'm cutely deluded for being protective of you."

He kissed his way up her body, pausing to nip at her pulse. "You're not deluded, but you are cute." Dancing his fingers along her collarbone, he said, "I'm going to cancel the event."

"No, we'll go ahead with it."

That surprised him, but then his mate often did. He was used to it at this point. "Baby, you had a rough—"

"We're going ahead with it," she insisted. "If we were ever going to cancel the shindig, it would have been for personal reasons, *not* because of the fucking Horsemen." She wouldn't give them that much power over anything in her life.

"You still aren't fully healed."

She snorted. "The wounds will all be healed by the time I need to get ready, and we both know it."

Yes, they did both know it. "You're tired." He could practically *feel* her exhaustion.

"Which I'd say is understandable, considering I expended a whole lot of psychic energy tonight. But I can take a few more hours to sleep it off. But only if you promise to wake me in time to get ready."

He rested his forehead against hers. "A couple of months ago, you'd be doing a happy dance—at least in your head—if I said I'd cancel the event."

"Because I didn't realize how important this was to you at first. Now I do. And almost dying makes a girl realize a few things."

"Like what?"

"Like celebrating an important event with your mate isn't really all that awful, especially when he looks seriously hot in a suit."

Chuckling, Knox brushed his mouth over hers. "All right, we'll stick to the schedule."

"And we'll make an announcement about the Horsemen, warn the other two that they'll be identified at some point, one way or another."

He nodded. "We'll incorporate the announcement into my speech, since that will be recorded and played around the

Underground." Then there was no way the Horsemen wouldn't hear it.

"Sounds good." She fisted a hand in the sheets as she forced herself to ask the question taunting her. "How did I call on the flames, Knox? I don't get it. You said it yourself: I'm not built to handle your level of power." She didn't *want* to handle it. She didn't like how it had practically drugged her demon.

He gently weaved his hand through her hair, rubbing the silky strands between the pads of his fingers. "I've spent hours puzzling over it."

"And?"

"When did the flames appear? What happened at that moment?"

"I was a mess; I was pissed and scared. My demon took over and unleased my wings. They were on fire." Which had never happened before.

That supported his theory—a theory he'd telepathically ran past Levi earlier, who agreed it was the most likely explanation. "Your wings share the same colors of the flames of hell—wings that didn't appear until a little of my power poured into you. I'm an archdemon; that means I don't just call on the flames; I am the flames. As such, you could say that your wings were born from the flames of hell, like I was." And that meant they would come to her as they came to him.

Her brows flew up. "You mean that could happen again?" Oh the hell no. Her demon actually smiled, the freak.

"Yes, it could. I know you probably don't like the idea of that because your demon's loss of control unsettled you, but I'll admit it brings me comfort to know you could call on them." She had the ultimate weapon at her disposal.

"I didn't do it intentionally."

"I know, but I'll teach you how to call them and how to send them away without even involving your demon in the process." He kissed her again, comforting her this time. "Just like I taught you how to control your wings."

"It was a good thing you made me practice so much. It meant I could call them easy, even when I was scared and drugged. If I hadn't, I wouldn't have escaped that rope. They burned right through it. Oh, about my demon ... convincing it to retreat wasn't at all easy. It was furious and blitzed on power, and it hadn't wanted to give it up. You did good. No, not good. Amazing. Totally *freaking* amazing."

"I wasn't sure it would listen to me."

"You're the only person it would ever have listened to." Nora had been right: only Knox could have helped her and her demon throughout their "trial." "Thank you for bringing me back." Harper kissed him, curling her arms around his neck and hooking one leg over his. "Come inside me."

He should ignore that sensual whisper, he thought. Should remind her that she'd almost died. Should make her take the next few hours easy, especially since she'd need her rest for the event. But he needed her. Needed to be in her, assuring himself that she was alive and well in the most basic way. So Knox took her right there, thrusting in and out of her soft and slow; pouring everything he felt and everything he was into it. She came with a scream of his name, and that sent him tumbling right over the edge with her.

CHAPTER TWENTY-THREE

———◆———

Knox hadn't taken more than four steps into the walk-in closet when he stopped dead. His mate was standing in front of the mirror, looking like every male's wet dream. That satin dark-red dress begged to be peeled up while he took her against the wall. The shade went perfectly against her ivory skin, seeming to emphasize how smooth and unblemished it was. The combination made him think of raspberries and cream. With the crystal gemstones that matched the ones on her red stilettos, the dress was as shiny as his mate. It also flashed some of the brand on her breast, which his demon liked a hell of a lot.

Slipping on her white diamond earrings, now that her ear was completely healed, Harper smiled at him. "Looking pretty dashing over there in that tuxedo, Thorne." Edible, actually. It made her want to crawl all over him like a kitten.

He prowled toward her, feeling every inch the predator that he was. His demon wanted to see what she looked like in that dress while bent over and begging to come. One track mind. But

Knox wasn't in a position to judge, given he was wondering the exact same thing. "You look stunning."

She gave him a mock look of reprimand. "You really shouldn't say things like that."

He raised a brow. "Oh? Why is that?"

"I'm taken," she stage-whispered, "and my mate is crazy possessive."

Cupping her hips, Knox pulled her flush against him. "So he should be."

"He definitely won't like you touching me."

Knox kissed her neck, inhaling her honeyed scent. "If he lets another male get this close to you, he doesn't deserve to keep you."

Harper smoothed her hands over his shoulders. "He deserves me just fine."

Smiling, he nipped at the fleshy part of her lower lip. "Are you sure you want to go out tonight? It would be normal to want a little time to assimilate what happened."

"It probably would be normal to need time to process and stuff," she agreed, "but *I'm* not normal. We both know that."

Knox splayed his hand over her breast, wishing he could tug at the nipple ring he could feel against his palm through her dress. "You're not weird." She simply didn't like to dwell or stew. She moved on from things fairly quickly. He admired that. "You're positive you want to go? I have absolutely no issue with spending the night fucking you while that dress is hiked around your waist."

The latter sounded rather tempting, but Harper was happy for that to come later. "If I didn't know any better, I'd think you didn't want me to go out."

"Maybe my protective streak is on hyper-drive and I'd like to keep you here where I know you're safe," he admitted.

He could be so cute sometimes. "But that would be letting those assholes win, wouldn't it? It would be giving them the power over us that they want. I'm not down with that."

His mouth curved. "All right, let's go."

Harper grabbed her purse and linked her arm through his. "Lead the way."

As they walked down the staircase, he said, "If someone would have told me just yesterday that you'd be smiling as we left for the event, I would never have believed them."

She was actually looking forward to the shindig. Okay, she was looking forward to flashing her rings at Alethea. "I like surprising you. It keeps you on your toes."

"It does," Knox allowed. He led her down the hallway and into the foyer, where the sentinels were waiting.

Harper smiled at them. "Well, don't you all look pretty." The guys were all in tuxedos, and Larkin was wearing a seriously cute black dress.

Keenan grinned, but it was slightly forced. "You don't look so bad yourself." He flinched when she punched his arm. "Ow! What was that for?"

"You're still blaming yourself for not checking the driver's seat. It's not your fault that I was taken. I've been meaning to ask, did you deliver the news to Carla and Bray?" she asked Larkin.

The harpy nodded. "We did it a few hours ago."

Harper bit her lip. "Just how badly did they take it?"

"About as badly as any parent would take the death of their child," replied Larkin. "I did worry they might come to the shindig—"

Knox sighed. "It's not a shindig."

"—to kick up a fuss and lash out at you in anger, but they seem to just want to be left alone. In any case, I have people keeping watch over them."

Harper wasn't looking forward to finally coming face to face with Carla and Bray again. If Carla truly hadn't hated Harper before, she would sure do now that her oldest son had died at Harper's hands. Well, at her demon's hands—there wasn't much difference.

Turning to Knox, Harper asked, "Do you think we made the right decision in not telling them ourselves?"

"Yes, it was the best thing for all concerned." As their Primes, Knox and Harper should have been the ones to break the news to Carla and Bray. But since Harper's demon had been the one to end their son's life, she thought it would be a little insensitive for her to deliver the news personally. Knox could have visited them alone, but he wasn't going to leave Harper's side until he could finally breathe without tasting fear and remembering how it had felt to hear she'd been taken. He wasn't letting her out of his sight for a while.

"Do you think Kellen will hate me for it?" Harper asked.

"No," replied Knox. "He saw Roan for what he was." But if the kid froze her out again, Knox would ensure Kellen didn't walk back into her life. She wasn't a toy he could put down when he felt like. She was a person. A good person who didn't deserve to be messed around. "You sure you don't want to spend the night at home?"

Harper straightened her shoulders. "I'm sure. Let's do this."

The Underground's dome looked nothing at all like it usually did. With the artistic flower arrangements, ice sculptures, the soft music from the live brand, and the scent of citruses and lavender, you could easily forget the space was usually a combat zone. Harper was impressed. Bitch or not, Belinda was good at what she did.

Chatter, laughter, and the clinking of glasses filled the air.

Waiters circulated, serving drinks and easy-to-eat appetizers to the mingling crowd—most of which was Primes. Some demons were swirling along the man-made dance floor. Martina was working the crowd, no doubt doing some pickpocketing. As long as she didn't set anything on fire, Harper was good with that.

Knox took two glasses of champagne from a waiter and handed one to Harper. "Hold this with your left hand."

Knowing he wanted everyone to get a good look at her rings, she said, "See, I told you my mate was possessive."

Mouth curved, he spoke against her temple. "Sorry, baby, but we'll have to do what drives you and your demon crazy."

She couldn't help that her upper lip curled a little. "Mingle."

He chuckled. "Yes, mingle."

Her shoes clacked along the floor as they moved. Thankfully she'd walked around the mansion in them to break them in, so they weren't chafing the back of her ankles. "Fine, but can we start with Jolene?" Harper gestured to the corner, where her grandmother was studying a sculpture of a naked male with Raini, Devon, Beck, and Ciaran.

"Of course," said Knox.

But, to Harper's annoyance, it didn't prove to be as simple as that. They *headed* for Jolene but got waylaid several times by people who wanted to chat, including Thatcher and Mila. As Harper smiled at each and every person, she couldn't help but wonder if she was looking right at one of the Horsemen. Some commented on the rings, others didn't, but they all seemed shocked—no surprise there.

The sentinels stayed close, all prepared for action. Just because Roan and Crow were dead didn't mean the other two Horsemen wouldn't strike at the event, though she seriously doubted they would. They'd have to come up with a whole new plan now that they'd lost yet another key player. She wondered if they even knew that Roan was dead yet. Well, if they didn't, they would find out when Knox made his announcement.

To Harper's extreme disappointment, Alethea wasn't one of the people who approached them. But Harper did catch a glimpse of her chatting with Jonas, Raul, and a few others on the other side of the dome.

Having Knox at her side should have made the mingling bearable. But every touch was sensual, possessive, and teasing. Really, it was like being subjected to a sensory overload. His fingers combed through her hair, trailed along her spine, and massaged her inner wrist. His hand kneaded her nape, cupped her hip, "accidentally" brushed her breast, or splayed on her lower back, taking up as much skin as he could and ensuring the heel of his hand rested just above her ass.

When he wasn't talking to the others, he was breezing his lips against her temple or whispering in her ear, making the hairs on the back of her neck stand on end. And he knew *exactly* what all the flirty touches were doing. Knew she was wet and flushed. The only reason she didn't reprimand him was that she worried he'd send those psychic fingers wandering—it wasn't something he hadn't done in public before.

As they broke away from yet another crowd, he whispered into her ear, "Tell me the truth. Just how wet are you?"

"You know my body well enough to know exactly how wet it will be."

He smiled against her ear, liking that answer. "You're right."

And then another group of demons came over. It was at least an hour later that she and Knox finally reached Jolene. And Harper felt like she'd just come up for air out of the sea. "Hey, Grams."

Jolene, looking as smart as ever, gave her a one-armed hug. "You're happy. I'm glad. I was worried that I'd find you sulking."

"I was worried we wouldn't find you at all," said Raini, mouth twitching.

Devon chuckled and took a sip of her champagne. "Honestly, I had that same worry."

Snorting, Harper turned to Beck and gave him a quick hug. She hadn't yet told anyone about what happened with Crow and Roan, not trusting that her grandmother wouldn't blow up Carla's home out of anger. Besides, Harper knew her family and friends had been looking forward to the shindig and she wanted them to be able to enjoy it. She also knew she'd need to soon warn them that Knox would be making an unpleasant announcement so they weren't taken off-guard.

"I like the rings," said Jolene. "Maybe Knox's demon will stop leaving brands all over you now."

Harper kind of doubted it. "Maybe."

Knox lightly tapped the black diamond. *I didn't think that the sight of them on your finger would make me hard.*

Smiling, she said, *I don't think it takes much to make you hard.*

Devon looked at the rings the way someone would gaze down at a cute little baby. "I think they're beautiful. So shiny and—*stop sniffing me!*" She glared at Tanner over her shoulder. "I mean it, pooch, stop."

Grinning, Tanner said, "But you smell like candy. How can I resist candy?"

Devon inhaled deeply, ready to give the hellhound ... well, hell. But then she smiled at someone over his shoulder. The smile had a devious curve to it. "Hey there, Belinda."

Oh, how wonderful.

The image of "well-groomed," Belinda appeared at Harper's side in an emerald silk gown, her hair styled in an elegant updo that must have taken hours. Her courteous smile was all for Knox. "Is everything to your satisfaction?"

Knox nodded. "It is. I'm impressed."

Belinda beamed and clasped her hands together. "I'm so very glad. My team will also be pleased to hear that our hard work paid off."

At that moment, Khloë sidled up to Raini, a skewer in hand. "This steak is cooked to perfection."

Belinda's smile faltered slightly. "I'm glad to hear it. Will you be making your speech soon, Mr Thorne?"

Snaking a hand around Harper's waist, Knox opened his mouth to reply when he heard a familiar voice to his right.

"I sure do like this sculpture."

Jolene smiled at the newcomer. "Well, hello, Lou."

The Devil sent her a narrow-eyed look. "Hello, vile woman."

"You buttoned up your shirt wrong," Jolene told him.

"What?" he squeaked, peeking down at the shirt. Realizing she was kidding, he flattened his lips. "See, vile."

Jolene rolled her eyes. "Let it go, Lou."

Sensing there was more to this than the shirt comment, Harper asked, "Let what go? What did you do, Grams?"

Jolene tipped her chin at Lou. "He was in a bad mood, so thought I'd take him to a nice, calming atmosphere to cheer him up. Only there is no cheering him up."

Harper wasn't buying that innocent act for a single second. "Where did you take him?"

"To a poetry recital."

Lou's face hardened. "The words hardly ever rhymed! How is that poetry?" And it clearly drove his OCD streak crazy.

Harper clamped her lips tightly closed to contain her laugh, but her shoulders shook. She didn't dare look at the girls, knowing she would burst out laughing if she saw them doing the same. "Will you never learn to ignore my grandmother's seemingly well-meaning gestures?"

Lou folded his arms, the image of petulance. "I'm done talking about it."

Skimming through a wallet, Martina hummed to herself as she came to Jolene's side. A gasp flew out of Belinda, making Martina's head snap up. The imp took in Belinda's emerald dress—the exact one that Martina herself was wearing—and grinned. "Ooh, snap! You have great taste."

Belinda gaped in horror, wringing her hands. "You—I— Where did you get that dress? Mine was specially made! It was supposed to be the only one!" She whirled on Harper with a scowl. "You set that up!"

Well, of course she had. And Harper had no intention of denying it. "Come on, Belinda, you didn't really think I'd just overlook all that stuff you said to me, did you? As you often pointed out, I'm a Wallis. We don't let crap like that go." She cocked her head. "Out of a simple yet admittedly weird curiosity, just how much do you hate me right now?"

Red faced, Belinda stomped off.

"Yeah, that's pretty much what I thought."

Knox couldn't help but chuckle. "She will despise you for life."

Harper shrugged. "I can live with that." Most happily. She looked at a laughing Lou and said, "So you hate it when anyone plays tricks on you, but you're totally okay with it happening to others?"

He pointed at himself and snickered. "Hello, the Devil."

Whatever.

The next hour was spent laughing and joking and . . . well, it was kind of fun. The one good thing about Lou being with them was that not many approached Knox. Their kind was wary of the Devil, even if there were much worse things in hell than him. He might be a nut-job, but he was a powerful nut-job.

Later on, Knox put both their empty glasses on the tray of a passing waiter and whispered into Harper's ear, "Come on, I want to dance with you."

"Just a second." She turned to their group. "I need you to all listen for a minute." Her sober tone made them move closer. "Something happened yesterday after I left the spa. It was bad and I was hurt, but—as you can see—I'm fine now. You'll find out all the details soon; Knox will be making an announcement."

Jolene's eyes flared. "You were hurt and you didn't tell me?" The others looked just as enraged, aside from Lou. He did, however, appear annoyed.

"Grams, I love you. I do. But you're batshit. I couldn't trust that you wouldn't do something wild. I couldn't trust that any of you wouldn't have somehow involved yourselves. I'm a Prime now, whether I want to be or not. I have to be seen to deal with things, not have my family and friends do it for me, or it will make me seem weak. I know you don't want that for me."

"She's right, you know," Lou told Jolene. "You can't be trusted not to overreact." His eyes narrowed at Harper. "And didn't I tell you to be careful? Baby Lucifer needs you to be on the ball. Knox, you need to up your level of protection if this delightful child is to ever be born."

Ignoring that, Knox looked at Harper's friends. "Harper will explain everything to you tomorrow. Then you can express just how upset you are with her for not telling you sooner. Let her have this night to enjoy herself."

Devon sighed. "I'm not mad at you, Harper. I long ago accepted that you aren't the type to call your friends and share your woes. I'm mad that we didn't leave the Underground with you."

Raini nodded. "Maybe if we hadn't gone to the mall—"

Harper raised a hand. "None of you are at fault."

"Well, *I'm* mad that you didn't tell me," said Khloë, "but I'll ride your ass about it tomorrow so you can enjoy your evening."

Knox's mouth curved. "Good of you. Now, if you'll excuse us ..." He guided Harper away by her elbow, leading her to the crowded dance floor. He drew her against him; one warm hand clasped hers while the other splayed on her back. Their movements were slow, smooth, and perfectly in sync. "I'm truly astonished that you're smiling."

She lifted one shoulder. "The shindig isn't so bad."

"Remember that next time I want to organize an event."

Not likely. "Hm."

"After this, we'll make the announcement." What would have been a simple speech would now be something else. "Then I'm taking you to the penthouse, where I plan to do very wicked things to you."

A flush creeped up her neck and face. "Stop. You're making me all tingly." Her rhythm faltered as an icy fingertip flicked her clit. "Don't, I'm already horny as hell."

He brushed his mouth over hers just as he slid a psychic finger between her folds. "Exactly how I want you." But he let the finger dissipate, knowing the sensation would make her burn even more.

Harper bit down on her lip, shooting him a look that swore revenge. "That was cruel." The music faded away and, smiling, he led her toward the podium ... only to find Dario, Malden, Jonas, and the dolphin. Harper's demon grinned.

As Knox lifted their linked hands just enough to flash their rings, Malden blinked and said, "Black diamonds." He whistled. "I can't say I'm surprised." He raised his glass in silent congratulations.

"Really?" said Harper. With the exception of Jolene, he was the only person to have claimed they weren't surprised.

"Knox is the kind of person who goes after what he wants and does whatever it takes to keep it," Malden rightly pointed out. Dario, not looking all that surprised by the rings, nodded in agreement. Harper wondered if his dear old grandmother had foreseen the exchange of rings.

"A little soon, isn't it?" Alethea said to Knox, voice like a whip.

"Soon?" Knox echoed.

"You hardly know her." Alethea's upper lip curled. "Declaring her as your mate was a rash move. This … this is beyond foolhardy."

"Foolhardy?" Harper frowned. "Who uses that word anymore?"

Knox returned Alethea's glare. "At what point did you get the impression that your approval means anything to me?"

"We've known each other a long time," she said. "This isn't you."

"Giving a black diamond to my mate, marking her as mine in no uncertain terms, is exactly who I am." He wanted Harper and the rest of the world to know who she belonged to.

Alethea gave a fast shake of the head. "You were never possessive."

"Not of you," he said, and she barely hid her wince. When her eyes cut to Harper and narrowed, Knox's demon rushed to the surface and growled at Alethea, "Don't even look at her."

Harper almost shivered as the temperature lowered by a few degrees. The others in the group froze, sensing the danger and not wanting to catch the entity's attention.

Alethea's eyelids flickered. "I just—"

"I never liked you," it told her. "Too easy to seduce. Too eager to please."

It was Harper's turn to wince. If the demon was aiming to embarrass the dolphin, it was succeeding.

"Do not ever again think to censure what we do or don't do," added the demon. It retreated then. "If you'll excuse me," began Knox, "I have a speech to make."

Pale and shaky, the dolphin stormed away without another word. Wise move.

Jonas cleared his throat. "I apologize on my sister's behalf, Knox. And to you also, Harper."

He didn't make excuses for her, and Harper respected him for that. "Apology accepted, though it wasn't yours to make."

Knox led her forward, causing the others to part and let them through. On the podium, Knox took a microphone from a demon hovering there and cleared his throat. Silence immediately fell and everyone turned to face the podium. "I want to take a moment to thank you all for coming," said Knox, voice amplified by the sound system. "And thank you to Belinda Thacker and her team for organizing the event and making it special."

A quiet, dignified applause rang across the dome.

He linked his fingers with Harper. "This event was not only to celebrate the 150th anniversary of the Underground's opening, but also my mating to Harper Wallis. I have every confidence that she'll make an excellent Prime and . . . "

Harper kind of shut off at that point, far too uncomfortable with the sort of praise he liked to lavish on her. She had no wish to stand there, flushing the same red as her dress. Looking around, she caught side of Belinda and the dolphin muttering to each other, looking equally pissed. Hmm. Harper wondered how they knew each other, but she supposed it was quite possible that Belinda had organized an event for Alethea's lair in the past. She'd have to look into that at a later point. For now, she'd do what her demon was doing and delight in their misery over the rings.

"Before we step down from the podium, we have an

announcement to make," said Knox, which snapped her out of her musings.

Harper was pretty sure half, if not most, people were expecting him to announce that she was pregnant.

"Earlier tonight, Lawrence Crow was captured and killed." Knox paused as people gasped. "We would have liked to help him, but he was beyond that. He was far too entrenched in his delusion, which is a sad thing. But he could in fact have been helped . . . had his mental state not been manipulated by another demon—a demon who convinced him that his pills were poisoning him and told him that he had a mission to complete."

"What kind of mission?" Raul asked, frowning.

"To kill me," said Harper. "But their plan didn't work so well, because a near-rogue can't be controlled."

"Crow's attention instead turned to me," began Knox, "and he tried to attack me on several occasions. You're wondering why anyone would do such a thing to Crow. It has come to my attention that there are demons who wish to see the fall of the Primes." The crowd exchanged shocked looks. "They call themselves the Four Horsemen. Isla was one of them, which left only three . . . until Harper killed another of them in self-defense—the same demon who manipulated Crow."

"Who was it?" asked Malden.

"The eldest son of the woman Crow kidnapped and butchered," Knox told him. "When he prowled through the Underground with a photo of his mother, asking if anyone had seen her, we believed he was concerned for his mother's safety. In truth, it wasn't really *her* he was attempting to find, it was Crow—he'd lost control of his puppet. Unfortunately, we do not have the names of the other two Horsemen. It would not surprise me if they were in this very dome." He ran his gaze along the crowd. "Know that I will find you,' he warned. "And I will destroy you."

"I've never heard of any demons calling themselves the Four Horsemen," said Thatcher, brows pulled together in confusion.

"Now you have," said Knox. "By all means conduct your own investigation. It might help us identify them sooner. You may all be interested to know that they are the source of all the rumors. They want the Primes to turn on each other and, in doing so, do all their dirty work for them. Be very careful what rumors you do and don't believe." With that, Knox handed the microphone back to the demon still hovering and then helped Harper down from the podium, where Tanner and Levi waited.

"Making the announcement tonight was a good idea," said Levi, looking at the muttering crowd. "The Horsemen's main advantage was the secrecy of their existence. They're not so secret anymore. People will be alert for any strange activity."

"They're also very suspicious of each other now, though," Tanner pointed out. "Paranoia can lead to fighting."

True enough. "The Primes had a right to know they were being played." Knox wouldn't have liked such information being kept from him. Turning to Harper, he asked, "Ready to leave now, baby?"

"Totally," said Harper.

"Want to say goodbye to your family and friends first?"

She turned to do so, but as she took in Lou and Jolene arguing, Martina flicking through another wallet, and Khloë attached to Keenan's back snapping selfie after selfie, Harper shook her head. "Nah."

The hotel they were staying at for the night wasn't far from the dome. The ride in the private elevator was a delicious agony; the air snapped taut with so much sexual tension, she was surprised she couldn't reach out and touch it. After all his possessive touches, she was flushed and aching, and more than ready to be fucked.

The elevator stopped with a ding, and the doors slid open. They stepped straight into a spacious entryway, and then the breath exploded out of her lungs as Knox slammed her against the wall. His dark eyes sparked with such raw need that she knew there would be nothing sweet or gentle about what came next. Awesome. She did *not* have the patience for soft or slow. Her demon was totally up for it.

"Open for me," he ordered, voice deep and dominant.

Harper parted her lips, and his tongue plunged into her mouth. He did what he always did when he kissed her. Dominated her mouth. Ate at it. Possessed it. Took and took until her head spun and she had to clutch his shoulders to steady herself. He tasted of him and power and champagne, and she was starting to feel a little drunk.

Harper sucked on his tongue, and his eyes flared. A growl rumbled up his chest, vibrating against her nipples—they pebbled at the sensation, almost painfully tight. A greedy excitement clawed at her; an excitement that was as demanding as his mouth and the confident hands that sank into her hair, holding her head how he wanted it.

Feeling acutely empty, Harper arched into him, grinding her clit against his cock; he was hard and ready. Knox growled again, pressing her harder against the wall and pinning her still with his hips. Every cell of her body cried out in frustration. She needed more, needed *him*.

Knox roughly peeled up her dress, heard something tear. Fuck it; he'd buy her a new dress. Snapping off her thong, he cupped her pussy. "Mine." All his. He slipped a finger between her folds, finding her deliciously slick. He spread her cream around her clit and gave it a gentle pluck. "You're going to come for me, Harper. Then I'm going to fuck you."

Well, that sounded super good to her. He took her mouth as he slid his finger between her folds, dipping it ever so slightly inside her but not thrusting, the bastard. Again and again, he did it as she moaned and bucked her hips, hinting for more. *Finally*, he slipped a finger inside her, and her head fell back as she moaned with both bliss and relief.

"No," he rumbled, fisting a hand in her hair and angling her head so he could watch her eyes. "Don't look away from me."

That bossy tone would probably never fail to make Harper bristle, which was why she almost swore at him. But then he curved his finger to rub at her g-spot and, yeah, he was instantly forgiven. He kissed her again, swallowing every moan as he fucked her with his finger. It felt so good, but it wasn't enough. She needed his cock. The addictive burn of his clever mouth fueled the hunger raging through her; a hunger so hot and carnal that she shook with it.

That was the thing: psychic fingers or not, he always made her frantic for him. Always made her feel empty and restless. Right now, her pussy was aching and throbbing, wanting to be filled. "Knox."

"Not yet." Knox used his free hand to scoop out her breasts and give one a possessive squeeze. "So perfect." Round and full and his. He swooped down and sucked her pierced nipple into his mouth, flicking the ring with his tongue. Her hips bucked again and her pussy fluttered around his finger. He knew she was hovering on the edge and it wouldn't take much to throw her over. Knox drove another finger inside her and hooked them as he fucked her hard with his hand. "Come all over my fingers."

Eyes a misty violet went blind with pleasure as her pussy clamped so hard around his fingers he wouldn't have been surprised if they snapped. Her mouth, red and swollen from his kiss, opened on a silent scream. "Fucking beautiful," he growled, voice thick. He couldn't wait any longer. He had to have her.

Shaking with aftershocks, Harper blinked, almost dizzy. That had been one hell of an orgasm and ... and now he was shedding his clothes. That brought her out of her daze. Anticipation ripped through her. She wanted him naked. Wanted to touch and taste. But when she reached for his cock, his hand snapped around her wrist and he shook his head.

"No, I want *in* you." He *needed* to be in her; needed to feel her hot pussy tightening and contracting around his cock as he took what belonged to him. "This is going to be fast, baby." He wanted to go slow and savor her, but he didn't have the control for that right then. Not when she was standing there in that dress and those fuck-me shoes; not when her taste was in his mouth and her scent filled his lungs; not when the knowledge that he could have lost her was still tormenting him.

He spun her to face the wall, and her hands shot out to brace her weight. "Yes, that's how I want you." Grabbing her hips, Knox angled her just right and slammed home. He groaned as her pussy clenched around him. She was wet, swollen and hot—so fucking hot that he lost all pretense of control. He pounded into her, fast and furious and so deep it had to hurt a little. She pushed back to meet each thrust, arching her back to take him even deeper.

He grazed his teeth over the crook of her neck. "I love your smell. I love it more when I'm fucking you. It gets warmer, sweeter." She moaned as his teeth tugged at the skin of her neck. "That's it, baby, let me hear you."

Harper couldn't have kept quiet if her life depended on it. Not when she was so full it hurt and her clit was throbbing. A shocked gasp flew out of her as icy fingers began to tweak and pull at her nipples, making them tingle and burn. "I won't last long if you keep that up."

His fingers bit into her hips. "You'll last as long as I want you to last," he growled.

Motherfucker. She didn't realize she'd said it out loud until a hand came down hard on her ass. "Hey!" Another sharp slap. She'd never admit she liked how the burn heightened the friction that was building inside her. With her nipples on fire, his teeth digging into her shoulder, his cock stretching and pumping in and out of her . . . "Knox." It was a warning. She was going to come and—

He pulled out, spun her, and lifted her up. "I want to look in your eyes when you come." Knox dropped her hard on his cock, shocking the breath out of her. He didn't give her any reprieve. Just held her gaze as he powered into her, groaning at the silken, fiery feel of her. "I love feeling your tight pussy squeezing me. Love how wet you get for me."

She was hardly ever going to have a dry spell when he was such a master at what he did. Harper wrapped herself tight around him, her nails and heels digging into the flesh of his back. "I really need to fucking come."

"I know, baby." He used his psychic fingers to part her folds so he hit her clit with her every thrust. "Tell me what I want to know, and you can come."

She didn't hesitate. "I love you."

Growling, he fucked her harder. Deeper. Never looking away from her eyes. "Come for me."

A scream tore out of Harper's throat as her release whipped through her, sending wave after wave of bliss washing over her. Biting out a harsh curse, Knox pounded into her once, twice, and then he exploded with a growl of her name.

Leaning her head on his shoulder, limp as a noodle, she asked, "How can you still be hard?"

He kissed her neck. "Why do you always ask me that when you know the answer?"

She gave a weak shrug. "It just amazes me that you even have the energy to go again."

Holding her tight, Knox carried her to the bedroom and lay them both on the bed, keeping his cock snug inside her. "No going asleep."

"I'm not," she lied.

"Your eyes are closing." He kissed her and she sighed softly into his mouth. "Stay awake. I have lots more I want to do to you."

Well, that seemed worth staying awake for. "Can I take off the dress now?"

"No. I spent the entire event imagining all the ways in which I'd take you while you had it hiked around your waist." He tucked her hair behind her ear, eyes drifting to the spot where the scissors had cut her lobe. And he remembered once again just how close he'd come to losing her.

"Don't," she said softly.

His gaze slid to hers. "What?"

"Don't think of how badly things could have gone. I'm alive, and I'm here. My wounds have all completely healed."

He rested his forehead on hers. "I'd like to say I won't worry so much now that you can call on the flames of hell, but I'll always worry about you. I'll always be overprotective to the point of making you crazy."

"You're not telling me anything I don't already know. I mean, you totally overreacted over the rodeo thing," she teased.

Overreacted? "You rode a wild bull."

"At least I didn't fuck a—"

"Stop. Just stop."

She chuckled and curled her arms around his neck. "It's okay. You can be as overprotective as you want. I'll love you anyway."

He smiled. "Good, because I love you, baby. Always will."

"And you finally fear my mighty wrath, right?" She frowned when he hesitated to answer. Why the hesitation?

"I'll admit your demon was a little scary."

"A little? She was freaking terrifying."

More like high on power and bloated with rage, he thought, but he decided not to say that out loud.

"She was!" insisted Harper. "I can be just as terrifying when I lose it."

"Is that so?"

"Yes." And she did *not* like the twinkle of amusement in his eyes.

"Terrifying?"

"I can be so totally terrifying that I scare even me. Why are you laughing? I'm serious, it's true. You just don't think so because you've never actually seen me that way. If you did, you'd freak out. Really, you would. I'm telling you, fully grown men have run the other way rather than face me when I'm in Berserker mode and – *stop laughing*!"

Do you love fiction with a supernatural twist?

Want the chance to hear news about your favourite
authors (and the chance to win free books)?

Keri Arthur
Kristen Callihan
P.C. Cast
Christine Feehan
Jacquelyn Frank
Larissa Ione
Darynda Jones
Sherrilyn Kenyon
Jayne Ann Krentz and Jayne Castle
Lucy March
Martin Millar
Tim O'Rourke
Lindsey Piper
Christopher Rice
J.R. Ward
Laura Wright

Then visit the Piatkus website and blog
www.piatkus.co.uk | www.piatkusbooks.net

And follow us on Facebook and Twitter
www.facebook.com/piatkusfiction | www.twitter.com/piatkusbooks

piatkus